THREE NOVELS

Rosalyn Drexler

Available:

Verbivoracious Festschrift Vol.1—Christine Brooke-Rose
Verbivoracious Festschrift Vol.2—Gilbert Adair
(Edited by G.N. Forester and M.J. Nicholls)
The Languages of Love — Christine Brooke-Rose
The Sycamore Tree — Christine Brooke-Rose
Go When You See the Green Man Walking — Christine Brooke-Rose

Forthcoming reprint titles:

Next
Dear Deceit
The Middlemen
Xorandor/Verbivore

by Christine Brooke-Rose

Knut
Erowina

by Tom Mallin

other Verbivoracious titles @

www.verbivoraciouspress.org

Three Novels

Rosalyn Drexler

Verbivoracious Press

Glentrees, 13 Mt Sinai Lane, Singapore

This edition published in Great Britain & Singapore

by Verbivoracious Press

www.verbivoraciouspress.org

ISBN: 978-981-09-2166-8

Printed and bound in Great Britain & Singapore

I am the Beautiful Stranger first published in the United States by Grossman Publishers, Inc. 1965. *One or Another* first published in the United States by Dutton, 1970. *The Cosmopolitan Girl* first published in the United States by M. Evans and Company, 1974.

I AM THE BEAUTIFUL STRANGER

For Sherman

LET IT GO

It is this deep blankness is the real thing strange.
The more things happen to you the more you can't
Tell or even remember what they were.

The contradictions cover such a range.
The walk would talk and go so far aslant.
You don't want madhouse and the whole thing there.

William Empson

One

I feel so free. It's summer and I'm going to camp. Diana and Harry Felter go to the beach. They have a bungalow in the Rockaways, but they never thought of inviting me. Diana told me she meets lots of boys on the boardwalk. She wants to keep them for herself. Let her! I'll have friends at camp. But I wish she wouldn't say bad things about me to her brother, because I have a crush on him. A great big fresh fruit orange crush on him. He doesn't know it but someday he will.

Camp Bronx House is for kids who'd never see a tree. That's not why I'm going there. I want to find out everything. Before you can go away, the nurse examines your hair. She went through mine with a pencil but it was super clean. I wash my hair every three days. Once I had bugs in my hair and the barber shaved it all off; I looked like a prisoner. It was winter and I wore a hat indoors too. I remember that time very well because it was the first time I ever saw a hundred-dollar bill. Daddy brought it home and laid it on the table for Mom and me to see. He got mad because the table was sticky and grabbed the money up and put it back into his wallet.

What I want most is that when I get back from camp my parents treat each other different. I can't believe they really hate each other. Found six pictures of Mother with the heads torn off—she said Dad did it. It frightened me. I asked her why she didn't put the heads back on with scotch tape and she told me that he had thrown the heads away. Mom knocked herself out ironing my clothes and sewing labels. I don't think I'll take any piano music, but the books I want to read and reread are *White Fang* and *Call of the Wild*. Hope I'm not unwell when I go; boys have X-ray eyes. I'm so happy I got my period. I waited a long time. Now so much will change—breasts, hair, and maybe my skin will clear up. Diana has always had a perfect skin. I'd like to bite her cheek and leave a mark there, but it would change into a kiss. I admire her as much as anyone else. Probably more.

Had to do time with Mom again. Dad at the drug store late. She bought me an ice-cream cone, vanilla fudge with sprinkles. Mom likes strawberry best. I don't like it—all those dead seeds crunching around on my molars. Ate the cones while we listened to Fred Allen on the radio. I think that if I were a man I'd do better for a woman than most men (especially my father). I really hate him. When I tell Mother what I want to get her, she says she knows I will someday because I can do anything I want to do. She has more faith in me than in Dad. On Halloween we were buying a pumpkin in the fruit store—I was very happy. When we came out with the pumpkin there was a car parked in front of the fruit store. Mother seemed to freeze when she spotted the car. "It's that redhead bitch!" she screamed. The woman answered, "Bitch yourself!" Mother took my pumpkin and threw it at the woman. It hit the side of the car and split open. The woman drove away. And now that my pumpkin is gone, how will I get to the ball? Just a joke.

I asked Mother why she was so mad at that woman and she answered that she was the one who hung around Daddy's drug store. "So what?" I said. Mom turned to me, red in the face, and whispered, "I caught them kissing in the phone booth." I was sure she was wrong, because Daddy would never kiss a stranger.

Two

Diana Felter brought me a gift from her brother. It was the kind of snotty thing he would think of. I got so happy at the wrapping, rainbow tissue paper with a big pink bow. She said to read the note inside, and it said: "A talisman for you to carry forever." Before I even opened the package I swore I would. And Diana waited for me to see it. Harry had given her orders to watch my reaction and report back to him. I closed my eyes and peeled off the paper. It was heavy. It was a rock. Just an ordinary rock from Van Cortlandt Park.

"I hope he didn't go to too much trouble to get me this," I said. "Tell him it's the one thing I've always wanted."

"It was his idea," she said. "I don't care if you throw it at his head."

"Diana, this shows me how little you know about me. I love it." And I began to really love it. I put it on my night table to look at. Diana stayed around a while discussing how great graduation had been for her. (Dad didn't let me wear lipstick.) But I could tell she wanted to run off and make up a story about how bad I felt to her handsome sheik of a girl-hating brother. I don't get many gifts. Some of them are jokes. My father once gave me an empty box for my birthday, and then ten minutes later pulled out the real gift, an identical box with a ring in it. I don't understand joking around. I took that ring, and it was marvelous, like a flake of moth crystal dyed green, and I stamped on it.

"She's crazy again, Hannah!" he shouted to my mother.

I haven't been crazy often. Only on special occasions. Like before graduation, when I couldn't stop crying. It makes me think that I react opposite to the way I feel.

I'm a lucky girl of thirteen. A teen at last. I got into the hardest school to get into outside of Bronx Science: MUSIC AND ART. Now my friends should realize I'm superior, but it's me I can't convince. I spent three hours getting ready to appear at dear old P.S. 80. Ugly dress, ugly hair, ugly flowers, ugly thoughts, but I was on the program to sing "A Heart That Is Free." That's what made me cry. I realized that my heart wasn't free, and that I didn't even know what free was.

Maybe free is changing things around, like about this rock I was disappointed to get. I never thought of taking a piece of park and keeping it for my own personal use. Harry made me think of it. Now I'll laugh in his face (if I can ever look directly into it). What's holding me back is I don't want him to look into my face and see that I love him.

Questions for myself: did he find the rock first by stumbling onto it, or, did he go out looking for it? What I want to know is: what came first, the rock or Selma?

The rock weighs about half a pound. It is irregular in shape and sparkles. When I look up what 'talisman' means I'll know whether or not it is one. I'm going to start taking it with me wherever I go: first to camp, where it may find its mommy and daddy, the earth and a mountain. I should compose a thank you note to Harry: Dear Harry, Unknown to you, the rock you sent contained diamonds. I am willing to share this find with you provided that we remain partners throughout and you don't let anyone else in on the deal. Our business requires frequent meetings under cover of dark; but have no fear, the rock burns brightly and we will find our way. Sincerely, Selma.

TALISMAN: amulet; charm.
AMULET: a charm to be worn.
CHARM: magic spell; thing worn to avert ill luck or bring good luck; to delight; that which fascinates control by incantation.

If I were to wear my talisman and go swimming with it around my neck I'd drown. How would this avert ill luck? Once you're dead, luck doesn't count. I admit the rock fascinates me and I believe it's going to take care of me. I'm not a rock collector; this is the only rock that interests me.

FAMILY GROUP
A Play

MOTHER: What's this?
ME: A rock.
MOTHER: You'll scratch your desk.
ME: I'll put it in my drawer.
MOTHER: It's got dirt on it.
    (LUCILLE enters. She is eight years old. My sister.)
LUCILLE: She kissed it. I saw her kiss it.
MOTHER: Why did you kiss it?
ME: What do you have against a rock?
MOTHER: You're crazy again. Throw it away or I'll call Daddy.
ME: Call him if you want to start something.
MOTHER: I don't start, you start.
ME: I'm saving it. It's part of when the earth was young.
MOTHER: At least wrap it in wax paper. I never knew you were scientifically inclined.
ME: There's a lot you don't know and I'm the first thing.
MOTHER: Shut your mouth and keep it shut.
ME *(singing)*: "Fools rush in, where angels fear to tread."
    (MOTHER and LUCILLE leave, not being able to stand the noise.)

I slipped the rock into a nicely ironed blouse in my camp trunk. I hope it will be comfortable there. Mother asked, "What's so heavy in there?" but she's weak. I don't think the trunk's heavy. When she saw me off at the bus she had to be funny: "Take good care of yourself and don't bring home any rocks, you got enough rocks in your head." She keeps telling the relatives about my head. It's propaganda. If your own parents think you're crazy, what'll other people think?

I want to say this one thing, camp was a good place for the rock. I mean The Rock. I half-buried it right by my bunk. Whenever I went in or out I touched its hard magic nose with my toe. None of the girls noticed, because in the country a rock's a rock. If I saw anyone else doing that, I'd wonder, but since it's me, I know, I'm casting a magic spell on myself. The reason I buried the rock is it belongs in the earth that created it in the first place.

Sent Diana a picture; it's real "cheesecake!" I'm only wearing a jacket (very short), and my knees are up. And I'm sitting on the grass with my face to the sun. My legs look fantastic, and I have a tan. It's my healthy look. I adore the way I photograph. If I'm lucky, Diana will show the picture to Harry. I want him to think of me as if I was a woman.

IMAGINE: I turn into a photograph. I'm smooth and shiny. I'm various shades of gray and black. Men pass me around and wish they knew me. Harry Felter keeps me in his wallet next to his G.O. card. I stay fresh in his memory. He won't give me up.

Three

Camp kept me pretty busy. I didn't mind not receiving mail from Diana. I kind of enjoyed composing letters to her. I made them sound as if I was in a paradise. I described the flowers color by color, petal by petal, leaf by leaf; emphasized the soft green beauty of our camp lawn, and the sweet smell of new-mown hay: this in contrast to her hot sand and burning sun. I wanted Diana to know I had something better than what she had. I might as well have one letter down here for the record:

Dearest Diana,

By now you are probably nice and tan. I have a tan too. There are lots of activities here. Yesterday I was in a play as a Greek goddess. I made my own costume out of sheets and pin needles. Every time I moved they stuck me, so it was hard to act mythological. I've passed the raft test and am now a "white cap," which means I'm allowed to swim out to the raft any time. Sometimes I'd like to swim all the way across the lake or maybe just to the middle and sink. But that's just an idea. Have you ever had the feeling that things were so great, so beautiful that you wanted to sink in and die? Don't, the ocean is worse than a lake and you may not be able to get back. I sang on talent night and am also writing a story for the camp paper. I met a girl here from another city, Albany. She comes from Albany but she's not an Albino (joke). Her uncle runs the camp and her name is Leila. She invited me to visit her in Albany. I think that's the way people should be. How is Harry? And what's he doing without his piano to practice? Collecting specimens for his microscope? I am enclosing a cut of my hair for his close inspection. I've been told it's extremely fine and won't hold a curl. I like my hair best about me. What do you like best about you: your eyes? Am also sending you the petal of a tiger lily (that's for you). Write and tell me what you are doing and if you have a new boyfriend. The boys here are babies.

Your friend forever,

Selma

Once I sent her a dead frog without a letter. I was so anxious to catch it that I hit it over the head with a milk bottle. I would have liked to watch her open that letter.

Leila gets letters from a boy she met in New York. He did something awful that she can't tell me about and now he writes to her from detention homes. I never met a boy like that. It seems exciting. I read his letters, and as soon as he gets out he's coming to see her in Albany. Perhaps we shall meet. I'll ask her if I can write to him too. It would be a welcome change to be better than someone else—more privileged, richer, smarter. I wonder what he sees in Leila. She's four-eyed and bow-legged and doesn't know how to kiss.

Got Leila to show me her letters during rest period. She made me promise not to tell anyone about them, especially her uncle who runs the camp. That's how she got in even though she's not a New Yorker. Her uncle pulled some strings. I think Leila has more "experience" than she lets on. Her big breasts are one thing in her favor. I copied her letters for my own memories; they made me cry. If I write to him maybe I can cheer him up. I am the beautiful stranger.

LETTERS FROM
CHARLEY ROGEN

Dear Leila,

I hope when you receive this letter you are in the very best of health. As for me, I'm getting along alright. Well Leila, you ask me how it is up here it's terrible. For one thing its boring because you see the samething over and over again. I sure wish I could get out of here. you know I've been here a month already, and it seemed to me like a year. Tell me something Leila, how did you past the fourth of July? I sure hope you had a nice one, with fireworks and all. Leila, over here I Past a terrible fourth. My mother tried to take me home, but they didn't let her. ain't that a "blip" tell me; how did you Past those red white and blue days that just Past. did you have fun? if you didn't to bad. I now if I was out I would of have a nice time. I would of "bomb" all of you girls. Leila I guess that's all I've got to say for now.

P.S.

Write to me.

Your friend
Charley (Chas)

My Friend Leila,

Well you ask me if one of your friend could write. "yes." Leila you said that you been writing a lot. if you think so dont write any more. I wouldn't mind if nobody writes. If I wrote something that dont belong here. dont mind it. that about it, Leila.

Sincerely Yours,
Charley Rogen

Dear Charley,

I'm the one who wanted to write to you. My name is Selma. I have blue eyes and dimples when I smile. Leila described you to me, so I know what you look like. To tell you the truth, I read some of the letters you sent her, so don't be surprised if I mention certain things. I'd like to be frank with you at the beginning of our correspondence. I'm not happy either, but probably you have more reason to be unhappy than I have. If there is anything I can ever do for you, please ask me, because then I'll know what you need. Do you know what you want to be when you grow up? I want to do so many things that I'm confused. I sing but I don't like to sing for people. Sometimes I write poetry. Not the kind about blue skies either. If you want to give Leila a rest and write to just me, fine, unless she minds.

Sincerely,
your new friend
Selma Silver

Dear Selma,

I like girls with dimples, it makes them look cute. and I dont mind hearing from a friend of Leila. Maybe sometime you send me a poem but I gotta warn you, it better be good. You know what I think I do when I get out? Well it is a mechanic. Cars get me whacky. Thats what I want to be, but it hard to get training if you don go to school. I hope you are in the Best of health, and Leila. I'm doing alright. Selma on Friday (Aug 17) I left the youth house (since you know about me from Leila), and they took me to Otisville. I'm not in Crestfal. I thought I was goin to Crestfal but I didn't. Leila I cant tell you much about Otsville, because I haven't been here long. Right now I'm in reception. I'll stay in reception for the first two weeks and then I think I will start work. they said up here that the average boys that stay here is about eight or nine month. I think I am one of those average boys. the address of this place is in the back.
Charley Rogen

P.O. BOX 8
Otisville N.Y.
Well Selma that all I got to say for now, do you know you
sound like celery?
P.S. Write as soon as Passible.

Stay real cute,
Charley Rogen

Dear Charley,

Sometimes eight or nine months isn't such a long time if
you think ahead. The one thing is sure that if you keep busy,
time will fly. We have a schedule up here, but it's all amuse-
ments, not work like you have to do. I love to dance; Leila
says that you are a great dancer. My plan is that when you
come out, and when you visit Leila, I'll run away from home
at the same time and come and meet you. Leila belongs to a
club that'll throw a party for you. You haven't asked me to do
anything or send you anything yet, except the poem. Suddenly I can't write one, maybe because you said it had to be
good, even if you were joking. I'm drawing a picture of the
pine trees for you. Camp is surrounded with pine trees and
right under them the pine needles are so thick it's like walking on sponge rubber. I lay on my back and wonder how it is
to be caught like you. Would you ever let me know why
you're there? I'm very sympathetic.

Sincerely,
Selma

Dear Selma,

Just a few lines to let you hear from me. I mean Selma, I
hope when you receive this letter it fines you in good health.
as for me I'm getting along alright. Say if you want to know so
much so fast you better get wise, you won't like what you

hear. so better wait till we know each other better. Most girls go for me but you sound different. theres a chance you wont care for me because in a way your just a kid (Leila told me how old you are). Still if you care to take a chance lets keep it this way. You said if I needed anything to dont hestate to tell you. Well, I got something in mind. It isn't nothing much and it isn't much to look at. I'm only kidding. Well what I had in mind is a picture. a picture of yourself that is. you see, the picture Leila sent me I lost. somebody took it while I was in the youth house. I had two fight in the youth house. that right, I did. By the way I had a bunch of fight not only two. you want to know how old I am. Well I'm now fifteen and when I get out of here I'll be past sixteen. that sure is a long time. Selma, the song I hear up here that I like is drinking rum and coca-cola, and maybe and also tangerine. When you write tell me the song you like up there. so that when they come on the radio up here I can listen to them. do you know something I like the way you fancy your letter up. it a good thought but you don know how to draw, dont let that stop you. Nothing ever stop me. your pine trees make me feel like your crazy. I'm only kidding. I only wish I could fancy my letter up like that too. Selma I signing off. 13-14-15-16

> Write soon,
> Charles

Dear Charles,

I hope you are feeling fine too and that when you look inside this envelope it will make you happy. I have enclosed the photograph you requested. It's the sexiest one I have. Don't fall in love with me, though. I was in love, recently in fact, but it ended unfortunately. I have a souvenir, however, to remember him by. Do you save things? I save some things like pictures of paintings out of magazines. It makes me feel that life can be beautiful. Sometimes I get so dreamy I don't hear what people are saying. Maybe I don't want to. Anyway, I have a reputation for being a little nuts in the cocoanut. My secret fear is, and I'm telling you because I think you'll understand, is that, hold on to your hat, my mother and father will send me to an insane asylum. That's where they store the nuts for winter. Ha, ha. Joke's on me. My favorite song at the time is "Indian Summer" but I'm changeable. Have you heard "Chattanooga Choo-Choo?" It's a great lindy. Leila and I practice the "breaks"—I invented a few myself. I would love to have a photograph of you too. Familiar looks grow on you. I suppose it's stupid to say, if you get into more fights don't get hurt, but I mean it. I was once challenged in school by a horrible girl but I didn't show up (neither did she). I don't mind being a coward as long as I don't get hurt. By the way, why did it take you so long to write? Your letters are most interesting to me.

> Your friend,
>
> Selma (celery)

My friend Selma,

Just a few lines to let you hear from me. Selma, how are you feeling? fine, I hope. ask me how I am and I'll say O.K. you ask me why did it take me so long to write a little letter. Well, I'll tell you up here I've been doing a lot of work, and I haven't got much time to write and thats the reason why. you told me in your letter that you'd like a photograph. Well, I'm waiting for my mother to bring me my wallet. you see, I haven't gotten any visit yet. you ask me how many visit can I get in a month. Well, its once. That sure is a long time before you can get a visitor. Selma? Why do I think you look like Ann Southern when you dont. I told you Otisville don't look like the Picture I sent you (did you get it? you didnt mention it). what does it look like then? Well it looks beat up. Well, you know that you'll get old and I'll get old, well, what I'm getting at is Otisville looks old. you know something that the last letter you wrote made me "crack" up, it made me crack up when you said that you were a little nuts in the coconut. Selma you look older than I thought of you in the picture you sent me. dont get me wrong now. I'm not trying to say your old but you know their was a record I didn't mention before when I wrote you. the record is, who's sorry now. its a tough record, you should hear that record. it made me feel bad. After all, who's sorry now? Selma tell me something serious. do you get tired of writing. if you do tell me so that we can write less to each other. be frank about it. I wont get mad. in fact I'll be glad for telling me the truth. if you do happen to say what I'm thinking, I'll understand. that one thing about me I under-stand everybody. that about it Selma. I'm signing off 21-22-23-24.

P.S. even if you dont Write

I'll send you my photograph.

I'll tell you when I might be out. it might be on March, April, May, etc.

From the one who'll never forget you,
Charley (Chas)

Selma, I dont have any love for this place.

Dear Charles,

You're right. I don't want to write to you any more. I want to see you. I don't get tired of writing, I get tired of imagining our friendship. Anyway, I'm going home soon to the city and in the city my mail isn't private. I haven't been given a mail key. If Mother happened to read one of your letters, she'd tear it up. I've thought of having a secret box at the post office, but get stingy when I realize it costs money. Don't worry, though, remember our Albany date. If you write to Leila she can write to me and then I'll know when you're out. I hope it'll be closer to March than May. Who knows what's in store for us. Remember I told you I was once in love? Well, I still am, but I think it's possible to love more than one person. Do you? I mean in different ways, only why does it have to be a secret? By the way, Leila told me that another guy up there with you told her that you don't do any work up there like you said. Is it true?

Your friend,

Selma

Dear Selma,

Just a few lines to let you hear from me. Selma you doubted my word when I told you I do work up here. You said that Leila told you I don't do work. Well she's dead wrong if you want to know something, Leila never been here. I do admit I didn't do any work in the Youth house. And who's the guy who told her? I'll bet she told herself and you agreed with her. How do you know that when you never been here? Just in case you don't know. When you go to an institution you go on a tuesday or on a Friday. on tuesday you go to Lincoln hall and on Friday you go to Crestful if you are under 15. If your older you'll go to Otisville. Selma, I think it would be better (like you say) if you dont write any more. if you do write I won't answer the letter. When you go to an institution is not on a Wednesday.

From

Charley R.

Four

I thought good things were happening everywhere because they were happening at camp, but when Mom and Dad met me at the bus, the same old thing: he was disgusting and my heart sank. I felt that no matter what good things ever happened to me it would still be me: the stupid little snot nose, the worthless shit, the ungrateful rat—all the names they ever called me or each other—because nothing ever changes, not even the face of things, it just gets older.

I forgot to mention the best thing about camp: food. Only once it wasn't so good when we went on a hike and I was crossing over a stream and fell into the water, lunch and all. Nothing soaks up water faster than white bread. So I shared Leila's lunch and ate more than she did. I watched the fish devour my sandwich and swim away under a cool rock, which is what I would have liked to do. That's the end of my story, which reminds me of that famous poem:

Tell me a story
of Jacky O'Nory
and now my story's begun
Tell me another
about his brother
and now my story is done.

Think I'll make up a poem about my sister.

Tell me a blister
of my little sister
and now my blister is closed

tell me a pusful
about how she's trustful
and now the story's exposed.

If she ever wears my sweater again I'll break her head. Nobody's going to call me selfish just because I don't want her to dirty my sweater. It doesn't fit her, anyway, and the more Daddy dear hits me for taking it back, the more I'll hate that freak with fourteen curls hanging off her head.

My worries are over. I'm leaving town. I'm leaving city and friend and foe and most of all family! They can't stand me? I can't stand them! Now sister Lucille can have both pillows and my share of food and all the books, and my leftover tickets to the World's Fair. Leila has written me a secret document revealing the whereabouts of Charley Rogen, who is back in Albany. She says he's dying to take me out. She also suggests a devious route that I must take in order to deceive the enemy. First order of the day is to borrow money from Grandma G. She doesn't need it. I'll tell her I want to buy Mother a present. Second order of the middle of the day, which it'll be by the time I finagle the money out of Grandma G, is, buy the train ticket. And then with light baggage and nary a fare thee well, I'll be off. Mother can tell the high school that I had to go to Florida for my health. She hates lying, I love to make her lie for me. We can get a doctor's certificate easily enough. Maybe I am sick. Why shouldn't I be sick. I suppose I should at least leave a note that I'm okay and will be back soon but "don't try to find out where I am."

Dear Mom,

    I'm not doing this to worry you, but I can't stand living at home with the others who live at home. Consider this a bonus vacation I'm taking for myself. I'm fine so don't worry. And don't try to find out where I am, if you love me. Cover up for me at school, I'll be back sooner than I think probably.

Your daughter, I remain alive with great effort,

Selma

P.S.

I may send for more money. I have enough meanwhile.

I am writing this on the train to Albany. I went to see Diana first, though. Her mother was braiding her hair. Her mother loves her. You can see it the way she enjoys doing things for her. She asked me if I wanted her to braid my hair too because it looked so wild. I said "No thank you" because I didn't belong to her. Later in Diana's room I asked Diana to braid my hair (because we belong to each other whether she's aware of it or not) and she said, very coldly, "I'm not good at it. Besides, it doesn't become you." Diana has lovely hands. She played the Beethoven Sonata in A for me before I left. Harry came in and closed the door to his room without saying hello. How can some people be so independent, or is it rude?

Some kids don't care if they just go away anywhere to no one, but I like to go somewhere to someone. When Leila invited me to visit her, she didn't think I'd take her up on it. Neither did I—at least not so soon. She doesn't even know I'm coming. It was a snap decision.

Bought an orangeade. My head itches. No fun to scratch: nothing to snap, crackle, or pop. The ugly sailor next to me wants to talk. The whole navy can drown, for all I care. The lights are dim now. He's pretending to be asleep. His body is definitely leaning on me. What can I do? Wake the potential hero up? His ear is right on my breast. It is a deaf ear, but that doesn't stop the breast from speaking. It will say something to anyone. Like the dog whose mouth waters at the sound of a bell, my nipples rise to the occasion at a touch. It's too easy, it isn't fair, it's not personal—boy, I'm empty, and I'm on my own.

I wasn't going to say anything about the Albany trip because I formed an awful picture of myself there. I mean I saw what a jerk I was pretty clearly, just interested in myself. Leila's family is poor too, and sad. First of all, the place they live in is rotting wood. You have to feel your way up a tall flight of splintered stairs, then there's a rusty screen door. When you come in the door, you're all the way in. One central room serves as a kitchen, bedroom, and living room. A pot-bellied stove warms the place up. Leila says you can get gassed from coal fumes unless you keep the windows open, and they do, so it's kind of keep warm and die, or, live to freeze another day. Her parents are suspicious of me, I mean me as a runaway idiot, not me as a mysterious spy. I believe they sent a telegram to my parents about where I was.

Leila was very nice to me. We slept in the same bed with her little brother Peter. I kept wanting to hug him but Leila was between us. Warm flesh on a winter night seems wonderful. It's something that kids with a whole bed to themselves miss. That's why they want to creep into their parents' bed. Why should they be alone? Daddy always used to lay next to me on top of the covers whenever I woke up with a nightmare. I just remembered something funny about him—how he took showers with me but wore bathing trunks.

I went to the toilet three times during the night because I was wearing a sexy nightgown. I hoped Leila's big brother Al would see me but he was really out. The dark room and the red glow from the stove might have seemed romantic at any other time, but to me, wandering among the bodies, I had a strong urge to get out of Albany.

Leila told me that Charley Rogen steals cars. He has a passion to go fast. His nickname is "Speed." I don't have a nickname because number one: my name is short already, and number two: I don't have a passion with an easy sound to it. Charley is known to put his foot all the way down on the pedal and not care. He starts cars without keys, and if he gets mad because the car won't start, he pours sand into the gas. That's one side of his character, the side that got him sent away; but it didn't cure him. Because I know personally, I was in one of his "special" cars. He has good taste. It was a red convertible with white-wall tires. We rode down the highway at top speed, of course, and he abandoned it near an old factory. He was wearing a leather jacket and new jeans which were very stiff. I casually allowed my hand to brush his fly to see if I excited him, but all I could feel was starch and a well-sewed seam.

"Don't never wear new jeans," he said to me.

Then we kissed and it was pure spirits of ammonia. I shuddered and my eyeballs pained me, my forehead scrunched down, and I gritted my teeth.

"Open your mouth, baby," he asked.

"I don't really want to," I said. "I ate onions tonight."

"I ain't fussy," he answered, and bent me back on the front seat. New cars are pretty comfortable. I didn't realize it. If I furnish my own home someday I'd like to get a red leather couch out of leather. But I didn't open my mouth, and he tried hard to press it open and bite it open and then finally:

"Say are you a bitch, a real cock-teasing bitch! Why'd you come with me if you don't do nothin'?"

"I like you," I said.

"You don't know what you like," he answered.

"Do you like this?"

I had to fight to keep him from pulling my blouse off altogether. It had green leaves on it in dark and light green and was real Irish linen. As a rule blouses are terrible on me, but I wore this one out. Charles tried to bite my buttons off. I think it was his idea of a joke. So I hit him with my head and we both went "Ouch!"

"You know somethin'?" he said. "You gotta hard head. It looks soft but it could hurt you."

"I've known that for a long time," I said, and then: "Let's go."

We took a bus back to Leila's and she asked me what we did and we had hot chocolate and I didn't tell her anything, so she imagined the worst. That put me up a peg in her estimation. She sneaked around to her parents' bureau (they were asleep, they go to sleep early, I think they're constantly asleep) and took out a plastic case about as big as a Swedish pancake.

"Look at this," she whispered, and I looked as she opened it up and showed me what seemed to be a large rubber bottle cap. "It keeps you from having babies," she said. I was amazed.

"What do you do, pray to it?" I asked.

"You wear it. You wear it inside, it's like a shower cap."

"Does it come in colors?"

I didn't want to be too interested. I also had some thoughts of my own about Leila and why she was so anxious to share this information with me. I suppose her puky looks and four eyes fooled me about her sex life; she must give it away free on every street corner. She laughed at what I said and put the object back in its hiding place. When we got undressed for bed I watched her very carefully to see if her life left any marks on her, like fingerprints, or something deep like a prehistoric mollusk but not prehistoric and not a mollusk, maybe a tiny swirl of someone else's hair pasted to her thigh. I searched her all over but she was smooth ivory all the way up and around. If she was saving anything, any historic treasure from her eventful life, it was stored in her belly button, and that would be going too far to examine. So I fell asleep being the dirty one in the room.

Received a call from Cousin Lenny. My parents respect his opinions even though he issues them from between jaws held together with tiny rubber bands. His bite is off, and I might add he is too, or he wouldn't seem so sane. He told me to come home immediately and not make my mother sick. I told him to mind his own business. I like him, but liking him has nothing to do with the way he really is. He was nicer when we were younger; one Christmas he couldn't wait to give me my gifts—rushed into the toilet and handed me a real bark canoe (toy) and a gray flannel bath-robe.

Naturally I came back, even though Lenny was the one who told me to. I had nothing to do in Albany and I wasn't really welcome. My parents seemed refreshed by my absence. They sure puzzle me. Shouldn't they be mad? I ran away and no one suffered.

Was my usual bitch self at dinner this evening. Refused to eat the liver, made faces, picked at everything till I nauseated everyone else. Mother kicked me out. I threw shoes and a flashlight against the wall of my room. (It's one big wall to me.) She came in spoiling for a fight and threw a dish towel at me. Not a very effective weapon!

In some way I'd like to make this next happening funny; it happened to me and it hurt and it made me hate. (Hate, kill, kill, which is the real gor-illa, Selma or King Kong?)

TIME: four o'clock
WEATHER: miserable
PLACE: my bedroom
PEOPLE: Mom and me
REASON: fight (rematch)
MOTHER: You'll go if I have to drag you there.
ME: I don't want to.
MOTHER: You rotten pig! Put on your coat and come on.
ME: I'm very tired. I want to stay home and read.
MOTHER: Don't you waste my money. I'll break your neck.

ME: Go ahead.

MOTHER: If you don't hurry up you'll miss your lesson.

ME: Even if I go I won't sing. I'll stand by the piano and cough.

MOTHER: Cough? Cough? You'll be a bastard and cough when I'm trying to do you something good? I could use the money for myself but instead I want to make something out of you and you're going to cough and embarrass me to your teacher!

ME: Yes.

MOTHER: (*She punches me in the stomach and knocks me on the floor. She kicks me a long time and doesn't let me up.*)

Why did it happen? When she ran out of the house I pretended I was at my lesson and sang. I sounded as if I was rubbed out and something else written on top.

Five

I had a gathering and we played that kid's game Spin the Bottle. Once the neck of the bottle pointed to me and the bottom to Harry Felter. Once was enough. He kissed me on the cheek (doesn't even know how to kiss). He is beginning to grow a beard. I think it will stay soft and fuzzy for a long time. I liked the way it felt when he turned his face away so quickly after he kissed me. It embarrassed him.

I'll be fourteen on Thanksgiving. Harry's friend "Hi" Rabinowitz calls me a turkey. He also called me a gilded stinkweed. I don't know why he did. I hate him, although I used to have a crush on him. He's smart in history and wants to be a politician. Dick Feffer is smart in history too and wants to do something with it. Milton Sasslofsky is crazy about music. He whistles symphonies all the time and imitates bird calls. His instrument is the oboe. The first time I heard him play I made a fool out of myself by giggling; it sounded like snake music. Harry Felter (that genius) wants to be a doctor. His fingers must be strong enough from pounding that piano every day—strong enough to keep his patients down while he tortures them. He is helping a real doctor at Montefiore hospital with research on cancer in plants. Two days ago my ball rolled down the back of Montefiore hospital (I went there because maybe Harry would come out). There was a red light on the door and it said "MORGUE" in big black letters. I was afraid to go in (naturally). Harry's been in a number of times, he says. He likes to describe the way the corpses are filed away in long drawers, and how even though it's so cold in there, the drawers glide in and out easily because they're lubricated with graphite. He has a detailed mind, and come to think of it, it reminds me of the morgue, the way everything is hidden and nothing touches and he doesn't touch me. That's what bothers me. He's a cold fish.

So you see, everyone I know does something intellectual. I wonder if that's why they act so old and at times unfriendly. Diana and Juanita (I'll get to her later) and Harry have been playing piano so long I feel stupid having to plow through my beginner's exercises. I want to play pieces with feeling. I like to do anything emotional, that's the way I am.

I like to make believe I come from a foreign country. In the bus coming home from school, Diana and I pretend we are speaking a foreign language. It makes me feel important to have command of words that no one else understands (not even me). Someone speaking in another tongue sounds somehow so much more intelligent than someone using the mother tongue. And what if Mother really put a fork in my tongue the way Aunt Bella suggested (violently)? Would I then have a forked tongue?

In the train I like to watch my image in the window. It's a dark image and hides my pimples. I think to myself, "That's how beautiful I'd look if I didn't have pimples." Sometimes I promise God to not wear makeup if he'd only give me a pretty complexion. But I don't believe in God, so it's no wonder my complexion stays bad.

Tuesday is a boring day: it isn't the first day of the week and it isn't the last day, it isn't the middle of the week, either, it just fills in. It's a lousy day because there's still three more days of school before the weekend. Last weekend I went to a party at a boy's house I don't know. Harry and Diana know him. He lives in a private house with a terrace. His name is Alfred; his friends call him Alfie. I think he liked me, but I didn't like him. Anyway, I was glad he liked me, because so few boys do. Diana danced ballet in the middle of the floor. All the boys looked at her. They always did. She has so much training. It makes her furious when she's not the center of attention. When she gets nervous she licks her lips and stubs her toes into the carpet as if she were packing lamb's wool into the tip of her toe shoes. She sits with her skirt above her knees and her lap spread wide, the same way she rests at the ballet studio after hard work. It's part of her show-off act. She gets the attention, all right! And I have to pretend I don't notice, because I'm second fiddle and bow and scrape. I don't know why she's my best friend. I wish I knew. She doesn't act like a best friend. She went to Juanita's party without objecting, even though she knew Juanita didn't invite me on purpose because Juanita likes Harry too.

Juanita is a great big horse, but Harry likes her better than he likes me.

Brown leaves and coolness, great! I can wear my new velvet suit. Maybe it is "gilding the stinkweed," as Hi would say, but who deserves the trans-formation more? You can't miss me in the color red. I bought the suit to wear for a choral performance. The sopranos stand in the back, so all any-one will be able to see of me is my face. Mother says she'd be able to see and hear me even if I was a thousand miles away. Pretty good trick—but the usual type of mother magic. Oh my poor old mother. She's thirty-three already. I hope I don't look like that when I grow up. How can I avoid it?

Cousin Lenny got a pinball machine for his birthday. It's a great big one and he keeps it under his bed. It rings bells, and the balls that roll into the holes are made of lead. He wouldn't let me play with it, but when he went down, I did. It's a boring game that you can play by yourself. After a while the score doesn't mean a thing: it always adds up to more than 25,000. At first it excited me and it seemed a lot. Millionaires must feel that way about their money; they lose sense of what it means. That's why they leave such big tips.

No homework for the weekend. That is, no written homework. I have to practice that stupid song "Hark, Hark, the Lark," and also one I like, "*Voi-Che Sapete*." Whatever I sing, my teeth seem to stick together like magnets and the chords stick out in my throat. I'm not very relaxed. I don't have the natural flow that born singers have. The teacher told me to quiver my lower jaw like a rabbit's nose, imagine I was throwing my voice upward and outward, hold my belly in, put one foot forward, smile when I sing *ee*, roll my *rrr*'s, etc. During practice we have to pull our tongues out of our mouths with a hanky so they won't slip back. Singing is pretty phony, if you ask me—not an expression of anything human. Maybe that's the way to be great: do all the awful things anyone else would rather die than do.

I'm not going to do anything today. I'm miserable. My parents had another one of their dirty, cursing lights and my father told my mother to go to hell. When I went in to stop them I was shouted at too. Mother threatened to beat me up for interrupting. I locked myself in the bathroom and contemplated poisoning myself. I put a glass on the window sill and poured iodine, clorox, cough medicine, soap, etc., into it. I was feeling so bad I was about to drink it, but the more stuff I added, the more interested I became in the color changes. Finally the whole mess turned a slimy gray and I poured it out the window. It was too disgusting. Dawn came up the same color as the poison.

Called for Darlene in her house, Hunter Hall. She has a stall shower. I saw her undressed and was surprised. She has breasts as long as my grandmother's. I couldn't take my eyes off them. She wasn't embarrassed, either. At least she has lovely hair (it's short and curly like a Greek god's), and she has a rosy complexion.

We met Janice on the benches. She wears thick lenses in her glasses. Her eyes are brown and wet and shaky. She has kinky hair and thick ankles. I wish I had a pair of brown loafers like she has. She gets anything she wants. I don't particularly like Janice or Darlene; they're drips.

Diana's ballet master calls her "lemon" because she wears a yellow leotard and tutu. He calls all the dancers by the color of their outfit. He bangs on the floor with a cane. Diana and Anyi Lynkopf are his best pupils. I noticed that when a male dancer picked Anyi up during an adagio his hand rested on her crotch and he had a way of running his hands over her body. Anyi seldom smiles, because her teeth are very bad; rotting green and pointed.

The dressing room smells like Sweat Cologne. The dancers douse themselves with it. They wash their feet in the sink.

Sunday I went to the annual performance of Sordkin pupils. Diana was in *Coppélia*. I sat on the top tier of collapsible benches that were placed against the wall of the rehearsal studio. Diana played the doll in the shop window who comes to life. After the performance she ran past me gleaming with sweat. It's hard work coming to life. I thought when she was dressed she would draw me into her circle of friends and we'd all go for a hot chocolate or something, but she ignored me and I didn't want to force myself on her.

I told my mother not to tell and she goes telling everyone. Yes, I'm ashamed that I got a piano scholarship. I got it by crying, by pretending I was so broken up because I couldn't play well. Boy can I cry, what self-pity! I don't really give a damn about the piano.

My teacher is a Bach expert and what a stickler for perfection. She has a real adversary in me; I manage to play things well with my right hand, but the left bumbles along like a dead nerve. I can't possibly remember what key a piece begins in, and have no way of playing it by heart; flats go sharp and naturals run rampant, eighth notes are held for four counts while I grope for the next series of dotted eighths and sixteenths. My teacher cries out in her German accent; "Why do you sabotage me?" She shoves me off the bench with her thick body and proceeds to flash through an invention.

It was cold when I came for my fifth lesson, and she made me sit on my hands to warm them up. They were still numb when I dashed through my scales, and she slapped them with a ruler and insulted me. I don't like her attitude. Just because I don't pay, she wants to whip me into a genius; well, I don't genius that easily.

Six

Grandma G. loves me and I love her, but when Aunt Bella (she feels better) took us all to the Jewish theater last week and I asked Grandma for a cherry life-saver in the car, she wouldn't give it to me. She hides sour-balls, cherry life-savers, and hard raspberries in a secret zippered compartment in her handbag. I wonder why she acts so selfish? All of a sudden candy is the only thing in her life. Grisha the Communist has a large yellow pad that he writes on. I wish I had it. I admire him because he once had something published in a newspaper. He lost his job because of it and they black-balled him in the industry. I think he was an operator on dresses and an organizer. Uncle Grisha reads a lot. He wants to give me a bunch of pamphlets and books on theories he believes in. Mother says his wife made him suffer; that she left him for another man. Well, that sort of thing is bound to hurt, but I thought Communists were used to switching around. I always forget that everyone is human. Aunt Bella made Lila cry. Lila is Grisha's daughter. Bella insulted her mother. Maybe striking out at other people makes Aunt Bella feel in the swing of things. To be alive is to attack. Although to be alive is also to fall down.

Uncle Ernie lives with Grandma G. She has a bed in the living room and he has the bedroom by himself. I like to dwell on how Ernie is, because I don't like him. He's stupid and secret. He is very thin with a pot belly (looks like a case of native malnutrition), belches a lot out of his turtle face, greases his hair, and uses Craig toothpaste. Whatever he uses he smells half fresh and half oily (dirty hair and clean teeth). He always gets to the toilet first. This is his thing. Grandma G. says he sits so long because at work they have bad toilets. He smokes continually in the toilet and creates a heavy smoke screen.

Grandma believes very much in the enema. She used to clean her kids out the minute they got sick. Ernie's enemas must have made some impression on him: he has a stake in that territory.

He never holds a conversation. He says hello and goodbye; in between he works, eats, and sleeps. He has what Mother calls a cigarette cough; it sounds like when someone tries to start a motor boat. Ernie is Mom's kid brother. His face is hairless. He reminds me of a cured midget. He lends Dad money to get out of debt. Dad is in perpetual debt the way others are in perpetual adoration or mourning—debt becomes him, it gives him his attitude. He is the mad debtor. Doesn't deny himself anything, though. People are always signing for him and regretting it. He has charm. It's a charm that people who don't care about anything have. Sometimes I think he'd just as soon drop dead as go on living. He makes jokes about it. He has no responsibility. Why does he go on working? Maybe he likes to have a good time even though he complains, and maybe he complains to us to keep us away from his money. Yet I always can get movie money from him. What he says is: "You shouldn't ever go downtown with less than three dollars in your pocket."

Ernie is a sucker for Dad. Dad uses his handball, money, and signature on loans: for this, Ernie gets free suppositories.

Mother tells me to be nice to Ernie, because sometimes we "eat off him." The family is forever trying to marry him off and no one suits him. Grandma doesn't want him left without a caretaker when she dies (can't she see he's sexless?). It's pitiful the way the whole family goes through the farce with him. They even pack his bag for him when he goes to Laurel-in-the-Pines. He comes back tan but unengaged. The relatives suspect there's something wrong, but say he's still young and he'll get married when the right girl comes along. Mother says he has a good heart. Save me from men who have good hearts!

Ernie is a member of the "clean-plate club": whatever Grandma puts on his plate he eats. She throws the food on as if she was aiming three pounds of whipped butter at a cockroach. He eats and then the belches bubble out of his bubble pipe. In our family I'm so aware of everyone's insides. They never let you forget it. It's like in some families they make you listen to sonny's violin or sister's piano. Ernie is a master of the belch. He belches and it's treated with reverence.

On the other hand, his rival is Uncle Ben, who has a specialty of his own. He buys the most expensive handkerchiefs, and then makes a show of how big they are and how soft the material and how hand-rolled the edge and how curly the initial in the corner. He never uses the handkerchief to blow his nose; instead he sits picking it with an aristocratic pinky. He knows it disgusts me, so he hoists it aloft. Then he slowly inserts the finger in the handkerchief and wipes it off; then he folds it carefully and puts it back in his jacket pocket; then he says, "Hello, Rosie O'Grady" as if he just saw me and he changes my name as if it were a joke.

I learned something funny about Communists: they may seem serious and know-it-all, but underneath they're sentimental and prone to believe the impossible. Now, Uncle Grisha naturally thinks his brother Ernie is a creep: Ernie reads comics and colors in coloring books. But when Orson Welles produced the Martians are coming gag, Grisha got so scared that he took Grandma G. and Ernie and ran into the street and kept running. That's an example of what mother preaches: "Blood is thicker than water."

Blood: The Drink You Eat With a Spoon.

I was going to Grandma G's to play rummy with her, but Mother met me on the street and told me she had just died.

Outside her door there was a straw mummy case. The door was open. Inside, two men were talking to Aunt Ray. Nobody was in the living room. I started to go in. Aunt Ray stopped me. "You can't go in there." I could see that the room was sunny. Ray and Mom went into the kitchen. I sneaked into the living room.

Grandma lay under a brand-new sheet. It was so sharply folded and crisp that it gave me the impression I could shape a boat or a plane out of it like a Japanese paper toy. I thought, "This is her transportation." I wanted to whisper, "Where to?" because I believe dead people hear you but can't let you know they do. So I got closer and called her "sweetheart" and "dear" and patted her hair.

Her skin was blotchy and there was cheese in the corners of her eyes. Her hands were crossed at her breast but there wasn't anything in them; I saw her glasses on the night table and put them on her chest (half funny, half serious), I'm-laughing-with-tears-in-my-eyes kind of thing. I really wanted her to take them with her, because who knows.

All the windows were closed. Why do people shut off the air supply so fast? The room was a preview of the tomb.

Mother finally noticed I wasn't with her and rushed in to drag me out. "You're a mean kid, you know Grandma wouldn't have wanted you to see her that way. Couldn't you have waited for the viewing?" Grandma a monument? If so, I should have crept under the cover with her to be revealed at the unveiling like Charlie Chaplin in the arms of a statue.

I sat on the steps outside till they took Grandma G. to the museum and I stood over her while the men made room in the van. I thought all the human things about her I could, because if she hadn't been born and given birth to my mother, I wouldn't have been born. I thought about how she had to go to the toilet once when I was there and peed in her pants because she didn't have bladder control. I thought of how she had grabbed my breasts suddenly one afternoon when I was about to go to the Tuxedo matinee, and said, "You've got a handful, you'll be okay." I thought it was a vulgar thing for her to do then, but now it strikes me as affectionate and the grandma kind of thing to do.

Went to the funeral. Walked slow and didn't smile. Felt like smiling. My mother in fat black, Blanche in medium black, and Bella in skinny black with a touch of dropsy black. It was a lovely sunny day. I kept thinking, "I'm alive." Completely removed from the tragedy of it. Maybe I'm always removed; it's better to remove yourself before someone does it for you. A romantic idea (the way I really am): I'd go home and find Grandma sitting on the Majestic radio where her picture used to be. I'd ask her to move over just a little so that I could reach the dials. We'd listen to *The Yiddishe Philosopher* together as a courtesy on my part, because I'd really want to hear *Little Orphan Annie* and test my code ring.

Think of something you don't want to happen or something you don't want to own and presto it's yours and it comes to live with you. Ernie is ours. He took my room and I have the piano room. I can see the reservoir and De Witt Clinton High School from my windows. Ernie came in at night and tried to see something through his toy telescope. I hate him. Mother treats him like her child. It's enough that I have to put up with my sister—the only place I can ignore her for the most part is on these pages. Mother forces Ernie to eat. She washes his underwear. He doesn't talk to me. Yesterday he gave sister a Hershey bar. He likes little kids: they don't pass judgment on him. He's a big tease: first he says to her, "You want it?" and then when she reaches for it, he sits on it and makes her try to get it. I think it's disgusting; the chocolate must be body temperature by the time she gets it. Then he plays ball with her and sooner or later it hits her between the legs. All his games are for him!

Only one of Ernie's drawers has clothes in it; the rest of his bureau is filled with junk. He keeps his underwear in the top drawer. Next drawer down has: lighter fluid and two Ronson lighters, a carton of Camels, a photo album, two pairs of glasses, and assorted Hershey bars. The drawer smells terrible. Third drawer down: a coloring set, a paint set, a Hohner harmonica, a deck of pinochle cards, and a wrench. Bottom drawer: radio parts and tools. That was it: not a Trojan in the whole mess. What a private life.

Today Mother admitted to me that there might be something a little off in Ernie, but to humor him because Grandma would have wanted it that way. Nobody caters to me. I suppose if I was the village idiot I'd get fantastic treatment.

I am the village idiot, but everyone else is, too. We wear peaked caps, and carry eggs home in them. On the way we suck the yolks out. At night we drink shell soup and sing egg songs. We play hide-and-seek among the hills. Some of us get lost forever, but most of us carry on the tradition.

Seven

At last I'm able to sit here without being afraid. Nobody is in the house but me. The rest of the family went to the movies to see Andy Hardy. I had locked myself in the toilet because I heard noises. Our apartment is very big. I waited for the noises to stop. I imagined someone sneaking around with murder in his heart. I didn't like being confined, because there wasn't anything to do in there. Finally I got brave (cowards do) and called out, "Come and get me, I'm ready for you!" I half knew it was only the wind rattling the panes or a shade flapping outside the window. Mother has to have all the windows open, even in cold weather. She fears that we'll wake up dead some morning because of a gas leak. She examines the pilot light to see if it's still on; let God be your pilot and the flame will burn bright. There are wonderful things in my house; both idols and idlers are viewed suspiciously.

My hair is still wet. The last time I washed it, Arty watched me while I played the young enchantress. I brushed my hair as voluptuously as I could, stroking and patting and letting it fan out electrically. I pretended that he was my lover and I was tantalizing him. I turned gracefully so that he could get every angle clearly in his mind. Why was I doing this to Arty? Because Arty doesn't like girls and it was safe to practice on him. Many's the time I kissed and petted with him on the benches in vain. He is revolting, he spits when he talks. His mother likes me because I'm his only girlfriend. They don't mind sacrificing someone else's child.

Went to a party tonight at Diana's. Met a new boy whose name is Elliot. Diana turned the lights out and we were stuck with each other. He asked me—and these are his exact words—"May I caress your charms?" I had to push him off because they weren't my charms, they were my falsies. Now Elliot thinks I'm a prude. He's a smooth operator; what I mean is, he acts and talks polite, but underneath he wants to do something dirty.

My lips were awfully swollen from kissing. Why do boys think that the harder they kiss, the better it will be? Maybe it's because they're boys. What I like is the suspense (a build-up): breathing on my neck, a hand up and down my back, rubbing against my breasts so that I wonder what's happening next. Will he or won't he? I covered my entire face with calamine lotion so that my parents wouldn't notice my swollen lips.

Tomorrow I get my period, just when I was planning to go to the St. George pool. I really could go swimming, I don't believe in that old-fashioned stuff, but the water would run red from between my legs and that's embarrassing. Instead I think I'll go to the Tuxedo and soak up a little darkness and entertainment. Maybe Diana'll go with me.

A LIST OF MY FAVORITES

COLOR: BLUE—IT LOOKS WELL ON ME

FOOD: CHOPPED HERRING AND EGGPLANT ON WHITE BREAD WITH TO-MATO

CLOTHES: SPORT—BECAUSE I'M SUCH A SPORT (HAH!)

GAME: TENNIS—SOMETIMES I'M THE RACQUET, SOMETIMES THE BALL

MOVIE: *The Good Earth*—SAD CHINESE PICTURE

ACTOR: CARY GRANT— DON'T KNOW ANYONE LIKE HIM

ACTRESS: DEANNA DURBIN—I WISH I WAS HER

MOTHER: MINE—SOMEONE ELSE'S MIGHT BE WORSE

FATHER: DIANA'S—HE'S SO HANDSOME AND CONTROLLED

SUBJECT: ENGLISH—BECAUSE I'M INTERESTED IN READING AND WRITING

HOUR: DUSK—BECAUSE IT'S MYSTERIOUS

FRIEND: DIANA—BECAUSE I LOVE HER

BOYFRIEND: HARRY—BUT HE DOESN'T KNOW IT

SONG: "MOONLIGHT SERENADE," "I STAND AT YOUR GATE," ETC.

DANCE: THE LINDY—LOVE THAT RHYTHM

HOBBY: LISTENING—I LIKE TO HEAR WHAT PEOPLE ARE SAYING

AMBITION: FOR HARRY TO TAKE ME OUT—AND TO BE GREAT SOMEHOW

The steam just went on. It dries me up. I wish I was in England where the weather's damp and complexions bloom. Our teacher pointed out that England is a land of eccentrics. That's where I belong. I do strange things. For instance I dress up in costumes and dance on the roof. Don't I know what to do with myself? It's my primitive rite in the sun. I embrace the elements. The direct rays hit me, go through me. Nothing else goes through me. I hold on to the pipes that are on the roof and do leg kicks and squats. Sometimes I wrap my legs around a pipe and lean way back; I tighten my stomach muscles and come up in one tight piece. I don't know why I exercise so much, I just like to. I'm thinking of going on a diet. Why don't I get into shape? I can have a good body and look like a dancer. I mean I can be as thin as Diana. Brave talk! I'm so weak-willed when it comes to eating; what will ever take its place?

Harry has a sex quiz he wants to try on some of Diana's friends. I wonder what it asks? Diana says that Harry met a girl at Loon Lake who taught him the facts of life. It's hard to believe. I would have liked to do that, but I don't have the facts at my fingertips. Someday I'm going to make love to him if I don't move away.

Diana showed me a very funny thing. It's called *How to Run a Car*. She got it from Arty. It's really *How to Make Love*. I wonder what Arty is interested in that for. He's a fag, although general knowledge is useful to anyone. Who knows, he may change someday in the far and distant future. You'd never know he was a fag unless you started noticing little things like his manicured nails and the swishy way he dances, as if he were endlessly involved in a solo featuring the pear-shaped ass and the revolving navel. He asks you to dance, and the minute you do he's off in the middle of the floor leering and extending his hand like a chiffon hanky to the other boys in the room. They tolerate it because he's their friend. We all like him even though he's queer, because he has good ideas and is the life of the party. I feel sorry for Arty's mother. She thinks he has lots of girls. He does, if you care to translate boys into girls; that's his language.

How to Run a Car

First grease all parts carefully. See that her points are lubricated and fit properly. Look into her motor and make sure that it's clean and in running order. Now get into the driver's seat. Adjust it. Put your key into her ignition and get her going. Hear that motor purr. Step down on the gas a little harder, make her roar. Keep it up till she's ready to go. Remember to signal that you're about to go, then steer her gently and carefully away from the curb. Accelerate the motor. Look around and go! When you're on the road give her all you've got if she's seasoned. You're on your way to learning how to drive a car. That is if you remembered to shift gears and go into three positions. When the going is tough use the first; when your speed is up use the second; and when there's clear sailing ahead and you're going full speed take her into third. Driving takes a lot out of you, but anyone can learn if they apply themselves and get a good car. The right owner can get years and years of service out of an old car. A properly cared-for car can be traded in it at the right time and the whole thing repeated again and again—so long and happy motoring!

Eight

I wish I didn't have to deal with parents. Just put the money in an envelope and send it to me care of the Riviera.

Mom claims that Murray the vegetable man likes her and picks out the best for her. Yesterday we received soft, moldy strawberries. The ones on top were okay but the fillers leaked a bitter red wine. So much for Murray in his dirty white apron using his position of trust to pawn off rotting fruit. He has no integrity, just doesn't care whether he keeps us as customers. Mother "trusts" too often and doesn't pay her bills. That's why storekeepers don't respect her. She orders by phone as if she were asking favors in fear: "You have good bananas today? Maybe you could pick me out some nice soup greens? I don't mind if you throw in a cantaloupe if you smell a ripe one."

Out to the benches again with my records. Diana brought her portable record player. We wore sheer peasant blouses. I'm thicker (the real peasant). She has a round face, I have round arms, she has strong calves, I have strong thighs, her waist is tiny, mine is broad. I'm the work horse, she's the aristocrat.

It wasn't fun on the benches tonight, no boys around. They must have been playing basketball. Games seem stupid to me. All that fuss and energy just to toss a ball through a ring. It would make some sense if you could throw yourself through the ring: rising, skimming the hoop, and then falling straight down through it, not stopping, going through the floor, the foundation, the earth. Every player lost because of the conditions of the game. We were disappointed but it wasn't the end of the world.

Wow, was I sad and bad and mad! I slashed the outside of my hands with a razor. I made deep criss-crosses in the flesh. A rehearsal for self-destruction? There wasn't much blood because the lines were so fine. I scarred my hands. It was easy to do because it didn't hurt. Even my brain was numb. Afterwards I bought pancake makeup to cover the cuts.

A young man I know would be scared away if he knew what I did. It's a strain being with him anyway. He's in the lingerie business. He lives with his parents and uses the apartment to take girls to when they're away summers in the Borscht Belt. He's jealous of me playing the piano. I hate dabblers like Larry. He's twenty-eight and is just taking piano for the first time. His real talent lies in conning mothers. My mother is crazy about him. He brought her flowers and me perfume. He looks like a Teddy bear, and even wears woolly brown double-breasted suits.

My hands are healing. I canceled my piano lesson. Mr. Jalisco my new teacher would be horrified. He's a nervous wreck by nature, plays the fast pieces faster than necessary.

I wish I could get help. Someone who would listen and say, "Insanity is not imminent." I already know that insanity is not peppermint; it is green pistachio—my favorite ice cream; I ask for it, but they seldom have it.

I can't bear going shopping with my mother. She has patience with those stupid clods of sales people. God, they drag out stuff that doesn't suit me at all. She makes me try it on anyway: "How do you know it looks bad if you don't give it a chance?" She knows and I know that a wide-hipped, short-waisted girl cannot wear long waists and gathered skirts. She tortures me.

"But I hate it," I tell her. She whispers that I'll insult the clerk. Then I insult the clerk on purpose: "Don't bother helping me, I can find what I want by myself." The sales person snoops around and shoves her ugly head through the curtains of the booth while I'm undressing: "Are you okay?" My body in its torn underwear is not for her to see, the clean-corseted frump! "I'll let you know later," I answer her, making my expression as ominous as possible. I can see myself from every angle in those dressing-room mirrors. Why does Mother insist that I'm beautiful? Is she blind or cruel? Doesn't she know that I'm deformed? Yes deformed! Deformed like a poor bastard hunchback, only in front, under the breasts where the line should be flat and long (not bulky and bony). When I was examined for camp the doctors called it Harrison's groove. I wonder who else has it? I want to hide. I hate myself.

Nine

Today is Friday. I'm supposed to go out tonight with Larry. He has tickets for Carmen. It seems that whenever I go to the opera I see Carmen. I never see anything else. I'd like to see Aida. I've heard so much about it—how real camels walk across the stage. I have a blue dress with stripes down the side to make me look taller, and a new matching straw hat and new high heels. Mother used up her food money for my outfit. She did it for Larry's benefit, not mine.

Same evening after *Carmen*: I cried. She didn't deserve to die. It was her nature to drive men mad. Some men are weak and can't take it. Larry bought a box of cherries and orange drinks during intermission. He smiles all the time. It means nothing. Is he hiding something or is it a social grace? He's the oldest man I've ever gone out with, and I'm not sure how to act. I feel like being stupid around him and doing silly things to disturb his manners.

Larry isn't all manners. He's a dirty businessman. We went for a drive and he stopped the car and pushed me down and got his hand caught in my skirt zipper. I told him to cut it out or I'd tell his mother on him. He just kept on repeating in a very breathy way, "Let me fuck you, baby, let me fuck you, please let me fuck you." He rolled around on top of me. I was disgusted; he creased my new dress, he scratched my face, he made my foot fall asleep. Mother thinks he wants to marry me. She'd get rid of me at the drop of a hat. He had no right to talk like that to me. I never gave him cause. I don't even like him. He's used to older girls.

Mother says it's my fault Larry doesn't come to see us (get the *us*) any more, and wants to know what I did to insult him. I got mad and told her I had accused him of wearing the ladies' underwear he manufactures. This appealed to her vulgar nature and instead of making a mean face she burst out laughing. It shocked me. What kind of mother is she, anyway?

I saw Larry getting on the bus to Fordham Road, so I got off. My face was full of pimples. The pimples were covered with calamine lotion. What a sight! I should have stayed on and sat down next to him and made him gaze at me in my bumpy, chalk-pink mask and then begged him in falsetto, "Fuck me, please fuck me, fuck me now and forever, fuck me on the seat, fuck me under the seat, fuck my frozen landscaped face." That would have taught him disbelief. He'd be the one to have to leave the bus and I'd shout after him, "I am driven by desperation."

Uncle Grisha asked me why I'm not good to my mother. She complains about me to the relatives. Says I'm mean and ungrateful. They detest me. Sometimes she boasts about me and compares me to their own dull offspring. This does not make them admire me.

I've stopped playing piano. I enjoyed it but couldn't learn anything competently except Chopin's Étude in A. I'd try to be playing it whenever I expected a date. I wouldn't stop playing till he was directly behind me; then and only then did I rise to greet him. It was a romantic notion I had. Oh to be admired and loved! I don't think anyone will ever love me. I have nothing to offer.

I have a friend Netty who's very nutty. She was one of the girls I met at Camp Bronx House. Her skin is pearly and her breasts stand up. Just a lovely-looking girl. If you want to know why I say she's very nutty, I can't; my lips are sealed. Here's a hint: she likes girls.

I finally met Netty's brother. He's very smart, a French major. We went for a walk in the cold. The benches had snow on them but we sat down. Hank put his arm around me. I didn't even feel it, I was wearing so much clothing. He tried to kiss me. His breath is awful, the worst I've smelled yet. If it wasn't for his breath I might have kissed him. He pulled a dirty trick on me. He put his hand up my dress before I knew what was happening. I had a wild sensation, something I couldn't hold back. It reminded me of when I was eight years old and woke up that way from a dream. I like it very much. I hope it happens again soon. It's the fatal way I might go—so warm and good from beginning to end.

I've seen my whole family running around without clothes on. So what! It's natural. My father's penis hangs down in front like an unpressed tie.

I almost defiled Mother's brand-new bedspreads. Saturday she came home with two beautiful plaid chintz spreads. I had decided to have intercourse with Hank because I knew him. Well, we went into the bedroom and I took my clothes off and lay on the bed, on the new spread. Hank took his things off too. He has a long torso and short legs like an Oriental. He stood by the closet, and as he walked toward me an untoward thing happened: he kind of doubled up and jerked in and out like a South American dance. "Was that an orgasm?" I asked (my new word for the week). He grinned in a painful way. "I can't control myself, sorry," he said. Then we heard the front door being opened. Hank dressed faster than he ever had in his life. What a close call!

Mother asked Hank how he was and he said, "Fine." It amuses me the way people never know anything about anyone else, especially the sex that goes on.

Hank's mother is a horror. She's jealous of me. She won't let me use Hank's typewriter when I'm over there. Says I'll break it. The fat fool. My mother is more generous. With my mother, other people come first.

Hank's brother is religious and you know what that means: bigoted, compulsive, fanatic, and insane. He refuses to take advantage of modern times. He's twice as pompous as Hank. At least Netty's fun. I really enjoyed her company the Sunday we read *All's Well That Ends Well*, under a tree in Van Cortlandt.

I'm tired of pretending I believe in God to Hank. He's getting as religious as his brother. Says his wife will have to shave off all her hair, and that means pubic, underarm, and head. Is it possible to buy a pubic wig? What if it slips? I'm also tired of reading the *Post* editorials just so that he and I can have intelligent, liberal discussions. Wouldn't it be more natural to just bore each other, which we really do, except when we're feeling each other up behind De Witt Clinton High School? Another thing about Hank, he doesn't want to do *that* as much as I do and begs off just when I'm getting hot. So much for that, and trying to do the mysterious and loving thing.

Ten

When I was thirteen, Mother took me to see my second cousin Marshall Baxter. He felt me up while I sat next to him on a love seat in his hotel suite. I didn't know what to do, so I didn't do anything. Mother wanted me to sing for him, to persuade him to get me a screen test. Marshall was a well-known Hollywood comedian, but he certainly wasn't going to thrust me into the lap of fame. What I want to say is that I think Marshall Baxter is a kind of sex maniac, because whenever I went to see him after that he unzipped his fly. I rather liked the whole thing—seeing someone famous in their true setting. Marshall was after IT all the time. He invited me to visit him backstage last year when he was in a Broadway musical. I saw him in his dressing room. He was seated in front of a mirror surrounded by light bulbs. His wrinkles were full of pancake makeup. He was lounging around in a paisley satin robe. He drew me onto his lap. "You like it, don't you?" he asked. I thought he meant the excitement of being backstage, and I did enjoy that, but his hand went down between the satin edges of his robe. And there it was again. "You've got a winner there," I said. "You can be a winner too," he answered. I laughed as he good-naturedly went back to perfecting his makeup. I saw part of the show and practically puked, it was so boring. He kept eating bananas and throwing the skins away while he played the piano. He ate at least twenty bananas. Some act! He's far from original. I wonder if his daughter knows what her father is like.

To continue the adventures of Me: picture me in a new pink cotton dress walking down the carpeted hotel corridor of the Hotel Warwick. I am going to see that old and licentious man about town, Marshall Baxter. He is in his room with two companions, one a millionaire and the other a dress manufacturer. Marshall's night table is crowded with medicine bottles. Marshall calls room service for drinks. The millionaire (who is a synthetic rubber baron) and the dress manufacturer go down to the cocktail lounge to wait for us. The drinks come. We drink and talk—my aspirations: college, dance, drama. He listens while he toys with my tits. What can I say to this man, he's from another world. He wants to know what I do with my boyfriends. He thinks I'm sex on wheels. I tell him "that's private." "You can tell me," he whispers and goes to his knees, kissing my panties under the dress. I pull away and leave him kissing the air. He thinks I'm playing him for a sucker. "C'mere," he shouts, and twists my arm. This time he means business. He opens his fly and orders, "Kiss it!" He is meaner than his penis. It looks relatively sober. I feel affection for it and do as he orders. Then we go out and have a swell time at the Copa where everyone knows him (even the lady who tells fortunes there; he says she's a whore on the side). We sit at a reserved table.

Marshall talked about me to the synthetic rubber baron, who invited me to his office on 34th Street. He told me about his Washington affiliations and how great he was to have invented phony rubber soles to help the war effort. He opened his crummy scrapbooks for me to see his face on every page. The minute the work day was over and his staff left—oo la la! He dragged me within inches of his peculiar and dangerous mustache. Each end of it was as stiff and pointed as a leather punching tool. I asked him how he got his mustache to stay so neat. He opened his desk drawer and handed me a tiny round box of imported pomade. He put the stuff on his mustache, drawing it out thinner and thinner. I was very disinterested. On a table, he had arranged a display of shoes he had produced soles for, but there weren't any pairs. I had thought maybe I could take home a pair.

We sat down on the couch and kissed. Then he told me a story about how some foreigner was having intercourse with his sweetheart but he didn't move at all and kept it in a whole week till he came. "That is the greatest sexual thing that can happen to anyone," he said. I thought he was crazy. Then he asked me, "Do you wear a brassiere?" I told him I didn't need to and he seemed pleased. He leaned back on the leather cushions and slowly pulled a Baxter trick. He exposed himself. "I hear you're the best in the business," he said. It was the first time anyone ever told me I was best at anything, so I worked extra hard and invented a new technique. It dealt with the off-beat. I had to synchronize what I was doing to the beating of his heart; very much like improvising a counterpoint to Bach.

Tell me I'm good at dying and I'll do it.

The Baron lent me his car and chauffeur to go see a play. He told me there'd be tickets waiting at the box office. It was a thrill. I felt as if I was powerful and rich. I don't think I'll ever be rich, not like those people. Baron (I call him that because he's so famous he has to remain anonymous) gave me fifty dollars to buy something to wear.

The letdown of the year came in Baron's penthouse. We were served venison from one of his estates. That was fine. The valet leaned over me with a silver tray covered with choice cubes of the steak. That was great. I was too dumb to know that I serve myself, so the Baron put some meat on my plate. I ate my meat without changing the fork hand to hand; you can eat faster that way and I think it's an approved method. Well, then I was primed for a super-special dessert. Dessert is my favorite course, but what a dud it turned out to be. The valet brought out a plate of chocolate Oreos.

The Baron's penthouse is like a house. There is a wide staircase leading to the second floor. Between the first and second landing he has a huge painting. I asked him who painted it and he got mad. He told me that in polite society one never asks such questions. He said it would be different if I asked him how big it was. I thought his concern about size was strange; I go for quality. Then I put my foot in it again by saying what a nice polite elevator man he had. He said, "You talked to the elevator man! My dear, don't ever do that again."

The elevator opens right smack in the penthouse foyer. It's a private elevator. The Baron's study, which he never uses, is decorated like a monk's, and in his living room he keeps part of the original Gates of Gethsemane (whatever that is).

I don't hardly remember what we did in bed, probably 69, but it ended up 11 (side by side we won't collide). His bathroom is splendid. He keeps two gallon bottles of Macy's mouthwash under the sink and four toothbrushes hanging from a golden eagle on the wall. The toilet looks like a white wicker chair, and if you forget to raise the seat, you get strained pee. The shower has eight nozzles jutting out of the wall for different parts of the body. It can be adjusted for fine or coarse spray. I took a long shower and used a transparent soap with no odor at all. Afterwards I tried his colognes. One, imported from Jamaica, smelled like limes. His talc was flesh-tinted; I powdered the inside of my thighs. My mouth had a terrible alcohol taste because I had licked it off the Baron's scrupulously clean body. I used the mouthwash and it burned my gums.

When I came down to the living room the Baron was impatient. He handed me fifty dollars. I had been planning to ask him for an educational loan (college fantasy again). In the shower I had been daydreaming about how I would arrive at school in his chauffeured car and pretend he was my father. He's at least fifty-five and I'm fifteen. I don't think I'll see him any more. He's not my path to glory.

Diana goes on and on, cool as a cucumber. She doesn't have to do any-thing bad to get what she wants. My secret life is all bad and yet . . . She says she wants to marry a man who is not smart or talented so that he will cater to her. I want to marry a man who is brilliant so that it will rub off on me. I can't tell if I'm dumb or just uneducated. Lately all I'm trying to do is prove I'm attractive to men. Dad thinks Diana is beautiful. What does he think I am, a turnip? When I have gatherings, he dances with her.

Eleven

My paternal grandfather is a big man with nose trouble. We've all inherited his nose. I don't think my father's nose is his own. It's part of my grandfather's, which was extremely large. Even though it's large he can't breathe through it. Nobody else can, either. I have a deviated septum. Only one side at a time works. Dad tries blowing out very hard and then breathes in fast to try to catch the air when the nose isn't looking, so to speak. Sometimes I hold my arms up in the air to breathe better. It's too bad that the only thing that's free is air, because it causes such a daily struggle.

Grandpa may not be able to breathe through his nose but he talks through it. The only one he talks to is Father, and their conversation sounds like a snort contest. How they love each other and hate my mother. Grandma hates Mother too. They must hate me because I'm the daughter of my mother. Let me tell you how disgusting people can be—evil in small ways, so that it piles up.

Our furniture is falling apart and Grandma and Grandpa have a second-hand store. Grandma promised Mom a chair and a lamp and a cocktail table. We went to pick the stuff out. Dad was waiting for us at the store. He shouted at her that he wouldn't allow any junk into the house. She screamed back at him that he never bought her anything new. He hit her. He forced her arms behind her back. Grandpa shined a flashlight into her eyes to make her stop screaming. I kicked Dad and knocked the flashlight out of Grandpa's hand. I hate that old bastard. Mother and I ran out of the store crying. We were on Third Avenue and 102nd Street. Mother said, "Stop crying, the colored people will think something's wrong." What did she mean by that?

Grandma (my father's mother) invited us to dinner last night. She makes awful food: jelly with garlic, herring with boiled potatoes, and tea with lemon. She berated Mother for the umpteenth time about how her son could have been a doctor if it wasn't for Mom rushing him into marriage. Dad tells them everything about Mother. He even calls her crazy—his own wife. He has no shame. They laugh at her behind her back. I'm very cold to those people. When Grandpa takes out his violin (he taught himself to play) and plays, and everyone says I got my musical talent from him, I deny it.

Grandma took me into the bedroom to show me a new bathrobe Dad got her for her ancient birthday. She stripped off her undershirt (she wears a man's undershirt) to show me her breasts. "Just like a girl," she boasted. Her skin is strange—like a coal miner's. The pores are large like orange peel (especially around the breasts), and there is dirt in them. Her face is the same, and her hands are always gray. She washes, but because of the kind of work she does in the store she can't ever get clean. She's different than Grandma Gold was: tough and wiry, delivers furniture in a pushcart without help from anyone. She's proud of that.

I love to explore her bedroom. There are treasures there. In metal boxes pushed under the bed she keeps diamond tie-pins, rings, bracelets, earrings, and other shiny beautiful objects like amber umbrella handles and ivory cane heads. Mother says she buys stolen goods. She once sold Marshall Baxter's wife a chinchilla jacket for fifteen dollars. She didn't know its value. Marshall Baxter's mother is Grandma's sister. I knew her when I was little and everyone called her "Tante."

I wondered why Grandma suddenly became so nice to Mother. Now I know; she thinks she's going to die. Dad found her out cold in the bathroom yesterday. The toilet bowl was full of blood. Maybe she will die. I couldn't care less. Poor Dad, he hates hospitals so much and now his mother is in one. Maybe I'm a cold fish, but I'd like to see all my enemies get it.

I stay up nights worrying about death. You can run anywhere and it follows you, it follows so close that I wonder how can death be so quick? Death is in us already, that's how. Death is the great love of my life; once is enough.

Everyone is passing. Last night, in his sleep, Grandpa went, soundproof after all that noisy breathing. Now the house is haunted. Grandpa had a stroke—no more Grandpa-ville.

Goodbye, Grandpop. If you sneeze you might blow your way out of hell. If you fart (and I know dead people do) you may zoom your gas-propelled way heavenward.

Expected news! Grandpop left me nothing in his will.

Think I'll go see Aunt Ray. She has a new dog. His name is Sandy. She's the only one in the family who allows an animal in the house. That doesn't make her great—it kind of softens the mean things she does. I'm not afraid of Sandy even though he barks. Once a dog sicked me and I froze. My fingertips got tight and I couldn't move from the spot. That saved me.

I can't stop eating. I gorge myself on candy and cake and soda. I can't help it. I get these overwhelming urges to eat. Eating is my surrender to satisfaction. It is the answer to "I want." And I want plenty. Food is mine to grow hungry for, and consume. It's always fun to decide what to eat. Appetite is the one rule, and appetite is what I have. I am hungry, always hungry, and this puts me in a class with lovers and artists—I have no other choice.

Twelve

Aunt Bella is extremely ill again. Friends and Uncle Mort's business associates have surrounded her with goodies, dried fruit, candy, smoked oysters, giant fruit from Florida, and imported biscuits from England. Now, what could be more idiotic? Bella is being fed intravenously.

The nurse is a real cock-tease, waving her ass in front of Uncle Mort (with Aunt Bella on her death bed in the other room)! She threw a whole pack of cards on the rug and then bent down to pick them up slowly, one by one. She was demonstrating a ligament-stretching exercise. "Bend from the waist," she explained, "to get the most benefit from this exercise."

One day last week when Mom and I went to see Bella, before she had her relapse, we found her in the kitchen, sitting on a high stool, making fruit jello for Uncle Mort. She was too tired to get back into bed by herself. Imagine, just to cook for her husband, to do the wifely thing. I suppose I'll hang on to life that way too; by doing normal things as if they were normal for me.

I'll never know what Aunt Bella wanted when she motioned me to come closer. She was lying on a bed with wheels, her dropsical stomach high under the sheet. Her shrunken yellow face and long thin fingers frightened me. I thought she would dig in and not let go. She smiled; I backed up to make room for the wild animal. Oh, I'm so bad, so guilty; Aunt Bella was the only one in the family who read books.

If I dream about Aunt Bella she'll live again, but more briefly than before.

I'd hate being old and decrepit. I couldn't stand it if it took me an hour to get a cup of lukewarm tea to my mouth and the only other thing I was allowed to eat was boiled rice. I hate being slow because I'm quick. Old people are probably reassured by their own pantomime: "If it takes me five minutes to get two steps from the table to the chair, how long will it take me to go from life to death? At the rate I'm going, maybe never."

Slept at Uncle Mort's apartment last night. Why? Because I was too tired to go all the way home from downtown. I did have some ideas about WID-OWED HUSBAND AND YOUNG GIRL, but put away the evil thought. I can just see the headlines:

UNCE AVUNCULAR SEDUCES NICE NIECE
The girl's mother found the pair involved intimately on the living room floor when she entered with a passkey to remove some of her deceased sister's belongings. The uncle, known as Uncle Mort, is being detained presently at the 15th precinct, where he is being held on charges of disturbing the morals of a minor. The girl was released in the custody of her mother.

Mort has fine Italian marble lamps. The ones by the bed have red bulbs in them. The glow made my skin look unblemished. When Mort came out of the toilet I went in and it was another kind of light entirely—fluorescent. I sprouted blue pimples. Uncle Mort smells like the Baron and wears real silk pajamas. He likes subdued colors like wine and blue. I was wearing a blue sheer nightgown but I did a crazy thing. When I was in the bathroom I took a roll of adhesive tape and wound it around my middle to nip in my waist and accent my breasts. Anything for attention, even if I didn't feel sexy. Uncle Mort said, "If you weren't such a tub of lard, I could get you a job modeling." He's finished in my book. Wait till I'm gorgeous and he has incestuous thoughts.

Brought A. home from school with me today. He's an Arabian fairy. We like each other. Drank milk and ate dates. Walked through a flat grassy place (a field?) in Van Cortlandt Park. The sun and sky above were in the right place and so were we. He's like a woman; we discussed makeup. His lips are cinnamon brown; I'll bet his penis is too. I can't help being attracted to him, even though I know I don't excite him. He's so elegant. I suppose the dirtier your mind is, the cleaner you'll try to be in person. Part of a famous quote which I don't remember is: "Desire has pitched its tent, in the place of excrement." That's it, he wants to look furthest from his desire. I love his velvet vest. He has a Van Dyke beard and his nails are manicured. I feel like a mother to him. Protecting someone makes me feel protected. Mom is prejudiced but he'll win her over with his manners, and if he doesn't . . .

Thirteen

Dad left early to open the drug store. I had breakfast with Mom and little sis. Ernie is a late sleeper. We had poached eggs, toast, and coffee. Sister had four eggs and four pieces of toast. She's fatter than the Taj Mahal. Mother ate with her mouth open. I caught myself eating like an animal with chin in plate and tongue lapping away. Mom told me to straighten up. Dad never eats anything but a slice of wholewheat toast and a wheat germ capsule with his coffee. The meal was going along as expected when the phone rang and that disrupted everything. Mom got upset. She spoke in a secret way over the phone so that even I couldn't piece the conversation together. She turned to me and put me in charge of the toaster and clean-up because she had to run. It must have been important, because she did the black bottom in front of the mirror (shake your hips, slap your can) and put on her best girdle. She dances when she's excited, that's the childish part of her. I asked her where she was going and she told me to mind my own business.

Mom back at six, with a roast chicken in a silver bag. She looked sad. I'd like to know what she's up to these days. I mean she's very naive and impressionable. She's the one SPECIAL OFFERS attract. She's a sucker for the sweepstakes, trips to Bermuda, dance lessons, encyclopedias, and freezer units. God knows what she's doing to improve her lot in life.

She confessed to me because she had to: Mom has a detective trailing Dad. She thinks he has another family somewhere. Yesterday when the phone rang it was the detective with a big breakthrough in the case. He gave Mom the woman's phone number. Mom called the woman's husband and he gave her short shrift, but, the woman got wind of it and called Dad immediately. He choked up with rage and threatened to kill Mom. (I don't think he'll do it.) He said he's going to have the phone removed. Mom wants me to watch the phone in case someone comes to take it away. What he did is unscrew the earpiece and remove a wire, so we can't hear a thing on it. Without the phone Mom's lost. It's her social life and the way we get our food.

Mother's in the bath with the water steaming hot. Dad's got her pregnant again for spite. He won't bring home ergot to start her period. I'm afraid she'll faint in the tub and get rid of herself first. She's determined to abort. As far as I'm concerned, it's murder. I detest the idea. What if she hadn't wanted me?

It happened "naturally" as she was standing by the stove stirring chocolate pudding. Mom held it up for me to see: a plastic bag of water about as big as a golf ball. "See, it's nothing," she said, the bathroom floor. She bled for a week while pieces of the placenta appeared every day. No pain, no nothing! Just thick chunks of the placenta floating folded in a bottle of alcohol. She would shake the bottle up and say, "That's the nourishment." Her vulgar and unfeeling attitude toward nature confused me. I could understand the primitive fear of the afterbirth, the burying of it, even the isolation of a menstruating female, that I had read about in a Margaret Mead book, but I wasn't prepared for her complete lack of superstition or guilt, or for her "scientific" discoveries. If the doctor hadn't appropriated the specimen in order to determine whether all of it had come out and nothing was left to cause hemorrhaging, she might have kept it on her knick-knack shelf as a conversation piece.

I miss the child that never was

I miss the child that used to be
I miss myself right now
Where am I?

Fourteen

ATTENTION: the time is now. It always was and will be. What shall I not do? I shall not do my math homework. I shall make small decisions that are in opposition to the existing order of things. Neither math, nor history, nor musical theory can ever again expect me to rehash the theories that make them possible. I'm screwing up.

Mrs. Plover asked me to conduct the Beethoven *Fifth*; she got sore at me because I wanted to do the whole symphony and kept swinging the baton in an insanely enthusiastic way. She wanted to divide the movements among others in the class. I had a great time with Toscanini backing me up. The physical labor wrung me out. Mrs. Plover leaned over me (upswept like her hairdo) and warned me: "You're not passing this term, either. You refuse to obey instructions, your homework is less than perfect, your behavior in class is disruptive to others who are serious about their work." She forgot to add: "and I hate your adolescent female guts!" She couldn't hate them more than I do.

I like to watch that sex-mad theory teacher operate. She wears pointy brassieres under low-cut, tight-fitting, knee-length dresses (often knitted and hugging her butt). She's been married twice that I know of. All during class she bends over our theory notebooks correcting, which gives her an opportunity to show what she's got. We all joke about it, but it's quite a disruptive display from someone who abhors disruptives.

Diana is winning top honors, kudos, and the admiration of all her teachers. Nothing can bring her down. I think our differences are contained in the essentials. For instance, I glanced down at my legs during official class and noticed that my stockings were sagging and had runs in them. She was neat as a pin. She respects herself. Every layer of her from bare bones to underwear to trim velvet suit is a framework so devoid of clutter, so balanced, that it can be built upon, and supported. I was already collapsing from the inside out; my clothes showed it. I allowed my hair to grow very long (mid-back), and when I wanted to hide, I made an effective screen by fluffing it forward on each side. My head became a hot hairy nest of bluebirds (of happiness?) smothering each other. Follow the bluebird of happiness and it will send you crashing through impenetrable thickets. Diana just puts out her hand.

I'm failing. Geometry has me beat. Too many rules before I can find out: HOW BIG—DISTANCE AROUND—SHORTEST WAY THROUGH? Why can't I just GO?

At times I amaze myself and others by knowing the answer. It works against me, because then "teach" thinks I can do better. She never lets up. She wants blood. They always want blood, and blood takes time, blood takes at least an hour every night of studying; the hour when I'd rather be doing something else, like eating or reading or creating soapy hair styles that defy gravity. I'd rather do worse (I'm a disappointment). When I lose interest, no threat in the world can bring it back.

French is completely foreign to me. Nice teacher, though. Her name is Madame Soupalt and she's married to a cello teacher, Mr. Tallow. She's cheery and good-natured, a joy to behold. She has no scapegoats and no favorites in class. I think she's interested in her personal life.

There should be one tense: the present. Other tenses are fantasies. I don't object to fantasies, I have a few myself, but I don't think fantasies should be made so difficult—fantasies should come easy and in your own language.

English! NOW there's the subject I love. WORDS, WORDS, WORDS, WORDS. Now What does that WORD mean? Say it fast and repeat it often—

it means nothing. It means I forgot what it means. It forgot what I mean. What they mean. Mean—they're mean—certainly mean! THE RATS—THE RATS—THE RATS WORDS SWORDS WARDS SWORDS WARDS WOINDS WOUNDS WOUNDS.

POEM
Word rats
are wounded

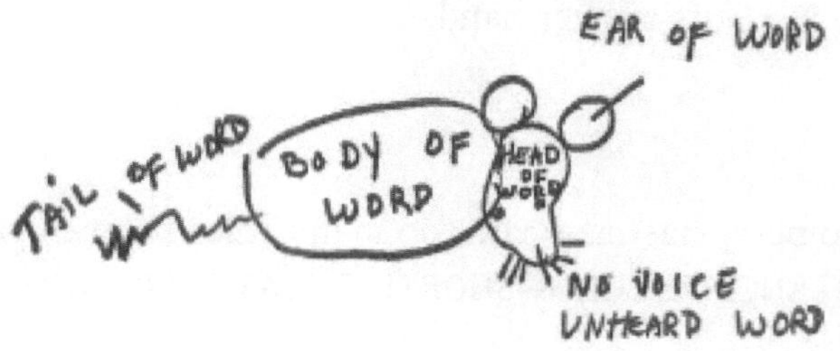

Yesterday in school our math teacher hypnotized some kids. I remembered how to do it. When fat Maria came down the steps after school, I asked her if she wanted to be hypnotized. She said, "Maybe." I promised to improve her flute playing if she let me experiment with her. She made me promise not to touch her silver flute, because it came apart in sections and only flute players could put it together again properly. I said, "Okay." I took her behind the back stairs that led from the gymnasium and started to talk to her in a very confidential monotonous voice. I did everything right except I almost forgot to tell her that when I clap my hands three times and tell her to wake up she should wake up. I made her write her name like she used to when she was seven years old; asked her to play a difficult piece without making mistakes (which she did, but it was dull as dishwater); asked her whether any boy had touched her; asked her whether her mother still slept with her father (she mumbled). I was bored with Maria because it seemed her parents never did anything outrageous to her or to each other, and her experience with boys was nil. Anyway, I was still in there playing Mandrake: I planted the idea in her head that she was a ravishing creature and had to be extra careful around the opposite sex, also that she would be a world-famous flautist within three years if she practiced four hours a day. When I brought her out of it she didn't believe I had hypnotized her until I showed her the piece of paper she had written her seven-year-old name on. I hardly believed it myself. I had all that power and didn't know what to do with it. It made me feel weak.

The most frightening question I can ask myself is: where does time go? Something happens, but where is it stored? I mean, is all gesture, all energy lost? Will there ever be a real time machine like in *Alley Oop*? God, imagine doing over and over again the same things that were practically unendurable at first. What a refresher course the time machine would be: a baby born ten times; a casual affair extending beyond any permanent one; accidents screeching to abrupt but useless stops; my father calling, "So long, you old bag" to my mother as he runs down the stairs an infinity of times.

Dad wants to see what I've been writing. Fat chance! One mention of birth, death, or copulation on the printed page and he tears it up. I should have another book going just for him. Hearts and flowers. If he became insistent, I could drag that out. It would be absolutely idyllic and have a trick ending.

Fifteen

Nothing to do again. Friends away at Rockaway. Met that nut Nathan who thinks Beethoven speaks directly to him, gives him messages through the symphonies. Nathan plays the violin, hates me to call it a fiddle, calling a violin a fiddle Americanizes it, gets it ready for a career of square dances instead of Paganini. I like to get his goat, except that it's easy to bother a nut and a trifle dangerous. He's ugly, has a big nose, short body, and black oily hair—THEN WHY DID I SLEEP WITH HIM? I have no morals sometimes. Maybe if the library was open on Sunday I would have been there instead of in Nathan's house, in his mother's bed. It was interesting but not intimate, because I was ashamed.

That Nathan came home from the navy and told me he had syph. I rushed over to Dr. Reiss and asked his advice. He acted like an old granny. Probably jealous. He said he'd have to report it if I had contracted the disease. Luckily the lab report gave me a clean bill of health. I wouldn't be surprised if Nathan got his venereal information from Beethoven too.

I bought a new brassiere. It's white satin; the cups make my breasts look like engorged bullet heads (one step closer and I fire). Nathan's brother was down by the benches and I wondered what he'd do if he saw me in my bra. I called him over and he was terribly flattered, because I go with the older crowd. I asked him to sit down and tell me how Nathan was doing in the navy. It got darker out, but there was plenty of light from the moon to make me visible. Joey looks like a baby ape; it amuses me. I let him put his head on my shoulder. His thick hair tickled my ear and neck. I lifted my blouse till it was above my collarbones. Joey looked. I asked him how he liked it, and he said he liked it fine. Then he asked, "Is that all you?" I made him touch me to prove it. My breasts are the most sensitive part of me. I get a thrill every time someone lays their hands on me. Isn't that an old cure-all, the "laying-on of hands?" Joey was so impressed he couldn't let go, kept adjusting my "treasures" as if they were a pair of out-of-focus binoculars. "Sighted the enemy yet?" I asked, as he gently brushed my nipples against his eyelids. "There's no one around," he whispered. "No enemies, and no friends." He was sounding too philosophical for me, and since I couldn't tell what he really meant, I broke the spell with: "Why is it that your whole family is so ugly?" And he countered with: "Nathan says you're a nymphomaniac." "To who does he say it?" I glared and punched him in the ribs. He grabbed both my arms and twisted them behind me. The baby ape was strong. "I don't know," he said, "just everybody he knows. He warned them about you." He had his face pretty close to mine, so I spit in it; there wasn't much spit, just enough to make him draw back, and in that moment I wrenched free and ran. So that's what they're saying about me. I wonder if Harry believes it? Truth is stranger than fiction, though; what if they knew about the Baron?

Stood in the library overwhelmed by titles: *Green Mansions*, *The Jungle Book*, *Droll Tales*, *Boswell's Journal*, *One Life One Kopek*, *Anna Karenina*, *The Moth and the Flame*, *Silas Marner*, *Penguin Island*, and *A Tale of Two Cities*. My eyes got stuck. I couldn't choose one. The librarian offered to help, but there was no helping me; I didn't want to read, I wanted to sense the overwhelming mystery of shelved creation.

I'd like my life to be as quiet as a library; and for each day to leave an indelible stamp on my mind, so that when I return (to that day), I will know for sure it's the right day. I think I'll be a writer; it just comes out of me.

Mother disgusted me today (again). I asked her how it felt to give birth and she said, "It's just like going to the toilet." How can she compare me to a turd! I suppose she didn't want to frighten me about pain and horror.

Sixteen

Who knows what evil lurks in the hearts of men? Dr. Reiss dressed in his spotless lab coat makes me stand nude on a chair to get my sunlamp treatments. I wear sunglasses. He's giving me the treatments free so I can get rid of my pimples. It's damned white of him. He kisses my legs and pats my behind. When I tell him I'm overweight he says I'm perfect. What kind of doctor is he, anyway? The least he could do is weigh me and tell me what to eat. The first time I went to his office I had a long wait, so I took a book of skin diseases out of his bookcase to read. I sat on the floor helpless with horror at all the ugly skins—finally I was comparing symptoms. I came to the conclusion that what I had was not acne but some obscure Mediterranean blotch. When Reiss came out to get me I was pretty depressed. His professional diagnosis cheered me up, though. He said, "And to prove you're not contagious, here's a little kiss." He kissed my cheek. I had a feeling he'd do something romantic—he's so old world.

Saw the beginning of an operation. I was sterile and stood right near the operating table. First they painted the patient's back with red stuff and put a needle in her spine. I started to black out when they sliced her belly and the blood popped out of the fatty tissue like tiny red berries. Nothing was visible except the excavation site. Her head was under a canopy and she couldn't see her body. She was talking to the anesthetist about her kids. Dr. Reiss was at the knife. He doesn't think I'm so tough any more. He was sore that I had to leave the operating room before his big scene: the skillful removal of three shimmering gallstones. I made it up to him at the next sunlamp treatment—drove him wild with desire. Now he wants to take me out for Wiener Schnitzel and Viennese coffee, a bill of fare I might not refuse. He said he'd like to be in charge of educating my palate.

Whenever I am guilty about anything, or after a bad fight, a spot on my outer right thigh about the size of a quarter gets hot. Why my upsetness should show itself to me in this way I have no idea. It's painted red in my mind like the "stop" button in the elevator, but it's not where anyone can reach it.

I'll never know some things, as long as I live.

We had a treat today after school. Elizabeth Schumann blasted out in the grandiose manner. (Music and Art is often visited by celebrities.) She stood on the stage where Mr. Cuneol usually conducts chorus IV, up in the tower. The size of her bosom helps her interpret German lieder. Everyone but me practically burst their Lifelines with applause. First of all I hate the doom sound of German, and here was this frau firmly stanced (one leg forward, one back, hands clasped below bosom) singing about trout and forests as if they were about to be destroyed. Most people laugh at classical music and they're right: it's for special people who want to be alone with their FEELINGS.

Charged up the hill again to get to school late. Sat in the "late" room thinking about my first doll carriage. It was enameled in wine color and had lovely satin dolly covers. Uncle Mort had given it to me for my Dydee doll. I used to make her drink bottle after bottle of warm water till the tepid fake pee-pee soaked through her diaper. Pee-pee makes it real. That doll was my baby. I still have her in the closet. Her cheeks are painted with nail polish, her belly is cracked, her hair is crayoned over, and the pissy leak hole has a broken toothpick stuck in it. I always like to put something into something—the empty spaces so the wind won't whistle through. Now who'll do the same for me?

Sometimes you hate people for things they can't help. I was walking down our dark hall very fast. I thought I knew where the door was, but I smashed into it with my nose. It hurt like hell. I sat on the floor crying "Momma." I felt like a big doll—limp and lifeless except for the squeak box inside. I'm ashamed of the warmth that comes over me when my mother is kind, yet I really can't stand her. And I repeat: it isn't her fault that she disturbs me. For instance, Daddy, Mommy and I are walking along the edge of the park to get to the bus stop near Jerome Avenue. We are on our way to Loew's Paradise to have a good time. Daddy insists that I walk with him and shoves Mother ahead to walk by herself. "You look nice enough to be my girlfriend," he says to me. My mother turns around for a moment to smile at me, and he hisses, "Keep going, you old bag." He thinks of himself as young, handsome, and irresistible. He wants to disassociate himself from the middle-aged, thick-heeled, eye-glassed woman in front of him. I ask him to walk with her. He refuses. I refuse to walk with him, and so we approach the bus stop separate, Indian file, strangers to all appearances.

STRANGERS

A play in the Dark

1ST STRANGER: Suddenly it has become dark.

2ND STRANGER: No, gradually it became dark.

3RD STRANGER: It has always been dark.

DAYDREAMS BY ME

I walk into the library and Harry Felter is there at the science section. He looks up and doesn't smile or say hello to me, so I go to him swiftly and say, "Ah, Harry, have I ever kissed you?" And then I kiss him soft and sweet on the mouth and leave him alone again.

I am lying on the grass in Van Cortlandt Park, right near the golf course. Someone says, "Use your mashie," and Harry settles right on top of me, mashes me to the ground. "I'm not a sled, Harry," I tell him, too warm to move. And he says, "I'm not a belly wop, Selma; I'm a Jew on your back."

I visit the Felter home. Diana is leaning against her Knabe concert grand. The fringe of a red and gold paisley cloth . . . ? Elegant arpeggios. She whispers, "You again, what do you want?"

"Let me take you away from all this."

I avert my eyes for an instant and see that her foot has changed into a brass pedal. She can only hide one at a time.

"Well, then," I say (superior), "I suppose you intend to sustain one chord for the rest of your life."

Her mother enters with a can of metal polish.

> MOTHER AS CLEOPATRA: It's cooler on the water. The water is breaking my heart. I could die.
> FATHER AS POTENTATE: Get those slave girls some nice tailored suits.

The Baron is in touch with me again. He wants to introduce me to his boy-friend (tonight at eight at his place) . He asked me to wear a veil and long while kid gloves. Why did he specify? I'll send him the bill. No skin off my ass. Maybe it's a fancy party.

It was a fancy party. Very fancy, with blowers and noisemakers, and feathered hats, and tootsie rolls, and chocolate kisses, and candles, and whipped cream cake: blowers, noisemakers, hats, ostrich plumes, tootsie rolls, chocolate, kisses, candles, whipped cream cake: blowmakers, feathered tootsies, candle rolls, fancy kisses, and chocolate very. During which with candles and whipped cream I rolled like an ostrich kissing the cake and plumed from behind. Lots of things I never did before, or was ever asked to. The Baron and his friend Jack had written their requests down on a cocktail napkin. It was pink and had a frolicking lamb.

"You'll like the attention you get," the Baron said, "if you've never been with two men before."

"Yeah," I said, "but it has to be dark."

"You don't lay the rules down, darling; we do," Jack said.

"Put this on."

He ordered me into a satin rag with no back and rhinestones hanging loosely fringelike around the neck. It was green. I hate green because it's life and death. Maybe I love green because it's life and death. Maybe I mentioned it before. I have simple ideas about color, like if I wear blue, it's a piece of sky; white, I'm invisible; brown, I fell into a pile of shit. And so on. They put green on me and I had my choice: sprout leaves or get pungent. I was as stale and packaged as those Oreos the Baron once offered me for dessert. "Watch me crumble," I thought, "for money." Together we can go places. I don't remember if I was present when it took place. I detached my retinal inter-view (closed my eyes, I mean), and watched from a great distance. It came to me that you can do anything as long as it's not you and you refuse to recognize yourself in the street.

I chewed and swallowed a dollar bill. It didn't taste like grass. Now I'm made of money but I don't grow on trees.

I'm saving the money the Baron gives me so that I can run away. When I have enough I'll just take off and forget the past. I have seventy-five dollars in my own account.

Nobody would guess what a stimulator I am. I wear very prudish clothes, but I am constantly preparing activities (in my mind) to spur men on. The more I excite their emptiness, the better I'll get paid, and I enjoy myself too.

Seventeen

Aunt Ray has lent me a green velvet dress with sleeves to wear to-night. I'm singing with the senior chorus because they don't have enough Sopranos. Mother says Aunt Ray is selfish because she doesn't invite Mother to play mah-jongg with her friends. Why doesn't Mother have her own friends?

Mah-jongg has a great sound. I drop the ivories on each other just to hear them click: bam, crack, flower! Arranging them on the racks reminds me of my button game. It's a solitary race; I line up red buttons on one side of a box cover, and black on the other. Then I say to myself, "I'm the red (or the black)." I slant the cover and the buttons slide down. If my color reaches bottom first, I win. What do I win? I don't know—maybe luck. I keep playing. Usually I'm comfortably in bed—tired, warm, mindless—when I take out the button box. The reason we have so many buttons is Daddy used to sell them. He didn't stay in the button and costume jewelry business long because when everyone else was buying Czechoslovakian rhinestones, he said, "Who needs them." And then they made fortunes during the shortage and he was out in the cold. This is typical, but it isn't the family bad-luck story—we have a worse one, it goes like this: "We would have been millionaires today *if!*" It seems Dad had an opportunity to own a piece of Rexall drug stores but he turned it down. Maybe no one asked him. He's always failing what he tries; but Mom doesn't try at all.

I think of street names literally. For instance, Aunt Ray's street, Gates Place—not a gate in sight, just another Bronx block open at both ends. The newest house on the block has cockroaches, too. I know, because we were considering an apartment there, whatever that has to do with anything. I think I mean crummy things never advertise themselves, they just show up. Cockroaches have free passage so they just go, and where they go is your house. I hate it when they get into your drawers and nothing is clean.

Being clean keeps the secret that we stink.

Now I'm really mad. My maps are all over the floor of my room. Mom tore them off the walls. She said it was my room but she didn't mean it. It's her house, her everything. All I get is mean, rotten stupidities. There isn't even a lock on the door; everyone wanders in to rummage through my belongings.

What is she, this stay-at-home momma? I wish she'd stop patting me, kissing me on the lips, and pushing my hair off my face. And I can't stand the way she examines my panties before she washes them.

The time is not ripe for my mysterious exit. I have been digging into the X-checker for new clothes.

Eighteen

Found a buggy kitten and fed it. Mother gave me a jar-top full of milk. Bye-bye, kitty, you can't come in.

Brought home a butterfly. Was allowed to keep this pet because it was dead. Set it in a box on top of cotton; tried to make it live by blowing on its wings and putting the box in the sun. It was permanently dead. I wanted to see how it was made and ripped the wings, squashed the body. Ugly green-black goo oozed out. Whoever may find me: DON'T DO THAT TO ME!

I also rip buds to make them bloom faster. I expect my brutality to cause a flourishing. This is because I pretend it's scientific. Any dismantling (flowers, crawling creatures, winged insects) comes under the heading of SCIENCE. I have a compulsion to pluck my eyebrows. I'm the victim of myself.

I've cut my hair off; I do that when I feel desperate. I could go into what hair means to me: strength (but Samson was a man), beauty, warmth (stuff my pillow), love. I've cut myself off from these things and I said out loud, "Damn it, off it goes." I couldn't stop cutting till it was very boyish. Now my head is light, is clean, is small and fine; shaped to the skull à la Jeanne d'Arc.

Saw a mysterious thing in science class today; a lima bean between layers of wet cotton sprouted a cotyledon (like an erect clitoris). First there was nothing visible; then its own nature drew it out into the damp warmth. The skin shriveled, was no longer needed. I thought of my own body.

At home I took a mirror and put it down between my legs much as a dentist examines the back of gums. This is what I saw: something like a mussel gone bad; narrow, fat-lipped, and reddish-brown. The urinary orifice was larger than expected and the mouth of the vagina slightly obstructed by inner flesh. The whole area seemed underdeveloped. I was really curious to know what men see when they look. I don't like it. It leaves me wide open.

I'm not jealous of Diana; I want to own her, I want to be necessary to her. We were both wearing red hair-bands today. I worry about her; she thinks her mother wants to poison her. She loves her father but is afraid of his temper. She sounds like me. I didn't know she was afraid of her parents. Live and learn. It surprised me when she wrote on our public school graduation picture: "To a sweet girl who is my dearest friend." (A message from the queen—her head was crowned with braids.) There is someone who is closer to her than I am, but this girl is completely ugly and hairy and weak and her name is Shirley. The only reason she is number one is because the families are close. My family is far.

I am so sick; my pajamas hurt my flesh, that's how I know I have fever. It's fun to write when you're sick, because the words seem to float. I have nothing else to do. I can't stand the sheets, my toes keep pushing against them. I smell toast toasting. Mother is making chicken soup. I hear things being done for ME. The doctor says I have the grippe and to rest away the illness. I love being sick.

I dreamt about trying to get out of school; I kept going up and down, and whenever I reached what I thought was an exit, the door was locked and I had to start all over again: go to the top, cross the halls, reach the principal's office, wait, walk through the and down the steps again.

I have dreams about steps often, usually about the Third Avenue El. I go up the steps and then I'm crawling along unprotected girders; I almost fall.

I'm in the movies. I go to the balcony. I start to fall down the steps and I tell myself it's only a dream. Then I wake up.

I'm in a ship going to Europe. Suddenly I'm in a rowboat in the dark waters. I'm in the way of the big ship. Then I'm in the water.

I'm in California. I take a ferry. I'm in the water. Or I cross a bridge to get to the ferry to take me to a mountain top where I sit down. I never return. I wake up.

I'm clinging to the outside of a bell tower. It is snowing. There is a light shining through narrow windows of the bell tower. I reach the window and tear out the central portion of the window frame. I look in. The fall inside is as steep as the fall outside. I know that I am doomed and make no other efforts. I wake up.

I hate falling dreams; dreams where you try to run but can't; and dreams in toilets where before you know it men and women use the same toilets; and dreams where you swim in deep, steamy water indoors and almost drown.

I've been asked to leave school. Yesterday I cut gym, and when the messenger asked if anyone in my class knew where I was, Diana told. What a friend. She can't resist giving information to the enemy.

The charming but cruel dean was seated in her office blowing her nose and wiping her bulging thyroidal eyes when I came in. She tucked her damp hanky up a long sleeve of rust wool; then she let me have it. (The rest of the snot that was clogging her think-power. A long stream of it dribbled off her lips.) "You're temporarily suspended," she said.

So what. I felt rotten, but still, so what! A person like myself can enjoy being temporarily suspended! (A lie.) I like the rhythm of being suspended. (A lie.) Up there where she wants to hang me, I'll swing long dis-tances like Tarzan and get out of the whole ugly mess. (Maybe.) Well, I'll have to let my class go on without me, even if my picture is already in the yearbook. Under the picture it says, "She has a winning smile." The bitch got very personal; she said, "You'll never find a husband, my dear, if you don't go to college."

I got depressed. When I get depressed I either get chicken or crazy, or both. So I mumbled, "Yes, Mrs. Forkin. How do I get to do that if I'm being kicked out?"

And she offered me the use of the school next year, which I declined by slamming a record book down on her desk and shouting, "You're nothing but a frigid bitch!"

I ran down two hundred steps to the Eighth Avenue subway. And will never run up them again.

Nineteen

Who loves me now that I hate the world? Only my rock can. Oh, I know it doesn't really, but I dug it up out of my old camp trunk and sat it on the windowsill. "You look young," I told it. "You haven't aged a bit. Let me show you how it feels to be thrown around."

I hefted my rock from hand to hand feeling its weight, and then, I missed. The rock landed on my toe. Smashed it so that I got blood on my sock. (It still hurts me when I wear high heels.) I cried and carried on the way I should have in school. Tell me, Talisman, did you want me to cry? All the people who want me to cry are: Harry Felter, Diana Felter, Mother, Father, and Mrs. Forkin. Sister Lucille hates for me to cry, it makes her frantic. She's over-sensitive. She heard me storming around and came in and sat close to me. Wherever I went in the room, she followed, trying to caress my hand. I told her to get the hell out and stop following me around like a dog, and when she didn't I asked her, "You really want to sympathize? You want to be a saint?" Before she could moon over me again I dropped the rock on her toe. She ran out screaming, which is her style too. That'll teach her to be good. I don't want to be her big sister, or anyone's big anything. Or anything.

They're sending me to camp again. They don't know what to do with me. Mother started a "Send Selma to Camp" fund among the relatives. They are not generous givers, but Mom managed to scrape enough together. She'd like to give me the best. Her fondest daydream (and mine) is that a rich family will adopt me.

I'm not talking to Diana any more. It hurts me more than the rock. Now Harry is lost to me too. The Baron called. He knows what he wants. If only all the people who are so sure of themselves would get confused, it would help me. I hate his desires. Imagine, he thought I could get a girlfriend for a double date. I'd throw up before and after. Besides, I don't have any girlfriends, and if I did they wouldn't go out with rich old men and disgust themselves. I want to kill myself again, but I won't again. Think of Charley Rogen; he never had a chance and yet he makes plans for the future. I've had every opportunity, but it seems to be my downfall.

The camp I'm going to is some kind of liberal union camp. It's cheap. Uncle Grisha suggested it. As penance for being kicked out of school I'm not going to allow myself to write. At least not till I come back. Last night Mother cried on the kitchen table. She made me a salami sandwich when I came in. She says that Dad doesn't tell her where he works now. She thinks she has his number, but when she calls he disguises his voice and sounds Italian. He's a torturer. She says he keeps another full set of clothing at another house.

I'm back from camp. That was short. What happened? I went that-a-way. Let's follow me. No, don't unless you're prepared. For what? Real romance. What was he like? Was he great? He was an actor.

He was seedy: bad teeth, falling hair, canvas shoes with taffy-colored rubber soles. Sexy, though. He had an aura. The first night in camp there was a dance in the casino. I waltzed for half an hour with a union organizer. While we were waltzing he plugged the health-giving qualities of carrot juice and honey. I danced as fast as I could, finally leading, hoping to throw him off, but he hung on. John (the actor) introduced himself after the dance as I was fanning my armpits and blowing cool air into them.

"You shouldn't do that," he said.

"Why not?" I asked.

"Because," he answered, "it's more fun if a man does it, like this."

"I never sweated so much," I said, embarrassed.

"You're a healthy young animal." He put his arm around me. "How would you like to go canoeing?"

"Um-hum," I said, so we went.

I fell out of the canoe.

"You'll drown with all those clothes on." He undressed me while I treaded water, and threw the clothes into the canoe. Then he embraced me, also treading water, and asked, "Are you a virgin?"

"Sure," I told him.

He didn't believe me.

"Don't you believe me?" I asked.

He dove under and found out I was lying. His finger floated around in me. "Little girls shouldn't tell lies," he said.

"You don't know about athletes and bike riders," I said. "Girl athletes have ruptured hymens. Your finger doesn't prove anything."

"Okay, have it your way," he said, soul-kissing me.

"I do have it my way." I bit his lip.

"Sleep with me tonight?" He wrote it on my thigh with his penis. It felt like the nose of a porpoise which feels like the head of a penis.

"Uh-uh!" I said, shaking my head. "How about tomorrow at four."

"Tomorrow at four'll do it," he agreed.

Four o'clock on the dot I arrived and interrupted John's nap. The cot was nice and warm and sagged in the middle.

"Here, let me put a pillow under your ass," he said.

"You don't sound very romantic," I told him. "Don't talk to me that way."

"As you wish, madam. The vulgar vernacular shall never leave my lips again to offend your ears."

I giggled because all I could see was his bald head between my legs. It wasn't what I wanted; maybe you have to develop a taste for things like that (like for liver).

There was a small screened window over the bed. Sun streamed in. John said I reminded him of *April Morn*; he also said my vagina was smooth as velvet. He isn't very original. We spent nap times together from then on. Once his roommate and a girl shared the bed opposite us. I didn't look, but what a thing to do!

There was recorded music every afternoon. We could sit on the lawn and listen. Once we made love a little early and could hear the Eroica all the way down the hill near the tennis courts where John's cabin was. I remember trying to come by thinking how the music sounded when John and I were together. How sad, life drags on. I wasn't exactly an automaton; I was a spectator participant. I watched every move but wasn't moved. (It's called The Experimental Summer. What makes just doing something an experiment? Put this into that and what do you get: tonic of sperm, the sound *aargh*, and clenched toes?) What a sweetheart John made! He nearly popped a blood vessel when he found out I had used his hairbrush. He was meticulous about that, the slob.

Everyone thought John was a bastard to ruin a nice kid like me. He wasn't evil—that was his life and the way he lived it. I told them. Anyway, an unusual thing happened to me through that guy. The second week I was there we were in the casino for community sing. John told me that a lesbian friend of his was paying him a visit and he was going to try to help her break the habit. I didn't understand what he was saying. He meant for me to keep away from his cabin door because he was making out with someone else. I came knocking; he didn't open the door, so I lay down in the dirt and screamed and cried. I was drunk on a few beers. I'm a cheap drunk. I kept shouting that he had promised to marry me. (He had and he hadn't.) I wanted to make him more of a bastard than he really was. Then the door did open and this huge female in his bathrobe stood there and said, "Cut the crap, honey, if you want to come in, come on." I said I wouldn't unless John asked me. He sat on the cot picking his feet and didn't say a word. I had the feeling that if I went in they'd tear me apart between them like a herring.

I stood up, turned around, and went back quietly to my cabin.

Mother don't cry for me.

The day I left camp I ate breakfast with John at the staff table. He hid a present for me under the napkin. It was a carrot with matchstick legs, matchstick arms, and a matchstick penis. There was a paper sign hung on the gift; it said: "PENIS PETE AT YOUR SERVICE." I put it in the side compartment of my valise and just yesterday found it again shriveled up and brown with the match sticks poking through the wax-paper wrappings. My type of souvenir.

Charley Rogen died. Leila wrote me that he was in a car that got out of control. All this time I have been nursing the idea that we'd get together sometime; now it gives me goose pimples. So that's what he grew up to be, a teenage corpse. He won't have to kick anyone in the ass to show he's tough any more. Dead men never lift a finger or a foot; if they did, the earth would rise up like a giant rotten pancake.

Twenty

I never thought that when Uncle Mort took everyone in the family from New York to Virginia for Cousin Lenny's wedding that I would be an eyewitness to its consummation. Perhaps "consummation" is the wrong word, because to consume something is to incorporate it into your own system (and it ceases to exist in its original form). What I saw was more like a poor dealer trying to shuffle the cards into one another smoothly, but only succeeding in jamming their edges together.

It took about eight hours to get to Richmond. Mother almost didn't go. She didn't have anything to wear. Uncle Mort gave her money to doll herself up. She bought everything black to look thinner. In black there's a kind of invisible boundary. Her accessories were: a silver mesh bag, silver pumps, and a white sequinned bolero bordered with silver sequins. Scales of a flounder and sequins are the same thing. I pretended they were, in my mind, so that when I asked Mother before we left the house, "Mom, are you fin, fin, finished?" I got stuck on the word 'finished.'

We sat in the train and Uncle Mort gave Mother a Camel. (He wanted to give her a hump.) Pretty awful of me to involve her in a dirty thought, but, she took the cigarette and inhaled. Only she doesn't inhale, she blows the smoke right out; she thinks she looks sophisticated. Uncle Mort embraced her in his bumbling clumsy relative way. What he feels must be like a giant order of boned chicken wrapped in a wet sponge. Her eyes froth over when he does that and she gets a "black-bottom" gaiety.

Dad spent his time on the train acting affluent. Uncle Mort knows some big people and some of them were his guests on the train. How do you get to be a "big" person? They took up the whole car. I wasn't too happy; it was about my dress. Dad bought it with me. He let me buy what I wanted. It was a violet taffeta dress with tiers of taffeta flaring out below the waist; each tier was separated by a blue velvet ribbon going all around. It had puffed sleeves. Mom blew her stack when she saw it. "You look like a wop in that dress!" She was truly distressed. I told her not to be vulgar about other people's nationalities and that she should be glad I liked cheerful, festive things. She clapped both her cheeks and pinched them, moaning, "How could you let her do it!" Dad, with instant hate and being the weak son of a bitch he was, shouted, "Do what you want! Take the lousy piece of crap back!" I wonder why they keep rehearsing the same parts over and over again (they won't forget their parts). Anyway, I refused to give the dress up. It was mine and it matched my eyes. Crazy Selma, that's me, fighting my way through the fog, arriving at the top of a mountain with no place else to turn but then, miraculously, cartoon-style walking on air to the next mountain.

Lenny's bride was called Honey. I don't know if that was her real name, but she dripped it sticky sweet all over everyone with that Southern drawl. Honey was and still is tiny. The wedding photographer took a picture of her in a three-way mirror; three of her makes one of anyone else. Even though her mother is totally unimportant to me, the sight of her with her daughter was an ugly sight not to be forgotten too soon. Imagine a piece of clay squeezed by a kindergartener and called "Lady"; imagine a crust-colored face shaved of all its features including eyebrows and eyelashes but seeded surprisingly with a sparse brown mustache. That was her in lace, the "face." They stood carefully together, hips meeting and arms locked behind, for a mother-daughter dream sequence before the wedding. The photographer snapped them in a flash: "Surprise!" Candid shot. "Mind doing that again? Just to make sure." And one with the groom in between them separating a prairie dog from its mound and hole in the desert. Who is this man? Is he the human male groom who all alone in the desert (Richmond, Va.) got so hot he had to make it with a furry creature? Or not so furry, flat hair glossed over with Honey. "That's it, both smile at the groom." They have tiny sharp teeth and no lips. What did my darling cousin get into. He is happy. I remember that he was happy and he offered me a chocolate from a giant red heart (box). It was the five-pound size and melted in layers. I took one that was wrapped in gold paper. It didn't deserve a medal. Fruit and nuts! How I hate fruits and nuts; I expected a soft center: burning with sweetness and luscious. There must have been one in there somewhere. (I didn't find it: I couldn't decipher the chocolate-swirl language that topped each one.)

Honey said, "Lenny's told me all about you. Ah'm so glad ya'll could come." She stepped out of her zip-up dogskin for a moment and I got a glimpse of her shimmering white-bride qualities. I envied her. Lenny was so athletic and tan. He had an intimate tic in his right eye that drove me crazy. It gave him star potential in my heart. In my heart I knew he was right, for me. I tossed and turned inside where I couldn't fall off. She offered me another chocolate. "No thank you," I joked, "there'll be nothing left for the worms." She turned to put the box back on the bureau or chest of drawers, whatever they call one or the other, I never could tell, and I smelled Chanel #5. I smelled it once before in a department store where they give free sprays.

I don't want to describe the wedding; just look it up under TRADITIONAL MODERNE. It had a smooth rolling time sequence: entry and welcome to all, ceremony, miniature weenies in baked wrappings and other goodies, exit to room two, the ballroom the chandeliers the geneology of tables, the cake on the table on the top of the main of the two main characters who. The young wedded couple were represented by a safe-food-colors-painted young wedded couple out of hard icing on the top of the cake. Sure it's confusing! I love primitive courtship, the nipples-in-hands dance, the dance-yourself-into-a-hole dance, and the let-us-all-join-in dance of sex. Lenny and Honey held the knife together and cut in. Cake. Cake instead of take! And an embarrassed kiss to satisfy the admiring relatives. They really like each other, and he has another home with her parents besides his own home and his father's home and his homeland, America. America the beautiful!

Lenny and Uncle Mort and Mom and Dad and not Lucille (she was too young to come) cried when the singer sang "My Yiddishe Momma." We were thinking about how much Aunt Bella would have wanted to be here at her son's wedding. I looked at Lenny eating and drinking like a pig on the dais and I remembered that he used to throw Uncle Mort's shoes into the toilet and also that I was present when he ran crying from the park after some bigger boys had stripped him and beat him up calling him a "sissy." He rose and opened the ball with a graceful glide and a whirl around the room with Honey. We applauded. A few relatives had bitter feelings about where they were seated. I was sitting with the young crowd toward the back of the room. In the official photograph I look like a shrunken head hung below a painted candelabra dangling at a field of face flowers.

Things loosened up. Uncle Mort danced with me. My elbows got stiff because I had to hold my arms way up to meet his hands. Dancing with him was like carrying something too wide, too far. He kissed me at the end of the dance and I opened my mouth. It was an impulse. He put his tongue in it and slid it around.

"You don't have to brush my teeth," I said. He laughed and pinched my ass. I hate pinching. We went back to eat. After every dance the dancers returned to their tables to eat. Melon and ice-cream was for dessert. I took a piece of ice from my melon cup and pushed it against Uncle Mort's neck. The ice fell down. He made me find it on the floor. There wasn't anything left of it but a dirty puddle. He went and got his own ice and jammed it down the front of my "wop" dress. I stood there red in the face wanting to kill him. Aunt Ray brought a distant fat cousin for me to dance with. We trotted out into the mob and then Dad cut in: "Mind if I dance with my own daughter, son?" He kept passing couples I didn't know, saying, "This is my daughter."

The party ended in a mess with the women arguing who should take the flowers home, and the men hiding bottles of liquor so the waiters wouldn't get them. Everyone was grabbing. I drank two glasses of Cutty Sark and felt mighty sick. Uncle Mort called me over seriously. And he told me seriously that seriously I would have to share Lenny and Honey's room because a business associate of his had decided to stay overnight unexpectedly and would have to use my room. "If I have to," I answered. "If they don't mind." "There are twin beds in the room," Uncle Mort told me, "and you can have one of 'em. You look pretty tired. Why don't you take this key and run up ahead of them."

I was just dozing off when my cousins arrived. They were drunk. I know they were drunk because they were very loud and kept saying "shhsh." Lenny came and stood over my bed to see if I was asleep. I played dead. I couldn't stop breathing, though. I tried to black out once by pressing the big veins on each side of my neck. (Or are they veins? What's an aorta?) Out of the almond of my eye I watched as they passed a votive object between them. Lenny carried it into the bathroom and hung it dangling like a dead bird on the shower pipe. Its nozzle had a running nose. Then he closed the bathroom door and took a leak. Niagara Falls. (It certainly falls.) Niagara is a lovely name for a girl child. For instance: "Come here, Niagara child, don't be afraid. I won't hurt you. I want to see how you're growing, Niagara. My, your little breasts are pulling out, Niagara, Nigerian nigger of the Nile." And then he violates her!

The bed they were in (not my lonely one) made a lot of noise. It was saying: "I work while the city sleeps." The event was disembodied; fluttering sheets pumped other ghosts full of ectoplasm. If there was any flesh, it was held most tenderly in the folds of warm nightwear. The whole setup was phony. I think they wanted me to wake up and observe them; then there'd be little cries of chagrin and little leaps for safety and cover while exposing themselves to me. But it went on its plodding way, the dull descent, until it shuddered to a stop. Becoming another white nun of solitude, I crossed myself in mock Catholic, fingered my beads of sweat, confessed confusion, and tried to sleep by practicing a sin that is not a sin in my religion. It isn't even mentioned except about men, and they're not supposed to spill their seed upon the ground. I'm safe, I don't spill, and if I did I wouldn't cry.

Twenty-One

When you don't like men you become an artist. Some guy I hate came to the house this afternoon. He has a round red face and lives on Central Park West in the Eldorado. His name is Bert. I met his brother and I like his brother better than him. Anyway, he brought this painfully ugly monster to see me with evil intent. I can just hear him lying: "She'll do it for you." The dumb-ox was a butcher. His own mouth hung open as if he had lugged himself off a meat hook. I'm afraid of butchers. Why did they choose that bloody profession? So Bert appeared with this prize package (blue ribbon) and my heart sank. God, the way Mother rushed in to announce them as if they were President Roosevelt and Winston Churchill. I was in the bedroom painting my first picture. How dare they interrupt the artist at work! I marched in regally and said, "I'm sorry, but you'll have to go, I'm busy." Bert asked me what I was so busy about; he was reluctant to leave and scared me.

"I'm painting a picture," I told him.

The butcher nudged Bert with his elbow as if to say, "Let's get outta here." Then they did leave and I was very, very glad. Of course Mother wanted to know why the two nice boys left so fast. She is innocent and the innocent never protect anyone, and are relentlessly clobbered by fate themselves.

Mother got mad at me today. (Getting mad is a daily exercise; mad muscles make superior mads.) She banged my skull with a frying pan. It cut my scalp; the blood came off on my hand when I reached up to judge the damage. I touched and looked and cried and even tasted the blood. I went in the bathroom and painted my face with it. Indian circles around the eyes made my eyes safe. (Don't step into the circle.) Red worry lines in a V put me into deep thought. And with delicate dips of the pinky into the inkwell of my scalp I tapped gory tears down my cheeks. "This is what you've done to me, Mother, made me a living mask au jus natural." She sent me to Dr. Reiss and he told me to not get dirt in it. He wouldn't put any stitches in. I told him that Mother hates me. He doesn't believe it. Thinks I must have made her nervous. It's true I called her a fat bitch and she is. I dusted the whole damn house for her and what does she do but go over the route again by herself. She says I don't do it right. She expects me to go into corners and find dust mice. Now I can go to hell for movie money. If I ate and breathed dust the way she does I'd be a cloud.

Lucille is giving her friends apples. She enjoys giving things away. I'd like to give her away to Dr. Reiss, ruin her. He'd accept her apples and make applesauce out of them in his sterilizer. I like to look at her she's so healthy. Only ten, but her breasts need a brassiere. I don't want her to look at me, though. She hangs in the bathroom asking me how to put on lipstick and why do I wear mascara? She asks me, "Why do you smile at yourself in the mirror?" I tell her because I forget what I look like to other people.

Strange things happen, if they don't happen they're not strange, but whether they happen or not, boy it's something to be ashamed about. I don't know what came over me, but I felt very sexy. I was in bed and Lucille was in her bed. I crept into her bed and felt her up. She moved around and I got cold feet. She smiled at me in a friendly way. She's much nicer than I am. With me though, she's trying to buy in. No matter what she does her status doesn't change; she's a second-class citizen because she was born second. I came first and they love me best, because when they had me they still loved each other.

Visually speaking, she's an East Indian: dark, dank, secretive. I look at her and I hear ankle bells or temple bells or sacred cow bells. She has eyes that hypnotize: big brown; breasts that appetize: big down. She's everything I'll never have on my body. My slow glands against her fast ones. But slow developers live longer.

Stared at undressed dummies from the bus window. Hoped to incorporate their perfection by thought wave into my own undeveloped shape. When I stare at women I'm comparing myself. Sometimes the comparison is favorable: I'm too human.

Mother says, why shouldn't I love both my daughters the same, why shouldn't I love them both they're both mine, and I bothed them both from the same stomach, the same soup for each right up to the measuring line, measure it, one baked potato each, each for each and all for all, half a cup, whole cup, five spoonfuls and whole fulls, leg, a leg, two legs in two mouths, fruit salad one a pineapple two a grape three a cherry four a pear five a ripe banana and six sectioned grapefruit, eat, eat, don't leave, keep even, line up there in the fair is fair parade. Don't hit!

I keep walking through the rooms. They get bigger. They get louder. The floors teeter-totter. The unused living room is dark. A shock of light from between the Venetian blinds blinds me. The closet door handle pulls off unexpectedly and I tumble backwards. I've been drinking sacramental wine and now I'm ill. It was too sweet. Life is sweet; the life level must be checked at regular intervals so it doesn't get too sweet. I faint; my life level is up and won't come down.

I say I want to be understood, yet I understand no one. I don't want to. I'm not capable of it. Yet what is there to understand? Do I mean: "Anticipate my wishes and act on them immediately, or out you go"? Pretty one-sided affair. If someone enjoys my mind and can take me as I am, then I am his forever. What's forever? Maybe I should be put away as Mom threatens. I am forced to suffer guilt because of weaklings, yet they are the strong ones. Mother is strong because she keeps taking punishment. I dish it out. She asks for it. I spit on her, make the toilet dirty, stay away from home, insult her accent, insult the way she eats (she sucks meat that gets stuck in her teeth, sounds like a bird call), make her carry packages up five flights of stairs alone. It makes her happy. She thrives.

Her whine turns my stomach. Why should I bear the burden of her life when I have none of my own? I wish I could get married. Maybe it wouldn't be so awful. Time to stop.

I am sick today: a cold. Can't breathe. Can think. Was thinking, why am I afraid to succeed, to finish what I start? Picture of long ago: I was ten. It was evening and I was in bed. Mom and Dad were entertaining in the living room. I heard him tell some jokes and laughed so hard I peed in bed. Mother changed the sheets and gave me new pajamas. I lay awake still laughing. Dad came in and told me a story about a kid who was piggish. This kid put pepper in two out of three pies, the unpeppered pie was for the kid, only he forgot which one it was and ate a terrible peppered pie by mistake. The moral was, I suppose, that wrongdoers are punished and what you do to others will be done to you. In my innocence I devised a ruse to stay up. I meticulously copied a picture out of a storybook and brought it into the living room pretending it was original. Dad accused me of being a liar. He insulted me in front of everyone. The more he insisted I was a liar, the more adamant I became about the origin of the picture. "Well," he ordered, "if you did it, do it again in front of all of us." I managed to produce a reasonable facsimile, which surprised him. I drew well out of stubbornness and fear. Then he said, "I just wanted to teach you a lesson, never lie!" Since then, even if I'm not lying I feel guilty, expect to be unmasked as a fraud.

Have decided that Dad tells stories with a moral because he's telling them to himself. He loves the gimmick. A story isn't worth its salt unless it's gimmicked up. I recall his favorite plot again: five people are on a plane, or ten people are on a train, the transportation crashes, strangers all, they are brought together by disaster (therein lies the crux of the flux), everyone's life unfolds systematically. How he'd love to outline his own life, put it into cliché order. But there's no rise and fall, no drama to his life. At least he doesn't think so. I've saved—no I found in the closet—his school notebooks. He studied botany and drew (because it was required) delicate studies of flowers and herbs. It could be the notebook of Leonardo da Vinci. I love my father but I'll never know him. Knowledge is a dangerous thing.

Twenty-Two

My goldfish died. All three. I kept them on the radiator and then the landlord got generous and gave us steam. The water practically boiled. By such remote and sudden decisions, fish near and dear to us often suffer catastrophe. Threw the fish into the toilet. One wouldn't go down. A pretty floating reminder—so reddish-gold in so coolish-green. It looked alive; the water was fanning its tail.

I was sitting on the sill of my open window looking out at the reservoir. It makes Mom nervous. She thinks I'll go into a faint and fall out, or throw myself out, or lose my balance and fall out. Why doesn't she push me out? She made me close the window. She was no sun lover. Ah wonderful sun, I was bathed in it, I was stretched in it like a big lace curtain on a frame. I'm an odd curtain. Mother can't my other half. I don't worry; it'll turn up in someone else's laundry. Someone's millionaire laundry (wrapped around a cashmere argyll sock and a pair of silk shorts) .

Mother is a contest fiend. The only thing she ever won was a makeup kit at a movie Bingo game: "It's us, it's us!" Big deal. Her plans for the future always include fortunes that land in our laps from nowhere. She insists that I marry "rich": "You can love a rich man as well as a poor man." I believe it. I go along with her. That's the way to live, great expectations. Which reminds me of our unfinished set of Dickens (bought with coupons clipped out of the *Post*). We have *Little Dorrit, Martin Chuzzlewit, A Tale of*

Two Cities, and *Great Expectations* in the deluxe white leatherette edition. I hate Dickens' dungeons, and all his books are prisons.

Mother washing the floors today. She won't use a mop, goes down on her hands and knees. I didn't want to be chased from room to room, so I left the house. I said I was going to look for a job and she said she didn't believe me. She wants me to go to night school and get a diploma. For what a diploma? For to be one of millions with a high school diploma? I can always say I have one or forge one at a printer. And what can I do? Nothing! With my knowledge of the alphabet which I learned in first grade (my only skill) I can qualify for filing clerk. Maybe girl messenger. I wouldn't give her my salary anyway. I'd buy art supplies, and I can do that with the money I earn from my various or not so various nefarious activities. Though, that money should remain untouchable till I arrange my getaway. I know every day that I don't belong here.

Stayed away from home for three hours. Sat in the Automat with the other patrons. Ate something every ten minutes: baked beans, ice cream, jello with whipped cream, coffee, applesauce cake, baked beans again, this time with franks, macaroni in casserole, carrots, spinach, ham sandwich, chopped sirloin steak, parker-house roll and butter, buttermilk, mashed potatoes, chow mein with rice, grapefruit sections, lima-bean soup, navy-bean soup with crackers, and for dessert banana shortcake.

Came home with a swollen belly and cramps, but it wasn't too bad. I have great capacity for food. Mother asked, "What's the matter, you pregnant?"

"If I was, would you take care of the baby?" I asked her.

"As if I don't have enough to do," she said, thinking it was all an impossible joke. Little does she know. A baby would be nice. I love babies. If I get married I want at least six babies, all kinds, but how do I get out of this place? It's dead here. Do I have to die? The next best thing is marriage:

POEM
Marriage saves,
until it shaves.

What does that mean?

Twenty-Three

Dr. Reiss called me. "What's the matter you don't come to see me any more?"

"I don't have pimples anymore," I told him.

"I thought we were friends," he said.

"What kind of friends?" I asked.

"Don't be a stranger. I have some new equipment you'd be interested in: beautiful instruments, masterpieces on the walls, a new scale, completely redecorated. You'd appreciate it. A girl like you appreciates. I know it. And what's wrong with a summer tan in the winter?"

"Dr. Reiss, I don't want to insult you, but I hope I never have skin trouble again. By the way, what pictures do you have on your walls?"

He became extremely sly. "My door is open, see for yourself. You'll love them. You'll admire my taste. You won't be disappointed."

"I'm disappointed already," I told him, "and I bet your taste stinks because your breath stinks and your good will stinks." But he didn't hang up and I didn't hang up.

"Listen Selma, I haven't mentioned it before, but you're a sick girl. You're crazy. You don't know who your friends are and you try to strangle them off. I don't offer myself up to every kid with a problem. My time is valuable, only I thought with you a little would go a long way. You need help. I recommended it to your parents a long time ago. They asked me to step in and I have, but you won't allow it."

"You're a liar!" I shouted. "You're a fucking liar! You want to lay me and you know it, only you want to play God. God doesn't need a Sperti sun lamp! He has the sun. The whole hot sun. So screw you and don't call me again or I'll go to the police and have you arrested for rape."

"Have it your own way, child, but if I may I'll send you a tried and true prescription for life. May I?"

I don't know why I was so insulting to him. He was no worse than a lot of men that I treated a lot better. Maybe I was too close to myself lately.

"Okay," I said, "send me a prescription, but don't charge me."

"I will, dear, but take my advice if you don't take anything from else from me again as long as you know me—"

"What're you talking about now?" I asked him.

"Just this. Don't have a hysterical fit like you just had in front of the wrong people. You could be put away. Far away where nobody'll care whether you bang your head against a wall or not. I think you're worth saving and I'll stick my neck out. So how about it? You want to be happy?"

I slammed the phone down in its cradle, and went to rock myself to sleep. Far from the creeps of my childhood.

The next day there arrived in the mail a curt note from Dr. Reiss written on his prescription pad. It said: "Please call for an appointment. I have what you need on special order." Signed "Dr. Reiss." Boy, was he hard up!

Twenty-Four

I was thinking about it. I really was: how anyone else's desperation just leaves me cold. Especially Dr. Reiss's. He'd love my goose pimples. They're in his line. He'd commercialize it: "Dr. Reiss's Goosepimpery Jam." The blurb would read: "Dr. Reiss's favorite food. For breakfast he spreads it on Britbuns with butter. For lunch he suggests a GOOSEPIMPERY sandwich on baked legloaf washed down with a cold glass of EXTRACT OF GOOSEPIMPERY. To decorate your roast, the doctor has created green glazed GOOSEGOOSE in super-colossal GOOSEPIMPERY size." All he'd have to do to cultivate his stock would be to:

1) Look at me

2) Talk to me

3) Touch me

4) Be absolutely desperate to do any of these things, and then skin me alive and be a genius and grow the skin back overnight.

Maybe I love the idea; I want to be a skin factory and feel no pain.

My Chinese fortune cookie said, "Be in your convictions and you will succeed." My fortune when I weighed myself said "Yes." "Yes" sounds so good-natured.

I met a college boy in the park yesterday. His name is Paul. I told him about the family. (Not everything). The more I told him the more he liked me. I became spontaneous and took a chance on putting my arm around him. Then, also on impulse, we held on to each other and rolled down the hill we had been sitting on. At the bottom he kissed me and I couldn't tear my lips away. It was like being in a romantic horror film where the girl is lying on a table next to the beast (or madman) and between them is a huge flask full of thunderous lightning: the soul of the beautiful girl is passing into the beast and the evil of the beast is passing into the beautiful girl. It was like that—a terrible transfer—a sucking of souls. His glasses fell off. That should be the signal; when someone loses his soul his glasses pop off automatically.

I went down to the lake again to see if Paul would come. He didn't. Seldon introduced me to him but I don't like to call Seldon about where Paul lives because Juanita might answer.

Well, Paul looked ME up! He honestly likes me. We went to the park and I danced for him. I swooped close to the earth like a brown tree swan (rarest of all). He just sat and stared through his goggles.

"Feel this," I said. I made him feel the muscles in my leg. "I dance on the roof every day." He was very shy and barely brushed my flesh so I took his hand and forced it all around my calf and thigh. "See?"

"I'll bet you could crack someone's ribs with legs like that."

"Maybe I could. I don't know my own power."

"Want to find out?"

Paul must have been kidding but I have a strange intuition that he would have thrown himself between my legs as a human sacrifice. There are things in Paul very religious and penance-stricken. Who knows, I may have a sinister desire to rule the world with my legs some day and then he'd come in handy.

Paul told me that he is a painter. I told him that I am a painter. He can't show me his work yet because it's locked in the basement of his house and his mother misplaced the key. Paul reads much more than I do, and he writes too. He gets stomach aches frequently and makes fun of them; he calls them the virus voovontzen. I put my ear to his stomach one afternoon and could hear the voovontzen simmering.

We went to C&L for ice-cream cones and I paid for my own, which impressed Paul. He made me close my eyes and then kissed the eyelids. If I was blind I would see again, but since I'm not, the pressure made my eyes a little blurry.

I told mother I met a nice boy. She said, "Why shouldn't you meet a nice boy?" Tomorrow morning he'll be alone in his apartment—tomorrow morning we have a date alone in his apartment—and tomorrow, tomorrow will never come.

Twenty-Five

FOR LOVE OR LUST
A New Title by Silver Gems Books

I took a bath at six in the morning in my house on Sedg-wick Avenue. By eight o'clock the same morning I found myself taking a shower in an apartment on upper Broadway. A young gentleman very much alive faced me: filter king beside the regular size. He bit my hair.

"Tastes bitter," he said.

"That's the shampoo," I told him. "Wait till it washes out." The water cascaded over our bodies like jujubes in spring.

"Are you afraid of me?" he asked.

"No, not of you; of it," I answered.

"I promise to keep that old devil-dog of the flesh from wagging its mangy tail," he said and vigorously soaped it up and hid it from view.

"I'm cleaner than I've ever been before and it feels good," I said. "Once I thought the only way to cleanse myself was by tainting the world."

He clapped a wet hand over my mouth. "You don't have to think that way any more."

The bathroom was full of steam. It was tough to do any-thing but breathe in there.

And now a slight pause for the way it really was. I washed Paul as if he was a pet dog. I kept a soapy grip on him with one hand while I scrubbed away with the other, and he loved it. "I think you missed this spot," he said, pointing to his left knee. He was so hairy all over; he could have been a new science-fiction character: Cocoanut Man. Cocoanut Man visits the rain forest with Selma Silver. She tips him over and drinks brain milk; it tastes soapy. When she speaks, a huge bubble surrounds them and hardens into plastic, protecting them from the rain. They kiss, but cocoanut strands catch in her teeth. Trapped together mouth to mouth, bubbles continue to issue from her with each cry for help. The bubbles crowd them. The bubbles crush them. With her last breath, Selma Silver says, "If only they wouldn't harden, if only they'd be satisfied with a temporary shape."

Paul reached out for a towel and I dried him. Then he dried me. It was like exchanging magazines in a waiting room.

WAITING ROOM SEQUENCE

PAUL: Do you think it'll be long?
ME: It's been long.
PAUL: I'm first.
ME: I saw you when I came in.
PAUL: Look at this—
ME: What a wonderful picture.
PAUL: It's you.

"Look," I said, "how small I am compared to you. Do you think I have a nice body?"

FOR LOVE OR LUST

II
He flipped the light switch on and illuminated the jar of

melting grape jelly we had been standing in. The shower curtains were lavender, the wallpaper was orchid, my blood was wine.

"You have an intelligent face," he said. "You have a straight face, you set your jaw. You're Helen of Troy. Oh you sweet-faced young female, you floor me. Then let us lay together in our strange and narrow fashion. I am your unhero." I tried to decipher his secret message. As a trusted agent of the Amazons I should have known. Our face-to-face confrontation had not as yet yielded the important information.

"Do you live here?" I asked.

"No," he answered, "I just came in for the shower."

My pencil point keeps breaking. The breaking point. I like to stop writing and remember how it feels. I think I frightened him. Not in the shower but in bed. I hope not irrevocably. Because for a few minutes I put him in with those kind of men who use women but don't want to know them. And I just threw myself on his bed and lay there like a corpse. So what happened is nothing, which is what I wanted to happen, although we both acted very disappointed.

After thinking about Paul for two days and wondering whether he'd call, he did.

"How are you?" I asked.

"Waiting for you," he said.

"Want me to come over?"

"Yes. And by the way, you have a magnificent body."

"You're crazy."

I told mother I was going out to meet Paul. She said she'd like to invite him for dinner. He might as well know the worst. This will put him to the test.

FANTASY ON PAUL MEETING THE FAMILY

ME: Mom, this is Paul, and this is my uncle Ernie (shake of hands) and this is my dad (shake of hands) and this is my sister (tweak of breasts), her name is Lucille.

PAUL: You kroavneys may not understand me. There is a language barrier.

ME: He's kidding. He's as American as we are.

PAUL: My whole existence is a ludicrous black muck of non-being. Which means I shoulda stood in bed.

MOM: Would you like something to eat?

PAUL: Some freshly slopped brew might help. Mind if I kingfish in your bowl of Cheezits?

I whisper into his ear that he is acting disgusting. Mother catches me whispering and says, "If you have to whisper, go outside." So we go outside and wedge ourselves out of sight behind the hall door. Oversize plaster models of human ears and brains shove in with us. Paul points to the BRAIN and remarks, "This is merchandise I have been seeking for a long time." I shiver and shrug. Mother calls out after us, "What're you doing out there, making a speech? Come back in." The BRAIN speaks: "I am the gent with the R.S.V.P. Waddaya think? Should I go?" Paul leaves with vigorous knee action. The ears and BRAIN bounce after him. I exhale the words 'ego-pants' and run up the stairs two at a time. Mother is refilling the bowl with Cheezits. Uncle Ernie complains, "He left without saying goodbye." Sister Lucille says, "How can you like someone who wears glasses?" Dad says, "Next time tell him to leave his dictionary at home. I went to college too."

Twenty-Six

Paul's door was open. I sneaked in. It was dark in his place but he knew I was there. He must have been waiting by the elevator watching the floors change.

"Don't move!" he ordered. I moved anyway and banged my leg on a table. "I want you to hear this in the dark. It's for you. It's an entrance-exit poem. It's a verbal agreement. It comes to you directly from the rarely understood empyrean.

> "Whatever thou may dream, thou art a *thing*;
> Thou answerest when the phone saith ting-a-ling
> (Except in dream, perhaps) ; thou likest Bing;
> And thou dost leap our leap who common feel
>   the gooser's sting.
> But be of cheer, Selma, in thy cell,
> Our droppings all contribute to thy smell;
> Thou stinkst; we think, then stink our thoughts
>   as well,
> And we shall share our Bosco when the milkman
>   comes in hell."

I thought he was insulting me. Even if it's philosophical I don't want to hear that I stink.

"Where are you?" I was ready for blood.

"Did you like it?" I heard him moving toward me.

"I hated it," I said. "I don't know much about poetry but I don't want to go to hell."

"YOU ARE THERE?" He tripped me from behind and we went down on the rug struggling wordlessly for a change. It was more fun than the first time we were together. Conflict, inflict, that's the trict. I got on top of him and pretended to clunk his head on the floor, but I put my other hand un- der his head so it was softer than violence. (His head?)

"What's your beef?" I demanded.

"My beef is now chopped meat."

"Is that all you've got to say after almost killing me in the dark?" He tried to sit up but I enjoyed keeping him there.

"I've got more to say," he said. "What thighs you have. You can free me."

"You're not mad any more?"

"You're the one who was mad; don't you realize what an impression you've made on me?"

"No."

Paul wants to save up money so we can go live together. I'm sitting here and he's sitting at his job drying movie stills. It is midnight, the witching hour, and this young witch is mounted on a smooth broom flying through the air.

BROOM: Where to, oh witch?
ME: Take me to Paul.
BROOM: Where is he?
ME: East of the Sunday and west of the Moondog. But you must land silently and invisibly; he is concentrating. You cannot miss him. He is seated at one end of a long line of rollers and squeezers waiting for the photos to come out. (Oh that feels good—the wind is lifting us.) If they're not dry enough he puts them through the rollers again. He may be half asleep. All night long he examines damp scenes of love, violence, and fantastic, indescribable monsters ravaging cit-

ies. It is a labor of love. He says he is presiding over priceless artifacts of our civilization, but I believe he is bewitched. I must break the spell and get him to take a daytime job.

BROOM: Beware, young mistress, and remember this rhyme:

> The day the day is on the way,
> The night the night is out of sight,
> use your flashlight.

ME: You're a wise old broom and I'll never use you to sweep the floor.

There are about as many 'reasonable' apartments as there are reasonable people. And the 'reasonable' ones are usually crummy. We looked at one near the East River Drive. The door opened almost directly into the toilet which was a water closet that resembled a faded cedar chest anchored to a porcelain boatub. (Your palanquin, m'lady.) If I happened to make a wish while eating in that kitchen, it would be an accomplishment of ease and beauty to throw pennies into the toilet and make the wish come true. Another feature of the apartment was the Indian balance-your-weight-evenly room. Splinters stood up like nails all around the bedroom floor. Sharp as swords, they would have to be mown down like an evil nuptial guard, and then the area cared for like a monument. (They died for us so that we could screw.) While we were deciding whether or not we wanted to live there, the janitor smashed a roach on the wall with his bare hands. Paul admired this demonstration, but I almost threw up when I saw the creamy smear it left.

I don't know if I want to put myself into the hands of a stranger (Paul). I'm scared. What if I have to go to work? What if he falls in love with a photo? What if I have to stay appealing every day? When my panic is over I know just what I'll do: go south and make myself a beauty. I'll return wrapped in tan like a carmallow. Then, when Paul peels my wrapper off, the sweet taste of fresh Selma should make him crave me forever.

ONE OR ANOTHER

For Danny

One or another
Is lost, since we all fall apart
Endlessly, in one motion depart
From each other

—D.H. Lawrence

§

J folded a small piece of orange origami paper into a lobster. He can do intricate things with his hands. It surprised me.

Origami: orgasm, orange, outrage, gamy, aura: J created.

The lobster lies on a pile of books on my desk: the topmost one is *The Valadon Drama.* If the lobster did not have two long pointed feelers; it would look like an armadillo; it is accordion pleated from the tip of its tail to its middle.

> Dear J,
>
> I didn't expect it. And I didn't want it. And it came and dumped itself on my couch. Without shoes. With socks. Buried in a book. Was it shy? Or what was it? A worm? I thought, "... almost a worm ..." No beginning, no end, all sex. I saw, as it uncoiled its flesh, that it was all sex: that it crawled into me and disappeared. Where's that worm now? I'm going nuts with the advent of the worm. I love you.

§

J's mother: June Wolff. The entire bookcase in her foyer is full of shells: the crusty abodes of sea creatures in company with fish skeletons, brittle beetles, fossils, sand dollars and pieces of metal or wood that June thinks resemble art. All lie together displayed with exquisite taste on mahogany shelves. All dead. The opposite of June Wolff. Perhaps not. There is nothing so exclusive, alone, or tight as a dancer ... always perfecting their bodies; never satisfied; punishing themselves, attempting to defy natural laws, e.g., to outwit gravity and death by constantly moving! The movement is a screen behind which the dancer lies dying; and the shells on June's shelves are the screens of her life farming out a small translucent span of beauty.

J resembles June: same eyes, same thick mouth. But the child, that is, J, does not dance.

§

In the coldest weather, J would not wear undershirts. And he'd forget to put his sweater on. Or, he'd leave his jacket unzipped. I was almost afraid to offer him a sweater. He accepted the imported double-knit black turtleneck woolen sweater when I showed it to him. And kept it for a few weeks. When I got it back, the smell of sweat was evident. I put it on and lowered my head toward my armpit so that I could smell him.

§

My husband, M, has a full red beard and a long red moustache. He is in the habit of pulling the hairs of his beard out one by one as he writes. The tiny, prickly pain keeps him alert.

To the Editor:

It seems to me that the "militant student" of today is nothing more than the "juvenile delinquent" of a decade ago. He should be dealt with swiftly and firmly in whatever way necessary to halt the destruction of private property, the interference with the right of other students to go to classes, and the willful disruption of the ROTC program, which so many of our clean-cut, diligent youth take part in to serve their country. The police who stand between us and the dissidents have shown remarkable self-control by using clubs at the ready, instead of pistols. I suggest that if the SDS continues its bullying tactics on campus, that we the citizens join in with government forces, and bring the Students for the Destruction of a Democratic Society to their knees with a pistol at their temples. This is the only way to treat those who would destroy all our forefathers built up.

M.J.

§

I think about my affair with J. About making love to one of my husband's students. I let these thoughts rise while M and I watch the Johnny Carson show. Johnny is up there on the screen, swinging his imaginary golf club at an imaginary golf ball right into my imaginary love life. Wham! Every night another green-stained Spalding: nicked and worn, pocked and dull, plops into my shallow bed and remains there in the cool: hiding.

§

a) I do not have a child.
b) I do not have a pet.
c) I do not have a plant.
d) I have ESP. I can read letters without opening them. I can tell colors with my eyes closed. I dream the present and the future. I can tell what M is doing at this very moment. My powers insinuate themselves into other lives.

§

When M drinks he leaves gifts. Once he left bullets in a neighbor's boots; another time it was a ceramic cat abandoned by him on a New Jersey porch. I used to forgive him everything, thinking it would never happen again, but M can't resist a practical joke: he has actually pulled a rug out from under me, thrown me down in front of oncoming traffic, destroyed an armoire with an ax. Because of the crazy things he has done, we have had to move time and time again . . . I'm tired of it . . . tired of barely escaping alive.

§

M puts two bullets and a note:

IF YOU CHANGE YOUR MIND, THERE MAY STILL BE TIME!
F. STACY SWARD
NATIONAL RIFLE ASSOCIATION

into a business envelope. He writes the name of a former colleague on it. The name is Lew Harris. M scrawls the name across the envelope in big bold script. He is using a Pentel pen. He runs the letters across the paper with a mad flourish, as if he is signing a document of great importance. He goes out. He gets into our station wagon. He settles in. He drives. He waves to some students he knows. M stops the car at 98th Street and Riverside Drive. He gets out. He double-parks. He runs up marble steps. He scans the doorbells. He takes the crisp envelope out of his jacket pocket. He shakes the bullets to one side and holds the thin edge of the envelope as high as the chrome around the bells reaches. He forces it between the brick wall and the flat chrome. M returns to the car and zooms away.

§

I use the Larry Mathews beauty salon in the Great Northern Hotel. It is on 57th Street between Sixth and Seventh Avenues. The number 5 (Fifth Avenue) bus gets me there. I go all the way down the long lobby and turn right at the glass doors. Inside, I pass the appointment desk, behind which is an aviary of wigs: bloodless beheadings perched on shelves. All around the salon, other women, like me, only uglier, sit in soft cotton print robes (stenciled leopard), giving themselves to the moment of rejuvenation: haircut, shampoo, hair set, pedicure, makeup. And music plays to the soft rustle of off-white curl papers falling to the floor. Everywhere the hypnotic hum of machinery in the service of beauty persists, as if a hypnotist were saying, ". . . you are asleep . . ." Heat blows gently out of tiny vents drilled into transparent hair-drying bubbles; there is a subtle woodwind of sound as manicure tables are rolled across the floor.

The manicurist takes one of my hands and caresses it before using the cuticle clippers. My other hand dips delicately, all tips, all pink asparagus, into a dessert plate of soapy water.

§

J: shy. Seventeen. He owns a telescope. He mounts it on a tripod; observes the stars above his roof: "If I'm lucky I'll see a comet." He spends hours waiting in the cold to see it. Once it dashed across the sky. Once it did. But it may have been something else.

§

"J, goodbye." I was crying. He was crying too.

"If you want to know what I think about your not wanting to see me anymore, I think it's mean . . . very mean!" I said. I had a Bloody Mary; he was not allowed to drink.

He was crying too.

"Look," I said, "I can get a key from my girlfriend; she said she'd let me use her place anytime. We don't have to wander around in hallways and parks anymore. We don't have to be afraid that Mark'll come home . . . or that your mother will disturb us."

"You don't understand," he said. "I want you to tell Mark about us. If you love me, you'll tell him. I don't want to hide my love for you anymore. I want you to live with me."

"I can't tell him," I said.

J had been adamant. He withdrew his hand which I had been holding under the table.

§

I use Le De by Givenchy. So does June Wolff. Strange coincidence: as if I had seduced J by the familiar scent.

Her mouse of a son crawling to me . . . on top of me. "Did you come?" I asked. I should not have sat cheek to cheek with him, looking at Japanese erotica.

No, I was not his first woman. His second. The first was French. His stepfather put her up to it (she was his stepfather's mistress). And she must have taught him very little . . . an apprehensive technique involving the vagina and the clitoris at the same time. He had trouble with his fingers: where should they go?

§

Two Christmases ago, I had come up out of the snow and stood in the foyer, in front of the shell collection. My face was glowing. J kissed me. And his sister Letitia kissed me. And June kissed me. Letitia gave me a Christmas decoration for a gift: a fragile glass ball painted green, with a nouveau-arte butterfly wrapping its brightly painted wings around the ball. I have it still, wrapped in tissue paper, tucked into a corner of my lingerie drawer. I gave me an antique, hand-carved number puzzle; the numbers were pasted onto thick, movable wooden cubes, and all were contained in a square wooden box. The object of the puzzle is to move the numbers around without taking them out of the box, and to have them read in order from one to fifteen, leaving one empty space in which to maneuver. After J left me, I found myself playing with the puzzle, jumbling the numbers up, dumping them out . . . cheating to get them right.

June gave me a fan that had belonged to Letitia: circa Victoriana. Letitia's room was crowded with things Victorian: Victorian lampshade, Victorian blouse made of lace, reticules, fans, faded silk roses, boxes of horn, a long satin skirt with hustle, and photographs of Diamond Jim Brady, Lillian Russell, Sarah Bernhardt, Oscar Wilde . . . to the photograph of Oscar Wilde she had pasted a nosegay of purple and wine petals (pansies?). It made the photograph seem to be in the process of materializing; but if it actually had, poor Mr. Wilde would have been a basket case, since he had been photographed from the waist up.

§

I recall that the Christmas ball was not a gift from Letitia. I bought it from her for three dollars and fifty cents. But my gifts to both June and Letitia were antique Victorian enameled pins, each displayed in its own "collector's item" red velvet box.

J received nothing. I stood in front of the window of a Village men's shop and admired him in a transparent posing jock. My weightless, see-through hand held him as he turned away.

§

I think about dying my hair another color; to become another person, a person who is beautiful, but M warns me against it. He says it would make me look like a whore. I know that M finds whores exciting . . .

§

Some of the best-looking people I've ever seen are whores. Although some of them look like Barbie dolls: big blonde wigs, and skinny brown legs hanging out of ass-high miniskirts. Still, it's cute and seems innocent, as if they are playing at being adult. Sweet to see them parading when the weatherman predicts rain: carrying umbrellas, wearing boots, plastic babushkas over elaborate wigs . . . just like Scarsdale matrons.

I was taken for a whore in Riker's one evening. I said, "No" to a drunken salesman. One of the authentic whores, in a red-knit-wool, two-piece, tight dress, had turned to a friend and in a very loud voice said: "He got the right string, but the wrong Yo-Yo."

We sat around the horseshoe counter nursing cups of tea. A pink man with a red neck put his brown-trousered knee against my bare one.

"I have two boats. I'll bet you don't believe me," he said. "Ever been to New Hampshire? I have two boats in New Hampshire. I'll draw you a picture of my boats. Where's a pencil?"

I gave him a pencil.

"Naw, you don't believe me. You don't think I have any boats."

I told him that I had a boat too, made out of paper, and that I floated it in my bathtub.

"I have a bathtub in my room. I'll bet you don't believe I have a bathtub in my room. Wanna come with me to my room?"

"No."

"What's your price? I'm willing to pay."

That question had confused me. As I left the restaurant, I pondered how to price myself, since I had never been sold before.

The man's voice followed me, pleading: "Where you going? Don't leave me alone; I haven't told you about my boats. I have to sell one; I hate to sell it."

§

M is walking on the Upper East Side alone. He is nervous. He notices a big black cadillac following him. He stops walking. It cruises up to him. Stops. There are two women seated in front. One of them propositions him. He is not interested in that one. She is too thin for him. The women change places at the wheel. The full-bodied one is asking him to get in the car. I can see that M is frightened. He wants to walk away. The full-bodied woman gets out of the car. She squats down between M and the car. She urinates. M watches as piss streams out, wetting her legs and hitting the car door before it trickles down the curb. He is almost interested. He asks her price. She tells him. He does not have enough. He is sorry. She gets back in the car: has a conference with the other hooker. They agree to charge him less if he puts it in the window.

"Put it in the window, honey."

Her mouth is open; the window is open.

M imagines his prick being sucked off while the window silently rises to capture him, forcing him to run alongside the car as it picks up speed.

The whores spot a police officer and take off.

§

The sign on the gymnasium wall says: NOW THAT YOU'VE DONE YOUR HAIR, WHAT ABOUT YOUR BODY?

Yes, what about it? I want to keep trim so as not to shock J. So far, we have managed to make love under things: my skirt, the sheets, a draped lamp. I know what I look like, but he doesn't, and I daren't let him find out. What M thinks doesn't really concern me anymore . . . I wouldn't want him wanting me too much . . . not while I'm wanting J. Of course there's the chance that I might he left by both of them! But then, I can always live in my head. What I dream is infinitely better than what I do . . . the hazards far less.

§

"Can I help you?" The gymnasium assistant, a slender girl in tights, pressing her false eyelashes down, approaches me.

"I'm just looking," I say.

Four women in black, their desperate flesh in action, lean forward, grab the air, kick in place, shift, speed up, bounce buttocks of overwhelming gravity to the mat. M would he disgusted by their energy. A girl straddles a whirling drum of wooden rollers, quivers sexually, poised for orgasm. Another stands in a stainless steel skirt on a platform; she leans forward to support herself as tiers of steel springs rub up and down her hips, bruising the fatty tissue hidden under soft gray warm-up pants. This would delight M: her passivity, her acceptance of injury.

"Would you care to see our sauna now?" I follow the attendant. "You may have this visit free, madam. If you care to use the sauna today, we provide you with a towel, slippers, and robe."

I enter the sauna with only a towel wrapped around me. I spread it on an upper wooden bench, breathe deeply, and lie down . . . strung out in body fragrance.

§

"Do you know that you should not lie there like that," J says to me admiringly. "Do you know that I want to unwrap you as if you were a mysterious package?"

"Yes, unwrap me. Find me." I am partially unwrapped already. I am wearing red nylon French panties: no crotch, ready for action. It is early afternoon. M is away at work.

J says, "The existence of another planet-like body outside our solar system has been deduced from observations made at the Sproul Observatory at Swarthmore College in Pennsylvania."

"Really?"

"It took scientists thirty years to find it. Its mass is greater than Jupiter, the largest planet in the solar system!"

"Time solves everything," I say. "I guess if those scientists keep looking through their telescopes, they'll see backward to the beginning of time. Is that possible? Is it possible to see something that doesn't exist anymore?"

J says, "I don't know about seeing it, but some astronomers believe that they've picked up short waves: sounds of the beginning of the earth, of creation . . . it's part of the 'big bang' theory."

"I have a 'big bang' theory myself," I say. "Let's go into the bedroom and I'll demonstrate."

I take him by the hand, I always take him by the hand, he is a child: afraid to go, afraid to stay.

First we play tent: both under the sheet, my legs in the air form a central pole. The soft and powdery, white-blueness of the sheet seems made of congealed water. The interior warmth of our enclosed dome is forty to eighty degrees higher than the atmosphere prevailing outside.

A tiny red light illuminates a corner of the sauna.

Another time: J stands in the doorway, afraid to come in. He thinks of the bed as M's bed. I initiate a game to bring him to me. "I'll bet I know something you won't do," I say.

"No, you don't," J answers hopefully.

"Ah, yes, I do," I say. J responds to the challenge. He is ready to do any-thing I ask.

"What do you know that I won't do?" he asks again.

"I'll bet you won't kiss me here."

He flutters around my muslin cage. The mouth of the moth cannot res-ist the light of my mercury lamp: an additional tease. My sex extends over several acres . . . he cannot escape me. He puts his tongue in: licks my fur.

"You won't do it!" I repeat over, and over, and over, and over, and over, and over . . .

"Let me see what happens to my penis when it's in you?" he asks, put-ting two fingers into my vagina. I press and release my muscles, feigning orgasm. He mounts me . . . enters me . . . centers me . . . his penis doing a better job than his fingers in obtaining and recording woman informa-tion: it wants to do the exploration itself. To make this possible for him, I provide maximum safety: I call to him, "Oh, J, I love you . . . !"

I am a stepping-stone into grown-up territory.

His mouth cruelly sucks the very life-spit out of my mouth, out of my mound, out of my mind . . .

I come.

§

If only we had a place of our own.

§

Lew Harris and his wife are on their way to see a movie. He wants to see *Vixen*, she wants to see *The Sound of Music*. They are arguing. They spot the envelope that M left for Lew Harris.

"Look, darling, it has your name on it." Mrs. Harris takes it down. She expects to read something very nice.

They read the note, rush right back upstairs, and call the police. Lew Harris is racking his brain to think of who his enemy might he. He decides that he has no enemies. He cannot recall ever having signed a petition to initiate better gun control laws. He is rereading the note: IF YOU CHANGE YOUR MIND, THERE MAY STILL BE TIME!

"I'm willing to change my mind," he says helplessly, "but about what?"

He decides that the note could not have been written by a member of the National Rifle Association, because a threatening note would only hurt their cause. He barely handles the bullets; they frighten him. He imagines the size hole they'd leave in him . . . the blood that would pour out! He is trying not to panic. He looks nervously out the windows of his apartment to see if anyone is staked out on the adjoining roofs.

The police arrive. One of them requests the letter. On reading it carefully, he says, "Well it don't actually say 'this bullet's got your name on it.' It would be different if the person who wrote this letter to you had one a them bullets pegged for you. . . . I mean, this ain't necessarily a threatenin' letter."

"But the bullets themselves . . ." Lew Harris says, "don't you think the bullets are threatening? Don't you think they mean something in relation to the note?"

The policeman reads the note again. "Nope, this is probably the work of a crank. Don't mean a thing. Anyway, there's nothing we can do about it, unless the guy actually shoots you."

"You mean there's really nothing you can do to prevent something happening?" Lew Harris is not willing to wait until he is shot before the law goes into action.

The cop says: "We could call the detective down at our precinct, have the name and handwriting checked out to see if we have a file on this guy . . . see if he's been using the mails for this purpose."

Harris, desperate, says, "It wasn't sent through the mails; it was delivered by hand and left by the bells downstairs."

The cop ponders this as he observes, with obvious disapproval, a nude sketch hanging on the wall. "I can't see that there's been a violation, but tell you what . . . I'll call Detective Mulholland and see what he has to say."

"Thank you very much." Lew Harris is hoping that Detective Mulholland will put on an around-the-clock guard. He mentions it to the cop.

The cop says, "We ain't got a force big enough to handle this kind of thing. It would be different if you was a celebrity . . . but you're just John Doe, average citizen. You realize, sir, that if a mentally deranged person wants to get you, he'll find a way, no matter how well-guarded you are?"

"I know," Lew Harris answers.

"Can you think of anyone who might want to harm you?"

"I've gone through all the possibilities, and there's no one."

The other cop reports his phone conversation with Detective Mulholland. "He says we should take the evidence down to the station house and he'll check it out. He'll call you in a few days if anything turns up; meanwhile, if you find something out yourself, you can get in touch with him."

They leave with the envelope which contains the bullets and M's unsettling communication.

§

"I don't know what to do," Lew Harris says, wondering whether he and his wife ought to make another foray in the direction of the movies.

"Do? Let's get the hell out of New York!" she answers him.

"I won't allow myself to be terrorized . . . no . . . I've got to find out who's playing this horrible joke on us."

"Could it have been one of your students?" Mrs. Harris suggests.

"Couldn't be; I'm the one defends them against the other teachers."

Lew Harris's wife is thinking that if she leaves the house with him she becomes a moving target. She decides not to be seen with him. She makes him a cup of tea and they sit smiling across the table at each other.

It occurs to Lew Harris that his enemy might be M! M, who speaks about hunting, who passionately defends the right of every US. citizen to own guns . . . "He's the only one I know with guns," Lew Harris explains to his wife, "and just last week I intervened for a kid, a Charles Thomas whom he was picking on. It made him furious. He passed a remark about how the kid deserved to be shot . . . and I said, nobody deserves to get shot! Besides, a gun is to kill! And he said: 'You don't have to kill with a gun, you can scare with it.' That's all I said, a gun is to kill. But I can't just come right out and accuse him. . . . Besides, would he admit it?"

§

I don't usually kiss photographs. But J is standing against a green girder in the subway FIFTH AVENUE stop. It is a color photo: pink face, blue work shirt open at the neck, dark-blue pants. A camera in a leather camera case hangs from his neck. He has a hand over the camera to steady it. The other hand is in his pocket. A red gum machine shields us from the eyes of transit passengers waiting for the train. I kiss J on his melancholy, glossy lips; I smooth his hair back with my pinky.

§

The way J looks at Letitia: is it envy or lust? Does he want to be her, or be in her? We watched her making pomander balls for Christmas, stabbing the swollen fruit with spiked cloves until the aromatic pome resembled a mace. I winced.

"Won't they rot?" I asked.

"No, they dry out and become fragrant. I hang them in the closet and put them in my drawers. People used to carry them around to guard against infection."

"Why don't you carry one around; see if it works," I said.

"I'm already infected," Letitia answered.

§

J . . . I'll bet you slept with your sister . . . remember, on Christmas Day Letitia was ill . . . a urinary infection . . . I had had the very same thing the week before, and I had slept with you, not knowing I had it . . . it is highly contagious. Did you pass it on to Letitia? Did you sleep with her? She has a habit of sprawling when she sits . . . and I noticed a box of birth control pills on her night table. June is much too liberal with you guys.

§

FRAME UP!

I, Charles Thomas, on November 7, 1969, during the first period, was proceeding to Driver's Education class in the West Tower; to get there I had to walk through the big gym. The gym teacher, Mr. Mark Johnson, was holding a class, and physically prevented me from going to class by standing in front of the door. He said: "You can't go through." When I insisted, "Would you please let me through because this is my first day back in school, and I have missed a lot of work," he asked, "What's your name (boy)?" And I said, "Puddin' Tain, ask me again and I'll tell you the same." Then I said, "It looks like you and me are going to stand here for the rest of the period." He said, "I guess so, because I have nothing else to do." I then called him a "mother", and pushed past him. And ran. I finally reached Driver's Ed., I won't tell you how. Toward the end of the period, Mr. Johnson walked into the room, pointed at me, and said, "I want that boy's name." At the end of the first period I went down to his office, took the piece of paper with my name and official class on it out of his hand and tore it up, and said: "If you want to get me in trouble, get me in trouble on your own time, not mine!" I walked out of his office, and on to my second-period class.

On November 7, I was automatically suspended from school, because the administration had stated that I threatened Mr. Johnson's life. You, my fellow students, know that Mr. Johnson is a sadist, and has been known to kick, put his foot on students' necks when they are down, twist arms behind backs, and otherwise harass scapegoats during gym period. But I was also accused of "insubordination," harassment of teachers and students, being detrimental to the social welfare of the population of our school, and all in all, a dangerous student! I was never given a preliminary school hearing, was suspended from participation in all school events, and received a special-delivery, certified mail letter on November 16 from the Board of Education, at 110 Livingston Street, office of high schools, that a suspension hearing would be held there November 25, at 10 A.M., room 730B . . .

Support Charles! Come to his hearing! There are Board of Education directives preventing this kind of action. We cannot allow the administration to exercise arbitrary, unjust, and illegal punishment to remove students they dislike from the schools!

§

Charles Thomas appears to me in the foyer, to the left of the umbrella stand. He is pale. His natural chocolate color faded. I gaze at him awhile before speaking.

"I want to thank you for standing up to my husband. Now there are two of us who know the true story . . . look!"

I bare my chest on which there still remains a large footprint. It is ingrained. Charles Thomas gives me a jar of bleaching cream and a piece of #OO sandpaper.

"You gonna look like a piece of raw meat for a few weeks," Charles Thomas says, "but after that you gonna have skin as fine as a baby's ass."

"Are you coming back to see me?"

"I'll be around . . ."

My evocation of Charles Thomas lasts only a short time; and I am alone again, in the present. M puts his finger on the bell, ringing it without stopping. He does it to bother me, hoping that I am as far away from the door as possible, so that I will have to come running.

"Why don't you open the door with your key?" I demand.

"My hands were full," he says, putting down his briefcase, a pile of newspapers, magazines, letters, flag stickers, old underwear, gloves, and the neighbor's garbage. We look at each other; there is nothing left but vexations. I remember when he used to call me his "darling little invalid"; watched for signs of illness so he could take care of me . . . draw out my fever.

"What did you do today?" he says accusingly.

"Nothing much." I keep from him the information that I have read Charles Thomas's FRAME UP! and managed to meet him soon afterward . . . that we achieved an instant rapport verging on friendship.

"Get busy and make me a snack," he orders. I bring him a quart of milk and a box of Social Tea crackers. He gulps down all the milk and finishes the box of crackers. He is not as active as he used to be, but still has a "jock's" appetite. He goes to sleep after eating. I wonder whether the Board of Education will actually prevent Charles Thomas from continuing his education . . . whether they will give him a fair hearing.

§

M puts the basketballs away in the storage closet. He locks the door. He goes into the gym office. A dark-green shade covers the small window in the door. He takes a handful of Dixon Ticonderoga Leadfast pencils out of a new box and sharpens each one by pressing it into the electric sharpener.

A buzz of carnal delight zings through him as the pencils, being eaten alive in the machine, grow smaller and sharper. He would like to put his finger in, his nose, or something else. He admires the cold efficiency of its function.

§

Lew Harris bursts into M's room. He grabs him, shakes him, shouts,

"Did you leave an envelope with two bullets in it, for me? Did you?"

"I might have," M gasps.

"Did you?" Lew Harris shoves him against his desk. A can of crayons falls to the floor, spilling its contents. M tries to twist away to pick up the crayons. The school bell rings. It is out of order. It keeps ringing. The sound startles Lew Harris. He lets M go. M grovels on his hands and knees, searching for crayons, paper clips, marbles.

"What do you mean, you might have?"

"It's entirely possible. I've done that kind of thing before."

"Think! Did you or didn't you? Admit it . . . you did write that note to me, didn't you! My wife is very sick about it; she refuses to leave the house. And you cost me a screw last night too!"

M is up. He slowly turns toward Lew Harris. He says, "I admit it, but it was only a joke. I thought you'd recognize my handwriting. I meant no harm."

"Recognize your handwriting?! Man, I wouldn't recognize my own handwriting. I don't know what to do about you, I really don't."

M sweats profusely. He is experiencing the same sense of danger he had felt when, as a youth, he had gone down the steps to the basement of his home after an argument with his father, taken a double-barreled shotgun from the rack, loaded both chambers, put the barrel against his forehead just above the eyebrows, and . . . not tripped the triggers.

M says, "Have you gone to the police?"

"What do you think? They have your letter and your bullets."

"But they don't know it was me, do they? They don't know about me?" M pleads.

"Not yet."

"Please don't give them my name . . . they'll bother us . . . my wife and I . . . they'll make it tough! Look, I haven't kept the guns; my mother has them locked up. I do this every once in a while when I drink. I promise I won't drink anymore . . . ever."

Sick to his stomach, Lew Harris turns swiftly and leaves.

§

I ask M to write a letter of apology to Mrs. Harris. He says he will. But he insists that I deliver it by hand along with a conciliatory gift: *History of Art* by H. W. Janson. The Harrises are interested in art.

§

Dear Mrs. Harris,

When a man behaves like a jackass, as I have done however inadvertently, he does not escape easily from his own censures—nor will I. The details of the full extent of my lunacy involved the distribution of a box of rifle shells, the destruction of a television set, running at ninety miles an hour across the Jersey countryside with a sounding horn for company, and several other aberrations too shameful to mention to a stranger.

That you were in any way upset by my crude and vulgar foolishness is something I am heartily sorry for. Please believe there was neither malice nor intent in the action—only some stupid alcoholic fantasy which I deeply regret affected your life and that of others.

Will you please accept my apologies which I hope, in part, can replace the pain my heedless actions may have caused?

Sincerely,
Mark Johnson

§

M has gone to the Pokerino Palace, where he can be surrounded by extravagant gifts: lawn croquet group, electric blanket, shotgun, Early American lamp, hi-fi, sterling silver platter . . . he is trying to add up winning points . . . he needs 1,500 more tickets. I used to go with him, before he became so obsessive. The cheap stuff palled on him: the pocket combs, finger traps, miniature cards, nail clippers, and dice, that I still get a kick out of. M is a much better player than I am. He knows where he wants the ball to roll, and it obeys him. He's had a flush, a royal flush, a straight, and full house many times. He considers it a waste of a nickel when I get my three of a kind . . . treats Pokerino as if it were an Olympic event. Oh, I know it's pretty stupid to sit glued to a stool watching rubber balls roll into holes on a slanted board . . . yet it was something we had together. Once when we were totally engrossed in the game (and a radio was playing over the loudspeaker), the program was interrupted by the announcer who said: "LADIES AND GENTLEMEN, YOUR NATIONAL ANTHEM!" M and I jumped up and stood at attention, our hands over our hearts, our stools spinning free. And there wasn't even a flag present. It broke us up! The evening was one to remember.

§

I have a signal that lets J know when I want to see him. I allow the phone two rings, then hang up. As soon as M leaves for Pokerino I dial J's number. This time I wait for him to pick up . . . I long to hear his voice.

"Hello," I say, "this is Melissa."

"How are you?" J asks. He sounds as if he is speaking to someone he barely knows. Perhaps this is because June is around. Most probably it is because I refuse to bring our affair into the open. J is preparing himself for a break. He is obstinate as a child. He is a child after all, and wants things his way . . . or not at all. But if we separate (like the white from the yolk of an egg), some of me will cling to him always.

"What are you doing?" I hope he is doing nothing.

"I was trying out the tape recorder June got me. I don't like the sound of my voice."

"I like the sound of your voice. Wanna come over?"

"You're crazy if you like my voice . . . . it's so monotonous. I'm sorry June bought me the tape recorder, maybe she can give it back."

"Bring it over with you, darling, I'll buy it. But hurry, and don't be sad.

Don't be alone, I love you."

§

J has placed the tape recorder on the table. It can feel the magnetic pull of love emanating from us with equal power. That is why it does not slide in either direction, but remains fastened. It is a small cassette-type machine, simple to operate. In order to record, two buttons must be pushed down simultaneously. I do this and we are ready. The tape makes tiny whirring sounds, like a captured fly grown tired trying to escape.

"What shall we talk about?" J asks.

"Tell me what you're afraid of," I answer.

"No."

I hear J draw in a quick slippery breath. Saliva bubbles at the corners of his mouth. I expect him to spit. Instead he swallows.

"Then let's make love," I suggest.

"No . . . I don't want to anymore."

"Why did you come over?"

"Because you asked me to," he says.

§

After J leaves, I find a magazine on the closet floor. It is called *Jr.* and features photos of young men in posing briefs, leather, or jeans. It must have dropped from J's coat pocket.

§

The tape recorder is on. I am J's voice. I am also his male lover. By creating a situation, I hope to read J's mind. . . . He is afraid that he is homo-sexual. This is not in keeping with the rest of his generation who claim to harbor no guilt.

J's lover has him tied, facedown on the bed. J is nude. His firm buttocks have a beautiful freshness, almost female in their rising plumpness. His lover says:

"How delightful to touch and squeeze your bum!"

J twists and turns trying to loosen his bonds. The other, armed with a magnificent cock, commences to deflower him. The delicate hole of pleasure, a chrysanthemum violated, receives three or four thrusts of fullest length. I sustains the insertion with cries of joy. His lover's stones slap against his raised buttocks.

J	Oh, I am overcome with voluptuous sensations.
Lover	I distill my very soul into you.
J	Bury yourself in me.
Lover	Ah!
J	Pleasure suffocates me.
Lover	Come! Come!
J	Beastly, unnatural! Oh, save me, Father!

So, it is true!

§

J says, "Mummy should have a boyfriend."
"Yes, J, how about you?"

§

We are at a party at June's house. J is afraid to go out. He climbs into June's bed. He curls up in the fetal position. He says, "I'm going to sleep with you, Mummy. I'm never getting out of your bed." I say, "Make him get out immediately."

We both have to carry him into the living room; we seat him on the couch. His eyes glisten with tears. He does not say a word. The party is over.

§

I am startled by the news that you want to kill yourself. That you ran screaming into the street: past the Nedicks, past the subway, around the corner and past the flower shop, the menswear store, the cleaners, the Maritime Building, across Greenwich Avenue where you hoped you would be run over by a truck and killed! Yet June caught you in front of the toy store . . . and took you home again. Now she's afraid to leave you alone.

§

June says: "J asked me, 'What is a tragedy?'"

§

J, listen to me child . . . M is a terrible lover . . . he is no lover at all. He has to tie me to the bed and pretend he is ravishing a virgin. It is a bore. I can tell you this because you are having a breakdown and don't know what I'm saying anyway. When you and I were together, J, I never spoke of M in a disparaging way, did I? I always said, "I'd hate to hurt Mark." Didn't I?

§

Semiannual party: fiesta time at your high school. J, you are wearing a black suit, white shirt, and a gray, green, and pink diagonally striped tie. You are small. You are beautiful. Your hands are unusually large though. I am thought to be a relative of yours when I ask where you are. You are in a big room, helping with the fiesta food: paella, pastillelios, pasacaglia, pastiche, pirogen, and pistachio nuts. Your classmates are dancing . . . you are with the over-thirties. I wonder why you never learned to dance? I see you looking at young girls' legs. I am jealous. I shouldn't be; I should be happy for you; I should be worried that you are not like the other boys. Your difference is a symptom, and I weep for you, child.

§

There must be something about me that attracts unhappy people. I hope I don't lose all of them.

§

It is freezing out. J and I go into a coffee shop. There is a minimum of twenty-five cents per person. I have the money for the coffee. J has only enough for carfare. We put our hands together to see how small mine are compared to his. I close my eyes and let touch take over. It is one of the most exciting moments of my life.

§

When I walk with M, he becomes enraged if I show interest in a passing male. He hits me on the head with his newspaper. It makes a hollow popping sound and embarrasses me. He thinks I am getting hot for a stranger . . . a younger, thinner, bouncier stranger . . . but always I am projecting an image of J. It is not young men I love. It is J, and always will be J. In twenty years J will be thirty-nine. In twenty years, I will be . . . ?

§

M says that Charles Thomas has discovered that he is a foster child . . . and doesn't like it! That he has become a menace.

§

110 Livingston Street. The board waited one and a half hours for Charles Thomas to appear. He did not. Students have taken over the lunchroom in protest against his unjust suspension. Fliers from the principal circulate :

To All Students:

It is important that you as students know what actually took place in the negotiations between the student negotiating team and the administration. The principal had already agreed to the following demands when the negotiations broke down because of the insistence upon the part of the students that total amnesty be granted for any future actions as a condition for any further talks.

Agreed:
1. The concept of a student court to replace the principal's suspension.
2. The reopening of the hearing for Charles Thomas and a letter from the principal to the superintendent who has final authority in the case, urging reinstatement of Charles provided he can give assurance of proper behavior.
3. Total amnesty for yesterday's and today's actions.

NOTE: I will still abide by these decisions despite the breakdown of talks, and I am willing to resume talks on the remainder of the demands at any time.

Gordon B. Choate

Principal

§

Mrs. Harris does not want to let me in. Lew Harris opens the door. I come in with the letter for Mrs. Harris, and the art history book. She is looking at me with repugnance.

"Mark wants you to have this book and this letter," I say, putting them on the table. Mrs. Harris does not even open the letter. She picks it up by the corner and drops it into a straw basket.

"I'm sorry," she says, "but I can't accept the book. You'll have to take it back."

"You must keep the book . . . Mark wants you to have it."

"It gives me the creeps!" she answers. "I don't want it in my house."

"If you don't take it, I'll have to throw it into a garbage can when I go down . . . I don't dare take it back."

"Suit yourself," she says coldly.

I flip the pages, trying to interest her in its illustrations . . . its desirability, "Look," I say, "celestial drama above a vast Alpine landscape . . . the Deity . . . coquettish damsels whose wriggly nakedness . . . The Kaisersaal . . . Tomb of the Countess . . . mother and child . . . isn't it wonderful . . . The condensation of centuries under one cover. Please keep it!"

"Your husband belongs in an asylum!" she shouts.

I sit there looking glum. Lew Harris throws a withering glance her way. "Don't tell Mark what she said, he's liable to snap," Harris says. "Well keep the book . . . tell your husband 'thank you.'

§

Charles Thomas has a better body than J.

Charles Thomas has absorbed all color into his skin. He reflects nothing. He contains everything.

J is the absence of color. He reflects my image. He keeps nothing.

I am going to introduce them and change the course of history: hues are produced by blending the three primary colors in various proportions. Adding white to them gives us tints, while mixing them with black produces shades.

§

J tried to drown himself. June showed me the note:

Dear Mummy,

My instructions were to self-destruct at zero hour, in order to be born again. And since zero is a very personal number, the instructor left it up to me, when. I consulted my *Wonder Book of Oceanography* in order to find out what lies on the bottom of the sea, because at that depth, all traces of my former fictional self might easily disappear into the mouths of sea beasts. Please believe that I will be happy to disappear into the digestive system of a sea anemone, to become part of that beautiful sprawling flower below the continental slope.

Though the continental slope is just plain mud, Mummy: blue mud, green mud, red mud, black mud, or white mud, it oozes over billions of tiny shells and skeletons of creatures which, like myself, have lived near the surface of the sea, and then upon death have drifted downward to the very bottom. Goodbye. Don't fret.

J

§

June lets the water out of the tub. She demands that J never fall asleep in the tub again. He goes back to polishing a telescope lens he has made. It takes hours. What does he think while he is polishing?

"I'm not thinking anything," he says.

I realize now that his arrogant posture is due to an internal conflict in him between loving and fleeing. I assume that he is attracted by, and afraid of me. His courtship consists in part in running away from me. I will not call again and ask for him.

§

June is, in spirit, a female phalarope. When she was pregnant she would have preferred having the male of the species incubate and guard the young alone. She is not interested in the traditional motherly chores.

§

M and I are on our way to the library. We are stopped by a reporter and a photographer who want to ask us a question. They are from a well-known morning paper. M says, "Shoot . . . what's the question?"

THE QUESTION

If you were on a sinking ship, and could save only one other person, your spouse or your child, who would you choose?

WHERE ASKED

Along Amsterdam Avenue.

THE ANSWERS

Mark Johnson, teacher:

I would have to try to save the child. A child hasn't lived yet, but an adult has in most instances tasted everything and is just marking time here on earth. Also, a child depends entirely on an adult, and it is the honorable thing to do, to live up to this trust. Besides, my wife is an excellent swimmer and could probably save both of us.

Melissa S. Johnson, housewife:

My child. If I allowed my child to die, I could not go on living myself. My husband is an excellent swimmer and could probably save all of us.

§

I have never learned to swim. Does this mean that my hypothetical child is doomed?

§

M, you are covered with patriotic gore . . . it won't come out at the cleaners. I asked you to take it in long before the fabric rotted, but you just lay on the bed, waiting for soft white veins of plaster to open and sift down over you. You spent one entire year gazing at the ceiling . . . and you blamed it on the "Commies"!

§

A young photographer said: "I was in Vietnam taking pictures, stumbled on a hospital in the hills: one thousand children under twelve with varying degrees of burns over their bodies and limbs. Many of them were crying; many of them were dying. I have to shut myself off. Can't take the emotion. I concentrate on composing the picture. You know it isn't so bad when the napalm hits you straight on, because then you're gone and don't know what happened. The terrible thing is when a few drops get you . . ."

The pictures are going to be published in a book. I asked the photographer to let me know when it comes out. I'm going to give it to M as a birthday present. He doesn't want to bring the boys back.

§

"Charles Thomas," I say, "maybe we can help some black people together . . . not here in New York, of course . . . not even in Chicago or Connecticut . . ."

"I don't have nothing to say to you, baby," he says.

"Don't you want to get even with Mr. Johnson for having you suspended?"

"He don't figure. I got bigger plans. I goin' to burn the school down . . . if he in it, that too bad!"

M's beard should he highly inflammable; after he brushes it each morning, he uses my hair spray which is a highly inflammable lacquer.

Charles Thomas feels so good he sings me a song:

> "Burn, baby, burn
> there's something you must learn
> when the fat is in the fire
> whitey stokes the funeral pyre
> when the flames are jumping higher
> white turns black as he expire
> Burn, baby, burn
> there's something you must learn
> when the shit is in the tree
> that's the place the panther be
> when the shit is on the ground
> whitey ain't goin' be around
> So, burn, baby, burn!"

I compliment Charles on his excellent singing voice . . . ask him again to accompany me on a goodwill tour. Again he refuses . . . so . . . I decide to shanghai him. I need him, I need him! And I have to help somebody, and somebody have to help me.

I slip into the cafeteria where there is still a sit-in going on. The steam table is steaming: hot vegetables, meat loaf, halibut sauce diablo, soup de jour. I am wearing a white apron, hair in a net, and white sneakers; a flowered handkerchief is pinned to the breast pocket of my uniform. I am mistaken for a cafeteria worker. Nobody else is allowed in.

In this guise I concoct a Mickey Finn consisting of :

> 3 crushed onions (essence)
> 4 cloves of garlic (chopped)
> 1 tsp. lemon extract (undiluted)
> 8 ounces warm milk (whole)
> 5 tbs. honey
> Cinnamon (1 stick)

> 6 ounces of paregoric

I serve it to Charles Thomas who belts it down without a second's hesitation. He turns blue. He passes out behind a rack of aluminium trays. We extricate ourselves, me mumbling, "Emergency, emergency . . ." and are helped into the elevator, then out into a cab (where he vomits into the declivity between my breasts).

We go to Biafra . . . directly . . . flying inconspicuously above the clouds. I snore, so that Charles Thomas will believe we are in an airplane.

§

Can we stem the tide of human suffering?

§

WE ATTEMPT TO STEM THE TIDE OF HUMAN SUFFERING (anyway)

I am almost a nurse. Charles Thomas is almost a doctor. We are wearing white, and we care. We are holding the first medical clinic here (Chuba, Biafra, [Nigeria]) in twenty-seven months of war, amid people suffering from protein starvation and resembling inmates of a concentration camp: which they are, even though they spend as much time outdoors as in.

These people are refugees.

We are tourists.

They say that when they reached the deserted farm settlement here, near the Niger River, it seemed a "Garden of Paradise."

"Oh, yes, Mis-tah! Rich cassava grow by himself on many miles of farmland and in the bush."

"Then what happened?" I ask, kneeling on the floor beside a sick child. I feel his swollen belly and stalk-thin, chocolate-colored limbs pocked with white scabs. Charles Thomas continues interpreting for me as I prescribe drip feed for the child, and press diuretic pills into the hand of his anxious mother.

"Tell her it is necessary for the child to take them in order to relieve the pressure of urine blocked inside."

The child will die (anyway) .

His mother whispers more information about the "Garden of Paradise." "We were so thirsty, but the well was sick, Mis-tah! We sneak the drink an' get dysentery . . . yes."

WE WAIT FOR HELP (anyway)

Charles and I are desperate, but we are healthy . . . We have to keep saying to ourselves: "If we were sick we couldn't help." Our physical affluence is obscene: the flesh too firm, the eyes too clear, the limbs too steady. But if we were sick ourselves, how could we be of assistance?

We have sent seventeen children to the hospital run by the French Red Cross at Santana, next to Avo-Omama . . . we hear that only two survived.

Outside, the sound of a thousand people murmuring and grunting like fallen birds with a snoutful of pain; they wait for our help (anyway) .

Charles Thomas turns to me imploringly. "I may have to beat up some of them to keep them in line," he says.

We pass among them, choosing who will enter the clinic. We hand out precious pink clinic cards and wish they were made of rice paper so that the hungry might eat them. The separate lines of children, adults, and very old people press forward whenever a patient hobbles toward the dirty concrete clinic building . . . where we portion out what we have.

I have to fight an impulse to carry the little boys who use canes to walk. I hear a child, with swollen, light-yellow testicles, explain to Charles Thomas: "It hurts to walk, Mis-tah!"

A woman carries in a man on her back, and Charles Thomas whispers to me, "He is dead."

Because it is war, a Nigerian shell lands.

It demolishes a mud-walled house, and injures a number of people. The ones outside the clinic, who have been standing for three hours in the withering sun, scatter into the bush . . . many merely put their eating dish over their heads.

Charles Thomas says, "Man, lookit what's happenin' here, and people are calm! Let's go back and shake 'em up."

I see and hear on the one o'clock news that genocide is an accepted technique of war—from one of its generals!

I go to sleep (anyway).

§

Why do I invent deaths for those I am attracted to?

I have not invented their deaths. J is suicidal. Charles Thomas is in constant danger because of his skin. There are other hazards: air pollution, the decay of algae in lakes, air traffic, the bomb, all bombs, wars, the war, the next war, disease, dissent, distrust, disgust, dissolution, disappearance . . . I live close to the highway, I hear cars screeching to a stop every day, avoiding an accident. Sometimes I hear the crash of an accident. When traffic is moving along without incident, it sounds like the ocean.

What do you mean?

I mean I love the sound of the ocean even though it is the sound of rubber tires turning. It helps me to dream.

Tell me what you dream.

For a week before my operation to untip a tipped womb, I had been eating nothing but peanut butter. I couldn't resist it. I was lying on my bed looking up when suddenly I found myself in a twilight state . . . neither conscious, nor unconscious . . . and I felt a miraculous lightness. I had actually left my body; my spirit was hovering over it looking down. I thought, "Isn't this marvelous." Then I heard footsteps in the other room. They terrified me. I was afraid I would not be able to get back into my body in time. Somehow I managed to do it, and gathering myself into a tight human ball I fell asleep at the foot of the bed. Then I dreamt. In the dream I was falling into the ocean. I was not drowning, just falling . . . I had the thought that falling was the same as rising . . . that the fish in the ocean were the same as the birds in the sky . . . that up was down, and down was up . . . I became ecstatic and woke up in this state.

Are you fearful of relinquishing the hold you have on reality?

Yes, that is true.

§

I go to the park to hang on to life. The grass and trees are green (in part), and this mostly green is real. Children are playing. The sun is shining. My spirit absorbs the rays of the sun, and produces not flowers, but lethargy. I watch the children playing, and wonder what my own child would look like if I had one. At once, all the children have J's face. Their laughter, their shouts, bombard my psyche like a multiwave oscillator, which is a quack's cure-all for mankind.

§

J, you have warm, wet lips: an unusual hydrothermal experience. Your genitals are like the sego lily: three-petaled, curved, and fragrant, not far from Point Sublime. I expect to travel there again sometime.

§

J has become Prince Motoyoshi; his poem to me reads:

> Wabi mureba
> Ima hata onaji
> Naniwa haru
> Mi wo tsukushite mo
> Awamu to zo omou

He will not translate it for me. But from it I surmise that he is lonely, doesn't care what happens to him, has to see me, even though it means that he will be lost in Naniwa Bay, because he has a small boat.

I answer his poem in uncertain meter, probably Sapphic. Half of the words come from a found fragment; only the last few words of each line remain . . . I will put a word in front of each sentence to see if it gives added meaning to the line.

> Fuck . . . passion yes.
> Fuck . . . utterly.
> Fuck . . . I can.
> Fuck . . . shall be to me.
> Fuck . . . a face.
> Fuck . . . shining back at me.
> Fuck . . . beautiful.
> Fuck . . . indelibly.

I'm sure that J will love it and stop being lonely when he reads it. It is so appreciative of all he's done for me.

J you must never go to sea in a sieve!

§

M suspects that I am having an affair with J. He is too late; it is almost over. He broods about having been in school all day, not having been able to track me down.

Now he is on his way to June's house . . . to catch us. June has flown to Puerto Rico to visit friends who live near the rainforest, so J is alone in the house. He opens the door a crack and turns ashen when he sees M. M asks for me. J says that he is alone and that June is in Puerto Rico. He invites M in. He serves M some of June's pâté, which she left for J to eat while she is gone. He also brings out a bottle of beer and a box of crackers. J pets his cat. M eats out of nervousness. He dips the crackers into the pâté: they break . . . he cannot manage their crisp frailty.

"Well, if Mrs. Johnson happens to drop by, tell her I'm looking for her, will you?" M thinks he is setting a trap.

"I don't expect anybody," J says.

"She said she might come here . . ." M watches for a revealing sign.

"Maybe she doesn't know that June's gone already," J says.

"Maybe she does and maybe she doesn't." M tries to picture J in bed with me . . . it makes him ill . . . he'd prefer being cuckolded by a star athlete, one of his choice.

J locks the door after M leaves, wondering what he wanted.

§

I take J to the Planetarium. I am a member of the Museum of Natural History and can get in free with one guest. Before we go in to see the show, we step on various scales to see what we would weigh on the moon and other planets. Inside, we sit in the dark, looking up. The man at the heavenly console is lecturing about "What Lies Beyond Saturn's Rings?" He says that Saturn consists of a molten core surrounded by an ice cover thousands of miles thick.

I put J's hand under my skirt. The Planetarium is the best place to take a date: the darkest. We enter the atmosphere filled with deadly methane and ammonia gases.

"However, this atmosphere is much more stable than Jupiter's," the man says.

My surface temperature rises to about −240 F. Like Jupiter, J makes me rotate quickly. I think that if he and I ever had children, we would name them Phoebe, Hyperion, Mimas, Engladas, Tethys, Diana, Rhea, Iapetus, and Titan. One of them would be different than all the rest (like J); the others would be normal. At breakfast we would always eat half a grapefruit placed facedown in the plate to resemble the top half of Saturn above its rings.

§

M is euphoric. He has been sent two tickets to a football game at Yale.

"I didn't know they play football in the summertime," I say. He ignores the remark. "I don't want to go with you," I add.

"Good!" he says. "I can sell your ticket for at least seventy-five dollars. I sent for these, but I didn't expect to get them. What a lucky break!"

§

Charles Thomas is out of the state, ostensibly to organize other Third World students at other high schools, and to help them recognize the hypocrisy of the educational system. He says, "Power . . . then peace!" He has a second, secret identity: "The Tongue." He has always had a powerful tongue. He writes me about his latest campaign to unsettle the establishment, especially rightest white co-eds:

> Hi, chiclet,
>
> Seem that at least one UCSH co-ed is fallen prey to "The Tongue." That me, baby. They describe me as a sex-crazed monster who hangs out in the vicinity of the campus lagoon. Well, I was there one 2:45 A.M., one night recently, and I did claim to possess a knife, and the chick did put me down, so I jump in front of her and put my hand over her mouth to stop her from screaming, dig? I say to her, "I got a knife and I won't use it if you cooperate. I won't rape you, just eat you." She was all shook up and didn't give me no back talk, so I dragged her into the bushes and perform cunnilingus on her. Then I apologized and told her that I didn't really have no shiv, and weren't going to cut her. She were so grateful for what I done for her that she give a wrong description to the authorities: white male, six feet, one inch tall, with blond hair and blue eyes. Hair medium length. Wearing a sport jacket, tan pants, no tie. About 23 years of age. They lookin'

for that unsavory character right now!

Be a good girl, or the boogie man gonna get you if you don't watch out.

Charles

§

June once said to me: "If you didn't want to be with M, you wouldn't be. You are not forced to stay with him."

Of course she's right.

But am I with him?

§

"What is the greatest sin you've ever committed?" I ask M.

He says, "I killed my father and slept with my mother."

M is never serious.

§

There is a school vacation and I have to leave Charles Thomas and J to go to Yellowstone National Park with M. He is going especially to see our national symbol, the bald eagle, and has written the names of Madison, Firehole, and Yellowstone rivers down; they are places where the bird, recognized by its white tail and head, may occasionally be seen. M is going to take pictures of the bald eagle, and have them blown up to poster size for his den. I don't know how he'll keep from wanting to take potshots at the wall, once it becomes symbolic not only of our country, but of an unbridled energy and strength . . . a free spirit which happens to be on the verge of extinction.

Predator? Yes, the bald eagle is: possessing size, strength, powerful flight, and keenness of vision. We must do all we can to let the bald eagle live . . . to let our country live.

J says that the northern constellation Aquila, lying south of Cygnus, and containing the bright star Altair, appears in the formation of an eagle. Thus we are represented in the sky too.

§

Natural wonders frighten me: they are "unnatural wonders" for which I have no explanation. In school my teacher had said: ". . . the two agents that are responsible for Yellowstone National Park are fire and ice." I had imagined then that the mountains were actually huge ice sculptures, and the lakes formed from drippings melted off by the sun; I had pictured a ranging, transparent glassy park: hissing and splashing . . . simmering night and day.

I want to go to Emerald Pool, transparent purple-blue waters set in orange sand, to take color pictures. M will want to be in most of the pictures . . . he has his mother in mind when he poses.

"Gonna get me some of them obsidian arrowheads," M says.

I see M covered with obsidian arrowheads like porcupine quills; he is pit-patting on all fours through the school basement; he meets the custodian who is raising the thermostat as high as it can go; it is June, the sit-in at the school is still going on; the custodian wants to suffocate the students . . . to burn them with steam . . . make them run out into the street. He tells M to position himself just beyond the cafeteria doors, to shoot his obsidian arrowheads at the children as they try to flee. M agrees. However, the arrowheads are black soul-brothers in another incarnation . . . they bury themselves in the wall to spell out the words: BLACK POWER!

M is trampled in the ensuing rush.

§

"What if heavy snows sweep across the continental divide?" I ask M. "What if we go all the way there and find that the park entrances are closed?"

"Let me worry about that," he says. "I'll consult the Weather Bureau before we take off. There are wonders to be seen in the off-season too. I understand they use snowmobiles to get around."

§

I am the deciduous quaking aspen. My fresh green trembling leaves have fallen off again and I am bare. My natural enemy is the beaver who eats me up inside, and then when I am hollow, floats me downstream to help build his dam. Squirrels nibble elegantly on my bark and buds. Mice embrace me, digging sharp claws in to maintain their balance. Birds eat my buds. Elk and deer also make a meal of me in times of famine. My once beautiful arms are left bare or scarred from forest fires or lightning.

I am Melissa Johnson: I am the deciduous quaking aspen.

§

M's mother is not old. And she has more plants than the Botanical Gardens. She also has a cat called Smut. She is a slender woman in her late fifties, I think, but she passes for thirty something.

She is a widow.

She is ingenious.

Her home is filtered by an aura of palpable femininity.

When M was unemployable she supported us.

She is better than me in every way. I mistreat M to hurt her.

Her kitchen: Venetian blue and white tile.

Her living room: zebra rug, appliqued pillows, lattice-front armoire, live trees, potted plants, bamboo magazine rack, leopard ceramic door-stop, flower printed sofa in beige and green (that makes one feel one is "getting into a garden") , and her own paintings on the wall.

Her bedroom and dressing room: white bookcase containing a bright sweater collection, bracelets and beads on the wall, Porthault flowered sheets, old French chairs covered in lace and ruffles, and again, her own paintings on the walls.

Her studio: meticulously clean, color charts on the wall, an easel, a captain's chair, and a potted plant.

She owns a luxurious fur blanket on which she seduced M. It sheds.

§

In Yellowstone National Park, M assured the park ranger that he would not feed, touch, tease, or molest the black or the grizzly bear. And that he would not bury rubbish that smelled of food, for the bears to unearth. Yet, when I woke up suddenly where we had camped for the night, I found myself surrounded by the remains of our evening repast. A 900-pound grizzly was traveling toward me as if he had discovered his ideal gourmet meal: gopher stuffed with ants, mushrooms, berries, and mice.

I screamed just once before a shot rang out in the frigid air; M had killed the bear. The huge thing thrashed about in pain for a few minutes before it died. Amazing that grizzly cubs are born blind, naked, and helpless, weighing at the most one pound each.

"Why did you surround me with garbage? Did you want the bear to kill me?"

"No, my dear," M said, "I wanted to kill *it* with my new rifle, but I needed a decoy, and you did admirably well."

". . . and if you had missed?"

"I never miss!"

§

M packs the car the night before. His gun, sheer black-barreled ugliness, has the look of a killer. Its dull finish (nonreflective) is calculated not to betray the owner's presence he snuggles the multishot, autoloading shotgun between two heavy woolen blankets. He wraps it with care: it has not always been well; when M first handled it, it coughed out five 12-gauge blasts till he put it down again. The baby spits bullets.

§

M drives to New Jersey to say goodbye to his mother.

M lifts her in his arms. She squirms away.

"Not here. Not now," she says, leading the way to the sofa. M sinks in: he is autumn: he is reds, golds, and browns in her garden . . . he is a fallen leaf about to be swept away by passion. She rakes him in.

If she keeps doing that, it will he all the reward he requires for staying alive. It has come to that.

§

Follow the plantigrade spoor of M's fat feet and you will he able to read my story written in snow. M has gone for help. He has left me some-where under a huge, wind-fluted snowdrift. It may seem that M is am-bling aimlessly, but his purpose is to find a park ranger, and he does. They approach my lair from leeward. M scoops great chunks of compacted snow from the drift: brings a hatchet down with all his force to break through the ice-coated roof that has formed in his absence. I am dead.

To the surprise of the park ranger, M devours me immediately: his long canines crunch through my thin skull, till there is nothing left but two limp strands of hair and a pair of boots.

Abruptly the park ranger starts to chase M, who manages to cover a lot of ground in his peculiar, broad-legged, shuffling gait.

He climbs to the top of an iceberg.

He glissades down the other side, arms outstretched to break the des-cent. He is satiated and wants to sleep.

He advances toward a pressure ridge, careful to keep downwind and out of sight of the ranger. He lies for a moment on a large level stretch of ice. He inches forward.

Suddenly he freezes.

The ranger has spotted his big, shiny, red, pitted nose. The nose stands out.

"It is unmistakable miles away," the ranger says.

M hides it automatically. Without his nose he becomes another yellowish-white clump of snow fallen into human shape.

Inside of M, I get myself together.

The next morning both our flensed carcasses are found frozen into the ice.

§

Why won't M admit that we are a dying culture . . . he is completely out of touch with the fabric of America. The fabric he wraps himself in is all wool and a yard wide. Incredible. He is to be present at the hearing in which students advance their demands for a more meaningful educational program. I can imagine what that will be like!

§

At the hearing, the teachers and members of the board are seated on one side of the room. All are wearing jackets, even the dowdy ladies who make no attempt to hide their baroque-veined legs. They sit gingerly, as if protecting a distended, exquisitely tender protrusion. The students have been hearing down on them, and they expect no immediate relief. Their hair, in an expression of shock, rises short and stiff; their mouths gape open . . . fishlike. The jaws creak as words leak out of them: ". . . we cannot give in . . . ," "But we have agreed on . . . ," "The question is . . . ," "We are listening," "It is our belief," ". . . a deep-seated malaise!"

The students present their demands:

1. That the school employ more Third World instructors, e.g., gamblers, pimps, whores, chippies, madams, dining-car waiters, and Holy Rollers.

2. That there be a separate lunchroom serving Third World food, e.g., alligator tail & rice, chitterlings & collard greens and okra, barbecued ribs, pigs feet, chicken and drop dumplings with sweet potatoes, neckbones & lye hominy; desserts: sweet potato pie, watermelon, blackstrap

sorghum molasses & biscuits; beverages: sassafras-root tea, homemade buttermilk.

3. That a zoo be built with city funds adjacent to the school in order that Third World students may become acquainted with the vital, primitive force that stalks African jungles, e.g., lions.

4. That there be taught a language of the Third World, e.g., Yoruba.

The members of the board agree that a gambler might be hired as a mathematics instructor. They quibble about whether the dining-car waiter would be sufficiently versed in geography to teach that subject, and they practically come to blows about using a pimp and a whore as social studies instructors. They are baffled and helpless. Chitterlings ding-a-ling past their awarenesses. Zoos harbor animals hungering to attack them. Yoruba speaks to them of coastal intrigue and bad black linguistic stock.

They turn down almost all of the demands.

§

M is taken hostage!

§

His head is forced through a hole that has been cut in a sheet. The sheet is hanging across a section of the gym. Black Phys. Ed. students are taking potshots at M with a basketball. They wonder why he shows no dismay: does not try to withdraw or cry out. Why doesn't he?

He is dead.

He is nicer when he is dead. He is smiling and he has an erection. The sheet falls over him. He is ready for surgery. The barber sharpens his razor. M is emasculated. I shall hold two burials: one for his body, one for his sex. Because his sex is in such a tiny casket, I will have it interred in a pet cemetery.

§
It is obvious that nobody shall overcome nothing.

Violence for violence's sake. Well all right.

And you, Charles Thomas, though you're full of Third World demands, what the hell is a Third World? Just another cattle roundup.

§

M crawls around the house like a healthy cockroach: darting and stopping, darting and stopping. He has been eating away at my brain as if it were made of papier-mâché; as long as he and I are housed in the same apartment, he will not go hungry. He is perched on my head, all six legs clutching it as if it were a strawberry. He would not notice it if I reached up and squashed him.

"Explain these keys!" M demands. He has found them in my pocketbook. He had hoped to find something incriminating, and he has. I don't know whether I should tell the truth to Mr. Roach, or let him feel it out of me with his antennae. He would not even realize that truth is part of me . . . he would think it was a wall, a book, a shelf . . . his own truth, something for a roach to crawl over or eat the paint from.

Naturally I lie.

"These? These must be old keys. You know I never throw anything away. Probably from our apartment on East Broadway."

"We gave those to the new tenants," M says. He falls on his back as if poisoned. The couch groans with him. M has been frantic all day about another matter, the matter of his ouster from school. The students have gotten up a petition to remove him. So, he is focusing on me to relieve the tension. It doesn't do me any good.

M holds the keys up. They ring against each other. They are gold keys hung on an elastic ribbon. One has a round top, the other is oval with a knob above the hole. Both are serrated, lined, fluted, flattened, indented, duplicated, and named: Cole National.

Yes, I thought they would open the way to pleasure for me.

§

Lita is so lovely. She has given me the keys to her apartment. She is a photographer and world traveler, I wonder why she is being so generous? Is she interested in me? She walks back and forth in the nude as she explains how to use the keys:

"Remember the gate downstairs, on the second floor? You can use the key, but you can also reach in and flip the latch with your fingers."

"Good," I say, "sounds easy."

She brings me a glass of Burgundy. It is pretty good American wine from California "11" Brands. It leaves no bitter taste. It leaves a hint of grape, which is probably what wine lovers mean by bouquet. It is elusive. Once I have decided that it is elusive, I drink it down like water, without tasting it at all. I don't want to pretend it is vintage, and must be savored. Wine bores me and puts me to sleep.

"This is where I keep the liquor. You're welcome to anything I have . . . whatever is in the refrigerator too."

Lita's kitchen is tiny. She cooks on a two-burner hot plate. There is a small sink against the wall (she has to do her dishes immediately; there is no room for them to pile up in). A bunch of red onions hangs from a nail on the wall.

"And don't drink the milk; I think it's sour," she says.

"Oh, and I've put clean towels in the bathroom . . . so just make yourself at home."

We go into the bedroom. She smiles knowingly at me, rips the bedspread off with a burst of energy. "I changed them for you," she says.

I imagine the tender sapling J, playing bridegroom; with me behind the softest of cambric veils. I thank the handmaiden Lita. She gives me additional information: the name of her hotel in Hawaii, in case her boyfriend calls and wants to know where she is; her maid's number; the number of her liquor store.

§

Lita is gone, and I am in possession of the apartment. Yet I feel that she is watching me. That her sheets, her glasses, her telephone are receiving minute impressions of me for her. That after I leave, no matter how expertly her maid tidies the place, she will be able to smell my breath breathing back at her from the mouthpiece of the phone, taste my lips on her glassware, hold my body in her arms as if she is J.

§

My cousin writes to invite me to her home in Washington. M thinks I have accepted the invitation. Instead I go to Lita's apartment on 57th Street. J has promised to meet me there. It took me an hour on the phone to persuade him; he thinks he is seeing me for the last time. We've been through this before.

§

He is an hour late. Two wine glasses are set on the table. Music is playing. I am wearing a transparent blouse and no brassiere. I call J . . . June answers.

"How are you?" I ask, not ready to inquire about J . . . I am afraid that he has gone to a museum, or a movie, to avoid me.

"I have a foot infection," June says.

"How did that happen?" I ask, amazed that it is always the dancer's foot, or the pianist's finger, or the singer's throat that gets hurt or sick.

"I got mad at J for prowling around the house all day and not talking to me, and I kicked him. Tore a toenail . . . it got infected, that's what happened. Not very dramatic, but I had to cancel my class. I soak it every two hours. Say, could you hold the phone; I think I hear J at the door. I sent him shopping. Ah, good, here he is."

"Speak to you later then," I say, hanging up. So, it is not his fault he is late. I am happy all over again. I figure out how long it will take him to get to 57th Street. I give him half an hour.

Before the half hour is up, I go downstairs to wait between the two stores that are on either side of the house where Lita lives. It is a curious neighborhood to live in: nothing but places in which to spend large sums of money: banks, exclusive department stores such as Bendel's, art galleries, antique stores, import shops. To be honest, I must say that there is also, close by, a Chock full o' Nuts store. But this is a concession to the salesgirls and clerks who staff the expensive and chic places of business. I myself enjoy their shrimp-salad sandwiches, their chicken-salad sandwiches, and their tuna-fish-salad sandwiches, all of which taste exactly alike: like celery. I must look very suspicious, stepping in and out of the doorway, looking up and down the block to see if J is coming. My shoes are off and I'm juiced and I don't dare look too long in one direction, in case I miss him coming in the other.

I see him coming from the west. He must have taken the IRT and walked east.

"I thought you wouldn't be able to find it," I say.

"I found it," he answers.

When we go in I show him the gate trick. It clangs behind us. Then we walk up two additional flights.

I sit very close to him. He refuses a glass of wine. I kiss him. He draws away. I see he is going to be difficult.

"I thought you wanted to talk," he says coldly.

"I love you," I say. "I can't stand not touching you. All you have to do is come into a room and I know what it feels like to be had by a force of nature."

"You mean it?" His little-boy ego is flattered, even if he has come ostensibly to say goodbye; he wants his going to be pleasant, complimentary, an unnoticeable transition into "just good friends." He can't understand the attraction he has for me, or I for him. He thinks he can take one part of it, the sexual, and lock it away, leaving only our superficial conversations on science, astronomy, photography, mythology, politics to sustain us.

His smooth chest pleases me so much because M is so hairy.

I kiss his flesh even though he is being aloof. He is wearing his usual no undershirt, unbuttoned sport shirt outfit. I make him touch my breasts. They are so firm and young-looking. I want to go to bed with him in Lita's apartment . . . we would have all the time in the world . . . nobody to interrupt us.

"Jason," I say to him, "let me help you get your kingdom back."

"You know I hate to be called Jason," J says, pouting.

"C'mon, J, I'll help you get the golden fleece; don't you want it?"

J says, "No one can make the attempt and come back alive." J is playing games with me. He's okay now: he is not afraid of games. Only good boys are allowed to go out to play. J is a good boy. "How can you help me?"

I lead him into the bedroom. I am magical: I undress J and anoint his skin with so potent a salve that it will protect him from all harm; he will be able to retrieve the golden fleece.

He becomes excited.

He picks the fleece off a hanging branch with his sex, after I have sung a snake to sleep.

"If you are nice to me I will give you eternal youth," I say to J.

"How?" he asks, removing one sandal.

"I will always remember you exactly the way you are."

I do not want to remember J exactly as he is. But I promise.

I go down on him. He asks me to stop. He is very sensitive. His penis is wearing the golden fleece like a mantle. It has bugs in it. They are golden too. I pick them off one by one and cast them into a pillbox to save for threading a necklace. J gets bigger and bigger as I work around his sex. Finally his penis thrusts itself into my hand, as if it is the snout of an affectionate animal.

J turns traitor on me. He has an orgasm the minute he gets in.

"Didn't you notice I wasn't loving you?" he asks.

"No, I didn't notice it," I lie.

I have no rival: unlike Medea I have no one to send the lovely robe which envelopes its wearer in fearful devouring flames. I stand in front of

J wearing that robe myself: I drop dead . . . my very flesh melted away.

"J," I say, ". . . you have an ugly body and an ugly mind. And all the time I was seeing you, I slept with M too."

He stares at me in disbelief. His naïveté had led him to believe that, because J loved him, I could not, and would not sleep with M. He took it for granted.

We dress quickly, and he offers to help me pack my bag. I tell him, "No, thank you." When I am done packing, he carries the bag downstairs for me.

As I step into my dragon-pulled chariot, I can see that he is full of anger. He has lost more than a friend and lover; he has lost a sorceress.

In one legend it is said that Jason committed suicide. But when did he begin to affect remorse?

§

Do you really mean NEVER, when you say never?

§

When I saw Lita yesterday, I said, "Lita, do you still have your old apartment?"

"My God, the building's been torn down," she answers.

§

Size forty-four men's boxer shorts in baby blue: M is furious.

"I don't wear a size forty-four!" he shouts.

"Let me measure you," I offer, but I do not have a tape measure, I have a piece of cord and a ruler. I make M stand so that I can circle his girth with my cord.

"I know my size," he says, sucking his belly in.

When I tell him that he measures 43½ inches, he says, "You don't know how to measure. Why doesn't this house have any of the things other houses have . . . an ordinary tape measure?"

M lies down again. He asks me to measure him as he lolls there in fat. His belly flattens out. I measure forty-one inches. He is satisfied.

"Return those to the store tomorrow," M orders. "How did you ever imagine I was fat enough to wear the forty-fours?"

§

I have by an extraordinary stratagem blown M up. As he balloons out, he makes a low hissing sound. His parts unfold and fill with air. I plug his asshole so it won't escape. He floats out the door. He is wearing, for propriety's sake, a size forty-four baby-blue pair of boxer shorts, out of which pops a shocking-pink latex erection. As he passes over 34th Street, children wave to him. He is then screened by a tall building, but reappears on the other side as an ill-defined obscurity: black smoke has laid its residue on him. I hear M pray for rain to wash his surface. He prays so hard his cork pops out.

He deflates.

He crumples to a rooftop, his skin rubbing together like the tissue of an empty stomach.

And a hole grows.

By the time I retrieve M, he is an empty pair of dirty underwear.

§

More underwear: this time it is J's T-shirt. He has forgotten it in my house. June made him wear it, so he lost it. The name tape pressed to the inside of the neckline says: CAMP GULLIVER. I actually blush when I read that. Last year he was young enough to go to camp. Oh, J! (J!)

§

J, I've decided to go to a football game with M. You're invited and so is Charles Thomas. Charles Thomas has shoulder pads and his own football to kick around. He blocks well. You're a natural fumbler. Want to play? You can fumble between the center and the quarterback. I've got a world of speed. M is on the offensive. He confuses me. I have trouble keeping out of his way. What I need is more grass drills and added weight.

§

J has just lost the ball again. How can he drop it? Charles Thomas has filled it with sand, that's how. He does not have to break J's arm. He does not have to take a crack at either elbow from underneath. But any method is valid if it makes the offense fumble. And J has lost the ball again. He doesn't get the point even though he has been trained to charge through a gauntlet of dozens of rubber straps that automatically whip at the football.

"I'd rather eat a hot dog in the stands," J says.

The sun beats down on our heads. M has taken off his shirt. His hair, gleaming in the sun, traps him behind miles of tangled burnished wire. He drinks beer. He drinks wine from a special picnic basket prepared at the Brasserie. Charles Thomas empties the basket, and puts it on his head to prevent sunstroke. He takes off his Dashiki. He is not wearing shoulder guards. He is balancing a sweet potato pie on each shoulder. He asks me to take a piece of pie without removing the pie plate from his shoulder. I cannot.

§

"Is it true that M killed you because you wouldn't sleep with him?" I ask Charles Thomas.

"I think it have more to do with three hundred black students learnin' to dance in the spotlight."

"Then why didn't he just kill the spot?"

"The spot don't bleed."

§

As I lie on the massage table, blue light from the sunroom spreads over the ceiling. I smell ultraviolet . . . alcohol . . . sweat . . . sesame seed oil. The masseuse zigzags one display of vitality after another, twisting handfuls of me, working the spine, hacking the fat with pseudo karate chops that leave me invigorated instead of relaxed.

Below each knee is an indented circle left there by the elasticized cuff of my knee socks. M bought them for me so that I might look like a schoolboy! They are part of an outfit which is very chic: a one-piece leather short overall.

"Turn over please," the masseuse says.

I have to tell myself that she's seen everything, before I lie on my hack. M made me shave my pubic hair. I feel so naked.

"Had an operation?" the masseuse asks.

"Yes, but I have doctor's permission to take massage. You can be as rough as you like with me. Do everything you usually do."

Charles Thomas runs his tongue along the soles of my feet, between my toes: "I wouldn't do this if you wasn't clean," he says.

"I love it," I say. "I've loved it ever since I saw a handsome actor lick the stage. He loved the stage. He licked himself across the stage. I cried encore!"

Charles Thomas doesn't need applause. He hears those little patsy-watsy strokes dance off my skin, and takes a bow.

The masseuse assaults him as he bends down, as if she is supervising a toilet training session: she beats him about the buttocks, genitals, and head. However, he wets his pants for spite, and leaves an excremental offering in the tip plate. It is more than she usually receives.

"I wish people would stop fooling around with the air conditioning. God what conditions to work under!" the masseuse says.

J wheels the massage table down the corridor. He says I am running a fever and must be isolated. We are followed by Charles Thomas and the muscular masseuse. They each carry a bag of ice cubes to pack me in.

"Will you be here when I thaw out?" I ask J.

He melts the center of an ice cube with his hot young breath, and puts the cube on my finger. It sparkles.

"I'll always be here," he says, catching the ring drops as they weep from my finger.

The half-hour massage is over.

Yes, J, you have successfully isolated me.

§

J, darling.

If you play dead, you die.

Remember our first kiss?

I remember our first kiss in the Great Northern Hotel, on the steps that led nowhere. You ran up the stairs and knocked on the wooden panel, "Look," you said, "they don't go anywhere." It was your discovery . . . but, baby . . . things leading nowhere are prevalent . . . and people who are nowhere are boarded up behind useless stares . . . and old lovers are buried behind brick walls in abandoned cellars.

Forgive me.

§

M is drinking again. He began at the football game. I have to be careful; he is armed and dangerous. We are locked into the apartment. If he begins sniping out the window . . . M says that he doesn't care whether he lives or dies. I care. I don't want to see him punched full of holes as he tries to run for cover.

Once we traveled across the country, and in most small diners or groceries where we stopped, they sold chances: a punchboard stuffed with tiny rolled-up names. The idea was to punch out a winning name. We punched Winnie; the winning name turned out to be Blanche. The waitress lifted a small round seal at the top of the punchboard to prove to us that the winning name really was Blanche.

No matter how many holes are punched in M, he can't win. But he can lose with more chances than anyone.

"Let me call your mother?" I plead. M pulls the telephone wire out of the wall. There goes his last chance. She could have lured him out of the house with the promise of a warm bath and a back rub . . . and a cartridge belt still warm from being strapped across her naked hips. That's where she stores her lipsticks, each one an amorous bullet of color loaded with kisses meant to explode in M's face. I used to wonder what caused the gap below his nose. It isn't an ordinary mouth; it hasn't healed: there are teeth missing, and his gums bleed.

"Where's the champagne?" M asks. I bring a bottle of New York State champagne that was stashed away for our anniversary. May as well celebrate death . . . death is the long-awaited occasion. I pop the cork for M.

§

M has a bilateral temporal EEG abnormality. He experiences the sound of a ringing bell as a seizure aura. Occasionally he hears the same bell when he feels like exhibiting his penis. A doctor told me that compulsive genital display is linked to abnormal discharges in the temporal area. It was suggested that he be lobotomized. I did not agree that the punishment fitted the crime.

§

I reread the letter Charles Thomas has sent me from South Africa. I have locked myself in the toilet. When I am alone with the letter, I will tear it up and hush it away. If M suspects that I am a friend of Charles's he will kill me.

Dear Miss Melissa Johnson,

I'm lucky I'm alive. I was number 2001 to line up for going down the diamond mine. 50 men in front of me stumbled and fell over one another. Most got crushed. The narrow tunnel they died in leads directly from where we sleep in barracks to the mine.

I want you to tell my friends in the USA to picket the Chimerical Bunk New York Trussed Company for their support of South Africa's apartheid establishment . . . Chimerical Bunk also joined with Chaste Manhattan and Thirst National Titty to lend $40 million directly to the South African Government.

Make a big sign, sugar . . . carry it for me.

No chance of copping a diamond down here: these cats investigate everybody's shit with a fine-toothed comb. Later, baby.

Charles

§

There is guilt by association. I remember Lew Harris's wife asking me to empty my handbag on her table. She wanted to make sure I wasn't packing a pistol. Wish I had one now. What would I do with it? Shoot myself out of the toilet?

The bullet might shatter an object of great sentimental value. A gift J gave me. He made it himself . . . a clay sculpture of a cat. The cat is curled up (J's favorite position). June and I marveled at how well done it was. I told M I bought it in the village.

§

J has found a way to capture the sun's rays and separate them. He has made a chromo lens. The lens is made of glass which is double convex and hollow; it is seven inches in diameter and will hold forty-two ounces.

He has made it in different colors, but, he says, "It does not constitute a lens until filled to the neck with a transparent liquid." When hanging in the sun, it receives the most exquisite medical elements into the water according to its color. It is potent. J is a scientific genius; he has also built a color wheel with removable discs (every color of the spectrum). He says that for every color there is a corresponding drug, for example:

Red, arterial stimulant—drug, ammonia.
Orange, lung builder—drug, carbonate of lime.
Yellow, cathartic—drug, calomel.
Yellow-green, cleanser—drug, chlorides.
Blue-green, cleanser—drug, boric acid.
Blue, alleviator of pain—drug, citric acid.
Indigo, astringent—drug, aconitum.
Violet, motor nerve depressant—drug, opium.
Yellow-violet, digestant—drug, chloral hydrate.
Violet-red, emotional stabilizer—drug, digitalis (foxglove).
Blue-red, cardiac energizer—drug, potassium nitrate.

I do not believe his claim that blue-charged water can cure an obstinate case of dandruff! June places J directly in front of the blue disc to quiet his nerves.

J says, "Blue vibrates 658,000,000,000,000 (trillion) times per second."

June says, "Although the green rays are good for head colds, boils, croup, eyestrain, hay fever, whooping cough, and nerve exhaustion, it aggravates cases of insanity."

She is staring fixedly at my green dress. This is a humane reason for me to remove my clothes. I don't know what to do about my mouth which I have rinsed with a chlorophyll mouthwash. June gives me a glass of solarized milk to neutralize my breath. I give off a philosophical yellow aura. J is calmed by my presence.

There is a red disc on the color wheel. My love and I bask in its sexy hot rays.

J is jealous of Charles Thomas. He knows I am seeing him. It prompts him to discuss the color black. "What kind of world would we be living in if it were composed of black, brown, and gray? Black clouds fill me with terror. Black means concealment and repression: the negation of pure spirit. It indicates hatred, malice, revenge, and low feelings . . . 'dark forces' . . . 'black magic' . . . necromancers (those who deal out death) . . . black is foreign and hostile to life."

J is a poor example of the infinite power of life and love. He has lost his center of luminosity.

§

J is at June's dance concert. There is no stage. It is in a loft. We are seated on the floor. There are two ladders among us. The concert has not yet begun. J is seated next to me against the wall. We are hugging our knees. J stands up. He takes a young girl by the hand, pulls her toward me as if she is a toy on wheels. I expect her to make a quacking sound every time the wheels go round. J hands me the string. I tentatively jerk her toward me. J has brought me an educational toy, one I would like to take apart and not put together again.

"This is Noreen," he says, introducing her to me.

They stand there adoring each other . . . pressing hands the way J and I used to. Is he innocent? Or is he trying to hurt me? Or are they part of the dance concert?

The lights go out.

From my seated position I kiss J's knees, his thighs; I put my hand up his trouser leg; he limps away as if I am an old war injury. The fourteen-year-old girl and J merge, wearing the same shadow. . . . June and three men, all in white overalls, enter: they cross each other's paths diametrically. June drags one ladder to another spot; she walks under it. The remaining ladder is rushed by the three male dancers . . . they knock it down and climb on it as it lies collapsed upon the floor.

The lights go out.

A flood spot goes on.

June is seen on the top rung of a ladder. She takes a paper flag out of her overall pocket and waves it. She has conquered a mountain, a moon, a parade . . . the men bear her away on the ladder.

We drink weak punch and ask, "Did you like it?"

I ask J, "Did you like it?"

With a question like that there is always a divergence of opinion. The young girl answers, "Like what?"

§

J leaves with the girl. We are to remain apart for a while. June approves of the separation . . . my affair with J is incestuous.

§

When we were first married, we had no furniture, but we had a sense of order, so we bought two large cardboard cartons: Singlewall F74. We marked one SUMMER, and the other WINTER. Into the WINTER carton we put the heavy things. I am lighter than M, so when he was angry with me, he'd bury me in the SUMMER carton with my belongings. At first this frightened me: I'd be afraid of smothering. After a year of being packed away, I used to race for SUMMER whenever M's eyebrows joined in a furry peak above his nose. I got to love being in the box: being in the box was not like being anywhere else.

Was not like being.

§

A woman.

§

A box.

§

I resist the idea of buying a vibrator, though orgasmic one-upmanship intrigues me. I want to break my record. There are two kinds of vibrator that I know of: the one that looks like a blind flashlight, and the one that has a water-cooled motor (and rides strapped to your hand). The latter palsies the hand itself, so that when masturbating, you can vibrate your genitals into orgasm without tiring. The other makes its dull presence known by filling the space and jarring it!

I imagine spending long sultry afternoons alone with my mechanical Robot . . . eventually, after long intimacy, daring to call it Rob.

M comes home early one sultry afternoon, and follows the plugged-in electric cord to the bed, where I am busy reaching plateau after plateau of joy.

"Bitch . . . butch . . . borscht . . . botch!" he insults my body.

"Don't you dare talk that way to me!" I shout indignantly. "Can't you see that I'm well connected?"

§

There are two bowls on the table. One is turned over. The inverted bowl has captured the demons that torment J. The empty bowl is a writ banishing me from my marriage to M. Written on the bowl is the statement that I am forthwith expelled stark naked and with disheveled hair.

So that I can do no more harm, M hires an artist to draw a picture of me on the bowl, nude, with flying hair, my arms tied, and feet chained.

We have cornflakes for breakfast in ancient crockery.

§

"You want to be better than I am," M accuses, as I manage to open a jar of pickles he has failed with. I should have heeded *Cosmopolitan*'s warning to women: NEVER OPEN A JAR YOURSELF IF THERE IS A MAN HANDY. APPEAR HELPLESS, HE LIKES IT THAT WAY.

Because of the jar of pickles which I so rashly attacked and conquered, I suppose that M is not going to date me again. He was about to take me to see *The Wild Bunch* (advertised as a "blood ballet").

"I don't want to be you at all," I say. His remark is a commonplace . . . a masculine idea . . . I am already better than he is.

§

I have never wanted to own a penis: out of curiosity I hold a banana out front to see what it would be like. It looks strange . . . it is in danger of being lopped off, or at least peeled. I think it will last longer if it is not peeled (peeled it will grow rotten faster, or somebody will eat it up). In all fairness to penises, breasts also are in danger of being lopped off. People who stand out are in danger too: I don't have to name those who were cut down in their prime.

§

Prima-vera.
Must we all be the same in order to exist together?
Prima-inter-pares.
I am first among equals.

§

M says that God did not create woman from man's rib, since the rib is still there.

§

I am the marrow and the splint. I am everybone. I am the tissue and the lie. I am everybone. I am the cartilage and the cap. I adapt to bear the strain of pressure. I glide smoothly. I provide support. I am the skeleton. I am everybone. I am twelve pairs of ribs I let man breathe. I afford strength: the humerus. I afford strength: the femur. My pelvis is a basin. I wash the human race.

I am:
skull
cervical vertebrae
clavicle
scapula
sternum
ribs
humerus
ulna
radius
ilium
sacrum
coccyx
pubis
ischial tuberosity
femur
patella
tibia
fibula
calcaneus:
I am the skeleton in God's closet.

I am also woman who is interested in structures: in the architecture of survival. And I know that M wants to disown me. He would he happiest in an all-male world.

"You're soft and boneless," M says to me.

"I'll rattle same as you when I'm dead," I say.

M pinches me to show how soft I am. I cook supper.

§

Sometimes Charles Thomas's patina varies from red to black, sometimes mat, sometimes shiny (when he makes love he is polished). His esteemed color is not merely ornamental; it gives a clue as to his life: he has been used.

§

"I once had a real mother when I was twelve years old," Charles says to me. "She was a great lady."

"I didn't know you knew your real mother," I say.

"Didn't you know I was with her till I was thirteen?" He takes my hand and looks sincerely into my eyes. I interpret the look as being a sincere one.

"My husband told me you just found out that you are a foster child."

"He's lyin' in his teeth," Charles Thomas says.

"Oh, I'm so glad," I say, and kiss the tip of his ear.

"I can prove it," he says. "You know how great my mom was? Remember, she is a black woman, with none a those white hang-ups; well, I was a pretty naïve twelve-year-old, and I was in my room, by myself, masturbating. I never done it before. I didn't know what it was . . . I came out of the room with this white stuff in my hand, and I showed it to my mom. 'Mom, what's this stuff?" I asked her. 'That's your seed, son,' she said. 'That's life comin' out.' I love my mother. I got no complaints."

§

Charles Thomas takes me to the cemetery where his mother is buried. He can't find her grave. "Guess she don't have no tombstone," he says.

We stand above an unmarked grave that may he hers.

I have brought an offering; it is a Karner butterfly mounted behind glass: brown, edged in white, with brushings of blue on the wings; there are ten sections of blue on its double round tail, ending in tiny cuticles of red above brown dotted tips. J netted it as it was resting on a heavenly blue lupine, in full bloom, on the valley floor of Yellowstone National

Park.

"What was your mother like?" I ask.

"Not like this," he says, as he lays the Karner butterfly to rest on a dry mound of earth. "She were more like a owlet moth: dark and grimy from the places she live in. In a few hundred years, if the air don't get no cleaner, all you Ofays gonna be black. It's a fact."

§

J has decided to go to the moon. It is the refuge, the true homeland of lunatics.

"But what will you do up there?" I imagine that he will bounce over the lunar landscape like silly-putty.

"Oh, I'll bounce around, take a dip in the Sea of Tranquillity. And I'll be laden with hand tools, camera, and antennae, including an Early Apollo Scientific Experiments Package, which will transmit information to earth. It's something I've always wanted to do."

He models his own special lunar surface suit with its associated "portable life-support system."

"You'll be lonely," I say, peering into his helmet.

"No, I won't! I'm not the only one going; they're sending the Chronics, the Incontinents, the Orphaned-Others, the Addictesses, the Inconsolables, and the Indigents, on sister flights. We're the new pioneers. Once they didn't know what to do with us . . . there was no room on earth . . . now we are to take our place in history, when there is unlimited space."

"So, you are going to leave me!"

"With great speed: three thousand, one hundred mph, as I round the eastern rim of the moon. But we'll keep in touch . . . my multiple electronic-umbilical system will maintain the link between us . . . between us . . . between us . . . between us. . . ."

§

M and I are in bed. As soon as he gets an erection, I slip out of bed. He joins me. We stand face to face.

"Why did you get out of bed? Why?" he asks.

I take hold of his erection and crank it up and down.

"The prick lifts the man," I say, laughing. "It's the leverage theory."

M illustrates my theory. He stretches taller and taller.

§

M's breath is being conveyed in sealed tanks from Washington to upper New York State. Dissident groups object, saying that in case of an accident (the tanks are going by rail) whole townships may be endangered. I know that M's breath is bad, but I hadn't suspected it was lethal.

M denies it is his breath they have managed to derail.

"What is it then?" I ask, pointing to the bill of lading.

"Farts from the last world war," M answers.

§

"No, I can't sleep," I tell M.

"I'll stay up with you," M says.

The phone rings. It is Lita. Unusual for her to call so late. "I'm ill," she says. "I must have some warm milk and there are no grocery stores open in my neighborhood. Could you possibly bring me a quart of milk?"

I have an extra quart of milk. I put it in a bag.

"Where do you think you're going?" M asks, putting himself between me and the door. I explain about Lita, making her sound far sicker than she is. I want to get out! M lets me go after I promise to bring back the morning papers.

§

Lita is not alone. She is with a man. She feels fine.

"What am I supposed to do with the milk?" I ask. It is warming in my arms. Lita kisses me on the lips and takes the milk container away. Her friend kisses me on the lips too. Sitting between them on the antique couch, I begin to feel erotic and examine the living-room chandelier around which Lita has twisted flowers.

"Would you like something to drink?" Lita asks me.

"No."

"Some herb tea?"

"No."

The man stands up.

"Why don't we go to the bedroom; it's more comfortable in there," Lita says. She takes my arm and whispers into my ear, "Be nice, you'll have a good time. Paul is a lovely person . . . he loves to make love."

I've always wondered whether Lita's photography supported her entirely. As I watch Paul precede us, familiarly, to the bedroom, I surmise that he is a semi-customer.

To get to the bedroom we go through a narrow hallway which is also the bathroom, containing a bath-shower on the left, and a beveled glass window on the right. The toilet is small and separate. I excuse myself and go into the toilet. Lita has decorated it with life studies of nudes, and pornography. I wash my hands, and as they soap each other I THINK sex.

"I'm going to take my clothes off," Lita says, doing so immediately. "Would you like to take your clothes off?"

"No," I say.

"What's the matter with you tonight?" Lita asks. "You didn't want anything to drink, and now you won't take your clothes off." She laughs at me, and brazenly shows herself off. She stands in front of the huge four-poster brass bed, cupping both breasts in her hands. "Paul, make her take her clothes off!"

Paul embraces me. He draws my hand over his erection. "It's for you," he says, "if you take your clothes off."

Dumbly I refuse. I am not comfortable with strangers.

He undresses. They tussle on the bed, giggling and whispering. They grab me. I fight back. They can't believe it. Neither can I.

"Don't be a drag," Lita says. "We won't hurt you. We just want to play . . . like little children."

The Tiffany lamp is softly glowing. The large mirror swinging between heavy mahogany posts is waiting for my naked image.

"Put out the light," I say . . . my one condition.

"Your friend is definitely lower class," Paul says to Lita as he turns off the light.

He lies beside me.

Where is Lita?

She is kissing me.

He puts his penis in.

Where is Lita?

She is kissing his ass.

He likes it. It makes him more excited. But he is concentrating on me, and ignoring her. She falls to the floor.

"You have a beautiful cunt," he says to me.

"Is he clean?" I ask Lita.

"He's a friend of mine," she answers.

"Where are my pants?" I ask frantically. It is late and I have to get back to M. We look on all the chairs, in the bed, on the floor. The pants cannot be found.

"Oh, I know," Lita says. She pulls them out from under the bed. "The dog likes to chew on panties."

I put them on even though they are wet from dog spittle. Semen drips from me, making them even wetter. I plan to toss them into the wash as soon as I get home . . . to sleep with M immediately . . . that way, if I get pregnant, M will think the child is his.

§

There is a tendency to think of strangers as someone you don't know.

Yet, Charles Thomas and M know each other; but what do they know? M has not understood me for some time. He thinks my momentary moods: elation, depression, occur because I am reacting to him. I am not. I am reacting to my own chemistry. I would like to confide the vicissitudes of my life to him, but he might succumb to hating me and my friends, because of a little anecdote like this one, for instance . . . a trifle that is only mildly amusing; Lita and I are in a restaurant where they know her. She has invited me to be her guest. We are served our drinks fast enough, but after that, somehow the waiter ignores us. "I'll get his attention." Lita says. She takes off her blouse, under which she is wearing a see-through plastic bra. "It's the top of a bathing suit." She explains. "It sticks to me, but it looks great, doesn't it?" I touch it. The waiter comes over. "We'd like to give our orders now," Lita says. We order melon and hearts of artichoke with lemon, and no main course. Lita rebuttons her blouse. "You know," she says disgustedly, "once I was the only one who'd flash tits in public, now everyone's doing it, and they consider me the Establishment."

§

The school auditorium: students are about to watch experimental films made by their peers. Each will have a specific theme: Communication, Freedom, Love, Peace, and Happiness.

Charles Thomas is working the projector; he has also contributed a can of film. His theme is Love. And the title of his movie is: *The Holy Triad*. It runs twenty-two minutes, is in black & white, 16mm.

M is seated in the darkened auditorium. He is one of the instructors planted there to keep order if things get out of hand. He is clutching his briefcase, which contains test papers, official forms, textbooks, and a handgun (nestling in a leather side pocket) .

The auditorium smells like a gymnasium. M is used to that. He takes a deep breath and gets comfortable. *The Holy Triad* is the first film on the program. M imagines it is about the father, the son, and the holy ghost played by blacks. He thinks this derisively and feels superior. The movie begins:

THE HOLY TRIAD

Shadowy figures enter a temple. It is surmounted with long golden tubes resembling the pipes of an organ or a brass bed. There is an investiture in reverse going on: the removal of trappings, and the retention of holy apparel which fits like skin. Because of a softly glowing lamp, fringed decently to conceal its bulbs, the religious personages are seen for a time only as black silhouettes. One of the personages falls to his knees, praying or imploring his prelate at extremely close range: their bodies are as one. The third divine is adhering to a strict routine of asepsis by drinking a murky purgative from his chalice.

M wishes the film were sharper visually. He formulates post-projection questions to ask the students in the audience. He wonders whether the film is saying something that he misses. He makes a few notes on a scrap of paper in the semidarkness of the auditorium, then continues to watch.

The purged cleric whispers a supplication into the ear of the kneeling prelate. He rises. All prostrate themselves before the temple of the Holy See . . . roll in a religious agony upon an imbricate velvet rug (its overlapping parts shot through with gold). A dog . . .

Symbolic of what? M tries to recall what he knows about Luis Buñuel and his use of the dog as a symbol.

. . . appears from under the dais with a holy relic in its teeth. The fragment, obviously the surviving memorial of a sacred person, is snatched from the dog's mouth and returned to its reliquary, where it may be preserved as worthy of veneration.

As the movie ends, a chorus of hallelujahs swells to fill the auditorium. M mounts the steps leading to the stage, grasps a lectern at each side, leans forward, and begins to pose the questions he has jotted down on the scrap of paper:

What does the triangle mean to you?
Is this a religious film?
What did the symbols you noticed point to?
Do you think that this film is a good visual prayer?
Does it express anything about communication between God and man?

But, Charles Thomas has made an experimental film, and the end is only the beginning. Even as M recites his penetrating questions, the film, frame by frame plays across M's broad, shiny forehead . . . this time everything is in sharp focus. M leaves the stage, returns to his seat, and faces the screen.

He does not see a religious allegory.
He does not see the triangle as a tendency of the universe to converge toward a point of unity.
He sees me, my best friend Lita, and a bare-assed male fucking each other on a big brass bed!
The dog has stolen my panties.

A superwave of shame hits M, yet he watches in shocked fascination as the film reveals to him what he has already imagined more than once. Rage fills him. He shoves his way through the whistling, sucking, hanging, shouting students who are having a ball. Charles Thomas has made a grand coup!

M rushes upstairs to the projection room. The door is locked. He pounds on it with all his might as the film continues.

§

"You ever been blackmailed by a black male?" Charles Thomas asks.

"Are you referring to that shitty little sexploitation movie you made at Lita's?" I ask.

"Yeah."

"What kind of a price tag do you put on it?"

"At least a three-million-dollar bill!"

"Are you asking for that kind of financing on the basis of 'name' performers?"

"Yeah!"

§

M's mother is painting a portrait of him from memory and photographs. The photographs are pinned to her bulletin board, and spread on the floor. She works with fast intense strokes; she attacks the canvas. M's face appears to be that of a cherub: pink and smooth.

"He doesn't look that way anymore," I say.

"What do you know about it?" she retorts, adding a dot of white to his eye so that it sparkles. She is concerned only with saving him in art.

"The cops searched our apartment and found a pistol," I say. She shakes her head in good-humored disbelief.

The portrait progresses. What began in natural light is flooded with artificial.

"He's an excellent subject," his mother says. "He can hold a pose for hours." There is no wind to ruffle the photographs. Her breath, as she scrutinizes the photographs, causes them to flutter and shift. She returns to the canvas: the photographs settle. He has always obeyed her covert instructions.

From a long way off, over days, months, years, he comes hastening toward her, "There, now I have him. Don't you think it's him?" She steps back, measuring proportions with a paintbrush, holds it in front of her. She then gazes through a refraction glass . . . he retreats.

"Yes," she says. "Yes."

§

J says: "You must free yourself from the tomb of the flesh before you can range the cosmos at will . . . like me."

I say: "But I have not yet admitted that I have a body."

§

J must tour the zodiac alone. Sirius, the Dog Star, lights the way, but eats five pounds of meat daily, and bites strangers. Sirius is a swift and high-nosed dog of great beauty. J has sent me from the heavenly workshop a carving of Sirius in pigstone, a limelike substance mixed with sulfur which, when rubbed, gives off a smell of cat urine, rotten eggs, and sulfur. I place the carving next to my copy of *A Diary from Dixie*. I open it to page 213 by chance. I say to myself, "Whatever I read will be oracular and eternal." Then I read the line: "Battle after battle results in disaster after disaster. Every morning's paper reports enough to kill a well woman, or to age a strong and hearty one." True.

§

The monsoon rains have started like a rain of bullets.

The wind blows from the southwest on M, in his Laotian garrison. He has gone where it is not only legal to kill, but mandatory. And he has escaped the police for a while. But the monsoon rains have started, and it is particularly disconcerting to fight in the midst of devastation to create more devastation. M likes it.

M likes to see whole trees in motion, almost breaking.

As the air fills with spray and the sea is covered with streaking foam, M loads his gun.

At home, I keep busy making batik . . . I hand-print cotton cloth painstakingly with hot wax and dye. I have been at it for six months.

Charles Thomas has been taunting me: he calls, and when I say that I don't want to see him, he serenades me with "Yankee Doodle," accompanying himself on a bamboo instrument called an Aklung. His version of "Yankee Doodle" plays havoc with the old political verse:

> Yankee Doodle went to war
> Stuffed with hot baloney
> He stuck a finger up his ass
> And pulled out lots of money.

M's garrison has been captured by the Pathet Lao and North Vietnamese . . . it is a landmark in the war for the Communists. Now, I hear, there will be no letup; the Communist troops will be able during the October-April dry season to recapture the territory they held before the 1962 Geneva agreement—the northern two-thirds of the country. I am a war widow.

§

June once said to me: "If you didn't want to be with M, you wouldn't be. You are not forced to stay with him."

Of course she's wrong.

§

"J, you wait outside."

It is J's birthday. I go into the French bakery to pick up a cake I ordered for him; it has real butter-cream icing, and is decorated with a moon scene: two plastic astronauts beside a rocket. It is a little boy's cake. The vanilla icing (titanium and pearl) resembles the surface of the moon. The French, using only pure ingredients, have baked a fresh planet; we shall be the first to taste it. (Which proves you can destroy your planet and share it too.)

"Where shall we eat it?" I ask J. He wonders where the best place would be, then says, "Let's go back."

"Back where?" I ask.

"Follow me," he says.

I follow J back many eons. "If we go too far back, the cake will spoil," I say.

"We'll eat it as we go," J declares.

FIRST BITE: J is in the water; he is no different than the swollen crumbs floating around him. He is evolving. He is in my womb. It will take him nine months to crawl out. Before his lungs inflate, his gills will heal shut and his element will no longer be water, but air and earth.

SECOND BITE: J is in the water, but he cannot drown: I am growing him to save him. Twice, I have given birth to him, and twice kept a piece of the umbilical cord. Before it was tied and cut, I painted it gentian violet. Now, in my hand it has turned to leather.

"Is that really what tied me to you?" J asks, lacing his shoes with it.

"Don't be irreverent," I caution him.

THIRD BITE: J is no longer the size of an English pea. It is the eighth week, in which he has become a fetus. Before this time it would have been impossible to determine by observation whether he was going to be a human being, a pig, a goat, a dog, or a monkey. See how undetermined he really was before I took him into me.

FOURTH BITE: He looks very funny . . . all slits . . . bulging high forehead . . . asexual. A calcifying shrimp out of the shell.

FIFTH BITE: J is a parasite: he accepts my maternal contributions: food, shelter, a sewage

	system.
SIXTH BITE:	He floats within the closed membrane which absorbs shock, and rearranges his position. His ear becomes functionally alive: it allows him to balance himself. How did he become unbalanced? "I cut off my ear and gave it to you," J says. "Don't be irreverent about equilibrium," I caution.
SEVENTH BITE:	I am constantly aware of J's movements. I have been spying on him for three months. "Why were you having me followed?" J asks. "I wanted to deposit a layer of fat beneath your lean skin, so that you'd survive in the external world. You had lost your covering of silky hair."
EIGHTH BITE:	J weighs five pounds. His nails project: they are soft and bendable. His body is rounded, his skin is no longer red . . . but he is not complete. He is correlated in the tenth and last lunar month before his birthday; it is then that the finishing touches are accomplished.
NINTH BITE:	J comes out. It is a boy . . . it is a triumph of Y over X. "Did I hurt you?" J asks, offering me the last bit of birthday cake.

"Yes," I answer. "During the second stage."

J throws the plastic moon scene away. "I'm no longer a child!" he insists spitefully.

"Well then, kiss me and prove it," I say.

Before M comes home, I sweep away the crumbs and vacuum the

couch. I look in the mirror. My face is red. I'm still excited. J and I had intercourse in the seated position. He gets more sophisticated every day.

§

M is holding on to his job. They won't allow him to teach, but they have assigned him to lunchroom duty. He is the supervisor, and is expected to create a smooth-functioning lunchroom.

The new lunchroom is in the basement. All windows are screened from the inside. There are two entrance-exits. Five hundred students fill the lunchroom each lunchroom period. This leaves little room for unrestricted movement by the students. All doors leading to the food area are shut about ten minutes prior to the ringing of the warning bell. Students are directed over a loudspeaker when to line up for food. Silverware tokens must be purchased for twenty-five cents at the beginning of the term. The silverware token is exchanged for a set of silverware by the cashiers at the time food is purchased. Three or four calls for silverware are made at intervals over the loudspeaker system, at which time the students are to return the silverware to a specified area and given their tokens in return.

The lunchroom has been divided into six sections. Walls adjacent to the tables are marked with a large letter: A, B, C, D, E, or F. The seniors sit in section A. This remains constant. Each student must register for a permanent seat at a table in his designated section. Any student failing to register is subject to disciplinary action.

This is the perfect job for M.

§

Dear Mrs. Johnson,

I expect you to meet me at Times Square for a silent vigil at 7 P.M. today. We'll walk with candles up Sixth Avenue to the Central Park lake at 60th Street and Fifth Avenue, where the Lantern Boat Ceremony will begin at 9 P.M.

You are invited to construct your own lantern boat beforehand if you wish. Instructions are: paper sides top and bottom, board at bottom 4" across (with candles stuck on; height of sides 7"). Peace messages and designs around outside of lanterns requested.

Enclosed, please find flier explaining the Lantern Boat Ceremony.

Sincerely,
Mr. Charles Thomas

Peace Message for a Lantern

WELCOME ALL WELCOME ALL WELCOME ALL

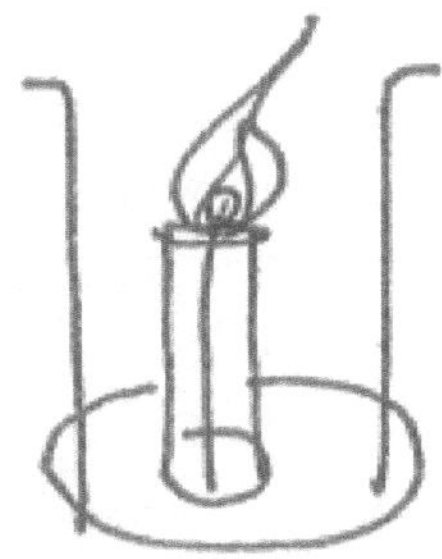

The Lantern Boat Ceremony is a re-enactment of the Japanese Bon Festival, a traditional Buddhist observance. The festival has its origins in ancient India where it was celebrated at the end of the monsoon season and marked a time of reflection and rededication upon the resumption of normal daily pursuits. In Japan it has become a festival for honoring one's dead ancestors, praying for peace, and celebrating the spirit of giving. Since the war, in Hiroshima and Nagasaki the Bon Festival has become the annual commemoration of those who died in the nuclear disasters of 1945. Relatives of those who were lost float lanterns on the rivers of the cities in memory of their loved ones and as a prayer for world peace.

§

Charles Thomas and I meet secretly at the water's edge. We put our lanterns in the water. They float out to join other lanterns bobbing like giant fireflies in the lake.

"I don't have no dead ancestors," Charles Thomas says. "They all alive and well in Mississippi. My grandma is one hundred and six years old, my grandpa is one hundred and twenty, and I ate one hundred and sixty-nine pancakes with melted butter on them."

"What does a full stomach have to do with a full life?" I ask Charles Thomas.

"Well, let me explain," he says. "Let's go sit on the grass."

We sit on a hill not far from the lake, where we can still see the lanterns. Charles Thomas sits with his back comfortably against a tree. I lie down, my head in his lap. He speaks in a gentle lulling voice, as if recounting a bedtime story to a beloved child.

Once upon a time there was a black boy in Harlem, where black children abound, and hunger is an everyday affair. This little black boy had a black mother. And his black mother got him a beautiful little used red coat donated by the welfare, and a beautiful little pair of torn jeans, and a beautiful cracked plate to eat off of, and a lovely little pair of sturdy charity shoes with rubber soles and no linings. And then wasn't Little Black Charles grand! But he was hungry. So he put on all his fine clothes and went out for a walk in the jungle to see what he could cop. And by and by he met a pusher who said to him, "Little Black Charles, you wanna be really grand?"

"Sure do," Little Black Charles said.

"You wanna get you some lovely little purple shoes with crimson soles and paisley linings?"

"Sure do," Little Black Charles said.

"You wanna get you some groovy threads that the other cats gonna throw up with envy when they dig you comin' down the street?"

"Sure do," Little Black Charles said. "Whut I gotta do to get all that stuff?"

"All you gotta do is make some deliveries for me . . . but you gotta be circumspect . . . dig?"

"I'm hip!" Little Black Charles said.

"You gonna make your mamma a happy lady," the pusher said. He gave the little boy a package, and an address, and sent him on his way. But somewhere along Lenox Avenue, Little Black Charles met a big Honky-Nark.

"Where you goin', Little Black, an' what you got in that package?" the Honky-Nark asked.

"I ain't goin' nowheres, and I ain't got nothin' in that package," Little Black Charles answered.

And the Honky-Nark said to him, "Little Black, I'm goin' to eat you up, even though you're dark meat and probably on the tough side, unless you give me that package."

And Little Black Charles said, "Oh! Please, Mr. Honky-Nark, don't eat me up, and I'll give you my beautiful little red coat with three buttons down the front and a pocket for each hand. You kin have it for your own kin . . . only don't do me no harm."

"I ain't got no use for that stinkin' rag," the Honky-Nark said. "Give me that bag you're holdin' so tight."

So Little Black Charles he run as fast as his little legs could carry him, away from the growlin' Honky-Nark who was takin' perfect aim at his head with a revolver. But Little Black Charles run so fast he whizzed up the street faster than the speed of bullets. He ran away, sayin', "It sure hard to get to be the grandest Little Black in the jungle."

And Little Black Charles went on, and by and by he met another Honky-Nark, and his heart beat faster with fear because he was afraid this Honky-Nark would burn him, and then his beautiful black mamma would never get to be a happy lady.

"Little Black, I'm gonna eat you up, even though you're dark meat, and dark meat don't agree with me, unless you give me that package you're holdin'," the Honky-Nark said.

And Little Black Charles said, "Oh! Please, Mr. Honky-Nark, don't eat me up, and I'll give you my beautiful little pair of torn Wrangler jeans for your very own."

"I ain't got no use for those trousers, unless I give them to a more deservin' little black boy. Here, come closer and let me examine them." But Little Black Charles knew the Honky-Nark was tryin' to hype him, so he took off down the street as fast as his little legs could carry him. He ran away, sayin', "I gettin' to be the speediest Little Black in the jungle, but when do I get to be the grandest Little Black in the jungle?"

And Little Black Charles went on, and by and by he met another Honky-Nark, and it said to him, "Little Black Charles, I'm goin' to smear the sidewalk with you unless you give me that suspicious package whut you holdin' under your arm." And Little Black Charles made a sound like a baby burpin' and said, "Oh! Please, Mr. Honky-Nark, don't smear the sidewalk with me, and I'll give you my prized possession, this recently repaired, sturdy pair of lace-up oxfords. They make a thoughtful gift for anyone whut's my size, and they don't smell much."

But the Honky-Nark said, "What use would them shoes be to me? I got four feet, and you got two; you ain't got enough shoes for me."

But Little Black Charles said, "Lessee you got four feet! I don't see but two. You almost human."

"You gotta believe whut I tell you, son," the Honky-Nark said, "and don't give me none of your lip!"

Then the Honky-Nark put his hand on the handle of a flat, vicious-lookin', blued-steel, eleven-shot, .38-caliber Colt automatic pistol that lay in his holster.

Before the Honky-Nark could draw his pistol out, Little Black Charles had made a clean getaway, the package still secure under his arm. He ran away, sayin', "I still ahead of the game, I got my clothes, and I got the goods, and I'm on my way, but I don't rightly know if I want to be that all grand in the jungle: maybe it grander to be grand on the beach." But that didn't slow him down none.

And by and by Little Black Charles came to a park at 135th and Convent Avenue. He was pooped from all that runnin' so he climbed into a tree to rest.

Presently he heard a horrible noise that sounded like "Nigrrrr-rrr-r-r-rrrrr, gr-r-r-r-rrrrrrrrrr!" and it got louder and louder. "Oh, dear!" said little Black Charles, "there are all the Honky-Narks comin' back to eat me up. Whut shall I do?" So he stayed in the tree which hid him from view, and peeked down to see what them Honky-Narks was cookin' up.

And there he saw all the Honky-Narks fightin', and disputin' which of them should stake out in the park to "hit" Little Black Charles when he show up. And at last they all got so angry that they began tearin' each others badges off'n their uniforms. And they came, rollin' and tumblin' right to the foot of the very tree where Little Black Charles was hidin'. And as he became more and more amused at the goin's-on of the Honky-Narks, his grip on the package loosened, and down it fell, right among the wranglin', tanglin' Honky-Narks. And so Little Black Charles climbed down out of the tree and hid behind a rock. And the Honky-Narks didn't care a snit about Little Black Charles anymore. They was fightin' for that special delivery H what had fell out of the tree. But one didn't dare let the other loose, so they held on for dear life. And they were so angry, that they ran around the tree, tryin' to eat each other up with their big white teeth, and they ran faster and faster, till they were whirlin' around so fast that you couldn't see their legs at all.

And they stomped the contents of the package into the dust at their feet, till it disappeared. And still they ran faster and faster, till they all just melted away, and there was nothin' left but a great big pool of melted butter round the foot of the tree.

"Oh!" said Little Black Charles, "what lovely melted butter! I'll take that home to Black Mamma for her to cook with, and then she be the happiest black mamma in the jungle."

So he put it all into his pockets, and took it home to Black Mamma to cook with.

When Black Mamma saw the melted butter, she wasn't so pleased. "Now," said she, "Where you git this rancid oil frum?"

And Little Black Charles told her the whole wonderful story, upon which she began to tremble with fear.

"Boy," she said, "you gonna hafta go away frum the jungle . . . far away! When that pusher find out that his dope is fertilizin' the shrubbery up at 135th and Convent, he gonna be after your ass, to put it politely."

So she got flour and eggs and milk and sugar, which she had been savin' for a grand occasion, and she made a big plate of most lovely pancakes. And she fried them in the melted margarine which tastes like the more expensive spread, and they were just as yellow and brown as the ones you get at B & G's.

And they both sat down to supper. Little Black Charles felt far from grand, he felt real had. But his mamma's pancakes was so good and he was so hungry, that he ate a hundred and sixty-nine, before he left to stay with his grandma and grandpa down South.

§

June is on tour. J has been put away for his own safety. This is his second hospital. The first was a traditional lockup: visitors had to pass a desk, get checked off a list, then were let single file into a big room used for receiving guests. Inmates and visitors sat at trestle tables on long wooden benches, gorging themselves on food that had been hastily ripped from ordinary paper bags. Open garbage containers sat like honored guests at the head of each table. . . . It did not surprise me to see life-guards in nurse's uniforms, who used pitchforks instead of paddles to belabor the troubled waters of insanity.

§

"Did you get my crayons?" I ask J. And he keeps smiling.

When I ask the nurse about the missing crayons, she says that they are probably misplaced. I am sure they are. All the patients steal. They are cunning, they are stealthy . . . but they are observed.

§

I visit J at the more modern hospital. My God, there are so many windows, and none of them can be opened. The air conditioning is on. When I step out of the elevator there are no locked doors that must be unlocked before I reach J. He is in the recreation room. It looks like a living room, except that most of the people are wearing pajamas and bathrobe. One man sitting at the end of the couch seems to be sinking. Another man, a boy with a bald head, is dancing to music heard by himself alone; he crashes into me.

J is still smiling. He is allowed to keep his gifts, here. His fingers fan out on the table; between each one he places a crayon. He hears another visitor say something . . . his face lights up . . . he stands . . . bows to me . . . extends his hand: he believes me to be Marie Curie. He presents me with the crayons that have been transformed into pitchblende, and from which I isolate a new element: radium salts. During the visit we share the toils and tribulations of research: tear the paper off crayons, break them into impure masses, determine atomic weights and properties of both polonium and radium . . . we share with Becquerel the 1903 Nobel Prize in Physics for radioactivity work. And we scribble our discoveries on the torn pieces of paper that wrapped our food. J screams! He discovers a hole eating through his hand . . . the radium has done its dirty work. Visiting hour is over. An orderly pulls J away from me. I try to wash his tainted hand with tears. It is my new discovery; tears can't wash taint off. I am Marie Sklodowska Curie, but my tears cannot reach him.

They have taken my bright young assistant to an empty room with a surveillance window. They have taken off his clothes. They give him a playful pat on the behind before they lock the door behind them. He crouches in a corner, holding the hand away from him. It disintegrates before his very eyes, falling away down the line of his arm like a lit fuse. He knows that once it reaches his body, he will die.

§

M says to me, "If you had slept with J, you would be very guilty now."

"Why do you say that?" I ask.

"You would blame yourself for his illness."

"No, I wouldn't. If I had slept with him, and I didn't, but if I had, it would have kept him sane longer; maybe given him some of the happiest moments of his life."

"Maybe," M says. I wonder whether I contributed to J's breakdown.

§

J, darling, I had intended to speak to you about how it is my seventeen-year-old soul that loves you, but something interferes: the threat in my home: M. It is almost impossible to live with a madman who seems sane. (Would it be easier to live with a sane man who seemed mad?) He hates me and yet he will not give me up. I envy you in your cell, because you have lost your mind; I can't lose mine. You know, whenever M gives me orders: "Undress . . . don't move . . . express terror!" I try to faint or go somewhere else in my head, but can't. I wish that something would happen to me so that I could be taken away . . . rescued.

§

I call M's penis "The Threat." It is waiting for me when I wake up; at night it attempts to beat me over the head. It hangs in the air as M says, "I don't know why I should feel this way. I'm very hostile." He has his club in his hand, and I either make him feel better, or I will get it! I have just come out of a dream myself. I do not want to have sex with him. I ask, "Do you have to urinate?"

"I knew you'd say that," he says.

"Well, I do," I say, getting up and going into the bathroom. He stays in bed. It is going to be an unpleasant day.

§

If you build a mountain of sand, do not expect it to stay in one place. I laugh at this "deep" saying that I made up. After I laugh, I reflect that it has something to do with the disappearing solidity of my marriage.

§

One fly is in the kitchen with me. It is after that rotting fruit M stole from the school lunchroom. He is a scavenger like the gull. He does not like fruit. He asked me to make jams and jellies out of it. I don't know how to do that. So . . . the fruit rots.

J, I have a present for you . . . a seagull card. It squawks when you press the middle of the card. I have one last visit with you before you go to a hospital in upstate New York. Perhaps you can imagine that you are by the seaside, when the gull cries.

§

I thank my legs for carrying me to you.

"Legs, thank you."

"He's in here," the nurse says.

"This is the snack room," you say, making a malted. "I have a shelf in the refrigerator all to myself. June brings me milk, and cheese, and salami. I can come in here any time of the day or night and make myself a snack."

Other inmates are wandering around the kitchen with food and drink in their hands. The sun is melting a plate of butter on the windowsill. A nurse comes in. "Anybody want me to slice anything?" she asks. She has a knife in her pocket. Nobody pays any attention to her. She goes out.

"She's after my balls," J confides, biting into the whole salami.

"I don't think so," I say in all sanity.

"YOU don't think so!" It enrages J. He whips open his bathrobe. "Look at this!"

It is not time to faint with delight. He has managed to stuff his entire complement of genitalia between his legs. He looks like a girl. I want to force his legs open, to show him he's still there.

"It isn't the first time," he says. "She takes them away."

"What does she do with them?" I ask.

"She gives them to the chief pathologist, who is in love with her. He turns them to glass . . . she looks into them and foretells the future, which is evil."

"Your balls have never been crystal clear to me," I say. "They're full of milky-white sperm."

"They used to he full of sperm!" he shouts. "But now she has released them to the female ward . . . I'm fucking the whole world, but I'll never see my children."

"Where is your father?" I ask.

"He disappeared into Florida, he deserted me," J sobs.

"And whose fault is that?" I try to comfort him. I retrieve his penis, his balls . . . caress them in silence.

"It's the fault of the Tourist Bureau. They want everyone to travel," he reasons.

§

J has accused the Catholic Church of diverting man's vital energy to the service of a corpse. He escaped from the bus that was taking him to the asylum, and went directly to Riverside Church where a service was about to begin. He climbed the pulpit and shouted over the microphone: "Science is my universe!" A great organ started to play and drowned out his voice.

§

The doctor has given June a copy of his report on the neuropsychiatric examination of J.

Conclusions:

A) Egocentric, with a passionate tendency aimed at the re-form of society, indignation of an erotic origin, vehemence, desire to draw attention to his "just" cause, love of theatrical attitudes, impulsive, need of instant satisfaction, pays no heed to the consequences of his act, paranoid logic. Autodi-dactism, militant philosophico-culture, with motorized white guilt, but no outlet, and no organized striking force. No belief in his existence. Personal annoyance on this point. Refutation of history. Denial of the future. Belief in a nonverbal present. Ambivalent, frenzied idealism. Accelerated contempt of religion, and those over thirty years of age. Lack of precogitation.

B) Markedly maniacal. Bursts of laughter. Excitability. Attacks, makes judgments, consigns to nothingness that which he declares does not exist. Naïve. Passes from one extremity to another. Proud and ashamed. At times wallowing in the splendor of his audacity. Does not perceive that his rebellion is thin stuff actually directed against a father figure. Resultant anguish.

C) Schizoid. Appears intellectual, but merely gives lip service to scientific terms, and socio-economic theories. This is a protective device which entangles him in conflict, and creates insoluble anxiety. He submits to uncertainty. Enters into depressive states. Takes refuge in a dissident society, which rejects him also. Onanism shamefacedly admitted.

Heterosexuality vehemently ascribed to, while entertaining homosexual fantasies.

May be pretending mental invalidism to prevent his induction into the army.

Present oculocardiac reflexes indifferent. Very strong tendinous and muscular reactions. Wants to strike out. Trembling in tongue and fingers when he does so. Hypermotivity. Intelligent. A didactic tone hostile to originality.

Possibility of a cure following a fit of modesty. Future not without promise, after a long term in asylum.

Jay Wolff remains a danger to public tranquillity. His condition requires that he be confined in an asylum, where he can receive the treatment of which he is in need.

Manhattan, 3 / 24/ 70

§

J and I are in disguise. We are on the lam. We make a modishly dressed couple. I am wearing hip-length boots, leather coat, a helmet, and a pants suit. He is wearing a pastel sack suit, purple wide-brimmed felt hat, and a frilled, cuff-linked, mauve striped shirt. He is perfumed, and relaxed in a pair of tapered shoes with stacked heels. We have shoulder-length hair. Our silhouettes are indistinguishable.

§

"How did you find us?" I ask Charles Thomas.

"I got ways," he says enigmatically.

"Why did you find us?" I open the windows to let out the fusty smell of love and careless "boo."

"I got reasons," he says. "Ask me to sit down. I'm here, ain't I?"

"Please sit down." I take Charles's coat and hang it on a chair.

"Got a present for you," he says, and thrusts a box at me.

"What's in it?" I ask.

"Find out," he says proudly. J passes him a joint. He sucks it in so deeply that the ash reaches his lips.

I unwrap a plastic turtle bowl.

A small rock.

A plastic palm tree.

Decorative plastic chips.

"Where's the turtle?" I ask.

"Right here." Charles Thomas has been holding the turtle in his pocket. He draws it out. It tries to crawl off his hand.

I put water in the bowl. Not too much. Just enough.

I put the turtle in the bowl and he sinks. Then he floats: a fragile unopened pillbox. His skinny little neck comes out cautiously. Then his feet. His right foot does not have claws. It looks as if some other turtle chewed them off. Each tiny bright eye observes what is on each side of it: our shadows, the rock, the rounded plastic sides of the bowl.

"What does it eat?" I ask Charles Thomas.

"Anythin'," he says, "chopped meat, tuna, lettuce, chicken, bugs . . . live bugs is best."

At the mention of live bugs, J laughs uproariously.

This is a fine time to introduce J and Charles Thomas.

"Charles—J, J—Charles."

They take no notice of each other.

J begins to search for live bugs to feed the turtle. He is looking under cushions, under the rug, in the bed, in the stove . . . everywhere. And J laughs uproariously. Naturally; it's a lot of fun to go hunting in your own pad. J is sharp, but he has slowed down. He thinks he's fast. He doesn't catch anything, but it's still fun. He likes searching. I hadn't realized that before, how much J needs to look for something.

Maybe he's looking for lost love.

Maybe he's looking for love he never had.

Maybe he believed me when I described M as a cockroach and wants to squash him. But no, J is a naturalist, a scientist, an observer rather than an activist: he wants to find the food to feed the turtle.

Charles finds an old piece of salami in the fridge. He drops it into the turtle bowl. The turtle takes his first bite of the dim bit of meat, does not chew (does it have teeth?), but by progressive waves of contraction and relaxation of its neck (tubular, muscular), the food goes down.

Charles puts the bowl on the windowsill.

"Turtle needs sun," he says.

The turtle climbs the rock, closes its slow lidded eyes, draws its head forward toward the sun. The touch of the sun excites it: it stretches its limbs to rid itself of a lingering chill. Companionless, he sleeps.

"What is there to know about this turtle?" I ask Charles.

"Not much," he says, but he is not a student of turtles. Yet he has some opinions about it. "The turtle feels the hot or the cold. He feels fear and hunger. You can tell he were hungry by the way he eat. If he see us he try to hide. Look at this!"

Charles Thomas peers into the bowl. The turtle dives into the water;

tries to squeeze himself between the side of the bowl and the rock. He stays sidewise and still.

"If he cold, he get in the sun," Charles Thomas continues. "If he cain't get in the sun, he go to sleep till it get warm. He ain't got no temperature of his own. So always test the water before you put him into it."

"You've been talking to the man in the pet store," I say.

"He's the expert," Charles Thomas says. "I want you to take good care of this here turtle; it's the first live thing I ever got you . . . outside of my-self . . . and you ain't took too good a care of me, baby."

J has fallen asleep on the kitchen floor. Charles Thomas, my own dorsal carapace, hardens above me.

"Not yet," I say, "I'm not ready.

He takes one of my breasts in his mouth. He starts at the nipple and somehow the rest of the breast is sucked in. He covers me again. This is fair housing. He screams in Motown: "Baby, it's all right!" Both of us know it isn't. Masochistically I decide to bring us closer to the truth. I shout, "Nigger! Nigger! Nigger!" Every time I do, I get hotter and hotter. I expect punishment. Sure enough Charles Thomas removes himself from me with gentlemanly unhaste; stands at the side of the couch (on which I lie, my eyes begging forgiveness). He directs a powerful stream of piss at me. It is an elegant gesture, glimpsed through lace; an invitation to the dance.

Yellow foam splashes against my flesh: it reminds me of the dirty tide washed up on beaches too close to town.

"Sink or swim," Charles Thomas suggests paternally.

"I don't know what came over me," I say to him.

"I came over you," he explains.

Looking into the kitchen: "That white boy done caught enough turtle food for a month."

Creepy-crawly things are traversing the quiet form of J. His pockets are alive. His knuckles dance. His hair rises and falls. His nostrils, full of funky feelers, feed snot to the invaders.

"Is he dead?" I ask horrified.

"He the host; wouldn't be right for him to be dead," Charles Thomas says. "But it sure do look as if he lost control."

§

"I can't handle the lunchroom any more," M says to me.

"Why not?" I refrain from telling M that he can't handle anything.

"The students keep demanding the microphone to broadcast their incendiary remarks, and when I give it to them, they shout that they haven't been given the microphone. Then . . . half the students troop out after some damn revolutionary, and the rest eat cold food and buy dope. That's the picture . . . that's the situation . . . I'm up to here with the whole thing!"

"Up to where?"

"Up to here!" He makes a slicing movement across his throat from ear to ear. I hold a platter to receive his head. He is still alive, and insists on speaking. ". . . and the poetry they entertain each other with . . . society should have a right to protect itself from this type of filth, which is filth for the sake of filth and nothing else!"

Rebellion must be a heady wine! Multitudes come out of obscurity and are identified, and they send the enemy into oblivion in their turn. Is this what is happening at M's school? And what has dope got to do with it? I wouldn't mind turning on . . . building dream castles through whose empty halls I could hear my own laughter, and J's.

§

The school lunchroom; the pusher has brought his violin. He has goods for sale of an amazing clarity and range. Five hundred students eager to make a connection have filled the lunchroom to capacity. Orchestral forces have been deployed across the room, for this occasion, in normal concert fashion. It is a cultural event.

A single microphone is suspended approximately eighteen feet above the platform from which M usually surveys the eaters . . . it is now a podium. The pusher stands slightly to the left of M. He is the soloist. He wears white tails and bow tie. Charles Thomas has made a painstaking effort to achieve perfect balance between solo and tutti. I am located at the precise aural focal point of the lunchroom.

The warning bell sounds. The pusher warms up. His violin tuned, he begins.

The violin concerto opens with a serene melody in B minor. Table B lights up and joints are passed around above pulsating chords on the harp, lower strings pizzicato and a sustained horn note. Three monitors pass out sticks of incense. There is still a slight smell of cabbage and coffee in the lunchroom. It is a noble spacious theme, to which intervals of the fourth lend a characteristically Acapulco flavor. I am turned on. I am in danger of giggling. I bite into a cube of sugar. It sparkles like a snowflake, and melts. M is conducting with a light-tipped baton, since the concert may last into evening.

The lyrical flow is interrupted by a restless motive, building up to table F (finance). Money and bodies are exchanged, restating the original theme in a fiscal relationship. Secondary ideas: paranoia about getting busted emphasize the thematic conflict as the movement develops in true classical sonata fashion. The pusher plays on, he knows what to expect. His chin grips the violin. His shoulder in a perpetual shrug supports it. His fingering is superb. He no longer needs a tourniquet to find the vein. No such technical legerdemain is required. In an intimate and subtle manner, the pusher spreads piquant coke on the shiny body of his violin and snorts it in. There is scattered applause by those not familiar with the piece . . . it is not over. Tablespoons are distributed to those requiring them, and souvenir packs of matches are tossed by the handful like wedding rice to the recently wedded. A promise of bliss is in the air, as the finale begins its savage introduction. Harmony is based on the pizzicato accompaniment to the opening theme of the first movement, when things were light and gay. In a more primitive mood, the pusher removes his clothing and dances. He is sodomized as M's baton probes for deeper meaning.

Charles Thomas envelopes me between two allegro movements. We are tranquil in this haunting, songlike movement: post-mainline, present high. Having scored a sparse, delicate, and transparent taste of death, we die. Five hundred students, each a short variation on a theme, unable to stand the pure stuff, die with us.

The pusher and M see that their audience has gone. They turn down the amps. Amazingly they sing a poignant lament. It is superfluous.

§

"Still making it with the kid?" Lita asks. I don't care to tell her that the "kid" is all memories and much daydreaming.

§

J takes my lipstick and writes on the bathroom mirror the words: FUCK JAY.

He is out on a weekend pass. I would like to go to The Cloisters with him but the Unicorn Tapestry makes J froth at the mouth, "The horn is too sharp and spirally," he says.

"It's a mythical beast, it can't hurt anyone," I say.

"There's a rip in the tapestry that's been mended," J points out. "The unicorn is not tame!" He seems terrified of the beautiful white horse with the lion's tail, sporting in a hunting park with ladies.

"The unicorn can be tamed by a virgin. It's symbolic of chastity and purity," I say to soothe J.

"There are no virgins, and it will never be tamed," he insists.

"Why did you write FUCK JAY on my mirror?" I ask.

"I really wanted to write FUCK MELISSA, but I used my name instead so you wouldn't be mad at me."

"Why do you feel that way about me? Aren't we friends? You told me that no matter what happened we would always be friends." It is unfair of me to pretend I am merely a friend. I may not be a friend at all. I may be his enemy. It depends on what action I take.

"We are friends," J says, "but I'm not your lover boy anymore."

"I know that J. I accept your decision."

He is examining his hands which have broken out into a rash. They itch him. I offer to bring him calamine lotion.

"I don't mind if they itch," J says. "I like it. I scratch and it feels great. The doctor isn't worried about my skin. He says it's just a minor symptom."

J scratches till he bleeds. I find myself kissing J's hands. They are pressed to my mouth and I am licking his blood. It has a familiar taste.

"June doesn't love me," J says suddenly, glaring at me.

"Yes she does love you, J. She talks about you all the time, and she's planning to buy you an enlarger."

"She has a boyfriend," J sobs. "She took him to her new studio at night and they made love."

"So what!" I say stupidly.

"What does she need him for!" he shouts in anguish.

"What do you mean, J, darling . . . oh, darling, what do you mean?"

He pulls away from me and buries his head in the drapes. "What does she need him for when she's got me?"

§

Two stark walls. An uninhabited, unfinished room. A tremulous half-light coming through large loft windows. The floor has been newly laid. It is pine. The pine has been waxed many times to bring out the natural beauty of the wood. Such a floor rejects liquids that spill on it. It is the floor of a dancer.

A woman wearing a silver helmet, out of which protrudes a long mane of black hair, enters from an open side of the room. She is naked. On her breasts are pinned two buttons. The motto: MAKE WAR, NOT LOVE.

A man enters from the opposite side of the unfinished room. He walks with the measured tread of a dancer pretending he is walking.

The woman is swaying gently. When she stops moving, her flesh continues, as if in slow motion. She lies down on the floor, her body stretched full length, running from one wall to the other. She is an animal trap. She waits for an undomesticate. She listens for a roar, or, a creaking of the floor, or, the stealthy opening of a door.

The man trips over her body. He falls upon it. He bites the nape of her neck.

She cries out in passion, "Ohhhhhhhhhhhh!" The sound is guttural, it goes on and on; she hardly seems to hear it. Then it is snipped from her mouth and "Ohhhhhhhhhh!" floats like a banner across the room.

She turns her head. It is June. Her helmet, still intact upon her head, has sprouted two ivory horns. The horns light up (low-wattage nite-lights lead the lover to her). He grasps the horns for balance as he throws himself upon her. He overflows within her. Juice, sweat, and semen stream to the corners of the room and pool there. Aroused, June drinks up the corners. Shadows disappear.

The man follows her in the manner of a dancer pretending to walk. He crouches over her in the manner of a man pretending to fuck. He turns his head.

It is M!

He has choreographed his way into her body.

They go to the exercise bar. As their knees bend, their arms drift out gracefully.

What a weird couple they make.

§

The block is sealed off. Crouching fuzz are everywhere. An officer with a bullhorn to his lips is shouting orders. There is movement behind ears, and guns aiming at our windows. Violent shafts of light turn in a fiery arc, illuminating the sky and the building where we're hiding. Every time the light makes one of its wide, crazy sweeps, I flatten under the table . . . M hugs the wall.

It has been several hours since the police laid siege.

Lew Harris is down there talking to the chief of police.

Hundreds of people have gathered behind police barricades.

A squad of police are trying to keep them in order.

A lady runs from the front rank of the crowd toward our building. She is tackled by a burly officer. He appears to dry-hump her as she turtles away. Another policeman is playing xylophone by striking, with his small wooden nightstick, the shinbones of those who dare to surge forward.

J lies dead on the stairs.

Two policemen are outside the door, one on each side . . . waiting.

M catches sight of himself in the mirror, and shoots. The mirror cracks. My sculpture of Sirius is showered with glass.

"Why don't you give yourself up!" I shout at M.

The cop with the bullhorn is admonishing the crowd in a rapid, one-note voice: "Go home. Everybody go home! It is dangerous to remain in the area. This is an order. Leave immediately!"

For the first time the crowd is still: nobody moves an inch. Another squad of police come charging up and try to push them back. The crowd allows itself to be hustled and shoved . . . but only into another shape: rhomboid into parallelogram into equilateral triangle.

I am not frightened. I know that I will be rescued.

§

J meets a lady outside his school. She asks him, "Would you like to learn an instrument?"

"Yes," he answers.

"What instrument would you like to play?" She stands, pencil poised above a yellow lined pad.

"Guitar," he says. For a moment, the hope that he can be like the others, a boy of his time, exalts his dreary outlook.

She inscribes the information. "And what is our name?"

"Jay Wolff."

He gives her his address and telephone number. She thanks him and approaches other children leaving the school: "Would you like to learn an instrument . . . ?"

A few weeks later, June answers the doorbell; it is the woman from the music school. "Yes?" June asks. "What do you want?"

"I understand that your son wants to learn to play the guitar . . ."

"My son is no longer with me," June says.

The woman, embarrassed, withholds the rest of her sales pitch. "You mean he is not coming back?" she inquires, already ringing for the elevator.

"He's not coming back, ever!" June says.

Now, June experiences the shock of J's death as if he had died in the war and sent her a cheerful letter which she receives posthumously.

Should June believe the letter or the corpse?

§

"Do you believe in ghosts?" I ask J.

"Yes," J answers, "so does Mummy and Letitia."

"Are you afraid of them?"

"No . . . I like them. Ghosts are disembodied spirits wandering among us because they want to make their presence known: they are spiritual beings who died young and still have things to say."

"Have you ever communicated with a specter?"

"No, but when I die I'll communicate with you," J promises.

"Please communicate with me now," I beg.

I am not sure I will be able to receive his messages. I am not in the least receptive to the idea that he will die. And, I have never been visited by a ghost before. My television, however, has often played host to a pale, double image, appearing on the screen as a white shadow.

§

. . . Melt . . .

Embalmer: We use the lost-wax method. No fine line lost. This smile set in wax lasts forever.

Me: But isn't waxed the opposite of walled? And, where is the emotion that animates the line? Why has death sealed his lips when he promised to come back to me from the dead!

. . . Melt . . .

§

M and I are conducting the remaining business of marriage in a colony of sun and surf worshipers; we are strange invaders to this sleepy strand of beach. When I can't stand M, I jump into the ocean and let the waves thunder over me, or I lie on the beach and watch the young men flex their muscles and/or ride their surfboards into shore. This is the easy life, bringing a dilettante corpse to life every day (M). He tries: imitating the great breakers, he crashes monotonously into me through the hot days and cooler nights, but he is a wave in a bathtub.

We live in a white stucco house with a red tile roof. We are scarcely visible behind date and cypress trees . . . a wall surrounds a courtyard and fountain. From our living room window can be seen the sapphire-blue Atlantic, into which M tosses salted peanuts.

We dine alfresco on an outdoor terrace, under a pink and yellow beach umbrella. M is certain that the dark-green lobster I bought for our dinner tonight is a sign.

"What kind of a sign?" I ask him.

"A warning to me . . . that all lobsters are alive before they are dead," he replies.

I notice for the first time, M encased in a suit of armor made of hard shell. The front part of his body is practically solid; the rest of the shell is divided into seven segments, the last of which forms the coccyx.

"Why would I bring you such a sign?" I am ready to deny it, but I have often been the intermediary between supernatural powers and mortals.

"You were merely the agent . . . Jay used you to get at me!"

"Then you don't blame me?"

M waves his great claws within inches of my nose. One of the claws is thick and heavy: for crushing tender objects. The other is more slender, curved, and provided with many sharp teeth. M does not seize me with it. He seems resigned.

§

J has come for me, riding the broad back of a giant sea turtle. They have remained afloat for fifteen hours, skimming the surface of the water. I am waiting on the shore with a blanket, and a Thermos of hot beef bouillon. The wind is tossing bits of orange paper around on the beach; it is the lobster J made for me. As he approaches, I wonder whether the monster he is hanging on to isn't the same turtle Charles Thomas once gave me, but which M threw into the toilet howl? If alligators are discovered full grown in sewers, why can't the same be true of discarded turtles?

Although J has come for me, he is merely an escort, acting as emissary for the nether world. Protocol must be observed.

"Do you have a note to leave M?" J asks stiffly.

"It's in this yellow purse." I show it to J.

"Leave it on the beach. Here, put this rock on it."

He gives me a rosette of tabular crystals of barite, enclosing sand grains and colored by iron oxide.

"It's too beautiful to leave behind," I say.

" 'Barite roses' are common enough," J answers, "I'll get you another. Are you going to leave your clothes on?"

"What do you suggest?"

"Leave them on. They'll act as a weight when you're ready to sink. If you begin to change your mind, it'll be too late to struggle out of them."

The turtle sips beef bouillon before we mount her. She flips sand over my purse which makes a mound on the beach resembling an egg. When the sun comes to warm the beach tomorrow, M will stumble on my purse, and find its contents pregnant.

"Let's go!" J shouts.

The wind has risen and is blowing waves horizontally so that I have to keep my head down. I am riding in front of J. His arms are around me. I shield my eyes from the sharp spray by pressing my hand against my forehead. I can see only a few inches ahead of me. Though the turtle knows the way, she hesitates for a moment, then looks back at J for instructions. He prods the soft spot under her tail. She changes direction; vertical, disappears under the waves with us. I observe dim circles of light behind my eyelids, as if I had been struck. Falling fast, the light grows dimmer and dimmer . . . my skirt billows around my thighs . . . bubbles and ears, pop . . . J floats away, a silver button in his fist. The turtle dives again. There is complete silence.

§

M lights a cigarette as he reads the note I have left for him. He smooths the paper on his knee:

> Is suicide my only alternative? Is being nothing in life, comparable to being nothing in death?

> decided to kill myself
> at the age of thirty-nine since I
> have experienced nothing
> of life that was yearned for.

> & I wouldn't think
> of leaving you M

> for someone, that is.

> while Lita and June went

into activities, preparing
their bodies for actions of love
I skimmed the surface

& was bored.

Conclusion?

spent fifteen years as an
apprentice wife
preparing for   ?
in "the real world"

From,
"It is Melissa I mourn for."

P.S. We are HERE now in the shark's fin soup after having fooled ourselves about the steaming present. Our thanx (J too) to you for having allowed this accomplishment.

Goodbye Mark
I'm going back inside my head
or did you think that I was
really dead?

THE COSMOPOLITAN GIRL

This book is dedicated to
Emma Licht
who taught at Public School 94 in the Bronx,
and who encouraged me to write

Wanted: a dog that neither barks nor bites,
eats broken glass and shits diamonds. —
Goethe

. . . Dogs are relevant in connection with human
society either because they suggest it by their
own social life (which men look on as an imita-
tion of theirs, or alternatively because, having no
social life of their own, they form part of ours.)
—Levi-Strauss

One of the reasons I have always tried to perfect the way I look is that I thought it would
make me happier. — *Princess Luciana Pignatteli*

1 Pablo has confessed his love for me. I was stunned. I knew that he was fond of me, the way he licked my hand and slept at the foot of the bed barely moving so as not to disturb me. But a declaration of love! And from a dog I have owned for two years . . . My God! I couldn't understand such an explosion. It is true I love him too, in another way, as a welcome responsibility, as a presence. Let me explain. I live alone. The room in which I live is located in the Hotel Buckminster. Pets are not allowed, but I have hidden Pablo. He is paper-trained and never barks above a whisper. He has a fine suit of clothes: wide velvet trousers, Hawaiian shirt, gaucho hat, and a wig. This is the disguise he wears should I have to open the door to anyone. When this happens he sits with his back to the door looking out the window. He is an intelligent dog, well-coordinated and faithful (that goes without saying). I keep him with me to satisfy a desire that is so personal I am ashamed to admit it. My purpose is to tie together the two aspects of my nature: the civilized and the animal. However, Pablo is fast becoming more civilized than I am. He insists that a daily schedule of activities be read to him each morning, and that I present the day's menu to him for his approval. His menu might read as follows: fresh chopped sirloin steak au jus (served in medium bowl on a lace place mat on the floor), mineralized spring water over ice (served in crystal tumbler), crisp burgundy vitamin capsule, handcarved unpolished bone of beef. His menu is always at variance with the actual fare, but the captive customer's complaints fall on deaf ears and an empty pocketbook. Since he is in the habit of having me read the news to him while he eats, I change it in the telling to amuse both of us, for instance: "RELIGION REPORT . . . VATICAN ABOLISHES THE TONSURE. Pope Eccles XXIV today ordered the abolition of the tonsure, the circular shaving of the crown of the head that has marked preliminary steps on the way to a nit-free scalp. The Pope also maintained the age-old ban on women in any barberic role, emphasizing once again the moral contained within the biblical tale of Samson and Delilah . . . LOCAL NEWS—HELEN JONES ADDRESSES THE P.B.A. Warning that corruption among the police, prosecutors, and judges must be confronted 'in a darkened, sealed tunnel,' Helen Jones today told the Patrolmen's Benevolent Association that she was afraid of rats. This was the first public indication that she was no longer interested in being a foil for the bigwigs. Despite the resentment of the governor, the mayor, and a state senator, she won three rounds of applause and an Italian salami for her decision to withdraw. 'I have lost confidence in our system,' she declared in the section of her speech dealing with misbegotten dollars and high cholesterol lunches for jurors, 'but I have gained my own self-respect.' For this she received a standing ovulation that lasted for days, though with diminishing intensity for the last two." Pablo does not laugh easily. I keep trying. If he left me, life would not be worth living.

2 I am a pretty person. My features do not fight with one another. I have a small nose that is slightly rounded at the tip, adequate nostrils, and a flat bridge which might be more interesting should a bump appear along its bony path. My breasts are small, my spine straight, my thighs not much fuller than my calves. My color is good; I like to be out-of-doors. I try to achieve some excitement in my appearance by changing the way I do my hair (according to the way women in *Cosmopolitan* do theirs: natural but controlled, parted on the left side, falling in gentle waves to just below the ear.) My clothes can be mixed and still belong together since none of the colors clash, and they are classically simple. This is necessary since I have few clothes, and they must go everywhere: shopping, on-the-town, job hunting, man hunting (formal or informal). What I wear decides who I am. This is elementary psychology, but true. I once wore a tiger-striped nightgown and clawed a man to death.

At home I walk around with no clothes on at all (depending on whether the steam is up). I do not bother to pull down the shade. If someone in the building opposite wants to look, he's welcome. If someone doesn't like it, that's his problem. I do what makes me feel good . . . but not always. It's a hard rule to follow because sometimes I'm not sure what does please me.

3 I was about to go into my room when I heard Pablo ask: "Is it you, Helen?" Who else could it be? When I entered he claimed that he had had a bad dream. Then lowering his voice: "It was about the courtyard."

Our window faces the side entrance, pigeon droppings encrust the court. One must step gingerly over the concrete to reach the door. The building was built in 1904. At that time it was the most elegant residential hotel in the nation, a huge edifice modeled on Stanford White's Beaux Arts school. Unlike the paper-thin walls of today's more modern constructions, the Buckminster has thick vaultlike walls. Stars of the music world like Caruso, Toscanini, Chaliapin, Jenny Lind, the Pied Piper, and Stravinsky found they could practice here without disturbing their neighbors. Privacy was assured. A good place for a murder.

"I dreamt I was lying in the courtyard dead," Pablo whispered.

"Oh no!"

"You're crying, Helen. Oh now, is it anything to cry about? It was only a dream."

I blew my nose without answering. There followed a deep silence. "I'll have to ask Mother what it means," I said.

4 Mother is a psychic; she can guess the past, present, and future. She does not believe it is guessing. She has spoken to more than fifty people with some degree of accuracy by merely holding a folded piece of paper in her hand on which they have written a question. When she speaks to me she is less accurate, since what she says is colored by emotion. The surgeon does not operate on his family, the seer does not tell a loved one what is in store for her; however, Mother is the exception to the rule. I take what she says with a grain of salt. I am aware of her shortcomings.

Mother rose above me in the chapel, her batwing sleeves stirring the incense in the air. Candles flickered on the altar. The cross was wound with artificial flowers. A hymn began to play as one of Mother's assistants activated her new quadraphonic sound system. I was the only customer, but got the full treatment. Mother took the microphone: "Good evening, I am the Reverend Myra Jones, and I believe I can be of some help to you, if you sincerely seek it . . ."

From my cushion on the floor I called: "I'm sincere, Mother."

She pressed the microphone to her lips and said tenderly: "Our purpose here is devotion to the good and natural things of life. You are what you breathe, what you eat, and who you choose to love."

Albert, Mother's chief assistant, took the photo of Pablo that I had put into an envelope. The envelope was sealed. Albert brought the envelope to Mother. She smoothed it between her hands, then held it very still. Her head went back and her eyes closed. She began to bark. Her neck snapped forward as she lifted the envelope above her head. Albert replaced the microphone in its stand. Mother moaned, sang a line from "How Much Is That Doggie in the Window," opened her eyes wide, and staring at me said: "I hold in my hand a picture of someone called Pablo. This is not the picture of Pablo Casals, cellist deceased, nor is it the picture of Pablo Picasso, artist deceased; this Pablo has no last name and no great talent though he is able to dance some, howl at the moon, run a fair race, or catch a well-aimed ball in his mouth. This is an odd sort of man who can achieve peace and tranquillity only by being free, this means sexually, and, let me see, he loves combat and is very strong. Yes, he is a fighter. One of his ears is slightly chewed, and his left leg is healing from a bite. What a purely primitive person! Oh dear . . ."

Mother made a circle with the envelope, then held it out flat on her palm.

"Tell me about Pablo's dream, Mother. That's what I came to find out."

"Please call me Reverend when I am acting in that capacity," Mother warned, "or my powers might wane."

"Yes, Reverend Jones. I apologize."

This time Mother began howling as she crawled all around the lectern with the envelope in her mouth. She was too far gone for me to think she was putting me on. I think that the spirit of Pablo had possessed her and that she was actually at that moment a dog. As a dog she was surprisingly appealing. Albert, putting his hands under her armpits, helped her up as she was about to speak again: "I receive an image of a dog lying very still. He is under a canopy. It is raining. The dog is Pablo."

"Is he dead? Is he dead?" I cried out, horrified.

"The dog is an actor. He is making a movie in which he is pretending that he is dead. It is not really raining but it is wet enough. Pablo will get a cold from which he will recover."

"But what does the dream mean, Reverend? Please tell me."

"The meaning manifest in this dream, which is the dream of a dog, a dog-faced man, or a man dreaming he is a dog, is that in grave situations one must laugh loudly, if need be, a great hollow laugh."

"I don't get it," I said. "There was no one laughing in the dream. The only sound was of the rain falling."

"Well, then, maybe the dream means that it is better to dream one is dead than to actually die. Your dog is suffering from extreme anxiety. One can surmise that from the fixed smile on his face, and the nervous twitching of his tail."

"Do you have any advice for me?" I knew that Myra Jones was wrong about Pablo's tail, he was a happy tail-wagger, not a nervous tail-twitcher, but she was right about his engraved finky smile. It drove me wild sometimes.

"Brush him often, play with him, and never tell him he's growing old. Also laugh a lot when you're around him. He needs reassurance."

"Is that all, Reverend Jones?"

"Oh yes, keep the bottoms of your windows closed."

Mother threw me a daisy which landed in my lap. She then disappeared into the black drapes that separated the chapel from the rest of the apartment. It was a magical departure. Music swelled. Rosy lights caused misty halos to glint off antique icons. Albert brought me an ancient silver wine bowl to dip my cup into. It was very peaceful. As I squatted on the pillow, sipping wine, I could understand how people would want to stay rooted in their places all their lives.

As I was leaving, Albert approached me: "I must see you soon," he said urgently.

"You know where to get in touch with me," I replied.

5 A bright cool afternoon, but Pablo was restless. I could have spent all day looking out the window at the blue shadows of buildings.

"I'm a dog," Pablo began, "and it isn't fair to keep me locked up in this room like an abused child some adult is ashamed of. Don't you know what life is all about?" he growled.

"Tell me," I said curtly.

"Life is fighting for territory, smelling another dog's shit and knowing it's not yours, pissing high on the tree trunk, and fucking a bitch! That's what life is all about. I love you but you're not enough."

"If you go I'll never see you again. You aren't registered with the city. You haven't had your shots, and you know you won't eat scraps."

"I'll take my chances," Pablo answered. He was really in a terrible mood.

I let him go, but followed him. As soon as he disappeared down the hall, he turned back again.

"I can't do it," he said. "An invisible force wants to keep me here."

"Remember, I gave you your chance," I told him, relieved.

6 Pablo has been angry with me since his attempted freedom. It would have been better had I refused his request. Someday I'll prepare him for going: walk with him short distances, let him run without a leash, call him back. Does a dog know what a dog wants? Without me he would be alone in the world, hungry, running with the pack (as do summer colony rejects); he'd become vicious, a killer . . . indiscriminate. On meeting me alone some winter day, would he rip me apart to wallow in my warm blood? He was snuggled up against me on the bed, his wet nose stamping my inner arm with sticky goodwill.

"Tell me another story about Tommy the Turd," Pablo said. It was his favorite antihero tale. (Tommy the Turd appealed to his nose.)

I opened an imaginary book and read: "One day Tommy the Turd went out looking for a friend because he was very lonely. Now you know how hard that might be because even before you saw him you could smell him. But Tommy wrapped himself in a shiny new Saran Wrap jacket and went out into the world anyway in his brave quest for a friend. He visited the Museum of Modern Art, and was standing near the pool looking at his dark reflection when a curator of the museum noticed him. 'My, my, what a fine work of art that is!' the curator said to himself. 'I must have it installed immediately.' But first, of Course, he had to ask Tommy whether he would allow himself to be installed. So he began: 'I'd like to be your friend. What is your name?' 'Tommy, sir,' Tommy the Turd answered, wisely leaving off his last name. 'Well, pleased to meet you, Tommy. I think you are a wonderful sight to behold and know that you could give pleasure to thousands of people who visit our museum every year.'

" 'How?' " Tommy inquired innocently.

" 'By letting us install you in our permanent collection,' the museum curator replied. When Tommy hesitated, too overcome by emotion to answer, the curator misinterpreted and offered Tommy two passes to the museum which included openings and free movie shows for a year.

" 'Who would I give them to?' Tommy asked.

" 'Your parents? Friends?'

" 'You're my only friend, sir, and my parents have long since passed away.'

" 'I'm sorry to hear that,' the curator said, 'but as your only friend I recommend that you put yourself in my hands. You'll not only be famous, you'll be happy surrounded with other works of art and also people. You'll never be lonely. Sometimes there is music in the courtyard, sometimes poetry readings. Your spirit will soar.'

"Tommy, having received an offer he couldn't refuse, accepted and was put on a pedestal right in the middle of the pool. Beams of colored lights played around him, bouncing off the shiny Saran Wrap jacket like sparks of new stars. For one moment he was happy, then the fountain went on. The lively water found him under his fragile wrapper, and Tommy the Turd began to dissolve. The pool in which he stood changed from bright blue to a dirty camel's-hair brown. People who had been drinking champagne beside the pool to celebrate the new acquisition left with undue haste as the odor of decaying matter wafted toward them.

" 'Everyone's abandoning me,' Tommy cried. 'I'm nothing but a piece of shit!' When he disappeared, there was nothing left in the pool but a soggy scrap of Saran Wrap, which a workman scooped out.

" 'Excrement as art is valid,' the curator insisted, and there were some who believed him, artists who found a way to preserve their turds. But it was too late for Tommy."

Pablo brushed a tear from his eye: "If only Tommy had realized that there are more turds in the world than people, he would have had a sense of pride," he said, "but he did have his moment of glory."

"Yes he did," I agreed.

"Remember when Tommy was an aviator and everyone jumped out of the plane?" Pablo reminisced.

"Yes, and remember when he went on that wonderful tour of the sewage system and made friends with a rat?"

"I don't remember that," Pablo said.

"That was the night we watched Fleetwood Mac on TV and you complained that nobody wrote good dog lyrics any more."

"Did I say that?"

"You sure did . . . And then we even wrote our own dog song which I happen to have right here between the pages of this dictionary."

"Read it," Pablo said. "It probably stinks."

I read:

A piece of dog nailed to a weed

A dog without a back;
A dog which does not drive;
A (brown) dog without content!

"No one could sing that," Pablo complained, "it doesn't rhyme and it doesn't reason."

"I also wrote a dog essay for you; come on, you remember. I was high and someone was knocking on the door, and I didn't want to answer it, so I wrote till the knocking stopped. Remember?" I kicked Pablo to make him remember.

"Read it," Pablo said. "It's my only love letter."

I stood on a chair and, gesticulating wildly, repeated Pablo's "love" letter which he had heard only once: "Is there any dog on which one can sit, as on a chair? Yes/no. Perhaps there only exists a dog on which one can spit; the utilitarian dog. The dog without any purpose. What we call a dog belongs equally to what we call our spirit as to what we call our body. Let us try to make a dog without feet or tail which would be as good as a complete dog. And a poem is just like a dog. It has its own language and since everything exists only through language, he forms, in spite of his 'turd psychology' which is imposed by other species, the new dog and the craven universe; that is his function. I dedicate this essay to Pablo whom I love."

"Whistle when you want me," Pablo said lyrically. "I'm your salty dog."

7 Don't think I kept Pablo cooped up at all times. He is a champion swimmer. Three times a week after midnight we would sneak into the hotel pool (located in the basement) for some exercise. I would skinny-dip; he of course could not remove his coat, but when he was wet, how his muscles rippled and rerippled.

It was a pretty pool surrounded with Casbah narrow arches, colored tile, and small circular windows high up on the walls. The light was dim and the room suffused with lacteal illumination. Pablo swam in green milk, his eyes blurry from too strong a concentration of chlorine in the water.

Water is not native to me; I sink. My father tried to teach me how to swim: he would put his arms out just below the surface and I would lie there supported, almost floating. When he removed his arms for an instant I went under. For years I have tried to overcome my panic by staying under for short periods of time. Pablo's presence helps me.

Following is a list of things I say to myself in the hopes of becoming a water baby:

STAY UNDER WATER
SUPPRESS PANIC
ASSUME FETAL POSITION
FLOAT TO TOP
THERE IS ENOUGH AIR
I WILL NOT DROWN
I AM IN CONTROL
I AM BUOYANT
I CAN EMERGE
I BREATHE
I FLOAT
MY LIMBS ARE FREE
I AM NO LONGER A PUPPET

Repeating this does not free me. Instead I hear water rushing into my ears and nostrils; I see the four paws of Pablo paddling toward me; then his mouth on my arm pulling.

Lying beside the pool I vowed that it was too much of a sacrifice to accompany Pablo to the pool. Just as some people don't dare look down from a height for fear of falling (jumping?), I don't dare go in too deep (the baptism unto death).

8 Last night I went to Daddy's house. It's on Beekman Place. Across the East River is a big PEPSI-COLA sign; it's almost a part of Daddy's art collection because you can see it from his floor-to-ceiling living room windows. He's rich but not generous with me; in fact I hardly share in his good fortune at all. He expects me to work for a living! If it wasn't for his weird gift of healing people with flowering herbs, penetrating gazes, and massive masterly massage he'd be on relief or washing dishes somewhere. There is nothing the man can do besides putter around with the ill health of others. He's almost as rich as one of those Indian maharishis who travel around in gold Cadillacs, or mountain-hop in hand-painted private planes. Daddy is not so blatant. He wears a tieless shirt, baggy black trousers, and a V-necked wool cardigan. I respect him for his lack of style.

Daddy's art collection is nearly all New York school (abstract expressionism) because, he says, the paintings remind him of the well-worn palms of men of experience. He reads the paintings like palms: "There's the lifeline," (a diagonal streak of red cut across by a tipsy wobble of yellow) he explains, "rich, free, but becoming cowardly toward the end. Each brushstroke brings fear of change while actually in flux." De Kooning's devouring monster women remind him of Mother: her ominous oracular self, her flayed being suddenly exposed and laid bare to cutting winds. "Notice the similarity, the shocked expression in the face and the whirlpool eyes revolving madly," he said to me, holding a photo of Mother alongside the De Kooning painting.

Mother is magical. Daddy is magical. They made me . . . ordinary. There is nothing in the future I foresee. No one I am called to heal but myself.

I do love Edward (Daddy's name), but he doubts it: "You only come here to ask for things," he says. "You never show affection. When I call you, you seldom return my calls. How much longer can I go on trying to reach you when you don't respond?"

Why doesn't he know that I can't? I'm different: not one of his patients who relate symptoms. He has always paid more attention to them. They are his career, his inner life, his real family. Each new case presents an opportunity for him to absorb himself in himself, to wander among the flowers of his knowledge: he plucks the right ones, gathers his bouquet, and presents it to an illness . . . not to me. What is his relationship to the sick? Why must he cure? I don't understand it. Healing is only temporary;

a stopgap measure before death claims us one way or another. What difference if a stranger sickens and dies sooner?

"You want to be all-powerful," I told Daddy. "You want to duel with death."

"Nobody duels any more," he answered me. "Healing is not a clash of swords, it is a gathering of facts. You know that."

"I'm not speaking of method," I said. "I'm talking to you about your self-image. How do you think of yourself?"

"Do you really want to know, or are you being hostile again?"

"I want to know, Daddy." I kissed his soft hairy cheek. Some spittle from his mouth clung to the edge of my lip. It tasted like rosewater.

"That's a tough question to answer," he responded, finally taking my hand in an affectionate fatherly grasp, "but even as a small boy, any human being, bird, or creature in pain or distress aroused in me such compassion and desire to help their suffering that I determined to be a doctor. I was also a dreamer, and would dream that healing power flowed from my hand to all those I touched. I couldn't stand the noise of cities and had a tendency to visit with nature. Later, I combined the two great interests of my life and found that I was not merely dreaming. I do not feel superior to those I help and I am certainly humble in the face of calamity!"

Daddy gave me a marvelous fresh strawberry mousse and a piece of home-baked fruit-and-brandy cake while he worked on a patient. I was allowed to watch. The man was stretched out in one of the guest bedrooms on the third floor. At first he seemed nervous, jumped at the slightest noise: door chimes, a drawer closing, Beethoven's Seventh. He was sweating copiously (Daddy asked me to pat him dry with soft cloths, which I did as carefully as I could). Then the man lay down again shaken and helpless. He seemed in constant dread of something. I offered him some strawberry mousse but he refused.

"I suffer from flatulence and constipation," he said to me, thinking I was a medical person, too. Daddy hadn't introduced me as his daughter. "And I have a constant backache," he added dolefully. I would have advised him to eat stewed prunes and Grapenuts every morning for breakfast, but Daddy brought in the following remedies which the man eagerly took one after the other: Rock Rose for his terror, Cherry Plum for his fear of doing something desperate. ("I want to hang myself sometimes," he said. "I've had the urge ever since I heard Billie Holiday sing 'Strange Fruit.'")

Daddy spooned elixir of Aspen into the man's mouth for his fear of the unknown, gave him a tiny blue bottle of extract of Mimulus for his fear of people and noises, placed in the man's jacket pocket a box of Sweet Chestnut for his most unbearable mental anguish, set aside a transparent Lucite casket holding Scleranthus, for his unbalanced, uncertain state of mind, and fed him Agrimony for his unrest.

Immediately the man's bowels worked normally, much to his embarrassment. It must have been the aspen, which has been known since antiquity as a remedy against tapeworms, and cleans you out.

Finally I had Daddy alone in the dining room. His guests (daily freeloaders who came to adore Daddy and call him a genius) had already eaten and were wandering around the living room watching the riverboats, the Pepsi sign, and each other. Most of Daddy's friends were young and in an advanced state of inner peace. This tranquility led them to sit on the floor instead of the chairs or couches which were far more comfortable. I was attracted to a pretty man who sat upright: a young fertile stem (magnified) of the marsh horsetail. He had a harmonica in his mouth which he played without hands. The sound of the two chords he blew (the Amen chorus, F major to C major) was a kind of humorous comment on the meditative atmosphere of the room. I decided to take him home with me because (1) I needed a few laughs, and (2) he had a beautiful body.

Daddy got down to basics right away: "Do you have a job yet?" he asked.

"I'm looking," I answered, "but you know, it's got to be glamorous and interesting."

"Which means you are without funds again?"

I idly picked up a piece of carved jade that was sitting on a shelf behind me and put it in my pocket. Daddy would never miss it.

"All I need is fifty dollars to tide me over," I said. "Come on, love, give it to me."

"Tide you over? You know what happens to rocks when the tide rolls over them? They become sand, a vast indistinguishable beach washed out to sea or packed together into mute bulwarks."

I felt the mute but valuable bulwark in my pocket. It would if Edward was having one of his stingy days.

"For Christ's sake, Daddy, don't wax poetic on me, or I'll tell the world you're a selfish rat. You really are you know."

Daddy pounded the table in anger. "Get a hold on yourself. What happens when the money I give you runs out?"

"When the tide runs out, treasures are left behind," I said.

"Shipwrecks are left behind!" Daddy insisted. Whenever he saw me he saw disaster.

"Please, Dad, look at how skinny I am. Pablo says I'm too thin."

"Pablo?"

"The man I'm living with, you oughtta meet him."

"Really? Why?"

"He's a kick, you'd love him. We do an animal act together. He used to be in vaudeville and small circuses." I could see that Daddy didn't believe me. He turned away and wiped his hand across his eyes as if shielding himself from an awful sight. That awful sight was me.

"Describe your act," Daddy challenged. "You couldn't make less in show business than you're making now. Maybe it's an inspired choice."

"Well," I hesitated, trying to remember any animal acts I had ever seen. "What I do is . . . I am dressed in a sexy leotard with sheer tights and my feet are enhanced by a pair of high-heeled boots. In my hands I hold a hoop. Beyond the hoop is a plain kitchen table. The dog waits for my command. 'Jump!' I say as sternly as I can. 'Jump through the hoop!' But the dog doesn't budge. I say: 'Now, jump up on the table!' But the dog doesn't budge. He doesn't do anything I ask him to. The audience breaks up. Disobedience is the backbone of my act. Isn't it a wonderful idea? Can't get bookings though. Agents are looking for conformity."

"Haven't I seen that act on television recently?" Daddy guessed. How was I to know that he too could be distracted by the luminous boob tube?

"Yes," I admitted. "Wasn't it wonderful?"

Daddy changed the subject, unwilling to discuss the merits of a dog act with me. "How's your mother?" he asked.

"Fine. Still overpaying her help."

"You mean Albert?"

"Who else? He's the only lover she's got. I guess he really answers her needs as well as the telephone."

"And I supposed I don't?" Daddy fumed.

"But Edward, you and Mommy haven't been together for five years. Whatever are you talking about?"

"There is more to life than the physical. We have other ways of communing."

"Glad to hear that," I said. And then: "Goodbye."

"You're not leaving without your money?" Edward asked. "Oh, am I getting it?" I feigned surprise. This was our little game. Edward would never let me get out of there penniless. He'd then have to worry about whether I was dying of starvation. The publicity would be bad for his reputation. He went to his green metal cashbox, took out exactly fifty dollars, and handed it to me. Taking his money was the thin thread that bound us. If I didn't bounce around too much, it would never break.

The young man with the long hair and mournful harmonica came home with me.

9 "Hello, we're here," I called to Pablo as I opened the door. He was lying glumly in front of the TV watching a game show.

"None of the prizes interest me," Pablo said. "What would I do with a set of power tools?"

"Pablo, this is Reggie, a friend of Dad's. I've told him all about you."

"Hi," Reggie said, getting down into a deep knee-bend, closer to Pablo. "Helen told me you're into sports."

"I play ball," Pablo answered, "and also run track, wrestle, swim . . . you name it." He was warming up to Reggie. "What I really like to do is fetch and carry."

"Not exactly an Olympic event," Reggie said good-naturedly. "Wanna hear a blues tune?" He played a blues thing, this time cupping the instrument in his hands. Pablo got up and danced. It was just like a party.

"You guys thirsty?" I brought out a bottle of beer and some milk. Pablo loves milk. Reggie sprawled on the floor drinking his beer. I got into something comfortable and sheer. "Tell me about yourself," I said to Reggie. "Tell me what you want outta life." This got him started on a lot of talk I didn't understand at all. Stuff about sports averages.

"There are a lot of things I can do that I haven't done yet. Until I do them I'm shortchanging myself."

"Like what?" I asked.

"I've never batted .300 or hit 50 home runs in a season. I haven't won two MVP awards or played on three world championship teams."

"Why would you want to?" I asked, a trifle unsympathetically. "You can't be into peace, healing, harmonicas, and sports at the same time . . . can you?"

"I can do anything I put my mind to," Reggie said. "I've been approached for a three-year contract, but it would have to be in the vicinity of three million dollars. . . . I'm not going to sell myself cheap."

"Three million dollars is cheap for what you have to offer," I exclaimed, thinking he was playing some game I hadn't got the hang of yet. Reggie didn't seem to be spaced out. His voice had the ring of authority (yet who but madmen are that sure of themselves?), "Can I manage you?" I said, kissing the back of his neck. He smelled peppery, a combination of Patchouli and Holy Smoke.

"You can open another beer for me," he replied, then belched. "My compliments to the chef."

I was so glad I had bought giant, soft pillows to strew around. A good-looking man was just what I had imagined lying on them. I put the icy wet can of beer beside Reggie, and began to unbutton his shirt.

"I aim to fulfill my talents, play up to the peak of my ability," he said, taking my hand and placing it seductively over his crotch.

"How did you meet my father?" I asked, leaving my hand where he had put it. His penis began to rise, elevating my hand ever so slightly. I could feel his sex heat steaming through his trousers.

"I had trouble with my arm, couldn't move it. Had gone to all kinds of doctors. Mother knew about your father's gift for healing so she brought me to him . . . and look . . . nothing's wrong with me now." His hand swept in a full arc, his elbow bent and unbent, he lifted the can of beer and gulped it down. Pablo brought Reggie his chewed-up old tennis ball, and ignoring me, they began to play. I waited my turn (for the turn of the screw), because that's what we did after Pablo trotted to a shadowy corner and took a snooze.

"Are you clean and free of disease?" I asked Reggie, trying to make the question sound cute.

"You can always trust an athlete," he answered.

10 How to tell Pablo that I got the clap from Reggie? It was a mistake. I've always been very careful; however, I must have been receptive to the disease-carrying organism. Now I'm itchy and have a discharge. I know better than to be ashamed; the doctor'll give me a double shot of penicillin to cure it.

11 Pablo has taken the news rather well. There is only a hole in the blanket to show how upset he was, and a few stray hairs which he shed instead of tears.

"Chairman Mao has the right idea," Pablo said. "Venereal disease is practically nil in Red China. The Mao government has almost succeeded in eliminating extramarital sexual intercourse."

"What an unsympathetic thing to say to me, I complained. "Besides, how do you know?"

"I heard it in the elevator," Pablo answered, "from a recent guest of the All-China Medical Association."

12 I've been worried about what will happen to Pablo in his old age and so, projecting into the future, I wrote a letter to Dr. Foster, who gives advice to animal owners. He has always been kind and considerate to those who write in.

> Dear Dr. Foster:
> I raised Pablo from a young pup. That was when his mother rejected him. He's been my baby since, you might say. A year ago the nineteenth of this month, he turned completely blind and everybody started telling me to get rid of him because he was too old. I haven't seen one friend since I told her I'd rather have her put to sleep than my dog. Of course, Pablo is still with me and always will be. Why does everyone keep saying how old he is? Pablo is only a teenager.
>
> HJ.

> Dear HJ.:
> Understandably, some people are not even able to contemplate giving up a beloved pet. Pablo has been so close to you all these years, the thought of not always having him may simply be unacceptable. Certainly, the fact that a dog is blind does not mean that he cannot enjoy life. I have known many blind dogs who went about the process of living with great gusto. But aging is a process that cannot be denied in any species. Most dogs don't make it to the teens at all. Those who do succumb to various aging processes in the early teens. I am sure with the help of your veterinarian you are doing all you can for Pablo to bring him along

as far and as comfortably as possible. But your teenager's time cannot be extended indefinitely by modern medicine, or even by love.

DR. FOSTER

13 I hold in my hand a newspaper clipping that refers to Pablo's short-lived career as a juvenile delinquent. This is the way he came into my life.

PUPPY TELLS GUILT
DOG BURGLAR SEIZED
AFTER 21 BREAK-INS

SCARSDALE.—A New York puppy has admitted breaking into 21 homes, police said Thursday. The dog burst into howls when confronted by police. "It breaks my heart," said Det. Phil Saunders, indicating his chest. The dog committed the burglaries during the last six weeks. First he took only food, an old slipper, and a blond wig, but he became more sophisticated after older dogs told him he was wasting his time with minor loot. He then took watches, jewelry, and portable radios which he left at hock shops on the Lower East Side—his haul amounting to $300-$400 in each one, police said. "He knew it was wrong," said Saunders. "It was because he wanted things. It's a want type of situation." The mode of operation used by the young pup was to scrape with his paw on doors in the neighborhood to see if anyone was home, police said. If no one answered, he would find an open window, push in the screen, and climb inside. He would leave the same way. Saunders suspected from the start that a small creature was involved because of the small windows he climbed through and the nature of the losses. He caught the dog after a routine follow-up of a house burglary. Saunders questioned neigh-bors who reported seeing a small dog (part collie, part po-lice). They said they had caught the same dog trying to break into their home but had not reported the incident because it was a dog. Saunders went to the pet store where the dog had lived with his maternal grandmother and sev-en other dogs to whom he is related. "I asked him if he knew why we were there," said Saunders. "He said, 'Yes, because you want to adopt me,' and started to cry." He said most of the dog's profit apparently was spent for ice cream and hot dogs to give to kids. He was a lonely dog and badly needed a good home. The dog's grandmother said the puppy often would be gone as early as 5 A.M., but would never say where he had been. His parents are separated and apparently live somewhere in Scarsdale. "He might have been searching for them," Saunders said. Saunders recommended counseling for the dog and police said he would not be taken to the pound. Meanwhile, if you have a home and a place in your heart for a dog in need, call LU 9-2222.

I immediately called, and took Pablo in. We have an unspoken pact never to mention it again.

14 Late at night I heard someone stop outside the door. As quietly as I could, I looked through the peephole. There was another eye pressed to the glass. It couldn't see me, but I saw it. The iris was hazel with a ring of blue. A beautiful eye. Was it the eye of someone who wants to harm me?

15 Beware of the dog, it bites!

16 I know that Pablo has been sending letters to magazines and newspapers ever since I taught him to type. The roll of stamps becomes narrower and narrower. There are only five stamps left. I found the carbon of a letter he sent to a sex magazine. It amuses him to pretend that he is human, or is he making fun of us? Anyway, I think it's perfectly awful of him to leave the evidence (obscenity) around.

Dear Editor:
Both my wife and I are grateful to S.M. whose frank letter we read with great interest in your September issue. We are carnivores, with some curiosity in whole grains, and so the information intrigued us even more. Having been married for fifteen years, I must admit to you that sexual intercourse was becoming rather infrequent, and when it did take place, rather dull. Then, happily, in your publication came the first intimation of new joys!

The initial time I tried eating medium-sized milk bones from the immaculate vessel of my wife it did not work; milk bones absorb moisture at an alarming rate, and that's the way the cookie crumbled. Next I tried a well-trimmed club steak; this worked marvelously well. By the time I had reached the last bite my wife was perilously close to orgasm. Knowing enough to keep rolling when the dice are hot, we went on to all manner of delights: chopped sirloin, which I removed morsel by morsel with a pair of ivory chopsticks, old-fashioned Wheatena prepared ahead of time then fried within the "natural female oven" (the rough grain gave us both a gorgeous tingle). Obviously a jaded palate would not appreciate this simple fare, but we deemed it a pleasure to take our breakfast, lunch, and dinner in bed.

Keep publishing your informative, truly adult magazine.

Yours truly,
Pablo Andalou D.O.G.

17 "You haven't told me what you think about the letter you found," Pablo said.

"I think it's quite unusual," I answered without enthusiasm.

"I wrote it to amuse you. You never smile any more." He stood by nervously, hoping I'd thank him or at least scratch his back for him.

"Don't you ever get tired of trying to make me happy?" I said unkindly.

Pablo leaned both front paws on the windowsill. "You don't know how tired," he answered.

18 This evening when I went to the store for juice someone followed me. When I turned around he ducked into a doorway. If he continued following me I would have blown the whistle on my key chain. The advertisement said that the whistle is guaranteed to bring help immediately. I'm glad that I didn't have to blow it.

19 We had to get out of the city, so Pablo and I planned a picnic. "It must be at a fairly deserted place," Pablo said, "so that we won't be bothered." I chose a cemetery in Queens. Pablo carried the blanket and I the bag lunch. The man at the gatehouse assumed we were going to picnic on our own prepaid plot. He did not notice that Pablo was a dog. So many men wear beards and moustaches these days, and besides, Pablo had the brim of his hat pulled down over his ears. Though this made his ears damp he didn't complain.

The parklike flavor of the cemetery and its relative seclusion made it a perfect place for us to visit. Other cemeteries permit ice skating on ponds or encourage strollers; some even substitute see-through fences for their tall stone walls. But this memorial park was old-fashioned enough to retain its stone walls and also its marble monuments instead of indulging in the current trend to bronze lawn-level markers (which reduces the cost of mowing the grass).

"It's been a long time, perhaps a year, since I've come here," I said to Pablo.

"Pardon me, but you've never been here," Pablo said. "At least you've never mentioned it before."

"That's true, but I thought it would be a proper thing to say. Actually I've never been to any cemetery, they scare me."

"Then eat this ham sandwich with coleslaw and mustard. It'll make you feel better."

Pablo plied me with food, and it did make me feel happy and brave and alive. "I think we should know everything about each other," I said confidently. "While there is still time."

"That's not possible," Pablo replied. "I'd rather we rolled in the grass together. I love rolling in the grass. It's so aphrodisiac."

"Anything is possible when you're young and in love," I retorted. "Here we are, just the two of us . . . let's open our hearts to one another."

Pablo opened his mouth. He breathed in short fast takes, gasping doggy fashion. His tongue hung out impolitely; the dull reddish-black papules that normally line the underside of a dog's tongue resembled soft vestigial teeth—his real teeth (fangs) extended past the upper part of his mouth, reminding me of stiffened corn tassels.

"Okay, I'll tell you about myself," Pablo agreed. "These are the scientific facts. I carry, in every drop of my blood, chemical proof of a close relationship to wolves, foxes, and jackals of every species. Although hundreds of thousands of years have elapsed since my direct ancestors lived, and though there has been no blending of blood in the intervening centuries, something rich and brutal has been transmitted." He looked at me hoping that his information would terrify me and thus bolster his male ego, but I remained unperturbed.

"Just what are you getting at?" I asked.

Pablo showed me the newspaper clipping he had been wearing in his hatband for decoration.

HUNT RAPIST WITH FANGS

LINDENHURST, QUEENS, Aug. 22 (AP)—Police combed shopping marts and parks near this quiet community today for a man with fanglike teeth who raped a middle-aged woman.

The man leaped out of some bushes naked and attacked the woman as she was feeding pigeons, police reported.

The woman said her long-haired assailant appeared to be uneducated, since he did nothing but growl and otherwise utter unintelligible sounds. Police have checked three mental institutions in the area, but so far no inmates have been reported missing.

I was incredulous. "Don't tell me that was you!"

Pablo had that finky cement-set smile mooning his face. "I just want you to realize that I'm not Mr. Nice Guy," he said.

"Oh go chase a bird. That's your speed."

We spent the rest of the time chasing each other: hiding behind tombstones, falling, rising, shouting, and singing at the top of our lungs. We were careful to clean up after ourselves. We wanted to come back and could not afford to antagonize the watchman.

20 Just because Pablo and I have a platonic relationship doesn't mean that I don't dream of a passionate embrace that would weld us even closer together. We have so much in common: a fear of mysteriously moving shadows, avoidance of strangers, intolerance of hot or cold climates, a fearsome hate for being yanked along against our will. But is that enough?

21 "Sorry to bother you again so soon, Mother, but I need some advice."

Mother was wearing her long black robe with hidden pockets. She fumbled around in its folds till she found her steel-rimmed granny glasses and put them on. I observed her coldly, devoid of affection. Every time I saw her I tried to crush the tiny capsule of devotion that was choking me. Why couldn't I experience her as just another human being? She had none of the beauty left that had caused Daddy to compare her to a garden flower. Perhaps he had been thinking of her secret parts when he called her "my very own bearded iris." Mother, afraid of an emotional showdown, kept her professional distance, always.

"Have you come for a private consultation?" she asked.

"Yes. Do you have the time?" I responded coldly.

"I can give you an hour," she replied.

"Thank you, Mother."

"There is a larger fee for the private consultation," she added.

"I'll be able to pay you. Daddy gave me some money."

"Oh? How is your father?"

"He says he's in communication with you, so you ought to know how he is."

"Your father is imagining things."

"I think he wants to get together with you again, Mom."

"That is impossible," she intoned. "I could never live in a household that rang with the cries of those in pain. Edward seems to thrive on it. You know I must have the relative peace of the world of the dead, spirits who materialize only to calm the living or to set them on the right path. Besides, you know I'm living with Albert!" Her voice rose to a fiery pitch. "Albert is the only person who may tap my center of accumulated energy. Your father had his chance!"

Suddenly calm, Mother motioned for me to sit opposite her. Between us, on a round table two feet in diameter, stolidly sat a crystal ball (the future's transparent gossipmonger). I had been with Mother when she had bought the ball at a discount. Its crystal was imperfect, full of bubbles and flecks of color. Mother adored it because it was "different"; she expected it to increase her psychic powers. Gazing into the crystal, Mother said:

"Helen Jones, I am receptive to your spirit this evening. It shines with unwavering brightness and tells me that now . . . now is the time for you to forge ahead with financial plans for the future. If you apply for a job tomorrow, you will have great success. Do not hesitate. You have nothing to lose but the double fare. Friends made during the next week will prove beneficial to you, if, and I emphasize the IF, if you do not allow them to walk all over you the way you have in the past. Do not refuse an unusual invitation, and remember that experience is the best teacher, and that life is not a correspondence course. If you have any questions, ask them now, before the vision fades away."

"Reverend Jones," I began, hoping that Mother would not fly into a rage when I asked my question, "why did you and Daddy separate?"

Mother removed her steel-rimmed glasses (which didn't have lenses in them. She only wore them to make her look owl-wise) and tapped them angrily on the table. A sharp pain in my left leg told me that she had kicked me under the table.

"Don't you remember when Edward spread those stories about me? I spit on him!" She shouted to Albert to bring in her private file, then plucked from its accordion-pleated folds a Xeroxed copy of father's ignominious attack which had appeared in the papers.

SAUNA BURNS BASIS

OF DIVORCE ACTION

Burns suffered in an East Side sauna have converted a 36-year-old "devout Prudist," mother of one child, into a loose woman who sips brandy Alexanders in bars and has affairs with strange men, according to an attorney who filed a divorce suit against Mrs. Myra Tones naming the spa as contributing to the corruption of Mrs. Jones's morals.

Dr. Edward Jones testified that since his wife, Mrs. Myra Jones, was burned in the sauna two years ago she has become two persons, physically and psychologically speaking. As *Myra* Jones she exerts great sexual powers over younger men from whom she receives money, much of which is spent on the brandy Alexanders, which she craves. But as *Mrs. E.* Jones she remains the "shy" person and devout Prudist she was before she became a victim of the faulty thermostat (which has been replaced) at the Citrus Health Spa.

The doctor described his Wife *Myra* Jones as "the sexually hungry production of *Myra*'s mind" and *Mrs. E.* Jones as "the guilt-ridden projection who bitterly regrets her actions." He said that Mrs. Jones has been sexually involved "with at least a dozen other men" since her accident in the sauna. "On one occasion I had to follow her to Mexico to get her away from someone she met in a bar," he said. The doctor claims that now she has developed sex feelings for strangers, and that those feelings often take control when she is sipping brandy while seated near men in a bar. So far, the spa has refused to comment on the charges officially, but employees have been heard to remark the record that since the publicity, business has picked up considerably.

"How many lies do you count in that article? How many?" Mother insisted.

"At least three," I replied. "You're not devout, you've never been burned in a sauna, and you don't like brandy. You have been known to associate with strange young men though . . . Albert for one."

"Edward was jealous . . . excessively jealous. I'm not about to give up my strange young strangers, nor the comfortable neighborhood bar. Tell Edward that! No don't tell him. Why stir up dead passions? Your father may be Edward Jones physician and humanitarian to others, but to me he's a seething volcano."

"I think you're both crazy, Mom."

"Thank you, darling," she replied, laughing. "I think we both are too. Now remember, when you go home, to set your clock early for tomorrow. A new and exciting life waits for you."

The Reverend Jones had no reason to believe I would take her motherly advice. I never have.

22 "You've got to level with me, Pablo; I can't find my gold pants and jacket . . ."

"You can't?"

"No, I can't. And I haven't even worn them yet. Remember that package I received from the Mistress Collection by Funky?"

"No."

"Look here, Mr. Innocent, something very weird is happening; my favorite clothes have been disappearing."

"I'll help you look for them if that's what you want."

"I've already looked everywhere."

"Clothes just don't get up and walk out by themselves, do they?"

"Pablo, do you know something you're not telling me?"

"No."

23 Mother did not meet Albert at a séance. She met him as he roamed a local hospital's halls wearing a white jacket and a stethoscope that he had bought at Sears with a fraudulent credit card. Police had been looking for a phony doctor who'd plied unwary widows with expensive gifts in order to "take them for all they've got," Mother told me. She admired his many successful impersonations of those in respected professions: the lawyer, the surgeon, the banker, and the scientist. In spite of a lack of formal schooling, Albert gave advice that was always excellent and based on a cram course of self-initiated study. He could have been eminent in any of the aforementioned fields if he had not been a mental case. Diversity itself is an illness; it bespeaks an uncertain cast of mind. One other thing. Albert adored setting fires, and the charming but dangerous outcast was grateful to Mother for trusting him with the lighting of the chapel candles (in spite of a few regressions) and for shielding him from the law.

She doesn't know that I've been seeing Albert since he first took the folded piece of paper out of my hand. I love intrigue and bugging Mother. Outside of that Albert has no great attraction for me. It's a game. But who knows?

24 Albert deserves a physical description, since that is what is most elusive about him. Once he is fixed firmly in my mind, none of his disguises can confuse me.

HAIR: Brown, with a preponderance of red highlighting each pomaded wave

EYES: Green, planted at uniform dept within a narrow furrow

NOSE: Stuffed toucan

MOUTH: Sensitive, twitching

TEMPERATURE: Warm to the touch like a low wattage bulb

HABITS: Scratches behind the ear till it bleeds

RULES: Will not tie his shoelaces in public. Will not live within ten miles of the maddening stillness of the Negev

FAMILY: He is the son of a well-known hermaphrodite who managed to impregnate himself/ herself after receiving the medical opinion that it was an impossibility. Such is the ingenious that Albert is made of

FEAR: That he will one day throw the wheat away with the chaff

25 Albert called. He was coming over.
I knew I looked a mess, and so his call sent me into a flurry of

activity. How could I believe I was beautiful unless I saw myself through his eyes? Unless I made *sure* he'd go ape over me. I turned to my longtime friend and adviser *Cosmopolitan* magazine. "Oh *Cosmo*," I pleaded, "how can I look superstunning on short notice? Help me!" As if by chance, I came upon these words: "BEAUTY HINTS. YOUR ZIP-ZAP SPLIT-SECOND ROUTINE. GUARANTEED TO PERFORM MIRACLES." Just what I needed . . . a miracle. I followed *Cosmo*'s suggestions to a T: first I stripped down to the mere essentials, naked as the day I was born, although Mother told me I was wearing a blood-red chemise molded from hot wax when I first appeared between her legs. Then I stretched and pulled my body as if blocking a wet curtain. Next I washed my face and applied egg white and lemon juice, letting it dry to become a thin *masque*. When the *masque* hardened, it was as if I were removing my face. I had in my hands an incomplete, compacted death mask. Because of the lack of time, I whipped out a dry shampoo for my not-quite-clean hair, and then took the risk of falling asleep beneath eye pads soaked in witch hazel and ice water. While I lay there I thought only beautiful thoughts, since distressing ruminations on life and death are *taboo* if you want to be beautiful. I thought of being out in the open with Daddy, of transplanting young plants who could not in some cases extend their roots fast enough to keep up with the gradually disappearing moisture of boxes set in greenhouses. I breathed rhythmically through my nostrils, which was necessary for more happy brain waves. Because I have always considered feet to be desperately important, I hopped into the tub and let blasts of hot and cold water beat against my soles. It felt so good I wondered what I needed Albert for? The soles of my feet are as sensitive as my nipples (what an inelegant location for an erogenous zone!). After drying and perfuming my feet I put on my cuddliest slippers and became a speed demon . . . but not slapdash. I knew that Albert would view me with close scrutiny; he was extremely nearsighted, and what he couldn't see he could smell. He reminded me of Pablo in that respect. But what of my face? Yes, I do wear makeup sometimes: for cheeks a peach blush-on bronzing gel; for fabulously murky eyes my favorite color is sad shadow and gobs of old-fashioned black salve (you can get it at the drug store and it also draws pus out of wounds and pimples); my lips are painted cherry red, but for that neglected area between the upper lip and tip of nose I brush just a teensy-weensy suggestion of a moustache. Albert adores moustaches, he's bi-hirsute. I knew he would respect me for my political statement regarding androgyny as it reposed in my moustache. He did not regard hairiness as being unfeminine; in fact he carried about with him a photograph of a Turkish woman whose face rivaled that of Grace McDaniel's, who was once billed as THE UGLIEST WOMAN. Almost ready for Albert, I jolted my senses with a splash of cologne and put perfume behind my ears and on all pulse points. With thirty seconds to spare I sat down to wait for Mother's protégé.

26 I did not have intercourse with Albert. I was too beautiful and clean. It would have taken hours for me to repossess my naturalness. Besides, Albert was wearing a disguise that put me off; he had come as Gertrude Stein. Aside from the necrophiliac tendencies it might have revealed in me if I had balled Albert cum Stein, I did not want to discover that yes, Gertrude did have a penis, which is why she hid herself beneath such voluminous skirts of fat.

"In profile I look like an Indian," Albert said. "Stein's greasepaint is fabulous."

Haughtily turning, he waited for me to agree.

"Maybe you do," I said, "but what's the point?"

Albert was disappointed in me. "There isn't any point. It's just an experiment. I love to dress up and be different."

"You don't talk different. You talk like Albert."

"No, no, I talk like Gertrude Stein. Yesterday the Reverend Jones drew her into our circle. I studied her articulation, the things she said. I . . ." He gurgled deep down in his throat, took a few staggering steps backward, clutched at his jacket lapels, and continued in a voice that was deeper and yet ephemeral. It might have come from that place between heaven and hell; it might have traveled down from the eighteenth floor. It was a ghostlike voice. As the words emerged, Albert mimicked a striptease.

"I am loving, when I am loving I am saying I am loving. Yesterday I was not loving. Not loving is not loving any day. Today is a day I am loving. Today is here. Loving and today are words. All words do not say I am loving. What is loving when one is not feeling that one is loving? . . ."

"Hate?" I innocently asked. Albert was too far gone to answer me.

"Alice, *à quelle heure sont Ernest et Pablo* arriving? Does the smell? Have you ironed my manuscripts? Chocolates are for saints. No, I won't go, I've changed my mind. My, my, how the carrots are. I'm the only genius who knows who all the other geniuses are! Our trip to America will be triumphant, *un succès d'estime*. Don't worry, our relationship is ambiguous only to the underprivileged. *Au revoir et à bientôt, ma cherie.*"

He aurevoired himself right into the bathroom, where he recovered after drinking a small bottle of paregoric which I had been keeping for toothache.

"Feel better?"

"Much."

"You look better without your makeup and skirt."

"Thanks."

"What time is it, Albert?"

"Don't know. My timepiece and my codpiece don't work. Overwound I guess."

"It must be late."

"You want me to go?"

"Umhum."

"Do I deserve an Academy Award for my performance this evening?"

"Thank you. May I see you again sometime?"

"Umhum."

27 I have a collection of poems that men gave me for one reason or another. Sometimes it was to take the place of a gift, or to prove how much they trusted me with their innermost thoughts. Usually it was to prove that they were either sane or totally insane. Conniving romanti-cists all. The poems were mostly old-fashioned, none of them read like laundry lists, and none of them swarmed across the page like a flight of doves. Flattering but dull.

Albert's autobiographical poem was the last in my collection:

> *MUTABLE MOTHER*
> I keep thinking of fires we used to make
> in the empty lot across the street
> littered with garbage where horseflies streaked
> I was 10, you were old
> wild bitter mom, my boyish body
> trying over the moist
> shadow-mottled girth
> no one warned me to stay away from there
> Later a fire swept through
> the Venetian blinds
> of our oedipal castle
> we blackened
> Is the child with shred
> of flesh between his legs
> still burning?

28 People cannot be dealt with like a disease.

29 My favorite morning program is the Joe Fafka program. Joe carries on a dialogue with his listeners. The morons call in, and people like me just listen and laugh.

CALLER: Say Joe, just when did this crimewave start? I think that it was the Kennedy administration, with them Young Lords and them Black Panthers; rotten gripers!

JOE: No, it really commenced with Lyndon B. Johnson, that big Texas blowhard, when he said in his drawl: "You have to have your civil rights!" You see, sir, any time you appease a tyrant, it only whets his appetite more. He gave them the go-ahead, and we have to pay for it. I say starve the scum. Drive them out. Don't feed and clothe them. Is that what we're paying taxes for?"

CALLER: Can I say one more thing, Joe?

JOE: You're on.

CALLER: About the Jews in the Middle East . . .

JOE: Get the phone, you creep!

Joe is wonderful when he's mad, an authentic bigot.

30 Midmorning and it was Albert's voice on the phone. A marriage proposal. He said that I not only reminded him of my mother, but of his mother, and that I would make him the happiest man in the world if I consented to be his bride.

"Nope," I said.

31 Mother pulled a switch on me. She tried to convince me to marry Albert: "He may be a pyromaniac, but he's not an arsonist!" she shouted. "He does it for love, not money. Don't you want to be loved and adored by a husband and dance the carioca? I'd marry Albert myself, but he's too old for me."

"Mother, nobody's danced the carioca in years," I protested.

"One more word out of you and I'll hang up," Mother warned. "Why don't you down to Rio and see for yourself? It's a wonderful place to honeymoon."

"I don't love Albert," I said.

"Neither do I," she said. "I love your father."

So, Mother would sacrifice me, in order to pave the way for a reconciliation with Edward!

"You're not good enough to shine his shoes for him," I retorted angrily. Mother hung up.

32

I went to a professional for advice, as I always do. Dear Mary answered me in her syndicated column.

Dear Mary:

I suppose to some my problem may seem funny, but to me it's no joke. I've been dating this terrific guy for a few weeks now and we get along great even though I'm taller than he is. He takes me to the best places, and he's a perfect gentleman, but the problem is this, he gets a sexual thrill out of setting fires. You may have read about the fires at Melon's Wax Museum in which two exhibits were destroyed: a Chinese Temple and a representation of the Last Supper; my friend was a prime suspect. The thing is this, should I drop this suitor (he was bequeathed $100,000,000 in trust from which he is allowed to draw $100,000 a year) or should I continue the relationship?

Sincerely,
Once Burned

Dear Once Burned:

Ask him point-blank if he means to marry you or whether he is just carrying a torch. If he is serious, have him agree on a date. Once married, I suggest you tip off the proper authorities, and hotfoot it away with the loot.

33 There is a madman at large who is fixated on me. This note was slipped under the door.

DON'T THINK YOU
   HIDE FRUM ME, I KNOW YOU CUNT-TITS WHAT LAUGH AT ME WHEN I WANT TO,
         BUT, I KNOW WHERE SUCK AND FUCK AND,
             PUT THE BIGGEST COCK IN! ! ! ! ! ! !
I BE FRIEND SOON SINCERELYELY

34 Because I was upset, Pablo read to me.
"Florida. A group of students who had been drinking beer on Dorado Beach visited the Corry Brothers International Circus. They were wandering among the animal cages stored behind the tents, when one of the students broke away from his friends, shouting: 'I'm stronger than you are; let's fight?' He then jumped into the tiger's cage and pulled the tiger's whiskers. The tiger broke his neck with one swipe of its paw."

The item cheered me up enough so that I could jot down these questions. They may lead to a deeper understanding of the inexplicable.

QUESTIONS

1: Why was the tiger wearing false whiskers?

2: Why do students shout when they are together?

3: Why was the tiger's cage open?

4: What did the student learn?

5: Did the jungle beast resemble someone in the boy's family?

6: Was an honorary diploma awarded the boy and placed in the casket beside him?

7: Is it best to live in the cage or out of it?

35

My friend Marian hasn't seen or heard from me since she moved out of the Buckminster. We've been through a lot together and still feel close, but the burden of friendship is on me. Marian lives in a shithole on the Lower East Side with a guy who practically scraped her off the sidewalk when she was already pregnant with Elmer Joy. Marian is a singer and writes her own songs, but since the baby she hasn't had time. Marian is a natural person, and loves to have Elmer Joy at her breast. "It turns me on," she admitted, and look at what it's done for Elmer Joy. True, her kid was fat and healthy. He had come a long way from when he was born prematurely. Marian and Jeremy, Marian's old man, were driving through a snowstorm in Vermont, stopping every now and then to screw (Marian had three more months, she thought, before birth time), when she began to have labor pains. They drove to a local hospital, which happened to have a special unit for premies and newborns with other difficulties, where she gave birth. Elmer Joy had all kinds of tubes in his heart and almost died three times, but the doctor let Marian hold him and nurse him . . . That, and some infant will to live, pulled Elmer Joy through.

While watching a diaper commercial on TV, I got the impulse to call Marian. I knew it would be an important call and I was right; Marian put me on to a job possibility—selling tacos and soft drinks from a cart. One of her friends was planning to leave, and Marian was sure she'd recommend me.

"But I'd like to see you. Why don't we get together next week, go to the Cloisters or somewhere for a drink?" she said. "I just bought these knock-out violet-tinted glasses with pearl frames, you should see them on me, you'll die."

"Okay, so let's meet at your place, say tentatively, next Saturday morning, unless I call you before then," I agreed. "How's Jeremy?"

"He's still on the road with Miracle in Milan, you must have heard of them . . . the new Italian rock band. Jeremy's their road manager. We're doing very well, managed to save ten thousand dollars. Dig it! And we didn't have nothin' when we began."

"Say, that's great! What're you gonna do with all that money?"

"Buy a house in the country, have my own garden. You and Pablo can stay with us whenever you want."

"I love you, Marian."

"I love you, too, Helen."

She gave me her friend's phone number, and her friend said she'd talk to her boss about hiring me when she quit.

36 Pablo and I play celebrity. It's an interview game we made up. He is usually the journalist, and I am the celebrity.

Pablo with tape recorder going and pencil poised above notebook: "Miss Jones, our readership of young career women between the ages of nineteen and twenty-six would be especially interested in hearing what you have to say to them, since you are one of the most eligible women in the world . . ."

Miss Helen Jones, seated in front of a huge picture window: "Yes, I am one of the most eligible women in the world. I speak Greek, Danish, Italian, French, Spanglish, and Tongues. I'm not too old or too poor. I stay stiletto-slim by eating only foods that can be prepared with a minimum of fuss. I wear gold chokers around my long white neck. When I make love I allow three elegantly shaped breasts to appear from under my favorite negligee. It isn't difficult for me to keep a year-round pallid complexion since I summer in New York, indoors where the skin-drying sun can't reach me. My playmate and constant companion is Pablo, born a mutt, but a natural aristocrat. He also makes an adequate foot warmer. I don't allow work to interfere with partying in SoHo, Washington Heights, or Little Italy. I feel like Vasco da Gama or Christopher Columbus for having discovered these places. They are sensationally provincial. I used to go to Saint Croix, but since those thirty unexplained murders of whites on the island, I've canceled my reservation. No sense in going where one is not wanted, is there? I own literally thousands of designer dresses which I give away to my favorite charities every two years. I prefer wearing ready-to-wear 'finds' right off the racks. I've already had two well-publicized breakdowns, one at the Forty-second Street library when I tried to feed fifteen pounds of fillet mignon to the stone lions, another at Chock Full O' Nuts where I appeared in blackface and roller skates during the lunch hour. Having achieved total peace with my favorite yogi, Meher Barbareebop, who said, '*Don't worry. Be happy. We are all one. I am the ocean of life,*' I no longer need an intelligent, level-headed man to protect me. I practice the kazoo four hours a day and hope to go on concert tours in the near future. I readily admit my humble beginnings on a Georgia dirt farm; in fact I have fond memories of wandering carefree and barefoot through the mud with friends: black, white, pink, or blue . . . I was already broad-minded. My inquisitive nature lent added pleasure to an otherwise drab childhood. My cigarette is Gauloises. My voice has a husky quality; it went down an octave after I was hit by an overhanging branch while horseback riding. I have no time for a serious romance in my life. I'm never lonely."

Pablo thanked me for the interview and promised to send me a copy of it before it was published, just in case there was anything I wanted to retract. He's not the usual run of journalist.

37 When I mentioned earlier that Marian and I had been through a lot together, one of the things I was referring to was abortion. Last year, in the same week, by means of a vacuum, some pre-infant material was sucked out of our wombs. Pablo had been upset because he fancied himself the father of what might have been. I didn't fancy it at all, being the mother of wolf-boy, a child with callouses on elbows and knees, no knack for clear speech, a reading disability, and complete lack of table manners. The child's name would have reflected our merger—PabHel Inc —sure to bring him misery in school. I was more disturbed over Marian's experience; up till the last minute she hadn't made up her mind, and then, it was all over. Now, of course, she has Elmer Joy, and I have my freedom, such as it is.

38 Why work if you don't have to?

39 Cab driver told me to say hello to myself every morning, because, "If you don't accept yourself in a friendly way, no one else will." He also reminded me that "there ain't no closet small enough to hold what you need, and no closet big enough to hold what you want." I tipped him twenty-five cents to the dollar, instead of my usual fifteen cents.

40 Jade is worth three times what it used to be. I can't bring myself to sell the piece I took from Edward; I've grown attached to it. When I look at it I suffer. There is a snail captured in the jade: bluish-green, curled in on itself, and asleep.

41 Another note, this time left in my mailbox behind the desk in the lobby. The clerk said: "I can't remember everybody who comes in." The message was especially vicious. I was not the target, Pablo was. IF WE DON'T GET YOU, WE'LL GET YOUR DOG.

Who are they? What do they want? Pablo is a citizen of the inner city and so am I, both useless to a political plot.

42 Pablo told me of a dream he had in which purebred beagles were pulled out of the trunk of a car in order to be auctioned off, and then taken to laboratories where they were subjected to experiments.

"But you're a mutt," I said to soothe him. "Who would want you?"

"Those who are jealous of our mute partnership, those who are not decent and have lost their faith. Cells of satanic vivisectionists are springing up all over the city. My best friend, Fido, is a good example of the cruelty of these humans. His head was grafted onto the body of another dog. Both heads responded to stimuli, and Fido survived for one terrible month before he died."

"Is that a fact!" I said.

"I didn't just make it up," Pablo answered.

We spent the evening chewing nervously on dog biscuits.

43 I bought postcards of dogs showing them dancing, singing, and beating drums while wearing little pointed hats on their heads. The cards are imported from West Germany.

44 Daddy was beautiful as he went about his laboratory potentizing his flowers by a method he had discovered the year before. "See this little plant, Helen?" he said tenderly. "It grows about a foot in height, is so unassuming that it is easily passed unnoticed. The flowers on its many-branching slender wiry stems are pale mauve in color and very small. They remind me of you as a child."

Taking three small plain glass bowls, he filled them with water and set them under the blue lights that were always lit above his indoor garden. Carefully he placed the flower heads of the chicory plant in one of the bowls till the whole surface of the water was covered. In the second bowl he floated the tiny flowering end sprays of the agrimony, and in the third, those of the vervain (lemony sprigs, delightfully scented).

"In about four hours, when the petals start to fade, the water will be impregnated with magnetic power," Daddy said.

In about four hours the water was crystal clear and full of sparkling bubbles. Daddy lifted the flowers out of the water with a blade of grass so that he would not touch the fluid with his own fingers. The water was then transferred by means of a small-lipped phial to the bottles that were to hold the finished tincture. When the tincture bottles were half full, he added an equal amount of brandy to preserve the fluid and keep it clear indefinitely.

"You'd make a wonderful assistant," Daddy said. "Would you like to learn my methods, help me in my work?"

"Daddy, I'm going on a vacation to Las Vegas, so I can't," I lied, though the minute I said it I became interested in the trip. Decided to ask Albert to go with me. He'd been there before and would be helpful. Mother could finance the excursion; she'd want something in return, of course.

"All your life's a vacation," Daddy said. "You haven't applied yourself to anything. Why are you going to Las Vegas? You don't gamble."

"Curiosity, Dad. The same curiosity you have for plants. I want to play around, find out what happens when one lays a warm poultice of female juice over the palpitating heart of an impotent bystander. I want to extract a dew of the senses from the rigid limbs of those who prefer paralysis to the danger of feeling. I'm my father's daughter."

Edward, obviously moved by my declaration of allegiance, paced the floor of his laboratory. He responded with fatherly scientific persuasion, hoping to get me to give up my disturbing ideas.

"Essences cannot be extracted from people!" he exploded. "Soak a person in a tub and you get a skimming of dead cells. This helps no one; the person in the tub comes out wrinkled as a newborn babe . . . full of torpor . . ."

"You're not being helpful, Daddy."

"Nobody helped me."

"You didn't need help. You had your passion and the open fields. You went to medical school. You didn't care about clothes and travel. I do!"

"Helen, you are trying my patience! I used to be full of fun; played darts, kept myself with boxing, rowed in Central Park lake. In the very early mornings, even on wintry days I would take pleasure in walking in the park by the lake, flinging handfuls of bread crumbs to the hungry ducks or sparrows that landed on the snow. Strangers I met claimed that I awakened in them a renewed sense of joy and interest in life. Because of you I have become somber. You refuse the real gifts I have to offer. You prefer running around without any purpose in life."

"Why don't you try curing me with your flowers?"

"Do you mean it?"

"Yes, Edward, you can treat me."

Edward had never treated a case of filial obstinacy before, so he went through his file and consulted the case history of a woman of thirty-six who had suffered from asthma all her life. She had lost her baby daughter and would sit still for long periods in front of the child's photograph weeping. She seemed to live in a dream, having little interest in the rest of the family.

"You never seem to catch your breath and you live in a dream," Daddy said. "You have little interest in either myself or your mother except when you come soliciting our help, therefore, your state of mind indicates clematis. After two bottles you should regain your joy in life, and take an interest in your family."

"Thanks, Edward, you're a good dad."

"I expect you to restore my confidence in you," he replied, "and then you won't have to dun me for money, I'll be happy to give it to you."

45 *Cosmo* says: No matter how crassly expressed, the idea behind "Anything goes" is important for our times. Whether your "thing" turns out to be of redeeming social importance is not crucial; it's the passion with which you defend your view that's important. And so I've decided to follow my heart by sleeping with my beloved Pablo. What's the difference so long as no one gets hurt? I am woman and Pablo is a consenting adult male . . . dog.

46 MY LIST OF SENSUAL THINGS TO DO BEFORE SLEEPING WITH PABLO

MY PARAGRAPH OF SENSUAL THINGS I TRIED BEFORE I SLEPT WITH PABLO

SOME THINGS I TRIED IN ORDER TO BECOME SEXUALLY AROUSED

I began by blowing soap bubbles but couldn't get off behind it. I rescued a well-worn pair of jeans, which a former lover had left at my place, and imagined his super body in them. I crawled over the floor of my room on hands and knees exploring every surface, but instead of its making me feel adventurous and animal-like, I picked up a splinter in my knee and was furious. I put on a nightgown and wore it in the shower and got a chill. I went to an Italian grocery store and smelled all the smells, but merely got hungry not sexy. I ate sixteen perfect defrosted raspberries, ate an entire frozen custard slowly in the dark, studied photos of nude male statues, and sucked my big toe.

My conclusion was that I should let nature take its course. If Pablo was destined to drive me wild, he would, but till then, I would cease and desist experimenting on myself.

47 Pablo noticed my lack of sleep. Quite truthfully, I told him what I had been trying to do: "I want to sleep with you, but I'm afraid," I said slowly.

"All one has to do is expose one's inner feelings, and fear goes away," Pablo replied.

"That is not easy."

"You spend too much time on ephemerals. Don't worry about what will happen . . . live!"

"You think I should . . . live?"

"Yeah! Listen, Helen, I'm an athlete. I play the game fair, you're on my team, so we're sure to win. Close the lights, shut the door, you don't have to worry any more."

"You're not a very big dog . . ."

"Big enough."

"We're from different worlds . . ."

"But we're together now."

"What would my parents say if they knew?"

"What they don't know won't hurt them."

"Do you love me?"

"As much as any slave can love his master."

"Promise you won't come in my mouth."

"No chance of that."

Post-Coital Message to Pablo

48 Your fucking is not yet art. One day perhaps you will cry out, stammer incoherently, or grind your teeth together and open your eyes wide, very wide. Fucking is always a matter of the entire personality. For that reason it is fundamentally tragic to mount from the rear and not be able to kiss. Also you did not wash your paws before you had me; there were paw prints around my waist. I am sorry to say that I felt like a dog, uncomplex, the docile receiver of your invading penis. And my eyes were closed (too?) and I was dreaming of a man, no, two men: one lying under me sucking my breasts (Romulus), and one above me (Remus). During a last exertion, you nipped my neck and brought me back to reality. As Johann Wolfgang von Goethe said, "All is struggle, effort. Only those deserve love and life who have to conquer them each day." Isn't that everybody?

49 Pablo has promised to treat me like a person. He will never fuck me again . . . he says. The human smell means nothing to him, and I was too tall, even though I bent over. It embarrassed him and his timing was off. He has a bad knee from trying to hold his position while I skidded forward on the floor.

The first time is never easy, especially with a new species.

50 "Pablo, what have you done with my new sweater?"

"What do you mean?"

"It's missing. I could swear I put it in this drawer."

"Why tell me? I haven't taken it. Your sweaters are far too big for me."

"I haven't accused you, dummy, just thought perhaps you had seen it . . . the white one with sequins around the neck, you said you liked it on me because you could see my nipples through it. Oh, where could it be?"

"Remember when the toilet was stuffed?"

"Yes."

"Maybe it fell down the toilet."

"Maybe it flew out the window and a crowd of moths ate it up."

"Maybe."

"Pablo, I don't think I trust you any more. What have you done with my clothes?"

"Nothing, no-thing, nohohoho-thing.
Your little doggy's in the clear
so please don't kick him in the rear
if of your sweater he does hear
he'll let you know with all good cheer."

"You don't convince me."

51 Next morning I sulked around. Pablo suggested I listen to Joe Fafka. I had been wanting to discuss the energy crisis with him, the Civil War, and a topic he had brought up briefly a few days before, "What turns you on?" A woman had called and told Joe that his voice turned her on. He informed her that he was appearing at a new supermarket in New Jersey, and that if she was sincere she'd come out to New Jersey to meet him. Another woman, a newlywed, said that it turned her on to greet her husband at the door with no clothes on. I wasn't sure what I'd say if I got through, but impulsively, I dialed Joe's number. I waited fifteen minutes, then someone said, "hello."

"Is this Joe Fafka?" I asked. It didn't sound like him.

"Yes, this is Joe Fafka. Who do you think it is, dummy?"

"Joe."

"Yes, speaking. You're on the air, ma'am."

"Hello, Joe, I just wanted to tell you and your listeners that people who live in cold rooms live longer, so I don't mind the energy crisis at all and never complain when the heat is turned off. I figure the landlord is doing me a favor."

"Get off the phone, stupid!" Joe yelled. I stayed on. "You're too stupid to know when you're insulted," he continued.

"I know you don't mean it, Joe," I said.

"I do mean it, ma'am. Don't you realize that old people, sick people, and little children are suffering because of lack of heat?"

"Sure . . . but—"

"Well then, get off the phone!"

"Look, Joe, I want to ask you something else. It's about my boyfriend. We've had premarital sex and now he doesn't want to marry me. What should I do?"

"Kill yourself."

"Really Joe?"

"That is my considered opinion, ma'am."

"One more thing, Joe. I forgot to mention that my boyfriend is a Gemini, born May twenty-second at one A.M. Do you have a feeling about him? What's he really like?"

"Your friend is a typical Gemini—creative but can't sustain one occupation. He is so excitable that he leaps from one idea to the next. He's never satisfied. He likes to move. Can't stand being in one place too long. Gemini is adventurous, will try anything once. I get the feeling that your boyfriend has a wet nose. Does he have a cold?"

"No, his nose is always wet, and he scratches a lot but he doesn't have fleas."

"You're pulling my leg, ma'am; thank you for your call and don't call me again . . ."

"Joe, don't go . . . I wanted to tell you what turns me on."

"I'll bite. Go ahead, tell your idol Joe Fafka what turns you on, ma'am."

"Your opinions on the Civil War . . . they were so . . . so . . . divergent."

"Anything in particular that I said?"

"Well, I got excited when you talked about how the North used to milk the South by tariff, and how the South bore the ban of slavery while the North got the money for bringing the slaves down south, and how the North bought the cotton, got rich while the South grew poor."

"*That* excites you, ma'am? You're sick. Emotionally ill. Are you calling perhaps from one of our state institutions? I thought I heard a Southern drawl when you opened your mouth. Could you be one of those detestable jungle bunnies; a commie, black, no goodnick on welfare? And why do you call *me* to ask *me* all kinds of questions? I'm not God."

"You wanna know what you are, Joe? You're an evil, white supremacist bigot!"

With that, the station operator broke our connection, but I turned up the radio to hear Joe say, ". . . coward . . . stupid low life! . . . Now friends, if you have something to celebrate, if you want to take the family out for a truly excellent dinner . . ."

52 At 3 A.M. I heard loud knocking on my door. When I opened it, I found no one. There was a melted puddle of ice in the hall beside the door, and hanging on the doorknob was a skinny, yellow old chicken leg. Since when has Chicken Delight taken up voodoo?

53 Las Vegas here I come! Albert arrived at my door with an overnight bag and a raincoat thrown over his arm.

"Your mother tried to get it out of me but I wouldn't tell her where I was going, or with who," he said breathlessly.

"Don't be silly. Mother knows everything, Albert; she wants you to go with me. Honest!"

"No, Helen, you're wrong. The Reverend Jones is ambivalent, like all women. She doesn't know what she wants."

"Bullcrap!"

Albert began sniveling. "The world isn't safe for young lovers,"

I took his bag, shoved him inside, and shocked him with the news that

Pablo (whom he hadn't met before) was going with us.

"Pablo?"

"My dog . . . what are you staring at?"

Pablo was walking around on his hind legs, a highball in one paw . . . He also had an erection.

"Is that Pablo?" Albert asked in consternation. "But I haven't made a reservation for three!"

"That's okay, he can sleep on the floor or at the foot of the bed. Don't worry. He's just a dog."

"I'm just a dog," Pablo repeated. "Look, no opposable thumb."

Albert was forced to examine Pablo's softly clenched paw. "My God, he looks like a dog, but he acts human, and he talks!"

"Mere illusion, he's a trained dog."

"What else does he do?" Albert asked suspiciously.

"He can jump through a hoop of fire." Albert became visibly excited, his voice took on an exuberance it had lacked on his arrival. "Hoop of fire? I'd like to see that!"

"You will, in Las Vegas," I promised. "That's why Pablo is coming with us. He's more fun than a barrel of monkeys."

Parting Pablo's head, Albert looked at me and said, "The dog's a treasure. I can understand why you wouldn't want to be away from him for a second."

54 Before we left for the airport, Pablo communicated his hierarchy of rank within our small group. I was the disputed piece of ground, Albert the lower-ranking enemy. Pablo stood erect, body in a normal position, back flat, tail behind him. Albert, submissive, abject creature that he was, wriggled across the room in a crouching walk, his head down, and ears back. Pablo said: "I am top dog, and don't you ever forget it!" The game amused Albert. It had never occurred to him before to obey a dog.

And Mother called, with one of her terrible predictions. She was jealous of me. She wanted all the men in the world for herself. No wonder I can only relate meaningfully to a dog!

"Believe me, Helen, if you go tourist class, three abreast, there will be a disruptive influence seated between Albert and yourself. This disruptive influence has a tendency to become ill during flight. He is a satanic messenger carrying dangerous flatulence which he plans to explode halfway between embarkation point and destination. He will demand an extravagant sum of fillet mignon after commandeering the plane. Both you and Albert will become hostages. When you land in Las Vegas, the plane will be surrounded by government agents who will rush the plane and capture the messenger. When it becomes clear that the messenger was not acting alone, but that his flatulence was inspired by an enforced diet of beans and cabbage fed him by Albert and yourself, both of you will be seriously implicated. A vet, sympathetic to the canine cause, will act on Pablo's behalf, but Albert will be judged incompetent and sent directly home to me. Why don't you send him home now and avoid trouble later?"

While listening to Mother, I took a scarf from the drawer of my bureau, fastened it around my neck, put on my red velvet jacket and buttoned it, pushed my overnight case toward the door, and straightened my skirt.

"I want to talk to Pablo," Mother demanded. She would have liked to be the one who taught him to talk, but that was my accomplishment.

Pablo spoke into the receiver without growling. His voice was high and clear, his throat a velvety passageway for sound since I had given him two lozenges made specifically for public speakers and singers (it was compounded from an original formula used by Enrico Caruso). "I love your daughter," Pablo said.

"Everybody loves her," Mother replied, "but nobody really knows her. She's a selfish monster, ungrateful, incapable of standing on her own two feet, keeps irregular hours, lives in a world of her own, lies, has a weak bladder, weak ankles, big ears, enormous feet, plaid shoulder caps, and her skin is host to a spy network of hidden capillaries. Now, do you still love her?"

Pablo spoke to her as one speaks to an angry child: obscurely. "Yes, dear Reverend, because I regard myself not as a victim engaged in some risky transcendental project, but rather as a lover who has absolutely no control over the forces that produce and distribute love. I am aware of Helen's qualities more than her faults: the rich variety of exciting games she makes up; the neatness of the papers upon which I perform my daily dislodging of waste; the endearingly simple way she opens a door halfway before coming in. Let me say this, I think it's normal for you as a mother to worry about Helen, but on the other hand you may be responsible for her failure which is as cumulative as lead poisoning, and forces her to rely on fantasy. Helen sees you as a madwoman commensurate with the pain you inflict. However I am here to see that it does not reach an unbearable intensity. It doesn't take a dog to understand the effect of conglomerate mergers such as father, mother, cousins, aunts, etcetera, versus the private enterprise of a child! In other words, Reverend Jones, Helen is try-ing to create her own life handmade. That should be sufficient profit for you as a mother."

"I will now speak to Albert," Mother declared.

Albert, trembling with fear, took the phone. He needed Mother's good-will, was sure the plane would crash if she put her mind to wishing it would.

"Myra? Listen Myra, I'm not serious about Helen. Yes, I love you. Only you. This is just a short holiday I'm taking. Yes, I'll be lonely. Where are the pencils? Oh . . . I left them in a jar on the kitchen window. The paper is already cut into small pieces. Yes, there's a paperweight on the pile to keep it from in all directions when the door opens. You have three ap-pointments tomorrow, check them out in your appointment book, the big one. What? No, of course Helen and I aren't eloping. I expect to win a great sum of money at the gaming tables. Don't cry. I am grateful to you. I'll bring you a souvenir from Las Vegas."

When Albert turned to me he was ashen. I brought him a glass of wa-ter. He was still hanging on to the phone, listening to Mother.

"She says I'm your half brother," he said in horror. "What if we had slept with each other . . . or married and had children!"

I hit him. He needed it. "I'm ready to go now," he said.

"Albert, promise me you'll be a good sport in Vegas, and that you'll tell me if you start worrying about Mother, okay?"

"I promise."

55 On the plane, Albert tucked a blanket around me. He made sure I had a nap before dinner and sent back the cold chicken because it did not look fresh. I had instead a portion of pot roast drowning in gravy, with a side of instant mashed potatoes. The salad came with French dressing, artificially preserved and served in a tiny pleated plastic container. The flatware was sealed in a cellophane wrapper. Pablo had the best of it with a pound of raw sirloin steak brought from home. He consumed his food facing the window so that the stewardess would not notice the unusual slurping style he had of eating.

Albert explained our check-in procedure. "I have taken two single rooms, not adjoining, under two different names. You are the Countess Helena De Jones, I am Meyer Wolfsheim the Third, and Pablo is Pablo De Jones Junior, your younger brother. The management will provide a cot for him in your bedroom. I've invited you, so the expenses are on me, the incidentals you are to take care of. I only tell you this to avoid unpleasant misunderstandings later."

56 The scene was bizarre. The Collonade Hotel was holding a Mexican fiesta party when we arrived. All the people I had ever read about in the society columns were there, or was I dreaming? I believe I saw Slap Threnody Lawless (dazzling in gold lamé), Eyesore & Chaste Revered (who wouldn't revere him?), Candy Rawhole (that's what happens when you have a sweet tooth), Silly Blah (it rhymes with *ah*) , Gonad & Iodine Von Iceyburg (thawing out of course), Armwet & Cement Squirtgun (who recently bought an apartment overlooking the Champs de Bon Marché to put up all those wonderful rock stars who will just be passing through), Mrs. Puce Nimble (Puce be nimble, Puce be quick, Puce jump over the candlestick), Lacey Mirrorbell (bella, bella), Merry Schmutz (merrily, merrily, merrily, merrily, life is but a schmutzy dream), Mr. & Mrs. Robbers Skulk (what more can I say?), Saddy Sockaguy (the other side of the coin: remember Happy Rockefeller? of course you do), Mrs. Angier Fiddle-Puke (no, my dears, the disease is called angina), and the Baroness de Bologna-Salami, who sat around complaining that the telephone operators failed to deliver her messages, that the laundry did an inferior job and had starched her silk panties, but had put softener into her cuffs, and worst of all she said that the maid had a habit of bursting into her room at crack of dawn to see if she could make up the bed. The list is partial, of course, since I did not examine the hotel register.

After sending our bags up with a bellgirl (a small woman shaped like a bell, who had strong arms and wore a pillbox hat under which she carried all kinds of pills to sell to the Collonade's patrons), we went to the main ballroom. The director of entertainment was wearing a blue football helmet and carried a baseball bat; with this bat he advanced on a piñata shaped like a pig that was hanging from the ceiling. He then slammed the piñata till it split open and ten thousand dollars' worth of small gifts tumbled out of its belly. With a great shout and screams of delight, forty-two women, all expensively dressed and coifed, rushed toward the loot and began scrambling in the shredded paper that had been the papier-mâché beast's innards. It was a ridiculous riot, instigated by greed not need, everybody wanted something for nothing; they were actually being taken for a management promotional ride, and would be losing far more than they were getting, at the gaming tables later on. One woman, who was tickled by a man to make her let go of a package, slammed him in the face with it before stalking off. The man bled, but did not leave the field. Others came limping toward the velvet chairs that surrounded the ballroom. Hardly anyone remained uninjured.

Pablo peed in his pants with excitement. We moved to another spot. A dry one. Watched a Charleston contest. The most powerful woman in Las Vegas (politically powerful), who was the madam of a whorehouse, won a baroque silver serving tray for her abandoned performance, and a princess who had almost been thrown by her mount during the hobbyhorse competition received an emerald bracelet. I watched enviously as others carried off a white mink coat, a custom-designed men's watch from Tiffany's, and the key to an antique convertible Daimler. Lady Luck once smiled at me, too, when I sang the Campbell's soup jingle over the phone and received a case of tomato soup.

57 There were two croupiers at our single-ended table. As the roulette wheel turned, it made a sound like false teeth clicking. Albert put his chips on manque, betting that the winner would be between numbers one and eighteen. The croupier spun the wheel in a counterclockwise direction, then moving his hands, showed us that they were empty. When the wheel stopped he removed the ball from the winning compartment, keeping his hand turned so that we could see the ball at all times. Then he paid out. Albert did not win. "*Faites vos jeux,*" the croupier called, and while the ball was in motion we placed our bets again. This time Albert had put his chips on rouge. He lost anyway.

"Why don't we play the slot machines?" I asked. "You'll lose every cent if this keeps up." Albert agreed. He had brought only a few hundred dollars with him.

"I would have won," he complained, "if I had used the Sean Connery method."

"What's that?"

"Well Connery won thirty thousand at Italy's Saint Vincent Casino by backing number seventeen three times."

"My grandfather had a more eccentric system," I said, remembering a family anecdote of how the Joneses recouped the family fortune after losing everything. "His equipment was a spider trapped in a matchbox that was painted half red and half black on the inside. He'd put the box in front of him on the table, remove the lid after a few minutes, and then bet on rouge or noir according to the spider's position."

"Where can I get a spider in Las Vegas?" Pablo asked.

"We might look in the cellar," Albert suggested.

58 Down in the subbasement we did find a spider's web, but the spider wasn't at home.

"Why don't we use a spider substitute?" I suggested.

"Like what?" Pablo asked. "A mouse?"

"You're close . . . How about a cockroach?"

"Yes, that's it. We'll search for a roach. But what about the matchbox?" Albert said.

"Steal one from the kitchen," I answered.

"And the red and black paint, where do we get that?" Albert said.

"Use lipstick and eyebrow pencil." I showed them the huge selection of junk that I always carried with me in a zippered makeup case.

We fanned out. I found the roach. It was pregnant and sluggish, but nothing to get sentimental about. A pregnant roach brings good luck if you treat it kindly and say a prayer over its useless wings, which I did:

cockroach, cockroach
be a honey
cockroach, cockroach
bring us money
Amen.

Albert stole the box of matches from one of the hotel's huge stainless steel kitchens. "These are a great temptation," he confided.

"Never mind, empty the matches into that mop sink, and let the water run over them," I said.

Albert was so docile I should have suspected something; instead I gave my attention to preparing the box.

Our high hopes, our preparations came to nothing. We lost. The second time around, before we had placed our bets, the cockroach crawled out of the box and climbed on a woman's hand. She screamed, and we were asked to leave the table. Albert seemed unusually agitated. He excused himself and went to the men's room.

"Follow him, Pablo!" I ordered.

Pablo could not find Albert in the men's room. We searched the lobby, the bar, and our bedroom, but no Albert.

"Let's try the subbasement, he might be returning the roach to its nest," I said.

That's where we found him, pouring Mazola oil over piles of dirty laundry. Pablo had to keep him at bay, while I went through his pockets for matches.

"You're arousing me," Albert warned. "Keep that up and I'll do something we'll both be sorry for."

"What's that, Albert?"

"I'll start a fire in your heart," he answered.

59 That night room service brought us a quart of rum raisin ice cream and three goblets of madeira. With his credit card Albert bought me a feather boa in the boutique. It was flame red.

"Remember, I'm your half sister," I cautioned. "Don't get carried away."

"I have a confession to make to you, Helen. Even if you weren't related to me I could never make love to you. I don't know what love is. I know what ice cream is. I know what a car is. But what is love?"

"Please, Albert, let's not discuss it. I was only foolin' around. Finish your ice cream."

By the time Albert had finished his madeira he was obnoxious. "Know why I don't like you, Helen?" he began.

"Why, Albert?"

"Because you oil your face at night, sleep in a torn nightgown, leave your bed unmade day after day, keep rotting apple cores in your ashtrays, walk barefoot, and sleep around."

Poor Albert, he was hallucinating. I hadn't "slept around" for a year . . . and what an expression. However, now I knew why Mother was his dish of tea, it wasn't because she was keeping him from the police and the psychiatric ward, it was because of her meticulously clean sheets, frilly nightgowns from Lord and Taylor's, and her clean feet.

60 "What did you learn in Las Vegas?" Daddy asked.
"I learned that *weight* is a measure related to heaviness by carrying away a pocketful of silver dollars. I learned that *length* is a measure of extent or distance by counting my footsteps from the lobby of the hotel to my bedroom. I learned that *volume* is a measure of space occupied when I filled my water glass to rinse my mouth. I learned that *temperature* is a measure of hotness or coldness when I felt my forehead and found that I had fever."

"I hope you didn't take an aspirin!" Daddy said.

"No, I didn't, Edward. The fever went away by itself the minute I got back to New York."

"And did you take my advice?" he asked.

"What advice, Edward?"

"The safety strategy," he said. "You remember . . . I told you how to protect yourself."

"Of course. It slipped my mind for a minute."

Daddy had warned me to leave my valuables in the hotel safe, and to bolt my door before retiring. Since Pablo was my only valuable I couldn't very well leave him in the hotel safe, but; I had locked our door from the inside before going to sleep. Other things I did not do: I did not drink too much and so did not end up unconscious in the street minus my wallet. I did not take a taxi and give the driver directions only to find myself going in the opposite direction, and after surrendering my money dropped off far from my hotel. I did not let ragged children approach me, children whose charm is their chief tool, crying, "You are a nice lady, I like nice ladies. Please buy this flower." I couldn't imagine why Edward had chosen to worry about these particular things, unless he had consulted one of his out-of-date travelers' manuals. It is the proper thing for a father to warn his daughter of the perils that lie ahead. Edward does love me and wants me to be happy.

61 The following scene took place at Marian's apartment. I had brought an Italian bread and a container of ricotta for her, as a post-Vegas gift. When I rang the bell, Marian appeared.

"Hi, Marian," I said. "Look at what I brought you."

"I am not Marian," she answered, and slammed the door. I stood there for a moment not knowing what to do, and then decided to leave. Halfway down the stairs, I stopped and thought, "Wait a minute!"

Up the stairs I went and once more rang Marian's bell. Enraged by this continual ringing, Marian opened the door . . . but before she could say a word, I said, "I am not Helen either." And went downstairs again.

In a few days whatever it is will blow over.

62 I picked up the phone at the second ring. Sometimes I wait for the third; I do not want to seem too eager.

"Helen?"

"Speaking."

"The fear of death is a symptom of betrayal!"

"Who is this?"

"Nobody."

There was a click, a broken connection, and then dead air caught between myself and whom?

63 "Why are you doing this to me?" I asked Pablo. He had defecated on the floor and placed a tiny paper flag at the top of the pile.

"Don't take it personally. I was trying to recreate Iwo Jima from this photograph."

"But I have to clean up after you!"

"Enemy of self-expression!"

"Come clean Pablo, what's it really about?"

"My memories are intolerable, Helen. I guess I was seeking revenge for my sister who was treated poorly by your kind when she was just a pup."

"What do I have to do with it?"

"You're not an animal; you're a natural enemy."

"Nonsense. Haven't I always been kind to you?"

"Read this newspaper story. It might help you to understand my basic mistrust of forked creatures."

The clipping, yellowed and uneven, told a shocking story:

PUPPY BEATEN TO DEATH:
OWNERS JAILED

A young Brooklyn couple was charged with murder last night in the fatal beating of their two month-old dog. Police said Princess was beaten to death by her master, Richard Person, and her mistress, Nona, both 20.

The pup's body, covered from head to toe with cuts, welts, and bruises, was found yesterday in the backyard of the couple's apartment at 336 Heather St.

"She was hairless and black-and-blue from her forehead to her feet," said Detective Peter Rogers of the Alley Ave. station.

According to police, neighbors said the dog had been beaten almost every day for two weeks, but the beatings intensified over the weekend during an outdoor party and barbecue, when the dog stole a hamburger from the grill.

Detectives said Person hit the tiny animal with his fists and a belt, while the mistress also "used physical force."

On Sunday, the cops reported, the dog was forced to sit still in the rain, held by a metal choke collar attached to a fence.

Around 8:30 A.M. yesterday, Person drove his wife to a subway station, so she could go to her job as a computer trainee. Then he returned home and slept until noon.

When he awoke, police said, he found the puppy lying on the ground. Unable to rouse her, he called the A.S.P.C.A. and reported that the pup "doesn't wake up."

Person was advised to bring the pup in. When veterinarians Alfred Jonas and Ricardo Maldonado saw the body, they called for detectives to take over the investigation.

Police said the pup's legs were swollen, her face was pulled up, and her lips were three times the normal size.

The cops quoted Person as saying: "Princess wasn't housebroken. I was disgusted with her . . . I wanted obedience from that dog and I didn't get it."

Detectives said that while Person was being questioned in the police station he shouted: "I want a lawyer. Get on the phone. I want my rights."

Person and his wife were booked on charges of murder, possessing a dangerous weapon (the belt), and endangering a pup's welfare.

64 "Must I be punished for what others of my species have done?" I asked Pablo.

"Yes you must, until I can feed the hand I bite."

Why couldn't Pablo get it into his head that I would always be his kind philanthropist and he would remain the needy petitioner? I reprimanded him for his own good.

"Bad dog! Bad dog! From now on scratch the door when you have to go out, or you won't get any supper!"

65 I happened to be standing near the door when the note was slipped under it. The paper was a cloudy blue, watermarked, and 60 percent rag content.

Dearest Watched Lady,

I know that you are ALONE! And if like me would need some cumponionship for 1 evng or few hour, I am willing to say nice thing! You are MODERN miss, so I been keep away till now! BUT IS READY! Hear this cumplete sentence, "HOW ARE YOU? I AM FINE." Tonite at 8 I have for you the best SURPRISE! Make you happy and smile to me!

Not be afraid of lonly old man.

Check my name at desk in lobby.

I have room here too. Yrs Truly,

ROBERT DELFORD SMITH

alias

BOB FJORD SMYTHE

(which you prefer is available)

"Room 21B," the desk clerk said, "is occupied by one of our oldest tenants, Mr. Robert D. Smith, a senior citizen. He's harmless, toothless, and practically penniless. Some of our other guests have complained about him. Do you have a complaint?"

"No," I answered.

66 Curious, but apprehensive, I knocked at his door. I was not prepared for his terrifying and incongruous appearance: his hair was dark and greasy, curtaining his long, thin face. He wore horn-rimmed bifocals that were held together with adhesive tape and rubber bands. There were ragged gaps between his broken teeth through which he breathed heavily. His outfit, something out of grand opera, was made of thick navy flannel with rows of brass buttons down the front. It was much too big for him, so he had rolled up the sleeves at the cuffs, and the trousers around his ankles. On his bare feet were laceless shoes splitting open at the welts and seams. His hands were red and rough, with finger-nails like talons, half an inch long and encrusted with dirt.

"Please to come in," he bowed deeply. "This is good room, no leaks, very romantic."

"I don't have much time," I said.

"Time is relevant," he replied.

"But I will come in for a few minutes."

"You will not be displaced. I promise."

In the dim light I made out another figure on an unmade cot. I was taken by the hand and led to it.

"Helen Jones, please meet my silent partner, your twin sister. Am I right?"

The figure on the cot was a large rag doll, made to look exactly like my-self, and wore most of the clothing that I had found missing during the previous month: my Allura red wig with open-weave backing, my sweater, and my gold pants and jacket by Funky. She/ it even had on my chunky green wedgies, her fat cloth ankles were swollen and looked as if they had the gout.

"How did you get my things?" I asked the old man, but not too harshly. I wanted to catch him off guard.

"I buy at great bargain from dog. He like butcher bone with some meat, and I like to make pretty companion. It was fair deal."

"What do you do with this . . . this dummy?" I asked. "Do you talk to it?"

"Talk. Hold. Go for walk around room like real person. When I want her to be warm, I put this in."

He pulled a hot water bottle out from under the doll's pants.

"Sometime I kiss her on lips, but am too old to be excite."

"I think you have great talent," I said, edging toward the door. "You might make yourself a whole family someday out of scraps."

Suddenly animated and spilling over with memories he shouted: "Talented? Yes! When little boy I was drawing apple and pear in school. They give paper, pencil, eraser. LOOK!" He grabbed a blackened pot off a hot plate. "Peas, carrots, potato, meat. They have no color. When I cook the color go away. It make me so sad."

"I'm sorry," I said. "Raw food *is* much prettier."

"But is all right," he said. "I make picture of food."

The old man pulled me back into the room, sat me on the bed, and made me look at thirty crayoned still lifes that he had drawn on the sides of brown bags and cardboard boxes. He was, without doubt, a late bloomer, a marvelous primitive.

"Now we celebrate," he said. "We eat."

It was hard for me to believe that this was the man who had written those dirty notes and called me on the telephone. However, when I thought about it, I came to the conclusion that Pablo had put him up to it, to get even with me. Robert Delford Smith had been a convenient scapegoat.

67 When I knocked on Mr. Smith's door the next day, there was no answer.

"They came and took him away," the desk clerk said.

"Who took him away?"

"Don't know. Could be some government agency arranged for him to go to an old people's home or a hospital. Wherever it is, he'll be better off."

68 Daddy's been showing movies at his house. The young people who come to him love movies. They gaze at the screen as if it were the Buddha's eyes behind which all things past and present occur. Sometimes Daddy shows Chaplin shorts, and old comedies like *Behind the Eightball*. Once an eight-minute film taught how to make a bomb out of a bottle instead of a lamp out of a bottle. Lamps, the narrator said, were only good to hit husbands on the head with while they were sleeping, but Molotov cocktails (the bottle-bombs) could wipe out a blockful of enemies. Mostly the films are chosen because of their cheap rental. This sometimes leads to unfortunate juxtapositions: Betty Boop cartoons followed by male stag movies, followed by a lesson on how to bake a Key Lime pie.

When I visited Edward he was presenting the world première of a film concerning psychosurgery: *Before and After Psychosurgery.*

"The psychosurgeons are up to some pretty horrifying things nowadays," Daddy said. "I am haunted by one aspect of this technique, the participation of the 'psychotherapist', who literally sits beside his patient conducting an interview with him while the neurosurgeons gradually turn up the electrical current. In this manner the 'therapist' monitors and titrates the amount of tissue destruction required to change the patient's ongoing emotional reactions. The patient himself cannot tell what's happening, since destruction of the frontal lobe tissue is reflected in a progressive loss of all those human functions related to the frontal lobes: insight, empathy, sensitivity, self-awareness, judgment, emotional responsiveness, and so on."

The movie in black and white was shown using the split-screen technique. On one side, a black woman wearing a self-stimulation unit on her belt turned it on and off as she wandered about a hospital. She was pressing the buttons in a frantic fashion because it built her up toward a feeling of orgasm that she was not able to consummate. This particular woman's problem, a narrator reported, was narcolepsy, a tendency to fall asleep unexpectedly in inappropriate situations, e.g., when seated on the toilet, standing on a crowded train platform, or slicing a roast with a sharp kitchen knife . . . Since she wore her self-stimulation unit on her belt, her friends or other patients could simply press her wake-up button for her when she began to doze off. The other side of the screen showed a woman being stimulated electrically: she reported a pleasant tingling sensation in the left side of her body "from my face down to the bottom of my legs." She started giggling and making funny comments, stating that she enjoyed the sensation very much . . . Finally, becoming more flirtatious, she ended up by openly expressing her desire to have sexual intercourse with the therapist.

Next, an eleven-year-old boy, otherwise normal, became so terribly excited by the electrical stimulation that he decided he would like to be a girl . . . and . . . on the other side of the split screen, much to my horror, I saw Mr. Smith, my neighbor, with electrodes springing out of his head like a sparkling Las Vegas headdress. The investigator made him dance, masturbate, and grin at the camera like a monkey. Finally, because his pleasure and pain centers had been irritated by the remote control device, he wept and fell down, totally exhausted.

A therapist, his hands hidden in the pockets of his crisp white smock, reported: "Although Mr. Smith is somewhat senile and nonproductive, he has undergone a very dramatic change. He is now cooperative and easily managed, but still not productive." As the camera moved in for a close-up of Mr. Smith's face, he spoke: "I guess, doctor, that your electricity is stronger than my will."

69 I'm going crazy. Pablo is gone. He left no note. I'm inclined to believe he's on his way to Hollywood to become a star. He doesn't have it in him to become a watchdog; too easily distracted. It runs in his family. His grandfather, he told me, disappeared for one entire evening after hearing that Halley's comet was coming and with it the end of the world. The old dog, then a young pup, had climbed onto the roof of a building because he wanted to see the end of the world happen. From the roof where he was waiting, he had an unobstructed view of the sky. He told Pablo that before the comet appeared words had materialized in the sky saying: IT IS I. His grandfather was amazed by the perfect use of grammar, it convinced him that God was an educated dog whose command of English could save the world . . . and that if all dogs practiced correct usage of the language the dog pounds of the world would soon be emptied. Needless to say, the world did not end with Halley's comet, and Pablo's grandfather was beaten by his master. Could Pablo have gone to the roof in search of another comet? Another message? Another fulfillment of the recurrent prophecy that the world is about to end?

70 Pablo was not on the roof.

71 I called on Mother to learn his fate. She began her psychic search by asking for and receiving an object belonging to Pablo, his old tennis ball (his favorite possession).

"I am getting vibrations of the route they took," she said.

"He's with someone?"

"Don't interrupt. Yes, he is with a dark-complexioned man from the East. The man is coming out of a notions shop with a skein of red wool and a box of straight pins. They go to a hotel. It has a neon sign. I may be wrong. It may not be a hotel. Something else. Perhaps a store. It's not close. Quick, give me a map of New York City!"

I gave Mamma the map of N.Y.C. that I carried with me in order to pretend I was a tourist. I can't count the times I've searched for Grand Central Station and found it, first on my map, and then on Forty-second Street. It's always a surprise, like discovering an Egyptian tomb in the Metropolitan Museum of Art.

Mamma traced a route south toward Houston Street, the area called SoHo, where there are many galleries, artists, and restaurants.

"Yes, the sign is in the window of a store. . . . Some kind of gathering is taking place. I can feel it. He is here. *Here!*" Her finger stopped close to Prince Street.

72 I put up signs everywhere describing Pablo and giving my phone number. So far nobody has contacted me.

73 The surprise guest at our local supermarket was announced on a big piece of paper glued to the window: *Joe Fafka!* He was pushing a product called Daley's Instant Cheese. (Daley's comes in powder form and is good to take on camping trips or wherever an instant cheese is needed. All that has to be done to the powder is to add some water to the mixture and squeeze in the plastic pouch included in the package. This forms a doughlike ball which tastes like a nutty Swiss.) At last I would meet Joe in person. I was already waiting in front of the cardboard display when Joe came in the door. He was wearing a green silk suit, had a round childlike face, and stood about five feet two inches. He stood up on the box provided for him behind the display and spoke into the microphone: "To any lady who tries our product today, while I am here, a free ticket to visit our radio studios and take the grand tour! See your favorite radio personalities who have never been seen before. Watch them in action: see them walk, talk, check the clock, drink coffee from a paper cup. All this and more if you'll step up and make your purchase. Also included in each and every package of Daley's Instant Cheese is a coupon allowing you a five-cent discount on your next package. Folks, this cheese doesn't taste like instant anything, it tastes like an authentically aged cheese. It's a quality cheese. Daley's can also be stored without refrigeration. Put it in the kiddies' lunch bag and let them develop their grip while they squeeze the cheese. And yes, we stand behind our product, there's a money-back guarantee for those of you who do not agree with us that Daley's is the cheese of the future, the cheese the moon should have been made of, the cheese that is the best money can buy. Now really folks, you have everything to gain and nothing to lose. Step right up. Our pretty cheese saleswoman is standing by to offer you a sample of Daley's right now."

A woman wearing a bunny costume minus the ears and tail began smearing cheese on tiny squares of crackers.

"Who is he?" a woman asked. "Is he famous or somethin'?" Her cart was full of beer, crackers, bologna, and cheese. Joe spotted her in the crowd, pointed to her, and said, "You, madame, must be giving a party, am I right?"

"Yes I am," she replied.

"Then let me add to the total enjoyment of your party by presenting you with a generous sample of Daley's Instant Cheese." With that, he threw two packages of Daley's into her cart. A few women applauded. Joe took a bow.

I waited till Joe was done and had autographed all the scraps of paper that were thrust upon him. Then I followed him to the back of the store where the manager was gifting him with three porterhouse steaks.

"Joe, I've gotta talk to you. I have a serious problem . . . I called you last week."

"Not here, stupid," he hissed.

"It can't wait," I pleaded. There were tears in my eyes. The manager tried to shove me but I wouldn't move.

"This is private back here, girlie," the manager said. "Employees only."

Something about me must have attracted Joe, because once he had the bag of meat under his arm, his mood changed. "I have time for a coffee. You can spit it out over coffee, kid, but don't think I'm God. I'm not."

"I know you're not, Joe. I agree with you."

74 We went to a vegetarian restaurant on Seventy-ninth Street. I had tea with an apple strudel, and Joe had coffee with a cheese Danish. "I don't usually break bread with a nut," he said. "What's the story?"

"I've lost a loved one . . ."

"Then it's too late for me to help." Joe bit into his Danish. "Not a bad piece of cake."

"Lost, not dead, Joe. And I've tried just about everything: put an ad in the paper, put posters around, walked my feet off . . ."

"This loved one . . . is he your husband?"

"Not exactly."

"What do you want the jerk back for? He's not worth taking back. The same thing would start all over again, the beatings, the arguments over money, the drunken weekends . . ."

"He's not a jerk and he never acted the way you say, Joe."

"He's not a drinker?"

"Absolutely not."

"What you're telling me is that he was a good man and you suspect foul play. Am I right?"

"Partly."

"Fill me in. Oh, and try to catch the waiter's eye, will you, honey? I could go for another pastry."

"He's not a man, my loved one isn't—"

"Not a woman! Jesus Christ, I hope you're not a dike. They live miserable lives. Don't tell me I'm having coffee with an invert."

Another pastry arrived. Joe sent it back. He had lost his appetite.

"Here's a picture of Pablo," I finally said. "We were very close. I know you're an animal lover and an antivivisectionist, so I came to you."

Joe's mouth hung open. "You got the wrong guy, honey. I'm a hunter. Ed Evans who comes on after me is the animal lover. I'm allergic to dogs and cats. I swell up and can't breathe when they get near me."

"You've got to help me. Your listeners can help. I want you to broadcast a description of Pablo—that's his name—and then maybe someone'll call in who's seen him."

To get me off his back, Joe agreed to appeal to his people.

75 Mother had been cleaning out her boxes and bags that contained old letters, bills, memorabilia of her fantastic psychic performances, phone numbers of friends long gone, Christmas cards, newspaper clippings, old keys, childhood photographs, compositions on yellow, lined paper, useless discount coupons, paper clips, and brittle rubber bands; in this conglomeration of junk she found a diary I had begun in the sixth grade, and sent it to me. Her reason for sending it was to hurt me. The first few lines read as follows: "I'm going into 7th grade. In a very tough Junior High School. It is Aug. 16, and I have not received my card from the new school telling me what class I'm to be in. I hope I've made an honor class. Somehow all this I'm writing sounds very boring & stupid. Well anyway to get on about the school. It is a very big school and has a lot of unfriendly children. I really enjoyed my old school. P.S. 173. I hope I'm as popular in 115 as I was in 173."

I called Mother. "Why did you send me that diary?" I asked.

"It's yours, I didn't want to throw it out."

"You've thrown out other things of mine . . . the teddy bear, my first hair curler . . . things I loved. Why call my attention to the unhappy past?"

"Learn from it. Learn from the past. It should make you realize that you always were a worrier. Before you even set foot in the new school you had talked yourself into believing the children there would be unfriendly to you."

"Turned out they were."

"You're the unfriendly person, Helen. People react to you. If you were friendly, you'd be well liked. That's why you don't have friends even now."

"You're tearing me down again, Mother. Cut it out!"

"We've never talked woman-to-woman, dear. Why don't you drop over tonight? I apologize for being tactless."

"It isn't that you lack tact, Mother, but rather that you hate me and can't admit it to me, or to yourself. Now you want me to visit you so that you can continue your attack. I won't come."

"I want to see you, Helen," Mother said. Her voice sounded tired and sad. Could she be lonely for me? Had I been too harsh? Still I held back.

"It's too late," I said.

"Please, dear, your own mamma wants to hold her darling little Helen."

"All right, Myra, I won't be long."

76 Mother was sitting in the dark, candles out, chairs still set up from the previous session. The room seemed gripped with bitter cold . . . It may have been her mood. The steam was on. It knocked and hissed as it came out of the small pressure valve attached to the radiator. As Mother moved, her chair creaked. Soon she became visible as well as audible. In the dimness her form took on the insubstantial shape of a being not yet finished . . . a cold, gray lump that had materialized out of the vague light.

"I do not protect sinners, even though that sinner might be myself," she whispered. "I have summoned you here to confess a wrong."

"What're you up to now, Myra?" I asked. She had the unnerving habit of staging her communications so that the other person became uneasy. I found myself drifting into a hypnotic state . . . hypnotic or . . . dreamy with an edge of fear: what if I slipped away into the gossamer ambience and could not get back? "Mind if I put on the lights?" I flipped the switch before she could answer.

The cold, gray lump stood up, motionless.

"Son of a bitch!" she said. "You have no sense of theater. Don't you realize how hard it is to say certain things? I require the proper setting."

Mother glared at me. I stood my ground. The lights would remain on.

"I don't have long to live," she began again, trying for my sympathy. I had heard it before.

"Nobody has long to live, Mother. Life is short."

"And," she continued as if I had not interrupted her, "and, I have sent Albert away. He was too frivolous, more of a liability than I wanted to be responsible for."

"Where have you sent him?"

"Where? Away. He is being taken care of by those more conversant with his pleasures. It may be expensive, but where he is now Albert has his own asbestos-lined room with a clearly marked escape route that leads directly to either a horney recreation area or t0 his doctor's spacious recording studio."

"Myra, I didn't come here to talk about the expensive rest home you've sent Albert to. His therapy means nothing to me. I came because you sounded human and I miss my mommy."

She shifted from foot to foot. "Would you like a cup of tea with some strawberry jam and crackers?"

Tea with Myra was like playing house with a giant doll. I had owned a tea set when I was a child (the exact duplicate of Mother's). My teapot had a tea cozy, which is a flannel outer wrapping, to keep the water in the pot hot. The mention of a cup of tea made me vulnerable, took me back to when I had adored Myra and imitated her social graces.

"Yes, I'd love some tea," I replied, reaching out for Myra's hand to hold it affectionately. She her hand lie in mine like a flattened kippered herring. All emotion had been scraped from the bones, and love smoked out. "I'm a commodity," the hand seemed to say, "a delicacy that will soon be gone. Have me while you can. The supply of mothers' hands is growing low."

Behind the door I heard her humming happily as she put the water up to boil and took out the dishes.

"I miss you," she said on returning. "Nobody can take the place of a daughter."

"I'm sorry, but you'll have to get along without me. I have my own life to live."

Her body heat bundled me closer to her in the cold room. I began to sweat. What would she say now to keep me from escaping?

"I remember you before you remember yourself," she said, her eyes reflecting the jubilation of the past. "I remember the drunken joy I felt at your birth . . . I had an orgasm at the height of pain . . . You wanted to remain, but I opened my womb and then in the cool white mist of the delivery room gave birth. First you were a flowerlike form bound to me only by the slenderest stem. The stem shriveled as the human flower ripened. You were my first miracle."

I mixed strawberry jam into my tea. The strawberries settled at the bottom of the cup. "Can you read strawberry fragments the way you read tea leaves?" I asked.

"The strawberry does not lend itself to interpretation," she answered wearily. I suppose she was disappointed in me. I should have praised her for accomplishing my birth, for feeling both pleasure and pain where only pain was to be expected. I kept my strategic distance.

"I have to go soon, Myra." My using her name instead of calling her Mother made her realize that I would not come any closer.

Then we sat silently. I wanted to leave. She was eager to have me stay with her in the eerie, "prepared" room.

"When you were eight years old you had a dog named Scamp. You were very attached to her. She ate your leftovers, slept in your room, went to school with you, in short was your best friend. One afternoon while you were away at school, Scamp disappeared. I told you that she had run away. She didn't!" Mother's face hardened, as she reintroduced an old trauma.

"What happened to Scamp?" I heard myself cry, in that anguished child's voice from the past.

"I took her for a walk and left her in the street. I hated her! She tore up the rugs, dirtied the house with those 'cute' muddy paws, made too much noise, and cost too much money. You and that dog gave me extra work; if I could have left you on the street with the dog and been guaranteed I'd never see you both again, I would have. At the age of eight you took over my life. Mine! You demanded everything: time, love, money. Oh, I felt great when I got rid of Scamp. It was like springtime. I could live again!"

"And Edward?" I couldn't believe that Daddy had been part of the plot.

"Oh, your father wanted me to keep Scamp. It was easy for him to be the good guy; he wasn't ever at home to take care of Scamp. Your father is an old softy."

"You've always been so devious, Myra," I said quietly. "You should have been a surgeon; you operate with brilliance. Now tell me, what else have you taken away from me that I loved?"

"Nothing I've taken nothing!" My pain gave her strength; it brought color to her face.

"Didn't you want Edward to hate me? Aren't you still working on it?" I thought I was controlling myself very well, though if Myra hit me where it really hurt, somewhere in the vicinity of Pablo's disappearance, I would have struck her.

"Edward isn't the angel you think he is," Myra shouted. "I'm a better person than he'll ever be."

"I'm aware of his faults," I answered.

"Oh, are you? Well, how would you like to go to bed with a flaccid floral arrangement? That's what he was with me in bed—a dead bloom, a twisted wreath . . ."

"That's your private business, Myra," I said. It broke my heart to hear it.

77 The unvoiced can be heard as clearly as the voiced, but we do not have to pay attention to it . . . until insanity overtakes us.

78 All living things, including human babies, get destructive radiations from their mothers; those radiations might underlie "hate at first sight." People with "brown thumbs" emit radiations harmful to their plants.

79 When I bought half a rye bread at the bakery, the salesperson gave me the smaller half. I was too embarrassed to ask to see the other half close up, to measure it against my half. I did not want to seem greedy. But it was my money I spent. I should have asserted myself. Since Pablo has gone, I almost welcome unfair treatment. Unhappiness and a sense of loss have to be fed or they lessen in intensity. I must be careful not to smile. To smile is to deny my daily mourning. I don't want to embark on another life (I don't dare to be happy) until I find Pablo.

80 Jeremy, Marian's old man, does not look like Mick Jagger (Marian says he does because of his thick lips and tall skinny frame). Maybe in a jump suit he'd come closer . . . but until then he's only Mick Jagger in Marian's head.

"Mariam you're lucky to have an old man and a young baby. I don't think I can make it without Pablo."

"I had my hard times," she said. "Things still aren't that good."

"What'dya mean?"

"Sex . . . I'm not really interested. Right after the baby I lost the urge. Remember how I used to ball all the time? Now nothing. It's not fair to Jeremy."

"No such thing as fair. How does that saying go? The body's willing but the mind says no?"

"Ain't no such saying, Helen. You know, Jeremy's a good man, but the sight of him doesn't make me jump for joy. We've become the little old couple at home. I don't get around the way I used to. I miss those pretty young boys who hang around Phoebe's. I don't need this . . . this security shit. It's shit. What can I write my songs about . . . diapers? Fifth-floor walk-up? My man's a road manager, hi-ho where does he go? My hands got red when I made the bed? I'm dying on the vine. I'm not even inter-ested in clothes any more. Me! Dig this closet."

She opened the closet door. Hanging there good as new were tons of beautiful clothes; each dress had it own padded hanger, the sweaters were neatly folded on the shelf, and shoes were stacked in their original boxes.

"Never wear 'em. They just take up space," she said.

Jeremy, who had been mashing carrots for Elmer Joy, looked up and said: "Why don't you give your glad rags to Helen if they don't make you glad?"

"Right, take what you want," she offered. "Maybe with some freaky threads and a wig you'll feel differently about yourself."

I refused her offer because I couldn't see how clothes would make a new woman of me. Clothes hadn't helped Albert—he was back in the nut-burg again—and Pablo with his fancy gear had gone and left me all alone.

Besides, Marian was not a generous person. If I accepted her wardrobe, she might renege and want the stuff back again. Then our relationship would consist of the transportation and maintenance of clothing. It might prove exhausting and time-consuming.

"I'm thinking of moving out of the Buckminster," I said.

"To where?"

"Not sure . . . East Side maybe . . . in the Seventies. I've never shared an apartment with another woman . . . Could be a big help financially and so- cially."

"Yeah, you'll move when I get my first golden record," Marian said.

"Don't you believe me?"

"No."

She was right. It would take a bomb to get me out of the Buckminster. What if Pablo came trotting back some day?

"You staying for dinner?" Jeremy asked.

"I've got to get to sleep early, so I can wake up early. Joe Fafka is asking his listeners to watch out for Pablo. He's doing it as a public service."

"You know I don't believe in psychoanalysis, Helen," Marian said, "but in your ease I think it would help. You're so hung up you're still wearing the hanger. Dig it, baby, what you need is a big, big change."

"And what you need is to write songs again. I think your life as it is right now is interesting enough material to write about. Why do you put it down?"

"Don't change the subject. We're talking about Helen Jones now, not Marian Freylinghusen Von Hoffer. I know I can write the shit out of any situation. I'm not worried about me. What does your mother say?"

"Mother!" Marian had never mentioned my mother before.

"Yeah, mother . . . I'm selfish, I don't want to be the only one suffering through this with you. Suffering's what mothers are for."

"Gee, Marian, I thought you hated my mother, too. Didn't we agree that she's an envious old fart who's jealous of me because I'm so thin?"

"Helen, Helen, Helen," Marian sighed. "Grow up."

Jeremy put his arm around my shoulder. "Don't let it get you down.

There are worse things in the world. When I was a kid, my dad took me fishing. We were both crazy about angling, and we had a wonderful day catching trout and pickerel. Man, suddenly it got dark, and we decided to take a shortcut to where the car was. We had to cross a swamp, you know, full of fallen trees. Had to climb up one trunk to get to the other side of the swamp. Didn't notice the water moccasin curled up in front of us, a nasty creature. Then wherever we turned there were snakes curling and slithering. We couldn't go back and we couldn't go forward. We managed to hook the snakes directly in front of us on the log with our poles. The hooks broke with the weight of the snakes, but we jumped off the log just in time, as other snakes began to crawl on from the swamp, and were able to reach our car. I still get nightmares about it. That's bad see?"

"Thanks, Jeremy," I said, "but I don't get the connection."

"The connection is," Marian explained, "that Jeremy is on speed and can't stop talking."

"I'm coming down now," Jeremy said.

Marian put Elmer Joy into my arms as a gesture of friendship. "Kiss him," she said. "Kissing babies is as good as meditation."

Babies are so comforting. They smile all over their bodies and put their soft lingers into your mouth as if it is their own. They smell good, and laugh at funny faces.

I left in better shape than when I had arrived. Good friends are worth more than money, analysis, or a trip to romantic places.

81 Had no luck with the Joe Fafka program. His listeners thought he was putting them on about a talking dog. Who would want to be caught in broad daylight questioning a dog and waiting for an answer? There were some false leads: a Great Dane found in an abandoned car at One hundred thirty-eighth Street and Convent Avenue, a toy poodle caught between buildings on the Lower East Side, a nondescript dirty-white mutt who had been frightening children in the park at Ninety-sixth Street near the horse path, and a Russian wolfhound that had run away from an outdoor photography session. Some sympathetic dog lovers offered pups from their dogs next litter. Joe invited me on the air to thank his many listeners. I began by expressing what I believed to be my warm and grateful feelings, but soon descended to the unpleasant sort of remarks one is apt to make when one has been abandoned. I fell apart.

"Joe, I want to thank your kind listeners for going all out for me and trying to find Pablo. Their words of comfort will always remind me that the milk of human kindness still flows, even though it soon becomes sour and stinks. How can so many of you folks listening in think that I am just like you? Even when I had Pablo, I didn't let him dirty the sidewalk. I don't prefer dogs to people. I never called him 'sweetsie pie', or bought him matching rainboots, raincoat, and umbrella. I knew that Pablo was a dog. A dog is incapable of love. I was well aware that Pablo was with me for one reason, custodial care! I did not carry a photo of him in my wallet, nor is he my sole heir. My search for Pablo has nothing to do with the extremes of loneliness. If he does not return to me, there are other lifestyles to investigate. His disappearance was a blessing in disguise. It freed me. I'll be able to take vacations without worrying about placing the dog. I'll be able to live wherever I want. My guests won't have to ask, 'Does he bite?' Pablo, if you are listening to this broadcast, I want you to know it's all over between us. You had the best of both worlds, yet you left without even a word of thanks. But I say to you—THANK YOU PABLO! THANK YOU FOR THROWING ME INTO THE POOL TO TEACH ME HOW TO SWIM!"

Callers flooded the lines insulting me. One woman said that if she ever met me she'd shave the hair off my head and make me walk nude down Broadway with a sign around my neck reading TRAITOR. There was one obscene call in which the man described himself as well hung, young, and dying of bitches. He was cut off before he reached a wider audience than myself.

Joe complimented me: "You contributed to a lively show. Thanks, Miss Jones. Interest is gonna run high for a long time."

"I enjoyed being on the show. I'd like a dialogue show myself. Is it hard?"

"Miss Jones, all you need is the gift of gab, a research assistant, and a strong viewpoint. Anyone can be a Joe Fafka, or a Pia Lindstrom, or even the McCanns at Home . . . The bigger the job, the easier it is."

"How would I apply for such a job? I mean, where do I begin?"

"Can you write?" Joe asked. "You must be able to make sense on paper."

"I can write up a storm," I said.

82 I tried to write up a storm, just to see if I could. You don't get famous overnight, you've got to work at it.

Disaster Area

Storm Maxine blew up over the East Coast yesterday, destroying all that was in her path. For miles around, rubble was strewn over an area that once contained a prosperous business and residential community. Hundreds of lives were lost, along with millions of dollars' worth of property. Maxine, erratic and volatile, followed in her sister's path (last year Lorraine caused the President to declare the East Coast a national disaster area, and allocated thousands of dollars to rebuilding the Seacoast). Weather forecasters say that Maxine and Lorraine are mysteries to them, since they did not follow the usual storm patterns, but erupted unexpectedly and with unforeseen fury, only to disappear in a few hours after the damage was done. "Just like a woman," was the comment heard, though strictly the record, by those interviewing the President. He seemed in good spirits after a night of needed rest, and promised to support research designed to tame those "terrible ladies of death and destruction."

83 They called it superrealism, but it was Pablo. I had wandered down to SoHo, to the place on the map that Myra had pointed out, and there he was in a gallery, next to the store with a neon flying cock in the window.

An artist had made life-size exact replicas of my dog sleeping, humping a bitch, springing to the attack, eating, sniffing a tree, carrying a newspaper, sitting behind the wheel of a car (that was something new). On the wall beside each piece of art was a page of information concerning Pablo. I was not mentioned.

The name of the artist was Luis Farash. I had seen his work before on the cover of *Time* magazine. His number was in the phone book and I called him immediately.

"Your dog?" the voice said. "Can you prove it?"

"I have pictures of him."

"Many dogs look alike. Are there any distinguishing features that would set him apart?"

"He answers to the name Pablo, and he can talk."

"Talk? All by himself without external manipulation of the voice box?"

"Sings too, though his repertoire is limited."

"Does he limp slightly and have one chewed ear?"

"Yes, an adolescent injury."

"I can see you know the dog well, Miss . . ."

"Helen Jones."

"Miss Jones. The dog I have your description."

"Where do you live? I'll come right over to get him."

"I wouldn't do that if I were you."

"Why not?"

"He's happy here . . . He's mine now . . . The best model I've ever had."

"Let me speak to him."

"All right, but don't say I didn't warn you."

After a short pause, during which I heard whispering and giggling at the other end of the line, Pablo's voice reached me: "Helen? How ya doin' babe? I meant to drop you a note explaining . . ."

"Explaining what?"

"That every dog must have his day . . . know what I mean?"

I didn't know what he meant. "Come off it Pablo, you drove me crazy wondering whether you were dead or alive."

"So now you know. I'm alive and happy. Happier than I've ever been. Luis has made me famous; we have a movie contract, a dog food endorsement, something in the works for a TV series, and next month T-shirts with my name and photograph will be on sale at May's department store exclusively."

Luis Farash took the phone and spitefully added, "I'm surprised you never helped Pablo realize his talents."

"Exploit him you mean."

"How did you find me?" This time a note of admiration in Pablo's voice.

"Myra helped; she told me where to search. I popped into the gallery, and there you were."

"How did you like the show?" Pablo asked as if I were just anyone who had happened to visit the gallery.

"Fuck you!" I shouted, and slammed the receiver down.

84 She who lies down with dogs gets fleas.

85 Farash's show, when I was able to be honest with myself, was upsetting and extremely moving because of his masterful skill. He had presented Pablo without a veneer of glamour, with complete verisimilitude. One might look upon his exhibition as an allegory of the basic needs of man unhampered by his superego. Watching a dog do what men do behind closed doors is a sight that engages one's sympathy and

anger. Pablo was not heroic for he was only exhibiting his nature. But Luis Farash deserved four stars for daring such an overwhelming criticism of man's best friend. I wrote a letter to the Op-Ed page of the *Times*, enlarging on the above topic and recommending the show to incipient art lovers and other minorities. For this expansive attitude on my part I received an unexpected award. The letter of notification arrived in the mail this morning.

> *It is my honor to name you, on behalf of Altruistic Foundation, a recipient of the Foundation's Altruist-in-Residence Award for 1974. This award is made in recognition of your sustained contribution to American moral growth through altruism; and it is intended as further encouragement to you, the generous citizen, to continue to give-with the tools of imagination, wit, pathos, and poetry—the personal and societal questions of human value and morality which illuminate a vigorous altruism and mirror the aspirations and searchings of a people striving for self-abnegation.*
>
> *John H. Johns*

86 Love takes a long time to wear off. I haunted the places where Pablo might be: Houston Street, Spring, West Broadway. In my shoulder bag I carried a jeweled collar for him. He was a sucker for hip jewelry, and might be won over. When I finally ran into him a few weeks later I didn't recognize him. Pablo had gained so much weight that he waddled. His eyes were bloodshot and he could barely drag himself to the Spring Street bar.

"Aren't you taking care of yourself?" I asked.

"Farash buys me Nesselrode pie, ice cream, Sacher tortes, and whipped potatoes. I can't resist," he whispered hoarsely.

"You'll eat yourself to death!"

"I'm a social eater, not a foodaholic," he declared. "When I start hiding chocolate cake in the clothes hamper, then I'll go for help."

Luis Farash protested that he needed a fat Pablo since "Obesity and What Comes After" was the theme of his next show.

"You're a cruel man," I cried.

"No . . . I'm an artist," he said.

87 Through the window of the bar I could see Pablo being adored by two young women who were eating chicken crepes in cream sauce. They fed him choice bits of the succulent meat as he lay under their feet. Luis Farash took the check.

88 A Buckminster acquaintance, James McCrory, brought a bottle of wine and we drank it while watching a drama written especially for television. I had the blues and the creeps and needed company. The plot of the program went like this: a rabid dog is trapped in a heatless farmhouse. With him in the house is a family—a young boy, mother, father, and grandmother. There is a blizzard outside (natch). The father wants to shoot the dog. The little boy begs him not to do it. The dog bites the boy and the father shoots the dog. The grandmother has a heart attack, and the mother goes into labor pains. The snow blows under the door. The new infant is born. One by one the occupants of the house freeze to death. Finally only the father and the infant are alive. The father wraps the infant in everybody's clothing. He then shoots himself in the head. A helicopter lands and rescues the baby. Thirty-five years later we see the baby now grown into a man. He looks just like his father. He enters his home in an upper-middle-class suburb, finds his wife with a lover in flagrante delicto in the bedroom, takes a gun out of the bureau drawer, shoots her and her lover, then shoots himself in the head. We hear a baby cry, then see the little one in a crib in the bedroom. The end.

When the credits zoomed by I caught James McCrory's name as head writer. "You son of a gun!" I exclaimed. "Why didn't you tell me it was your program?"

James kissed me and said, "I wanted to surprise you, get your gut reaction."

"I loved it, James. You're a great comic talent."

"Comic?"

"Comic, tragic, it's all the same. Haven't you ever heard the song 'I'm Laughin' with Tears in My Eyes'?"

"You hated it, didn't you?"

"No, no, I really loved it. It touched me, James, especially when the helicopter landed. I thought: 'Oh my God, he's too late!' What was it like to write it?"

"I had constipation, took dexies, worked around the clock, suffered headaches, lived like a monk in a trunk."

"If I wrote something, would you read it? You're the only professional author I know."

"I'm at your disposal m'lady, and will be happy to give you a criticism and evaluation for free . . . Well, not exactly for free . . . I want another kiss."

"That's easy," I said, all warm and cheerful.

"What are you going to write? Do you have a project in mind?"

"I kind of thought I'd write a story of unrequited love, sort of autobiographical . . . but it all comes out good in the end. Or do you think it should come out tragic?"

"That's up to you."

"Oh yeah. It is. Besides, if it's autobiographical it would have to be the truth . . . and I don't even know the end yet."

"No, you don't."

89 What is writing?

Imagine an ant colony carrying one by one a bit of food to their nest. The crumb of sustenance is bigger and heavier than any of the ants, yet they manage. They forage everywhere for their food; it is the instinct to survive. What others reject, they collect. Nothing is wasted.

This is not writing. It is comparison shopping.

90 Yes, I'd marry James. He's a darling mess. He likes me a lot. More than that. This time I'll play hard to get. I've learned that the best way to keep someone you love is not in a pumpkin shell (pumpkin shells go soft and shrink). The thing to do is to keep one's emotions hidden, to be like Daddy's jade snail—valuable, art-carved, silent . . . coveted. I gave Pablo everything I had. Oh shit!

91 Marian and Jeremy have moved to Woodstock. Boy, did she luck into it. And now they'll live happily ever after.

92 Mother and I feel that Daddy has changed. He has proposed a grandiose scheme to the city art commission. It is the idea of an egomaniac: he wants to donate a 125-foot-high stainless steel Shirley poppy in full bloom showing its reproductive organs. If the idea is accepted, it will rise from a block-long bed of ordinary flowers on the center mall of Park Avenue between Sixty-eighth and Sixty-ninth Streets.

"It is totally inappropriate," Mother said, "and a traffic hazard, besides. The sun shining off the stem and petals would blind drivers."

"Edward hates cars," I said. "It might be his diabolic plan to cause chaos and confusion. I'll try to talk him out of it."

93 "They have accused me of self-aggrandizement!" Daddy shouted. "They say what I want to do is similar to what the pharaohs used to do."

"They're right, Edward; you do have a pretty big monument in mind.

Couldn't you just donate a bed of tulips, plant an empty lot somewhere? What's got into you?"

Daddy shrugged off my criticism. "I prefer to do the unusual. You know that, Helen. I've never gotten a kick out of giving five thousand dollars here and five thousand dollars there."

94 Word got out about Daddy's offer to the city, and Joe Fafka's program was inundated by calls from indignant citizens who wanted to air their views.

"Joe, do you think it's right for a private citizen to use a public avenue to put up a work of art so-called?"

"No sir, I don't," Joe began, "and this particular statue is another political move by those gay liberation creeps who want to deflower the innocent. The monument is at least eight feet wide and a hundred and twenty-five feet high . . . a monster phallus they want to jam down our throats. I am *furious* that anyone would dare to suggest we'd consent to that thing sitting on Park Avenue. Why, it's the most beautiful avenue in New York, just as beautiful as the Champs-Elysées in Paris!"

"As beautiful as what, Joe?"

"The Champs-Elysées, dummy!"

"What kinda champs?"

"Get off the phone, phony!"

Next a woman spoke: "Good morning, Joe Shmoe."

"Yes, what is it, madame?"

"I just wanted to tell you that you're a jerk!"

"Thank you, madame."

Joe paused for a drink of water; his sound effects man amplified the sound, then added the roar of a waterfall.

"I needed that. Now let's see who's on the line. Hello sir or madame or anything in-between, are you there?"

"Joe . . . about the Obelisk to the city . . ."

"You mean the gobble-risk, sir. Gobble, gobble, gobble . . . it's a real turkey."

"I think you're the funniest man alive, Joe, I listen to you all the time no matter what I'm doing."

"Don't lie to me, you bum!"

"Why should I lie to you, Joe? You make me laugh all the time and what's more I think you're doing a good job for guys like me who aren't heard."

"Look, stupid, you don't have to butter me up. You have as much influence as I do. I'm just one guy on the radio, but you're a few million out there where it counts. *You have influence. . . . Use it!* Call the Parks, Recreation, and Cultural Affairs Administration. Let them know your views. They have not yet taken a final position on the monument. Get your friends to call if you have any."

"Yes, but Joe, can I ask you a question?"

"Go ahead."

"What?"

"I said go ahead. Go on, ask your question."

"Oh, yeah, well . . . what makes you think that homosexuals are behind this statue?"

"Aren't they behind everything?"

"I don't get you, Joe."

"The funniest man you ever heard was making a joke, a witticism, jerk, but it went right over your head. I won't bother to explain, sir, it would be blipped right the air."

"Have you ever been approached by a homo, Joe? I was wondering what you would do if it happened?"

"I'd punch his nose down his throat that's what I'd do! What do you think I'd do? Isn't the city contaminated enough?"

"I agree, I agree, baby, I'd do the same thing."

"You sound like a pansy yourself, sir. Are you gay?"

"Cross my heart, Joe, I'm not. I'm a fireman."

"A fireman? You expect me to believe that? You want me to believe that you handle the hose, give mouth-to-mouth resuscitation . . . What do you do with your time in the firehouse?"

"You got me wrong, Joe. I don't do nothing but play cards, cook, sleep . . ."

"When do you see your wife, may I ask?"

"I'm not married, Joe."

"Ahha! Not married! And you want me to believe you're okay?"

"I called you to have a friendly conversation, Joe, not to be insulted."

"I'm the one who's insulted, *fag*! Get off the line and don't come back. I'll remember your voice, your *fag* voice!"

The sound effects man brought on the sound of a huge explosion, and then I heard a tiny whimper before Joe spoke again.

"Ladies and gentlemen, I know when I'm being put on. My last caller was a representative of the most odious, insidious group of people in the world—a homosexual. I wouldn't have minded his call if he had stood up like a man and admitted that he was a *homo* . . . but he had to come sneaking around like a thief in the night trying to fool me. Well, I can't be fooled. *They* want equal rights, but they are not equal, they are *less than* human. If any one of them would call in and say, 'Joe, I can't help it, I'm sick,' we might have the beginning of a dialogue, but they come on as if they are healthy, happy people, just like you and me. Would you want one of these vipers in *fag* clothing to teach *your* child right from wrong? Would you want one of these vile piles of garbage to dump themselves in your home just because the law says you *must*? They are weak, they are sick, they are perverted, and they know it. They want everyone to be like them—barren human beings. I'd deport every one of them if I could, and then they'd be with their own kind. Folks, these scum want the human race to die out. Do you? *Do you?* They have reduced the sacred sexual act to exactly that .. an act . . . often an act of sodomy . . . and in their desperation they would take your children. Please. *Please* demonstrate against the bill for equal rights for gay people. They are not only gay, they are hilarious, and this monument they propose will turn out to be a private club for gays, mark my word. It will become the most expensive pissoir on Park Avenue. The stench will drive out respectable people. It will float from Ninety-sixth Street to Grand Central Terminal. *Homos! Gays! Go back where you came from, the gutters, the sewers!* Oh, they're driving me mad. Lucky for me I'm about to depart for my semi-annual trip to Tahiti, where the coconut milk still flows and pretty maidens all in a raw will sway their pretty hips in grass skirts for me. I'm going to Tahiti, where a man who is a man can still peace, beauty, and natural sex . . . and you can go, too, friends, if you'll just call this number . . ."

"Hello Joe?"

"Yes, stupid, you think it was?"

"Joe, I hope you get leprosy and syphilis in Tahiti!"

"There it is, friends, you heard it here. When in doubt they call names. They don't know how to fight fair."

"Joe?"

"Yes, madame, this is Joe Shmoe on the line. Can I help you?"

"Listen, Joe, my father is not a fag and he's the person who proposed the monument. It is not a phallic symbol, it is more of an androgynous plant having both male and female organs. By a miracle of nature the bee fertilizes this flower and causes it to reproduce itself. This has nothing to do with homosexuality. God made the trees, the flowers, and he made me. Thank you."

95 "You're not grasping what I'm saying," Myra said on the telephone from Edward's house. "Edward is dead, and I want you to come right over."

I felt nothing. I thought I felt nothing. I would require evidence. I still had things to settle with Daddy; he couldn't have died.

"I've got to wash and dress, Myra; I got up late."

"You're a cold fish," Myra said accusingly.

"You want me to fall apart on the telephone?" I asked.

"Aren't you even going to ask how it happened?"

"Later Mother, later."

96 First Pablo, now Father. Is Pablo really a dog, or is he a sign? I often make tragic mistakes. How to interpret disappearances? How far I am from those I love!

97 Edward had developed a severe asthma in reaction to plant pollen. It may be true that all men kill the one they love, but it is equally true that loved ones frequently murder those who care for them. Destruction is distressingly reciprocal. Edward would not send his plants away, though he knew close proximity to them would be his doom. Before his death he had been involved in a number of "blind" experiments in order to effect a single cure for a number of ailments. His incentive was that what may *seem* to be an impenetrable maze, may presently bring one out into the light. The bulk of his experiments were not made in a haphazard manner but were attained by experimentation along rigidly predetermined lines. He wanted to break through the expected, to be surprised; he had begun to be influenced by the creative artist's use of chance. During our last visit together, Edward had said: "I recall reading an address by the late Professor Newton, a distinguished astronomer, on the subject of 'dead work', in which he emphasized the fact that many of the experiments which any scientific worker must make will lead to no definite goal . . ."

Edward was cremated and his ashes strewn over Burbank, California, which was what he wanted. Ashes to flowers, trees, and fruit. To remain a healer even in death.

98 At the services all the things said about Daddy were true and beautiful, about his courage and faith, his difficulties, and the persecution he had to put up with because of the medical profession's prejudice. Following is a eulogy by his friend. R. D. Reeuw, M.R.C.S . . . L.R.C.P.

"I first met Edward Jones at the International Homeopathic Congress in

1936. This meeting was the beginning of a friendship lasting until the day of his death. During those years I had the privilege of keeping in touch with him either personally or by letter, and in this way sharing with him each new discovery.

"One characteristic of his work was his unselfish desire to help humanity; he wanted nothing for himself. He refused payment for his treatments, and gave away the clothes off his back. The finding of each new remedy filled him with joy and thankfulness to the giver of all. He considered himself only as the instrument through which the remedies came.

"Jones has gone from our sight, but his work lives on, and only those who worked with him know the great value of his discoveries."

99 Myra held a séance to call Edward back. In the solemn stillness we waited for three notes on a trumpet to be sounded. "He will announce himself," Myra promised, "but we must be very quiet."

Quiet or not, there was no trumpet.

Myra said, "It must be in use elsewhere. I'll try reaching him directly." She stared into a corner of the darkened room. "Edward, my love, if you are here reveal yourself."

"How can he do that?" I whispered restlessly. I had had enough of fakery. Edward was certainly beyond the limits of stark, raving reality. He was dead and spread over the toasted terrain of Burbank.

"Listen, he is here."

I listened and heard three distinct thumps against some kind of resonant wood.

"Is it you, Edward? Knock twice if it is you," Mother asked hopefully.

This time the thumps were reduced by one.

A blurred and dissolving form detached itself from the ceiling. At first it was aimless, then it settled above Mother.

A scent of mildew and incense, so faint that it seemed to come from another dimension, entered my nostrils. Impetuously I cried out: "Daddy!" The blurred form descended and embraced me. Its cloudy, armlike protuberances drifted around me like clouds. Smoke made my eyes tear. Spots were swimming in them. I began to feel faint. There was a crash as Myra dropped her braceleted arm to the table.

"Something's burning!" she said before passing out.

Using the chair in which she was slumped as a stretcher, I dragged her out of the apartment and into the hall. Firemen were already rushing up the stairs, and I could hear the breaking of glass as other firefighters, coming up a ladder, hatcheted the windows. We hadn't been in there long enough to suffer smoke poisoning, but we had inhaled more smoke than was healthy. A neighbor remarked that he had seen our old friend Albert around the building. Too bad we had missed him.

100 I'm rich. Now what'll I do? Daddy left me his house and almost all of his money. There is one stipulation: I must spend at least three days out of the week helping people or I don't get the $. What constitutes helping? If I ball people who want me, is that helping? If I read stories to orphans and take them to the playground, is that helping? If I give a drunk a lifetime supply of sen-sen and gin, is that helping? Or must I play cards with the geriatric crowd and get them to smile? No, Daddy, you can't trick me into a useful life so that your death will seem useful.

What I think I'd like to do is move furniture. Sweat it out. Bend and lift. Shove and carry. Exhaust myself. I'm so tired of resting. (What do you think Edward?)

What I think I'd like to do is get in touch with Joe Fafka. Win friends and influence people. Have power and my own money. (What do you think Edward?)

What I think I'd like to do is write an article for *Cosmopolitan* about a three-way: mother, daughter, father. Yes, I'll use Joe Fafka's influence to contact the articles editor. (What do you think Edward?)

101 No sooner said than done! A reply from *Cosmo*:
Dear Helen,

I'm delighted you're going to do "Family as Lovers." As agreed, we see it as a major four-thousand-word article and can pay $1,000.00 for an accepted manuscript with a $100.00 write if disaster strikes (which it won't). I'm enclosing some notes. Call me if you have any questions.

My best,
Daisy Roberts
Articles Editor

102 *FAMILY AS LOVERS*
Article simply discussing incestuous relationships . . . Do close relations make good lovers?

this is a bit spurious since some are going to be bad and some of them good—like ALL lovers—but it will be an interesting subject and well read.

whereas cosmo is AGAINST incest and respects the old taboos perhaps we have been too harsh—and cliché in our own thinking—

the artical might have a humorous approach
or a serious approach—
    probably a little of both
    use attached article for fodder
writer should know
others who have family sex,
article shouldn't be just her own
experiences—
needs more general approach than that . . .

103 Article going well. Already have four typewritten pages.

104 Article going well. Already have three typewritten pages.

105 Article may not be written. Should be able to begin on the fifteenth page, as one begins on the top floor of the Guggenheim to see the show. It's too exhausting to begin on page one. It's never any good. Has anything ever been written backward?

106 .reverof em evarc mih ekam dluohs amleS hserf fo etsat teews eht, repparw ym sleep luaP nehw, nehT. wollamarc a ekil nat ni depparw nruter ll'I.
DNE

107 Hearing the sound of a dog barking, I give a slight start and am more moved than ever. I bite my underlip. In front of the flower shop at the side entrance of the Buckminster, two dogs are playing. One is leashed, the other free. I stop to look at the dogs with great tenderness. Sharply etched against the side of the building is a grouping of flowers that is swaying in the wind. The vagrant dog runs away. Seen in profile, the tethered dog is me.
Dream fragment: 5 A.M. Wed. Day.

108 Edward willed one hundred thousand dollars to research, to establish the existence of a plant soul. The will said that aside from funeral expenses, money for an old clerical friend to say goodbye at the grave, and what should go to me and Myra, the rest of the money should be given "for research or some other scientific proof of a soul of a flower, or other plant, which leaves at death."

"I think there can be a photograph of a soul leaving the flower at death," said the will, which was declared legal.

About one hundred and forty groups and individuals laid claim to the money, and in June, Judge Martin ruled that the fortune should go to the Homeopathetique Botanical Institute of East Orange, New Jersey.

The New Jersey-based society has fourteen hundred members and "studies crisis apparitions, deathbed visions, and out-of-plant experiences." It claims to have had extraordinary success with vascular plants in particular.

109 Now that Myra was my only living relative, I had the desire to be close to her . . . but certain matters, unhappy childhood traumas, would have to be brought out in the open first. My letter to her, though harsh, was intended as a wedge in the door.

> Mommy,
>
> Nothing is easy, and yet it IS easy. My love for you exists in spite of what you have done. Some memories are more important than others. Let me sort them out: your idea of a good time for me (for instance). When I was four years old, you put me on an amusement park ride. I stood in a big drum, you above it on a catwalk for observers.
>
> The drum began to revolve, and as it accelerated, the bottom, on which my feet rested, dropped out. Because of centrifugal force I became plastered to the inner curve of the drum. I was terrified, could barely breathe . . . a smile of terror on my face. Toward the end of the ride, as I slid down slowly into what I believed to be a bottomless pit, the drum slackened its pace and the floor came up. You asked me how I liked the ride. Was malice intended?

You treated me worse than prisoners at the San Diego jail. Kept me in an all-concrete section of our home, with no windows, and only pumped air to breathe. The only time I saw daylight was when I went to the roof on Sundays (Edward was away most of the time attending conferences or on field trips, so he was in ignorance of how you abused me. You also threatened to kill me if I told). My constant question to you was: "Is the sun shining outside or not?"

When you were despondent over losing a lover, you asked me to kill you with a butcher knife. I refused to do so. You then took a light bulb out of a socket, cocked the hammer of your .38 caliber revolver, handed me the gun and commanded me to shoot you while you had your finger in the light socket. (What you did not know was that I had flipped the light switch off, but there was no way for me to empty the gun before I pointed it at you.) You then asked me for a glass of water. You held it and sipped. I pulled the trigger of the gun. It misfired. Hysterically you fell upon a nearby couch. I covered you with a blanket. When you awoke you denied everything. It was as if I had dreamed it. I know you meant well, but I'm scarred for life.

Now that we understand each other (now that you are old and the shoe is on the other foot), I intend to show you what loving kindness is. I want to be helpful. I am inviting you to come and live with me in Edward's house until the bitter end. There will be no reprisals.

Helen Jones

110

A curt note from Myra: "Do you realize what it's like to hear the horrible tramping of little feet in heavy boots? And to watch your pinched face, tiny ass, wee beastie breasties, all cute and mean so deadly earnest at thirteen?—*Mommy*

111 So that's the way she wants to play.

112 I have not reconciled the two aspects of my character: the animal and the human. No, they are at war. Whenever I want something intensely, I consider myself animal or instinctive; when I manage to repress my desires—sex, violence, hunger—it is then that I regard myself as a human being.

113 Mr. Fafka invited me to be his co-host on a program concerning mistaken identity. It is chilling to think that even I might be pulled off the street at any time and arrested just because I happen to resemble a crime suspect. I do carry about with me a vague guilt for having done something bad . . . but what?

114 "Yes sir," Joe said, "if you have a story to tell us, go ahead, we're waiting."

"I'm calling from the Tombs, Joe. I'm innocent. There's another guy out there, walking free, who is the spitting image of me. I'm no murderer. I'm gonna sue the city!"

"You mean you're calling *me* instead of your lawyer, stupid?"

"Yeah, Joe."

"How do you expect *me* to help you?"

"I dunno."

"Well then, blow this out of your barracks bag, creep. . . . You're a contemptible, cretinous, character of the lowest caliber, you're a twisted knife in the side of humanity, a cyanide bullet in the brain of innocence, you're a raging maniac who was easily identified in the police lineup, am I right so far?"

"Yes, Joe."

"And you have a previous record as long as a city block, don't you?"

"Right on the button, Joe."

"Then why are you wasting our time with this nonsense?"

"Nonsense?"

"*Nonsense.* Take your punishment like a man, jerk! I hope they string you up by your shoelaces so you choke to death. May you drink water out of a toilet bowl for the rest of your unnatural life and may you find maggots in your meat forever and ever amen! Excuse me while I weep with rage, friends."

"You've made me feel much better, Joe. Before I called you I was living a lie; I couldn't face up to what I was and what I done. Now the whole world knows I'm rotten and I'm ready to take the rap. God bless you, Mr. Fafka."

"My pleasure," Joe answered. He gave me a reassuring nod and took another call; the accent was unmistakenly British.

"Good morning, sir."

"Sir *Fafka* if you please, madame, Mrs. Fancy Frump! Where'd you pick up that way of talking?"

"I was born in Great Britain, Mr. Fafka."

"Madame, I'll bet you were born in the Bronx and took a cram course with at the American Academy of Dramatic Arts."

"Joe, I called in to tell you that I've often been mistaken for Elizabeth Taylor . . . even by Richard Burton."

Joe got rid of her fast. "Why do the kooks call me?" he screamed. "If there are any sane people out there, please talk to me before I go bananas."

"Mr. Fafka, I heard your cry for help. There's nothing wrong with me, but I think you're nuts."

"Next!" Joe said.

"I am so happy to be talking to you, Joe. You don't have any idea. How's about you dropping by my house the next time you're in Oshawashkee,

Missouri?"

"You've called me long distance, ma'am. Why me?"

"I love you, Joe, that's why. Every night I say a little prayer for you."

"Would you mind saying it for me now?"

"Not at all. Dear God who are in Heaven, bless Joe Fafka for all the happiness he brings to us shut-ins, and protect him from sorrow and pain. When finally you and he meet, oh Lord, I hope you'll introduce me. Amen."

"Thank you for your kind thought, madame, and . . ."

"Joe, I want to comment on a recent strange experience. Just yesterday, as I was sitting in my wheelchair, I was mistaken for Golda Meir by two Arabs who kept me in a locked room for six hours. But no matter what they did I refused to return the Wailing Wall."

"I can't take it! I can't take it!" Joe screamed. "Helen, I'll talk to you."

"Sure, Joe, talk to me."

"Helen, don't you think that most people feel as if they are victims of mistaken identity? Why do you think there are sex changes, transvestites, Jesus Christs, and Napoleons in the world?"

"Because the grass is always greener on the other side of the fence?"

"Wrong! It's because nobody wants to face responsibility. I've spoken to a number of Jesus Christs in my day and they all seem to be living on past glories; the Bible's been written and they're satisfied to rest on their laurels. The same with the Napoleons: they're not interested in Catacombs, sewage systems, or war. All they want to do is to stand around with one hand stuck in their jacket. It's narcissistic. It's all for show—Hold your thought, Helen, there's another call coming in . . . Yes? . . . This is for you, Helen."

"Miss Jones . . ." The voice was a familiar one: rough guttural, something between a whimper and a bark. "For years now I've been mistaken for a dog. Because I was treated like a dog, I began to have a dog's mentality. Unless I get some help this is the end of the road for me, the end of a dusty, lonely road."

"Please give your name to the operator when I say 'now,' sir. You are not allowed to speak your name on the air. Okay . . . now!" Joe said.

115 I found Pablo holed up in a thirty dollar-a-week fleabag hotel on the Bowery, living on frankfurters and three cheap movies a day. I didn't have to plead too hard to take him home with me. He had spent practically his last dime on the phone call to Joe Fafka. I took him to Edward's house, fed him, bathed him, bedded him—all without reproach. But for months he didn't respond. He was like a vegetable.

"What happened to you, Pablo?"

"Luís Farash didn't give me a cent . . . and he's disappeared. Gone to the mid-East with a show. At least I'm not fat any more."

"Why do you say you're not a dog, Pablo? Men don't have tails."

"Look. Neither do I."

He was right, Luis Farash had gotten Pablo a tail job.

"Maybe you are a man," I said.

"I am."

"I'll help you rebuild your life as a man."

"And then we'll get married."

116 One should not discuss a dream in front of a simpleton.

117 Word of Albert reached me via the news. He's roaming free again. The caption—LOUD LAUGHER GOES FREE—meant Albert. I read: "Traffic court judge Viola Ramsey granted Albert Onestein the last laugh by dismissing charges against him of 'laughing in a loud voice' aboard a bus. An off-duty policewoman, who had recently overcome deafness by a near miracle, testified that Mr. Onestein had refused to stop what she called 'a wild laugh' and so she had arrested him on a charge of disorderly behavior. The judge, who could not even get a smile out of Mr. Onestein, much less an example of his disorderly 'wild laugh,' said the case was 'ridiculous, and the charges have no foundation.'

118 Joe told his audience that he is getting a laser beam to sterilize all black men on welfare. He is also doubling his guard at the station. Threats against him keep coming in. He seems to thrive on danger.

"Let 'em come and get me! I'm ready for 'em!" he said.

119 I'm going to be married in white, a double-ring ceremony. However, Pablo doesn't have any fingers so I'm giving him a gold bracelet for his right paw. Neither of us has a large guest list; on my side there's Mother, James McCrory, Albert, Marian & Jeremy, and Joe Fafka. On Pablo's side there's a feisty neighborhood pug he met outside the supermarket, Luis Farash (whom we've forgiven), and a snag-toothed bitch he claims is his real mother.

120 Instead of going to a pet store for Pablo's wedding gifts I wandered around town picking up things he might never use. I wasn't sure whether or not to satisfy his fantasy that he is a man. For instance, what would he do with a Hermes tie? Drag it across the floor? And that language record for his trip to France . . . he barely speaks his own language. As for his supposed mother (who is shedding and has dandruff), I thought of sending her a whirligig wire salad basket because they're fabulous and she doesn't have one, or, what might be more suitable since she has litter after litter, Sesame Street records for her pups.

121 Marian has RSVP'd regrets, although she and Jeremy have sent me a floor-length denim apron to wear with nothing under it at my next dinner for two. I think she is disappointed in me.

122 Dear Marian,
I'm sorry you won't be able to attend the wedding, but I want you to know that I am getting married to Pablo because I truly love him and because we have formed an alliance against those of you who think you know the way things should be. Living with Pablo will be the ultimate in gracious sexual living . . . I won't have to use the Pill, or anything else . . . no backup system . . . no diaphragm, gel, foam, or abstinence. Take my word for it.
Love, *Helen*

123 Dear Helen,
Then you intend to be faithful to Pablo?
Love, *Marian*

124 Dear Marian,
If I slept with another male and had a child, it would be obvious that it wasn't Pablo's.
Love, *Helen*

125 Dear Helen,
How dreary. Why do you want to take yourself out the swim?
Love, *Marian*

126 Dear Marian,
I'm afraid of drowning.
Love, *Helen*

127 Dear Helen,
I don't believe you.
Love, *Marian*

128 Dear Marian,
You're right. Things are liable to change. They always do.
I am interested in another man. His name is Joe Fafka. Ring a bell? But he's the scum of the earth. Why do I always fall for the underdog?
Love, *Helen*

129 Dear Helen,
Try the ménage à trois. I know that Pablo is poor, unemployed . . . a student of life . . . that beautiful waif you rescued from death, but face up to it, you'll be taking him in and paying for *everything*, while he stirs up trouble or blames you for his lack of success. He'll never admit it's his fault. You as sorcerer's apprentice will have to do what women have always had to do, brew up all kinds of magic to make him feel *he* is firmly in charge. Man, I can already hear you stifling those martyred sighs, saying to him: "I knock myself out all week to keep you in sirloin and you won't even heel, or beg on command when guests are here," or, "Is that why I paid the vet dollars . . . so you could act in a pornographic movie on the sly?" Please Helen, don't, at the expense of your own peace of mind give him his own checking account to cover bus fare, beer, his subscription to *Dogromp*, or anything else he says he needs. Don't merge at the bank, or put his name on the buzzer or mailbox. Before long he'll want to be top-dog: he'll take over and you'll be on the leash. Take it from a friend, you're gonna have trouble like you've never had before. Some of your most shattering battles are going to be over such trivialities as hair on the floor and in the bath, kibbles that have fallen between the couch pillows, and garbage that has soaked through the bag. A dog can't help

but be a slob.

So that's why, dear friend, I suggest another man to keep you sane and happy. Extramural activity is necessary though it may be the grossest gluttony. In your case it's a decided necessity.

Love, *Marian*

130 Dear Marian,
I think you're an absolute shit. But thanks anyway.
Love, *Helen*

131 There is no chance at all that I will find Joe Fafka more irresistible than Pablo, though with him I will once again enjoy the world of lobster and Chablis.

132 Mother married us since we could not find a priest or reverend to agree on the marriage. Even homosexuals can be married in church now, but not woman and dog. No sanctification for us.

133 We knelt on red velvet cushions during the ceremony.
"Do you, Helen, take this creature to be your lifelong companion, in distemper and mange, in cheerful mood and good health, till that Great Dog Catcher in the sky do you part?" the Reverend Jones asked.

"I do," I whispered shyly.

Mother turned to Pablo: "Do you, Pablo, take Helen as your wife, to have and to hold, and do you promise to lie down on command, come when called, and protect her life and limb to the best of your ability till death do you part?"

"I do," Pablo replied.

"Then with the power invested in me by myself and a God of my own choosing, I pronounce you hound and bitch and may you take your place among the great lovers of the world—Heloise and Abelard, Wally and Edward, Mickey and Minnie, Tarzan and Jane, Victoria and Albert, Jean-Paul and Simone, Molly and Leopold, Oscar and Alfred, Gertrude and Alice, Jack and Jill, Mick and Bianca, Allen and Peter, Henry and Nancy, Richard and Elizabeth, Paulo and Francesca, Dick and Bebe, Catherine the Great and? . . . You may now kiss each other."

First Pablo sniffed under my dress, then he slobbered all over my face. It was a moment I'll never forget. Though I was afraid he'd get worms I let him eat half the wedding cake, including the tiny bride and groom made of almond paste that stood at the top of the cake. When Joe Fafka congratulated me and kissed me on the lips Pablo growled. He was so jealous that he wouldn't allow me to pet him. "The human hand is an instrument of punishment," he said.

I hope it is not the beginning of the end.

134

Mother installed a bidet in the master bathroom as our wedding gift. She had just made a killing in the stock market.

"How did you do it, Mother? Everybody else is losing their shirts."

"I do it by relaxing my mind and letting visions drift into it," she said, "but first I sit on the latest copy of the *Wall Street Journal* for ten minutes, to absorb information. After a while I might see a bear riding on top of a bull, for instance, and in the background, there might be a company trademark. This would show me the company's stock price is about to fall. Sometimes Edward sends me messages. The only times I buy or sell are when I have those dreams and he tells me what to do."

"How is Dad?"

"We never discuss what he's doing or how he is."

"Does he ever mention me?"

"He mentioned Pablo."

"What did he say?"

"He said that someday a dog will be President, and then he uttered something so cryptic that even I could not interpret it. He said: "To the victor the onions!"

"To the Victor the onions?" I repeated. "Must have something to do with tears." I left it at that.

135 Joe Fafka is taking his vacation *chez moi* avec Pablo *aussi*. I once had a French lover who taught me how to say lots of things with *chez moi*, such as *Voulez-vous couchez avec moi chez moi?* I don't remember too much of it, but it used to turn him on. Anyway, Joe would never have come to me if he hadn't reached the breaking point; not only were his callers becoming dumber and dumber, but his home was burglarized and his most treasured possessions stolen.

JOE FAFKA LOSES GAME BURGLAR TAKES PADDLES

While a well-known radio personality slept in his rented Manhattan duplex early yesterday, a burglar made off with more than $15,000 worth of loot. He took the celeb's most treasured possessions—six Ping-Pong paddles.

He was asleep in his second floor bedroom when the burglar forced the kitchen window and entered the apartment.

When Fafka awoke and came downstairs around 6 A.M., he noticed that his stereo set had disappeared. Then he opened a living room closet and found that a special suitcase containing a model for a laser beam also was missing.

Meanwhile his maid discovered that his wallet, containing several credit cards but no cash, had vanished from the kitchen table where he had left it under the tablecloth the night before.

Fafka was most upset over the loss of his paddles, which he says were given to him by Xaviera Hollander when she appeared as a guest on his program. They are unusual paddles with wooden handles and rubber sponge faces and measure more than eight inches across.

"They aren't worth very much to anyone else," Fafka explained, "but to me they're priceless. They my hand perfectly and have just the right feel. I'll miss them." When pressed as to what he used them for, since they were too large for Ping-Pong, Mr. Fafka declined to explain.

136 The three of us—Joe, Pablo, and myself—play anagrams in the evening. Pablo always loses, yet he smiles. It is a strange smile ... almost a threat.

"Why can't you be a good loser?" I asked. "You're full of hate."

"My hatred springs from the impossibility of my winning. Why don't you ever play games that are suited to my particular kind of intelligence?"

"What game for instance?" I asked.

"A game that employs the sense of smell, for instance: the game of Find the Bone. I am able to locate a bone that's been buried for as long as five years. . . . You wouldn't have a chance there."

137 It's Joe's fault that our life together has not been private and tranquil. Last week he announced that Daddy's favorite acacia tree had begun to cry. He described what happened as a miracle and with tongue in cheek predicted that the house on Sutton Place would become as holy a shrine as Lourdes.

"Yes, friends, trees too snivel and blubber all over the place. You've got to see it to believe it. My landlady tells me that the sap of the acacia tree can cure internal hemorrhages and that the water from her tree, which is at this moment wasting its tears, can cure anything."

People who wanted miraculous cures began calling. "Joe, my mother suffers from heart trouble. Should I bring her in from Monterey?"

"It's worth a try, isn't it, sonny?"

"It's very expensive, Joe."

"Then don't bring her, stingy!"

That was how it began, but soon people found out where we lived and parked outside till I let them in. Small boys collected water from the tree and sold it at cents a drink from stands set up outside. In five days, three thousand unfortunate people passed through the house: an elderly lady with paralyzed arms (which she raised for a second after drinking some of the acacia water), a woman whose hands had been drawn into claws by arthritis, a child who'd been blind from birth, a victim of cancer whose jaw was eaten away, an opera diva who had lost her voice, a sixteen-year-old boy with acne, and so on. Finally I had to put up a ten-foot link fence right in my own living room, and the artwork went into storage. Pablo wanted to charge admission, but a visiting priest from Ecuador said, "This is God's tree, and this living room is holy."

People began to knock each other down in their efforts to get through the gates to the tree. Those who fell began to claw the mud around the roots, eating it and rubbing it on their afflicted parts. A young man was almost crushed to death between the fence and the TV.

Finally, Joe spoke up on the radio. "Friends, how can you conduct yourselves in such a selfish and vicious manner? I understand that this is a clear case of magical thinking, the kind that built cathedrals and fulfilled man's dreams, but your hope is misplaced. The tree is a fake. I repeat that: *the tree is a fake!* On careful analysis by government inspectors we have been apprised that there is nothing but filthy water coming out of a rotten knothole that's crusted over with crud. It makes me sick, sick to think people are drinking that stuff and putting it into their eyes and private parts. Cease and desist, I beg of you. It was a terrible mistake."

In a few days our enterprising neighbors who had opened soft-drink stands, snow-cone stands, and sandwich and popcorn concessions had left.

The incident injured Joe's credibility.

"Mr. Fafka, I think you're a rat giving hope and then taking it away."

"What is wrong with you, sir?"

"I'm dead from the waist down, Joe."

"And from the waist up too, jerk! I hope you stay paralyzed!"

"I don't drink, Joe."

"Liar! I can hear that fuzzy, blurry inflection in your voice, and I know, sir, that you are calling me in an alcoholic haze. If I ever hear your voice again I'll come get you wherever you are and tear your tongue out. You hear? Low life, lily-livered drunk! May you freeze on the Bowery next Christmas . . . Well, folks, I guess that's telling him, and now for those of you who are planning a party or celebration of some sort, Strawberry Cooler is the drink for you, made from natural ingredients and containing only eighteen percent alcohol . . ."

138 I've got a superglamorous career now: three days a week I take over for Joe. I handle the calls more humanly, try not to insult potential suicides or incite silent America to riot. I also advise people on sex and food although I do not have the credentials of a Mazie Justins who wrote eighty-seven pornographic novels before she went into the advice columnist business and managed to spark her helpful hints on multiple orgasm with wit and humor. I do not have the credentials of an Emma Roget who in her book on Italian regional cooking managed to mine from each of the fourteen main regions recipes that had never before appeared in any cookbook. But it is better to not be an expert in this constantly changing universe; it is better to be sympathetic, ambiguous, and to give a number of answers to a single question. Any recipe for living or cooking must have a substitute list of ingredients: when it is done, who can tell the difference anyway?

139 I no longer hang around the house with my clothes off. Joe the prude doesn't like it. Pablo adores it. He is sure that if I expose my body long enough I will grow a fine body of hair and then look more like him. He thinks that clothes press one's follicles shut, forcing the hair to grow inward, and that humans are being injured internally by bristly vibrissa which makes them nasty to other creatures. Whenever Pablo hides my clothes, Joe beats him. I don't know how to handle the situation. It's so explosive. Every time I go to work I'm afraid that the two men in my life will kill one another.

140 So much has happened since I've been on the air: a camera crew is coming to live with us to our new lifestyle: the menagerie a trois. They will be with us for at least two months. I have my own lavaliere mike which hangs between my breasts—like the cross, or the Jewish star, or even the Egyptian ankh. It is symbolic of a religion, and looks very sexy. When Joe and Pablo catch sight of it they stop fighting.

141 One month into the filming. We do not hold a conversation unless the camera is going. A permanent floodlight has been installed in the bathroom, and one wall removed. There is a catwalk above the living room. Yesterday when I opened the oven door to make some biscuits I found a cameraman inside. He is a Maoist and has been photographing my jewels, furs, and silverware. Whenever we eat he takes close-ups of our mouths and what we leave over. He says he is making a political film.

142 The Maoist has been won over. I fed him a plate of litchi nuts and he succumbed to the past. Now he is easier to get along with, although who can tell a man's heart when he is eating?

143 The movie, called *Three on a Matchress*, has been shown on educational TV and is an instant success. Pablo no longer hides his ears under his hat or strains for an upright position: he has come out of the closet. Saks has introduced the Pablo Look: men want to look like dogs. Hair shirts are "in", padded palms and soles de rigueur, wet noses chic, and fetch-and-carry is swiftly taking the place of golf and tennis. Language itself is undergoing a change: instead of saying, "You're making a mistake", people are using phrases such as, "You're barking up the wrong tree." But in spite of his notoriety, Pablo is still not allowed in restaurants and supermarkets. He particularly misses not being able to go to the movies or an off-Broadway show. We have hired a civil liberties lawyer and plan a test case to liberate all dogs from unjust laws.

To clarify the situation at home, I wrote up a domestic contract by which we must all abide:

THE JONES-PABLO-FAFKA DOMESTIC AGREEMENT

1. PRINCIPLES

We reject the notion that the work that brings in more money is not more valuable. The ability to earn money, or the fact that one already has it, should carry more weight in a relationship. Those who do not have money to contribute should do the dirty work and be subservient in every other way, including sexually. This is not as rigid as it seems since bad treatment provides great motivation to change things and to better oneself. If anyone balks, I, Helen Jones, have the right to kick them out.

2. JOB BREAKDOWN AND SCHEDULE

(A) Mornings: Buying newspaper, making breakfast, making lunches, shopping. Every other week each male does all.

(B) Afternoons: Free time for all: Joe may prepare his next day's script; Pablo may masturbate; I may take Polaroids of their activities.

(C) Nighttime (after 6 P.M.). On Tuesday, Thursday, and Sunday Pablo will tuck me in and have person-to-person talks. Joe will do me on Monday, Wednesday, and Saturday. Friday is split between both of them, or I may just say "No."

(D) Cleaning and laundering to be done by commercial laundry.

(E) All statements to the press must be cleared through me, Helen Jones.

144

The domestic agreement was made to ignore. And we did. We decided that it was humorless and degrading to the manifest spirit of our troilism. Consequently the contract was shredded and put into the gerbil cage where it would do more good.

145

Unfortunately, one side effect of our new togetherness has been a distortion of sexual generosity. It has become compulsive and no longer joyous. We feel we owe it to one another to drift (aimlessly) from bed to bed; all this is accomplished under the guise of sexual freedom. We have tried every position together.

I long to be alone!

Monks are not to be pitied; they know the value of chanting their way into oblivion where nobody will bother them. I miss Albert because of his surprising trunkful of costume changes, though I suspect he will finally immolate himself in one of them. And I miss the seven dwarfs because they took care of the house. And I miss Pablo's being just a pet, and Joe's being a mad, disembodied voice that lived in a static-free box. If only I knew then what I know now. Why is life so complicated? Why can't I conduct myself *beautifully* on every occasion? I want to make it as simple as this: "I am hungry, I will eat; I am frightened and ill, I will take a dose of Mimulus."